DOES GOA...
TO S...

"Who knows?" Vand...

"And who cares?" sa...
. . . like telling someone's fortune. All you have to do is
hold the hand firmly and keep track of the pulse and sweat
to know if you're saying what he wants to hear."

"No!" Vandien feigned astonishment. "Would the Romni,
holders of mystical powers for generations, practice such a
deceit?"

"Practice? Hell, who needs practice, we're already perfect
at it."

LUCK OF THE WHEELS

PRAISE FOR MEGAN LINDHOLM'S
PREVIOUS NOVELS:

"A bright new talent in the fantasy field!"
—Charles de Lint

"Lindholm has created a refreshingly different magic!"
—*Locus*

"Fascinating, absorbing and well-written."
—*Fantasy Review*

The Ki and Vandien adventures include:
HARPY'S FLIGHT
THE WINDSINGERS
THE LIMBRETH GATE

Ace Books by Megan Lindholm

HARPY'S FLIGHT
THE WINDSINGERS
THE LIMBRETH GATE
WIZARD OF THE PIGEONS
THE REINDEER PEOPLE
WOLF'S BROTHER
LUCK OF THE WHEELS

Megan Lindholm

LUCK OF THE WHEELS

ACE BOOKS, NEW YORK

This book is for James LaFollette.

Because every kid deserves the kind of uncle who, when he babysits small nephews, staples them to the wall, or hog-ties them with duct tape and leaves them on the front lawn, or handcuffs larger nephews to the bumpers of cars and abandons them, or offers to teach you how to swim while wearing tire chains or threatens to flush your favorite disgusting army hat down the toilet.

And every kid also deserves the kind of uncle who takes you to the doctor to get the ring you borrowed cut off your finger, or sits by your hospital bed for ten hours on the day you're facing surgery and comforts you with stories about how humiliated he was when he had to go to the hospital because his cousin shot him in the butt and makes off-the-wall remarks that rattle the nurses, or buys you hordes of books on archaeology and takes you out to look for arrowheads and stone implements, or uses you for a gofer at the gun show, or gives you fencing lessons in the garage on rainy days or brings you a genuine cavalry bugle to blow while your mom is trying to work on the final draft of her book.

And every writer deserves the kind of brother who stays up until midnight choreographing fencing scenes in the kitchen, and proofreads scribbled-on drafts, and tells her when her character is acting like a real wimp and organizes expeditions to Shoreys in Seattle just when the walls are completely closing in on her.

Garf, you've been all that and more. We love you.

But I'm still going to nail you for that damn bugle.

ONE

"And I'll tell you another thing," the owner of the caravansary went on as she refilled her own glass and then Ki's. She leaned heavily on the table they shared, shaking a warning finger at Ki so that the tiers of bracelets on her arm rattled against one another. "I'd never take a green-eyed man into my bed. Mean, every one of them I ever met. I knew one, eyes green as good jade, and heart cold as the same stone. He'd go out of his way to find a quarrel, and then wasn't happy until I'd apologized for starting it. Mean as snakes."

Ki nodded absently to her host's litany. A soft dry wind blew through the open portals and arched windows of the tavern common room—if common room was what they called it in this part of the world. The wind carried the scent of flowers and dust, and the sounds of foot and cart traffic from the streets outside. The floor of the tavern was raked sand, the walls of worked white stone. Trestle tables were crowded close in the common room, but most of the other tables were deserted at this time of day. Cushions stuffed with straw, their rough fabric faded, were fastened to the long low benches. This far south, not even the taverns looked like taverns. And the wine tasted like swill.

Ki shifted uncomfortably on her cushion, then leaned both elbows on the low table before her. She had wandered in here seeking work. Up north the tavernkeepers had always known who had work for a teamster. But this Trelira only had news of what men were best left unbedded, and the disasters that befell women foolish enough to ignore her warnings. Ki

1

hoped that if she sat and nodded long enough, Trelira might wander onto a more useful topic. She stifled a sigh and wiped sweat from the back of her neck. Damnable heat.

"Trouble most women have," Trelira was going on, "is how they look at a man. They look at his face, they look at his clothes. Like buying a horse by how pretty its harness is. What good is that? Prettier a man is, the less you get out of him. I had a man, a few years back, looked like a laughing young god. Sun-bronzed skin, forearms wide enough to balance a pitcher on, black, black hair and eyes as blue and innocent as a kitten's. Spent all his days in my caravansary, drinking my wine and telling tall stories. And if I asked his help, he'd go into a sulk, and have to be flattered and petted out of it. Fool that I was, I would. Ah, but he was beautiful, with his dark hair and pale eyes, and skin soft as a horse's muzzle.

"Then one day a man walked in here, homely as a mud fence and dressed like a farmer. Walked up to me and said, 'Your stable door is off its hinges, and every stall in it needs mucking out. For a good dinner and a glass of wine, I'll take care of it for you.' I tell you, it hit me like a sandslide. Kitten-eyes was out of my tavern less than an hour later, and the other fellow got more than wine and food for his trouble."

Ki tried to smile appreciatively. "Ah, handsome is as handsome does," she said blandly. "No doubt about it. Now, not to change the subject, but I've a freight wagon and . . ."

"Not always!" Trelira blithely ran over Ki's words. "Appearances can be just as important. A man with a dirty beard is bound to be dirty elsewhere. . . . You know what I mean. Bloodshot eyes and a red nose, and he's going to drink. Nor would I take a man with pale skin. Never met a healthy one yet. Nor one with scars. Working scars on a man's hands, they aren't bad. A game leg or bad back might mean he's just clumsy, or stupid. But scars elsewhere don't come from being sweet and gentle."

"Oh, I don't know," Ki ventured to disagree. She glanced down at her own weathered hands. "Anyone who's lived much is bound to have a few scars. And," she added as she smiled to herself, "certain scars add character to a man's appearance."

"Don't kid yourself, girl," Trelira advised her with maternal tolerance. "I know what you're thinking. But only silly little girls think a duelling scar means romance. Quarrelsome is more likely. Most times it just means a nasty temper. Look at that one, for instance. You can bet he's a mean bastard. Don't stare, now.''

Ki swung her gaze obediently toward the portal. A narrow man, a bit taller than Ki, was framed against the bright daylight. He pushed dark heat-damped curls off his forehead as he squinted around the room. His eyes were darker than one would have expected, even in his deeply tanned face. The easy sureness of his quick movements hinted at ready muscles beneath the loose white shirt. In a land where many wore robes and went barefoot, he wore a wide leather belt and tucked loose trousers into the tops of his kneeboots. He could have been handsome, but for the scar that seamed his face. It began between his eyes and ran down beside his nose past a small, trimmed moustache until it trailed off at his jawline. It was a fine score, nearly invisible against his weathered face but for a pull that tugged at one of his eyes when he smiled, as now. The warmth of that small smile belied the grimness of the scar. He caught Ki's gaze upon him. The smile widened and he came toward them.

''Here comes trouble,'' Trelira sighed warningly.

''Don't I know it,'' Ki replied wryly. The stranger dropped onto the bench beside her, and picking up her glass, drained it.

''Vandien.'' Ki made it both a greeting and an introduction. Trelira rose hastily, looking abashed.

''No offense meant,'' she murmured.

''None taken,'' Ki replied smoothly, adding in a wicked undertone, ''You're absolutely right, anyway.''

Vandien had swallowed the wine and was coughing politely to cover up his shock at its sourness. Ki thumped him on the back pitilessly. ''Meet Trelira, the owner of this caravansary,'' she invited him when he could breathe again.

''A lovely place,'' he managed. His smile included her in the compliment. Ki watched with amusement the sudden reappraisal in Trelira's eyes. With that smile and a story or two, Vandien could scavenge a living anywhere. Ki knew it. A shame, she reflected, that Vandien also knew it.

''It's a very dry day out there,'' he added smoothly. ''Could I trouble you for another glass, and perhaps a bottle of Alys?''

Trelira shook her head at the unfamiliar word. "This wine is all we offer, this time of year. Tariffs are too high on the rest; no point my buying what my customers can't afford. But I'll bring a fresh bottle." She departed the table quickly, her bright, loose garments fluttering around her.

"Not even the water in this town is drinkable," he confided to Ki when Trelira was out of earshot. "It's redder than this wine, but not as sour. Leaves more dregs in the cup, though. Did I interrupt something? Smuggling offer, perhaps? That woman looked guilt-stricken when I sat down."

"Nothing important. She had just observed that no woman in her right mind would put up with an evil-eyed wretch like you."

"I'll bet," he scoffed loftily. A serving boy crept up to set a bottle and glass before him, and scurried off, his bare feet soundless on the soft sand floor. "Any luck here?"

"None. How about you?"

"Not much better," he conceded. "I spent the whole morning with some minor official, getting our papers renewed. I told him we had bought our journeying permits at the border already, but he said they were out of date. So we have new papers, with a different seal, for twice as much coin. Made me wish we were back where the Merchant's Councils ran everything. This Duke everyone speaks of has his officials too scared to take a bribe. And his Brurjan patrollers are everywhere. I never saw so many Brurjans in one place before. Could pave a courtyard with their teeth." From inside his shirt he drew a roll of parchment and a flat coin-bag. Ki took them silently. Her face was sour. He shrugged and continued.

"Then this afternoon, I damn near fell asleep on my feet in the hiring mart. Trouble is that the wagon looks like a peddler's wagon. Folk ask me what I have to sell, not what I can haul. We did have one query, though. Two sisters came up and asked if we were taking passengers. I gathered that the older girl was running away from home to join her sweetheart. A very uncommon-looking girl she was. Her sister had curling dark hair and blue eyes. But she who wished to run away, she had hair red as a new calf's hide, and one eye blue and the other green. She . . ." He let his words run down in disappointment. Ki was already shaking her head. "I know," he conceded reluctantly. "I had the same visions of outraged kinfolk. I told them we didn't haul people, and they went away, whispering together. Did hear of one other thing, secondhand. A fellow has twenty chickens he wants to send to his cousin in Dinmaera, about three days from here. A gift of breeding stock to celebrate a wedding.''

''Damn!'' Ki hissed. ''Much as I hate hauling livestock, I'd have taken it, if we had the proper wagon for it. But as it is, they'd be inside with us. In this heat.''

''They're supposed to be in stout wooden cages.''

''They'd still stink. And make noises.''

Vandien was taking a cautious sip from his own glass. ''I left word with the fellow next to me that anyone looking for a wagon and team to hire could find us here. I'm starving. Is the food as bad as the wine?''

''I haven't been that brave yet,'' Ki replied distractedly.

''Shall we order something and find out, or go back to the wagon and fix something ourselves?''

When Ki didn't reply, Vandien turned to her. She was staring moodily at her wine glass. Her elbow was on the table, her chin propped on her fist. Deft as a cat's paw, his hand hooked her elbow off the edge of the table, snapping her attention back to him.

''The wagon,'' she said suddenly, ''is the whole damn problem. All house and no freight bed. I don't know why I bought a caravan like that.''

''I do. It was cheap, and it was there, and we were both in one hell of a hurry to get out of Jojorum. If you wanted a wagon like your old one, with room for freight in the back, you'd have to have it specially built.''

''Maybe,'' Ki conceded. ''But that peddler's wagon hasn't saved us time or coin. It's built all wrong; top-heavy and unstable in a river crossing or on a rough road. And where it should be built sturdy, it's built flimsy. I nearly went right through the door-step yesterday. You know what we should do?''

''Get a new wagon built?''

''Yes. Go to the wainwright in Firbanks and get him to . . .''

''No.'' Vandien's denial was absolute. ''Too many of the people between here and there would remember us too well. And a good number of them are Windsingers that could sing up a killing storm. There's no going back north for us, Ki.''

"Just for a short time," Ki argued grimly. "To get a decent wagon. Look at the thing we're driving. I can't even make a living with it. It's an ugly old peddler's wagon, not a freight wagon. There's no space to haul anything. It's all closed in."

"Just like every other Romni wagon I've ever seen," Vandien cut in smoothly. "They seem to cope just fine with their wagons being all living quarters. They don't worry about how they're going to pay their expenses. They just travel and live and trust to the luck of the wheels to provide for them. But not you. Sometimes I just don't understand you. You were raised Romni, but you won't put your trust in their ways. Think of your old wagon, only half caravan and the rest left open for freight. Some might say due to a lack of faith in the luck of the wheels."

"And some might say due to a streak of sanity. I've lived by the luck of the wheels, Vandien. You notice they don't call it the good luck of the wheels. Sometimes it's very bad. Especially in places like this, where they want a piece of paper sealed and stamped for every breath you take. I've seen Romni with a wagon full of children, in the middle of a hostile town, without a bite of food to eat and only the family gold to their names. Gold they'd sooner die for than spend."

"And no doubt they all starved to death?" he asked shrewdly.

"Well, no," she admitted reluctantly. "There are ways of getting by. Ways that can get your hand cut off if you're caught. I'd rather have an open-backed wagon, and a load of freight to haul."

He tried a new tack. "Well, we could pick up a load of trade goods," he offered speculatively. "You've still enough left of Rebeke's gold to do that. We could get scarves and pans and bells and earrings and lace. . . ."

"And live in the middle of it all, and open up our home to every customer's prying eyes. No. I've gotten used to the cuddy being private. And I won't use up the rest of the Windsinger's gold. It was too hard come by to part with for bells and buttons. No, it's going to buy me a new, decent wagon, built to my specifications. And that means the wainwright in Firbanks."

"It means any wainwright who can build a square corner," Vandien contradicted her irritably. He dipped his finger in the wine, idly drew on the tabletop with it. "Don't get so stubborn and set in your ways. Just because he built the last one doesn't mean he has to build the next one. I don't think we should go back north. Even if this Duke's iron hand bothers you. It's just another set of rules to get used to. We can manage.''

A tired smile broke on Ki's face. ''Listen to us. What's happened to your impulsiveness, that devil-may-care attitude?''

''A Windsinger scared it right out of me. And you're a fine one to talk. What's happened to all your cautions and planning? You're talking about walking back into the lion's den.''

Ki refilled both their glasses from Vandien's bottle. ''My caution isn't gone,'' she revealed after a sip. ''I'm just regaining it. We've worked too far south, Vandien. It's been obvious since we crossed the border into Loveran. I don't have any contacts here, I don't understand the coins, I detest the regulations, and I don't know where the roads go, let alone how safe they are or where the short-cuts are. How can I make a living down here? We've been in sunny, dreary Keddi for a week now, with no offer of work. What happens if we don't get work?''

''We'd survive.'' He sipped the wine, grimaced.

''How?''

''By the luck of the wheels, Ki! Just as all the other Romni survive.'' He paused and looked at her shrewdly. Ki narrowed her eyes warily, but he opened his wide, declaring the innocence of his intentions. ''Look. Let's compromise. For a month, let's live by our wits. Seeing new places, no delivery dates, no pushy customers, no spoiling cargoes. For a month.''

''In a month, we could starve.''

He gave a snort of disdain. ''I never starved in all the years before I met you. Lost a bit of weight, learned to be charming to strangers, and not particular about what I ate or where I slept, but I never starved.''

''We can't all be stray cats.''

''No? Let me teach you how.'' He made the offer with his most persuasive smile. His dark eyes, brown half a shade short of black, were inches from her green ones.

''And at the end of that month?'' Ki asked coolly.

He leaned back with a sigh. ''If we aren't successful, then we'll go back to the wainwright in Firbanks and get a new wagon.''

''And take up my old trade routes,'' Ki bartered.

Vandien emptied his glass, winced at the taste, and then shook his head. "No. The first Windsinger who heard of us would report it to Rebeke. She wouldn't let us go again."

"If we were careful," Ki began, leaning forward and speaking quietly but intensely. "If we were cautious . . ."

"Are you the teamsters for hire?"

Their heads turned in unison. The speaker was an old man. No. With a start, Ki realized that the man standing by their table was only a few years older than she was. It was his eyes that were old, and his voice. He looked as if some task had so wearied him that he had already spent the years of his mind if not his body. Like the child-mystic she and Vandien had seen in Adjutan, who could recite all six thousand of the sacred verses of Krinth. Ancient, weary eyes.

"We are," said Ki. "Not any more," Vandien chimed at the same instant. The man looked confused. Ki kicked Vandien's booted ankle under the table.

"We may be. It depends on the cargo, the distance, the road, and of course, the coin involved. Please, share our table and wine," Ki invited him graciously.

Trelira had seen him enter, and was setting an extra glass at the table before he was seated. "Brin!" she greeted him, smiling pleasantly and kissing his cheek. But her eyes darted past his shoulder anxiously. "You didn't bring Gotheris?"

"No. I left him at home this time, with Channry."

"Oh." Trelira paused overlong, and Ki wondered what she wasn't saying. "Well. Do you have enough? Something to eat? Well. Good to see you, Brin."

After each shake of their heads, Trelira had paused, but when at last she could find no excuse to hover by their table, she departed. Ki noticed that almost immediately she was back, raking smooth the sand floor by the next table. Old gossip, Ki thought to herself, and ignored her.

"I am Brin, as Trelira has let you know," the old man began. Vandien had filled his glass for him, but Brin made no move to touch it. "Your names are not known to me."

"Ki. And my partner, Vandien. You were asking if we were for hire. We are. What cargo?"

"Well. Not cargo, exactly. Tell me, have you any children?"

Vandien glanced up, startled, but Ki answered succinctly for both of them. "No."

"Aah. I see. Well, then, that might affect how you might

feel about . . . you see . . . I have a son. Gotheris. He is come of an age to be put to a useful trade. Years ago, when he was but a tiny child, he showed certain instincts and skills that made my brother, Dellin, most anxious to have him as an apprentice. Dellin is a Jore-healer, you see, a skill that has been long in my family, though not one I chose to follow. So we agreed that when the time came, Gotheris would be apprenticed to him. At that time, Dellin lived in Dinmaera, and we saw him more often. But since then, he has moved to Villena, and so it has been several years since we have seen him.''

Ki and Vandien exchanged puzzled glances. What had all this to do with a freight haul?

''We've had word from him over the years. And I recently sent a message to him that the boy was ready to learn now, and that idleness could only teach him mischief. So he has sent back to me that he is ready to receive the boy at any time.''

''You want us to take your boy to Villena?'' Vandien guessed.

''Yes. Exactly. I am willing to pay you three georns now, and at his arrival Dellin would pay you another full orn.''

''No passengers,'' Vandien said flatly. The cuddy was simply too small a space to share. But Ki raised a hand in a ''wait a moment'' gesture, and asked quickly, ''What can you tell me of the roads to Villena this time of year? I won't pretend that I'm familiar with them.''

Brin looked unshaken by her admission of ignorance. ''The roads are well marked, but they are caravan roads, soft and sandy, more difficult for a wagon than for men and beasts. There is only one river, low at this time of year, but it has eaten its way deep into the grass plains. The banks of the river are high, steep and rocky. Bridges do not stand in flood time, as has been proven many a time. So all folk go south to the fording place at Rivercross, and then north again to Villena. It is not an easy journey, but the ways are clearly marked, and there are good inns at the towns. It is a journey of, say, ninety kilex, which is . . .'' Brin paused, converting the distance into time in his mind. He shrugged. ''Perhaps fourteen days for a wagon, if one takes it at a pleasant place. There were rumors of thieves and rebels along it last year, but the Duke sent his Brurjan patrols to clean them out. It is a heavily travelled trade route, so the Duke keeps it free of trouble.''

"If there's so much traffic between here and Villena,'' Vandien butted in despite Ki's scowl, "why send your boy off with two strangers, instead of with a caravan driver you know, or a trader you've done business with?''

"I . . .'' The man hesitated, clearly flustered by the question. "I saw your wagon. It looked like a comfortable, even pleasant, way to travel. He is my only son, you know. And I would rather he went directly to his uncle, without long stopovers for trading and visiting. The sooner he is with Dellin, the sooner he can begin to learn his trade and become a useful man.''

Vandien rubbed his moustache and lips to cover the twist of his mouth. The man's reasons did not sound authentic. But Ki was nodding thoughtfully and asking, "And how old is Gotheris?''

"He has seen fourteen harvests,'' the man said, almost reluctantly, but then added brightly, "He is large for his years. The Jore blood does that. He will be a good-sized man when fully grown. And he has Jore eyes,'' he added hesitantly, as if they might object to that.

"I see no problems, then,'' Ki was saying, to Vandien's total amazement. "I'd like to meet the boy, though, before we touch hands on this agreement. Is that acceptable?''

A facial tic twitched Brin's cheek. "Certainly. I will bring him by first thing tomorrow. I will have him bring his things, and I will bring the coins for his passage. That way, as soon as you have agreed, you can be on your way. Acceptable?''

"I'd have to take on supplies first,'' Ki hedged.

"Then I shan't bring him by until you are ready. Noon, shall we say? Nothing makes that boy more impatient than waiting. Better not to make him stand about while things are got ready. We shall meet you here at noon, tomorrow. Good evening.''

Vandien frowned after Brin as he vanished through the portal. "There's a strange man. He doesn't seem to believe we might not take him. And what was his haste? He didn't even pause to finish his wine.''

"Given a choice, would you sit here and drink this stuff? Besides, he takes leave of his only son tomorrow. Such a farewell takes time. What's flustering up your feathers, Van? You questioned him like a jealous lover.''

"Vandien," he corrected her absently, watching the serving boys pull stiff hides across the portals and peg them into place. A dry wind from across the plains rattled sand against the leather. "Didn't he seem awfully anxious to be rid of the boy? I think there's trouble in this somewhere."

"Your tail's just tweaked because we aren't going to run off and start a month of vagrancy tomorrow. You think I'm backing out on our agreement, don't you? Well, I'm not. But why not start the month off with a little coin in hand? Take the boy and drop him off on the way. New places, you said. Well, I'd never heard of Villena until this night. And neither had you, I'll wager. So why not start from there? Trelira!" Ki called suddenly across the room. "What direction is Villena from here?"

The haste with which the portly caravansary owner trotted to their table betrayed her interest. "To the southwest, about fourteen days away. It's right on the caravan routes. There's Algona, Tekum, Rivercross, and then Villena. A lot bigger town then Keddi. It was originally a T'cheria settlement, but nowadays there are quite as many Humans there. And a group of Dene have settled at Rivercross. Thinking of going there?"

"Perhaps. Perhaps not. I was just wondering." Vandien played her out on her own curiosity. "What are you serving for the evening meal tonight?"

"I've mutton pastries and tubers with onions baked in soft gourds. Barley and bean soup, and a good fresh bake of bread. What takes you to Villena?"

"Nothing, probably." Vandien replied easily, pressing his leg against Ki's to ask for her silence. "Brin wanted us to take his son there, but Ki's not much for taking passengers. She likes her privacy. Just curiosity made me ask. Neither of us had heard of the place."

Ki picked up her cue. "I'll have the tubers and onions baked in the gourd, the soup, but no . . . ''

"Goat? He wants you to take Goat to Villena?"

The avidity of the question trampled over Ki's attempt to order food.

"Gotheris was the boy's name, I thought," Vandien ventured.

"Aye, but he's been called Goat since he was four or five.

He was a spry little fellow then, always gamboling about, so full of energy and mischief. There wasn't a mother but wished he were her child, when he was small." Trelira's eyes journeyed to some dreaming place and remembered some regret. "Why must children change and grow?" she asked sadly of no one in particular. Then her attention snapped back to Ki, and her eyes went shrewd and businesslike. "How much did he offer you for the trip?"

Ki opened her mouth to protest this prying, but Vandien hastily pressed a filled wineglass into her hand. She held her words back behind tight lips.

"Three georns and a full orn on safe arrival," Vandien told her with disarming frankness. His smile made her trustworthy. "Have pity on a stranger, Trelira. I can't even remember how many georns or fiorns in an orn. Given the roads and the distance, would you say that's a fair price for the trip?"

Trelira took a deep breath for speech, then shut her mouth and gave a quick nod.

Ki took up her part in Vandien's game. "I wonder why he doesn't wait until he has friends going that way?" She glanced casually at Trelira.

"They'd know the . . . he wouldn't know anyone. Brin doesn't know that many folk here. His land is on the edge of the town, alone but for his sheep and his three sons. His wife's sister was my cousin's wife," she added, speaking softly to herself.

"Well, we haven't said we'd take him, yet," Vandien admitted casually. But Trelira was no longer listening. She rose and turned, walking slowly back to her kitchen, her head full of her own thoughts. Ki and Vandien exchanged glances.

"Interesting." Ki sipped at her wine.

"Nice mess. Brin says his only son, Trelira says one of three. Brin says he wants the boy comfortable, Trelira says he wouldn't know anyone else to take him. Whatever smells funny here, she's got a family tie to it that's keeping her from gossiping. Suppose he's a half-wit?"

"To be apprenticed to a healer?"

"I could tell you stories about healers that would make you believe it," Vandien offered lightly. Then he shrugged, and became serious once again. "What else could it be?"

"Maybe nothing but your imagination. Maybe a boy grown

too big for home and small-town life. Don't sour the deal, friend, before we've even seen the boy.''

Food arrived, a double order of everything Trelira had mentioned. Ki frowned as the serving boy set it before them. ''What's this?'' she demanded.

The boy stared at her as if she were daft. ''Food?'' he suggested.

''We didn't ask for any yet.''

''Trelira ordered it for you. Oh, I'm to tell you there's no charge. To give you good strength for an early start tomorrow.''

Vandien raised a mocking eyebrow at Ki. She only snorted, and pushed her share of the mutton pastries onto his plate. He accepted them gravely. ''Still not eating meat?'' he asked the soup gravely, smiling behind his moustache.

''Don't push me, friend.'' The smell of the pastries was driving her crazy, and her resolve seemed in question. But she'd stick to it, if for no other reason than that he teased her about it. She was breaking her bread over her barley soup when Trelira's shadow fell across the table again. ''Goat,'' she began without preamble. ''He's family. I'd never speak ill of him. Those that do, don't know him. That's all. Actually, I wish him a good journey, with every comfort. So I'll add two georns of my own to his passage money. And any trader in town will tell you that adds up to a handsome fee for a trip to Villena.''

The two crescent coins clicked onto the table. Ki and Vandien stared at them, unmoving.

''What if we decide not to take him?'' Vandien asked.

''You'll take him,'' she said with decision. ''One look in his eyes, and no one can refuse the boy. And everyone in town knows that he wants to go away from here.'' Trelira turned on silent feet and was gone.

TWO

"The boy looks ordinary enough."

Vandien leaned out of the cuddy door and let his gaze follow Ki's. He had just finished storing their provisions in the cupboards and drawers inside the caravan. The two georns had been enough to take on generous supplies, and at Trelira's urging, they had done so. Vandien was more than a little disgruntled about it. Ki didn't usually spend advance money until she had decided to take on the job. So much for meeting the boy first. Well, whatever problems came with him, Ki had bought them in advance.

"Fourteen?" he observed skeptically.

"Looks more like sixteen to me. But you never can tell; some boys grow fast," Ki replied.

Gotheris walked beside his father, and nearly matched him in height. That put him half a head taller than Ki and the equal of Vandien. His brown hair clung to his head as smoothly as a cap and was cut to one length on the sides and back. In front it touched his eyebrows in a straight line. His eyes were light, though at this distance Vandien could not tell what color they were. His face was long and narrow, with the unfinished look of a boy who is sure of all the answers while still discovering the questions. His young body was lanky, as if growing bones were outracing the meat and muscle that should cloak them. His cream-colored shirt was lavishly embroidered in red and yellow, in gay contrast to the rough brown robe Brin wore. Goat wore loose brown trousers that fluttered around the tops of his sandaled feet. The boy strode empty-handed, but Brin had a large basket buckled to his back and a woven bag in his arms. Vandien frowned at the boy's laziness, then decided it was none of his business.

"Well, here we are, all ready to go!" Brin greeted them. His words rang falsely hearty in Vandien's ears.

Ki made some noncommital reply, studying the boy. The boy's eyes were very large, and slightly protruding. So that was what the father had meant by Jore eyes. Up close, they were so pale a green they verged on yellow, and the pupils were not those of a Human. A little crossbreeding, then, somewhere back in the family line. The rest of him seemed Human enough. He had a sweet little pink bow of a mouth, but when he smiled he showed teeth long and narrow and yellow as a goat's. Goat looked brightly from Ki to Vandien as Brin set his burdens down by the wagon and wiped his sweaty face with a stained kerchief.

"This is my son, Gotheris. Gotheris, make your respect to the teamster and his wife. Vandien and Ki."

"The teamster and her partner. Ki and Vandien." Vandien corrected him mellowly.

"I see. Beg pardon," Brin flushed, but Ki ignored the stumble. Gotheris giggled, in a high pitch more like a girl-child's laugh than that of a youth on the verge of manhood.

"Well, at least I'll know from the start who I must hark to!" the boy burst out, grinning delightedly from Ki to Vandien. "Is this the wagon?"

"You'll have to hark to whichever of us speaks," Ki said firmly, but the boy had turned from the group and was climbing into the caravan.

"Please excuse him," Brin said hastily, trying to speak smoothly. "He's so excited to finally be on his way, and full of curiosity about you and your caravan. I'm afraid his manners flee before his impulses sometimes. You may find him a bit uncouth, I fear. We have lived an isolated and rural life for so long that Gotheris has none of the graces or sophistication you would find in a city-bred boy. It is unfortunate that boys of that age usually believe themselves the very soul of wit and judgement. With just the two of us, he has grown up speaking his mind rather bluntly to adults, and often gives his opinions before he is asked. But aren't all boys his age like that? He is a bit coarsely mannered, I'm afraid, but the training and discipline of a healer will soon take off his rough edges." Brin's eyes darted from Ki to Vandien as he sensed their reluctance. He kept nodding at his own words and smiling so earnestly as he explained and excused that finally Ki nodded to make him stop.

"There's only the one big bed in here! Do we all sleep together then, tumbled in a pile? I'll warn you, I'll ask to be on top!" The boy was half-hanging out of the caravan door, a wide smile on his mouth. The ribald note in his voice shattered the just-made accord. Before either Ki or Vandien could speak, Brin stepped forward and seized him by the shoulder.

"Gotheris! Mind your behavior! Do you want these folk to think you witless and rude? Show them some respect, or you'll never be on your way to Dellin."

"Yes, Father," Gotheris replied, his manner so suddenly meek and chastened that Vandien felt his disgust abate somewhat.

"Have you ever been away from home before?" Ki asked casually.

"I'm afraid not," Brin answered for him. "You can see how excited he is; he has wanted to leave Keddi for so long, to see more of the world. I'm afraid he shows himself in a bad light in his excitement."

"I'm familiar with the way of boys," Ki answered, addressing them both. "No one could travel with the Romni and not become accustomed to the antics of children. Even the most disciplined will kick up their heels at the start of a journey. But," she added, turning gravely to Gotheris, "we must understand things before I touch hands with you on this. If we take Gotheris, he must be willing to obey Vandien and me. I will expect him to help with the camp chores at night, to clean up after himself, and help care for the horses; that means fetching water if needed, helping to unharness at night, that sort of thing. In short, although he will be our passenger, he will have to be a responsible member of the party as well."

Gotheris's face had grown more and more indignant with every condition. The words fair burst from him. "But my father is paying you to take me!"

"Hush, Son." The man's big hands flapped at him beseechingly. "I am sure you understand that all must cooperate on such a journey. And, Gotheris, think of all the things you'll learn!"

The boy made no reply, and his eyes dropped to look at the dusty ground. But in the instant before Ki began speaking again, his gaze leaped up to meet Vandien's in a rebelliously measuring look. Vandien met his look gravely, and the boy looked down, but a half smile rose and lingered on his face. Vandien suppressed a sigh. Soon enough, boy, he promised himself.

"He must be courteous, not only toward us but to any we meet along the way. And, in such close quarters, I must insist on personal cleanliness, and his awareness of the privacy of others." Ki was going on with her list of requirements. Brin was nodding earnestly to all she said, but the boy didn't appear concerned. First he picked at his yellow teeth, and then squatted down to scratch his ankle vigorously.

"I'm sure he'll be no trouble, once he settles into the rhythm of the journey. He knows he has to behave if he is to reach Dellin without delay. He'll do his best to be useful. Won't you, Gotheris?"

The squatting boy cocked his head up at his father and gave a quick flash of his teeth. "Of course I will, Father. What boy wouldn't jump at the chance to travel to hot, dusty Villena, there to study his eyes out with his humorless uncle, so he can spend the rest of his years looking at smelly sick folk and birthing squalling babies for screaming women? What else could I possibly want to spend my life doing?"

The words were unforgivably rude, but the tone was so earnest and sincere that Vandien felt himself at a loss. Was this the blunt speech of a young man who had lived isolated for most of his life? Was it familiar teasing between father and son? Brin more ignored than smiled at the remark.

In the awkward silence that followed, Ki met Vandien's eyes; he suddenly relaxed. Her look told him all. The boy's last words had decided her. She wasn't taking him anywhere. Vandien breathed an inner sigh of relief. Oh, she'd be fractious about having to convert some of the Windsinger's gold into georns to pay back Trelira's advance, but that was better than being saddled with that boy. He hadn't realized how much he'd been dreading the trip until the threat of it was removed. Breaking the news to Brin was Ki's task. After all, it was her wagon and team; she had the final say on all decisions. Thank the Moon, he added to himself.

He casually wandered over to the horses and began checking their ears for ticks. Two things he didn't enjoy about these warmer lands they now travelled: the new bugs they encountered, and the spells of watery eyes and running noses that afflicted them both, even in the hottest weather. He wondered idly if they would still follow the caravan route to Villena, even though they had no passenger. He found he hoped so. There would be interesting traffic on the road, and fascinating towns to pass through. Maybe even other Romni. Ki had heard there were tribes this far south, but they had yet to meet any. Even if they met no other Romni, there'd be new towns to explore. Maybe he'd find a leatherworker competent enough to turn out a new sheath for his rapier. His was all but worn through. He thought idly of the sword he had seen yesterday; a peculiar weapon even more flexible than his rapier, but fitted with barbs along the tip. A slapping, ripping weapon, someone had told him. Between a whip and a blade. He'd yet to see one in use. He'd bet on his rapier against one, though. He could imagine such a weapon entangled in an opponent's clothing, while his rapier could dart in and out swift as the lick of death.

"Ready to go?" Ki's voice was right at his elbow. He turned quickly, hooking her into an impulsive hug, kissing her before she could dodge him. Her skin was dusty against his mouth, but warm. He trapped her against him. "Where are we off to?" he demanded, feeling free as a child.

She worked her elbow up between them and levered herself free. She glanced over her shoulder to where Brin, scandalized, was studying his feet. He didn't look as disappointed as Vandien had expected him to, and Ki looked more annoyed. "Villena, of course. Goat's putting his things inside the caravan. Oh, he said he doesn't mind being called Goat; in fact, he prefers it. And the coins are in my pouch. So stop being an ass and let's get started. Did you check Sigurd's hoof?"

"We're taking the boy?" Vandien asked in disbelief. His arms dropped away from her.

"Of course. Well, I nearly backed out of it for a moment there; he has an unruly mouth. But when I asked him if he thought he could do things our way, he changed his attitude at once. He apologized and assured me he'd try his best. I think he embarrassed himself. He's very anxious to go. I think a lot of that tongue was just showing off for his father, letting him know that he's a young man now and ready to be off on his own. Boys say the most unfortunate things when they are trying to be clever. You know how they are; they show off their worst manners just when their parents are trying to impress a guest with how well behaved they are. I left him alone with his father to say their goodbyes. Vandien, are you all right?''

"I was so sure that you weren't going to do it." The bright plans of a moment ago were no more than dancing dust motes now.

"So was I, for a minute there," she conceded, smiling. Her face grew thoughtful. "But there's something about Goat's face, when you look into it. There's a man in there, trying to get out. And I suspect he'll be a pretty good man, once he learns to set childishness aside and deal with people on their own terms."

"Oh, Ki." He gazed at her reproachfully.

"Now don't you get sulky on me!" She began checking Sigmund's harness fussily. She spoke over her shoulder, not meeting his eyes. "Our deal is still on; I'll be as irresponsible as you like, right after we drop Goat off. It's only a fourteen-day trip; you can put up with him for that long. Besides, I don't think he'll be that bad, once he's used to us. Children imitate those around them. If we treat him like a young man, and expect him to behave as one, he will. Every boy has a bit of growing up to do. Goat's overdue for his, that's all."

"That's not all he's overdue for," Vandien muttered under his breath. Ki shot him a warning glance.

"Give him a chance," she protested. "He's only a boy."

Vandien glanced over in time to see Brin clasp his son's shoulder, then turn and stride hastily away. Goat's eyes were very wide as he stared after his father, as if Brin's back were the most amazing thing he had ever seen. Brin lifted a hand to rub quickly at his eyes as he went. A sudden flash of anger ambushed Vandien. "When I was his age, if anyone had called me a boy, he would have had to face my blade!"

"Exactly my point." Ki picked it up smoothly. "But you grew up, and so will he."

"In two weeks you're going to convert him into a responsible young man, I suppose," Vandien observed bitterly.

"It's not impossible." She blithely refused the quarrel. "Look how far I've gotten with you, after only a few years.

Don't act so put out; I thought he was the spoiled child,'' Ki added in a more serious tone.

Vandien just looked at her.

"This trip is only going to be as bad as you make it,'' she observed.

"That's right,'' he agreed sourly, and bent to pick up Sigmund's hoof. Ki began checking Sigurd's harness. The big greys stood quiet and passive in the sun. Vandien let down the hoof and made a conscious effort to shake off his ill humor. It wasn't only disappointment. The thought of travelling with Goat filled him with dismay. Vandien couldn't recall that he had ever been that callow and immature. When he had been as old as Goat, he had been making his own way in the world. He flinched as those early memories touched him. Sleeping in stables and ditches, telling stories by inn fires to earn a bit of bread and a rind of cheese. Being waylaid once and losing everything to the robbers, even his clothing. Stealing garments from a woman washing on a river bank, and being chased by her dogs. Travelling with a group of Dene through Brurjan territory, and being abandoned by them when he slapped a mosquito on his arm and took its life. Such lovely memories, he thought wryly. The ideal shaping for a young man's early years; no boy should be without such experiences. Maybe he was jealous, he reflected. Jealous of a young man still in the grip of childhood's innocence and frivolity.

He had been checking the harness straps as he pondered. He paused and leaned against Sigmund's wide back, watching Ki. She had tied back her long hair, but brown strands of it already dangled around her face. This southern sun had browned her face and arms until her green eyes stood out startlingly. He remembered buying the soft yellow shirt she was wearing tucked into her trousers. The bodice was embroidered with tiny green leaves and pale blue buds. She looked lovely in it. When she wasn't upset. Lines divided her brows. She took everything so seriously. He cleared his throat and she looked up. He grinned. She stared coolly at him for a moment, then turned her head to hide her answering smile. "If you'd told me it made you feel warm and protective, I could have started acting snotty and rude a long time ago,'' he offered, and saw her relax.

"Dung for brains," she observed fondly. "Let's get these wheels turning."

Ki mounted the high seat at the front of the wagon. Vandien started to follow her up when the door of the cuddy popped open and Gotheris scrambled out onto the seat. He sat down squarely in the middle. "I want to drive the team first," he announced.

"Perhaps later," Ki suggested. "After you've watched for a while. It's not as easy as it looks, especially with all the foot traffic there is in a town."

"You said I'd have to help. And my father promised me I'd be learning new things. So I want to drive."

The whine in his voice grated on Vandien's nerves. But he could be tolerant. He'd engage Goat on an adult level. "One thing about Ki: she always drives, unless she's sick, or bored with an arrow-straight flat road. So by the time she lets you take the reins, there's not much fun to it. With this team, there's not much challenge anyway. Sigurd and Sigmund pick their own pace and path. So relax and enjoy the ride."

Goat cocked his head and looked down at Vandien, his eyes shining. "Why do you let her say how everything will be? No woman would treat me so. But if the horses are so smart"—here he rounded on Ki—"why can't I drive the wagon now?"

Ki looked away from the strain on Vandien's face and spoke directly to Goat. "Because it's not what the team might do that I worry about. It's the fool that comes dashing out under their noses, or the horseman who thinks he must gallop, and takes the center of the road."

"But my father said . . ."

"And besides," said Vandien, clambering up onto the seat, "Ki said no. And I say no. Now move it over so we can get out of here."

Goat stared up at him, his eyes more yellow than Vandien had yet seen them. "For this treatment of me, my father paid good coin," Goat commented bitterly, but he edged over on the seat. Ki settled herself and took up the reins. It rankled Vandien that Goat had usurped his seat beside Ki, but he refused to give it a word. He settled beside Goat.

"Let's go," he suggested softly.

"Get up!" she called to the team, shaking the reins lightly. The greys were ready. They set their shoulders to their collars and the tall yellow wheels of the wagon began to turn. Their heavy, feathered hooves were near silent in the sandy streets. The town of Keddi drifted past them like trees on a riverbank.

"Is this all the faster they go?" Goat demanded petulantly.

"Mmm," Ki nodded. "But they go all day, and we get there just the same."

"Don't you ever whip them to a gallop?"

"Never," Ki lied, forestalling the conversation. Vandien was scarcely listening. His attention was focused on a street phenomenon. As Ki's wagon rolled leisurely down the street, all eyes were drawn to it. And as quickly pulled away. All marked Goat's passage, but no one called a genial farewell, or even a 'Good riddance!' " They ignored him as diligently as they would a scabrous beggar. Not hatred, Vandien decided, nor loathing, nor anything easy to understand. More as if each one felt personally shamed by the boy. Yet that made no sense. Could they have done something to the lad that they all regretted? Some act of intolerance carried too far? Vandien had once passed through a town where a witless girl had been crippled by the idle cruelty of some older boys. She had sat enthroned by the fountain, clad in the softest of raiment, messily eating the delicacies sent anonymously out to her. The focus of the town's shame and penitence, but still untouchable. This thing with Goat was kin to that somehow. Vandien was sure of it.

"But they could gallop if they had to?" Goat pressed.

"I suppose so," Ki replied, her tone already weary. Two more weeks of this, Vandien thought, and sighed.

The black mongrel came from nowhere. One moment the street was quiet, folk trading in the booths and tents of this market strip, all eyes carefully bowed away from Ki's wagon. The next instant, the little dog darted out of the crowd, yapping wildly at the team. Sigurd flicked his ears back and forth, but calm Sigmund continued to plod along. Why be worried by a beast not much bigger than a hoof, he seemed to say.

Then the dog darted under the very hooves of the team, to nip at Sigurd's heels. The big animal snorted and danced sideways in his harness. "Easy!" Ki called. "Go home, dog!"

The dog paid no mind to Ki, nor to a woman who hastened

out from a sweetmeat booth to call, "Here, Bits! Stop that at once! What's got into you? It's just a horse! Leave off that!"

Around and beneath the horses the feist leaped and snapped, yapping noisily and nipping at the feathers of the huge hooves. Sigurd danced sideways, shouldering his brother, who caught his agitation. The great grey heads tossed, manes flying, fighting their bits. Pedestrians cowered back and mothers snatched up small children as the team seesawed toward the booths. Vandien had never seen the stolid beasts so agitated by such a common occurrence. Nor had he ever seen a dog so intent on its own destruction. Ki stirred the team to a trot, hoping to get out of the dog's territory, but the feist continued to leap and snap, and the woman to run vainly behind the wagon calling for Bits.

"I'll pull them in and maybe she can call it off," Ki growled irritatedly. She drew in the reins, but Sigurd fought the restraint, tucking his head to his chest and pulling his teammate on. Vandien was silent as Ki held steady on the reins, baffled by the greys' strange unruliness.

There was a moment when the dog seemed to be relenting. The trotting woman was almost abreast of them. Then it sprang up suddenly, to sink its teeth into Sigurd's thick fetlock. The big grey kicked out wildly at this suddenly sharp nuisance. His next surge against the harness spooked Sigmund, and suddenly the team sprang forward. Vandien saw the slip of reins and gripped the seat. The greys had their heads and knew it. Dust rose and the wagon jounced as they broke into a ragged gallop. Vandien heard a yelp and felt a sickening jolt and the dog was no more. Behind them the woman cried out in anguish. The team surged forward as if stung. "Hang on!" he warned Goat, and tried to give Ki as much space as he could. She drew firmly in on the reins, striving for control. Tendons stood out in her wrists, and her fingers were white. Vandien caught a glimpse of her pinched mouth and angry eyes. Then Goat's face took his attention.

His sweet pink mouth was stretched wide to reveal his yellow teeth in an excited grin. His hands were fastened to the seat, but his eyes were full of excitement. He was not scared. No, he was enjoying this. The last of the huts of Keddi raced past them. Open road loomed ahead, straight and flat.

"Let them out, Ki!" Vandien suggested over the creak and rumble of the wagon. "Let them run it off!"

She didn't look at him, but suddenly slacked the reins, and even added a shake to urge the greys on. Their legs stretched, their wide haunches rose and fell rhythmically as they stretched their necks and ran. Sweat began to stain them, soaking the dust on their coats. In the heat of the day they tired soon, and began blowing noisily even before they dropped to a trot, and then a walk. Their ears flicked back and forth, waiting for a sign. Sigmund tossed his big head, and then shook it as if he too were perplexed by his behavior. Silently Ki gathered up the reins, letting the horses feel her will. Control was hers again.

Vandien blew out a sigh of relief and leaned back. "What did you make of that?" he asked Ki idly, casual now that it was over.

"Damn dog" was all Ki muttered.

"Well, it's dead now!" Goat exclaimed with immense satisfaction. He turned to Ki, his mouth wet with excitement. "These horses can move, when you let them! Why must we plod along like this?"

"Because we'll get farther plodding like this all day than by racing the team to exhaustion and having to stop for the afternoon," Vandien answered. He leaned around the boy to speak to Ki. "Strange dog. Living right by the road like that, and barking at horses. I wonder what got into it."

Ki shook her head. "She probably just got the feist. She's just lucky it picked a steady team to yap at. Some horses would have been all over that road, people and tents notwithstanding."

"It's always been a nasty dog," Gotheris informed them. "It even bit me, once, just for trying to pick it up."

"Then you knew it?" Vandien asked idly.

"Oh, yes. Melui has had Bits for a long time. Her husband gave him to her, just before he got gored by their own bull."

Vandien turned to Ki, heedless of whether Goat read his eyes or not.

"Want me to go back, talk to her, explain?" he offered.

Ki sighed. "You'd never catch up with us on foot. And besides, what could you say besides we're sorry it happened? Maybe she'd just as soon have someone to blame and be angry with.'' Ki rubbed her face with one hand and gave him a woeful smile. ''What a way to start a journey.''

''I think it's begun rather well, myself!'' Goat announced cheerfully. ''Now that the road's flat and straight, can I drive? I'd like to take them for a gallop down it.''

Vandien groaned. Ki didn't reply. Eyes fixed on the horizon, she held the sweating team to their steady plod.

''Please!'' Goat nagged whiningly.

It was going to be a very long journey.

THREE

Ki yearned for night. She had listened to Goat nagging to drive the team for what seemed a lifetime. When he got no response to his begging, he had tried to reach over and take the reins. She had slapped his hands away with a stern "No!" as if he were a great baby instead of a young man. She had seen Vandien's tensing, and shot him a glance to warn him that she would handle this herself. But the man's eyes had a glint of amusement in them. The damn man was enjoying her having to deal with Goat. After a long and sulky silence, Goat had proclaimed that he was bored, that this whole trip was boring, and that he wished his father could have found him some witty companions instead of a couple of mute clods. Ki had not replied. Vandien had merely smiled, a smile that made Ki's spine cold. Handling Goat on this trip was going to be tricky; even trickier would be preventing Vandien from handling Goat. She wanted to deliver her cargo intact.

Now the sun was on the edge of the wide blue southern sky, the day had cooled to a tolerable level, and in the near distance she could see a grove of spiky trees and a spot of brighter green that meant water. Suddenly she dreaded stopping for the night. She wished she could just go on driving, day and night, until they reached Villena and unloaded the boy.

Ki glanced over at Goat. He was hunkered on the seat between her and Vandien, his bottom lip projecting, his peculiar eyes fixed on the featureless road. It was not the

26

most scenic journey she had ever made. The hard-baked road cut its straight way through a plain dotted with brush and grazing animals. Most of the flocks were white sheep with black faces, but she had seen in the distance one herd of cattle with humped backs and wide-swept horns. The few dwellings they passed were huts of baked brick. Shepherds' huts, she guessed, and most of them appeared deserted. A lonely land.

Earlier in the day, several caravans had passed them. Most of them were no different from the folk they had seen in Keddi, but she had noticed Vandien perk up with interest as the last line of burdened horses and Humans had passed. The folk of this caravan were subtly different from the other travellers they had seen. The people were tall and swarthy, their narrow bodies and grace reminding Ki of plainsdeer. They were dressed in loose robes of cream or white or grey. Bits of color flashed in their bright scarves that sheltered their heads from the sun, and in the bracelets that clinked on ankles and wrists. Men and women alike wore their hair long and straight, and it was every shade of brown imaginable, but all sun-streaked with gold. Many of them were barefoot. The few small children with them wore brightly colored head scarves and little else. Animals and children were adorned with small silver bells on harnesses or head scarves, so there was a sweet ringing as the caravan passed. Most of their horses plodded listlessly beneath their burdens, but at the end of the entourage came a roan stallion and three tall white mares. A very small girl sat the stallion, her dusty bare heels bouncing against his shoulders, her hair flowing free as the animal's mane. A tall man walked at her side, but none of the animals were led, or wore a scrap of harness. The little girl grinned as she passed, teeth very white in her dark face, and Ki returned her smile. Vandien lifted a hand in greeting, and the man nodded gravely, but did not speak.

"I bet they've stories to tell. Wonder where they'll camp?" Vandien's dark eyes were bright with curiosity.

"Company would be nice," Ki agreed, privately thinking that Goat might find boys of his own age to run with while she and Vandien made the camp and had a quiet moment or two.

"Camp near Tamshin?" Goat asked with disgust. "Don't you know anything of those people? You're lucky I'm here to warn you. For one thing, they smell terrible, and all are infested with fleas and lice. All their children are thieves, taking anything they can get their dirty little hands on. And it is well known that their women have a disease that they pass to men, and it makes your eyes swell shut and your mouth break out with sores. They're filth! And it is rumored that they are the ones that supply the rebels with food and information, hoping to bring the Duke down so they may have the run of the land and take the business of honest merchants and traders.''

''They sound almost as bad as Romni,'' Vandien observed affably.

''The Duke has ordered his Brurjan troops to keep the Romni well away from his province. So I have never seen one, but I have heard . . .''

''I was raised Romni.'' She knew Vandien had been trying to get her to see the humor of the boy's intolerance, but it had cut too close to the bone. That conversation had died. And the afternoon had stretched on, wide and flat and sandy, the only scenery the scrub brush and grasses drying in the summer heat. A very long day. . . .

At least the boy had been keeping quiet these last few hours. Ki sneaked another look at him. His face looked totally empty, devoid of intelligence. But for that emptiness, the face could have been, well, not handsome, but at least affable. It was only when he opened his mouth to speak, or bared those yellow teeth in his foolish grin, that Ki was repulsed. He reached up to scratch his nose, and suddenly appeared so childish that Ki was ashamed of herself. Goat was very much a child still. If he had been ten instead of fourteen, would she have expected the manners of a man, the restraint of an adult? Here was a boy, on his first journey away from home, travelling with strangers to an uncle he hadn't seen in years. It was natural that he would be nervous and moody, swinging from sulky to overconfident. His looks were against him too, for if she had seen him in a crowd, she would have guessed his age at sixteen, or even older. Only a boy. Her heart softened toward him.

''We'll stop for the night at those trees ahead, Goat. Do you think that greener grass might mean a spring?''

He seemed surprised that she would speak to him, let alone ask him a question. His voice was between snotty and shy.

"Probably. Those are Gwigi trees. They only grow near water."

Ki refused to take offense from his tone. "Really? That's good to know. Vandien and I are strangers to this part of the world. Perhaps as we travel together, you can tell us the names of the trees and plants, and what you know of them. Such knowledge is always useful."

The boy brightened at once. His yellow teeth flashed in a grin. "I know all of the trees and plants around here. I can teach you about all of them. Of course, there is a lot to learn, so you probably won't remember it all. But I'll try to teach you." He paused. "But if I'm doing that, I don't think I should have to help out with the chores every night."

Ki snorted a laugh. "You should be a merchant, not a healer, with your bargaining. Well, I don't think I will let you out of chores just for telling me the names of a few trees, but this first night you can just watch, instead of helping, until you learn what has to be done every night. Does that sound fair?" Her voice was tolerant.

"Well," Goat grinned, "I still think I shouldn't have to do any chores. After all, my father did pay you, and I will be teaching you all these important things. I already saved you from camping near the Tamshin."

"We'll see," Ki replied briefly, stuggling to keep her mind open toward the boy. He said such unfortunate things. It was as if no one had ever rebuked him for rudeness. Perhaps more honesty was called for. She cleared her throat.

"Goat, I'm going to be very blunt with you. When you say rude things about the Tamshin, I find it offensive. I have never met with any people where the individuals could be judged by generalities. And I don't like it when you nag me after I have said no to something, such as the driving earlier today. Do you think you can stop doing those thing?"

Goat's face crumpled in a pout. "First you start to be nice and talk to me, then all of a sudden you start saying I'm rude and making all these rules! I wish I had never come with you!"

"Goat!" Vandien's voice cut in over the noise of his protest. "Listen. Ki didn't say you weren't nice. She said that some of the things you say aren't nice. And she asked you, rather politely, to stop saying them. Now, you choose. Do you want Ki to speak honestly to you, as she would to an adult, or baby you along like an ill-tempered brat?''

There was a challenge in Vandien's words. Ki watched Goat's face flood with anger.

"Well, I was being honest, too. The Tamshin are thieves; ask anyone. And my father did pay for my trip, and I don't see why I should have to do all the work. It's not fair.''

"Fair or not, it's how it is. Live with it,'' Vandien advised him shortly.

"Maybe it seems unfair now,'' Ki said gently. "But as we go along, you'll see how it works. For tonight, you don't have to do any chores. You can just watch. And tomorrow, you may even find that you want to help.'' Her tone was reasonable.

"But when I wanted to help today with the driving, you said no. I bet you're going to give me all the dirty chores.''

Ki had run out of patience. She kept silent. But Vandien turned to Goat and gave him a most peculiar smile. "We'll see,'' he promised.

The light was dimming, the trees loomed large, and with no sign from her the team drew the wagon from the road onto the coarse meadow that bordered it. She pulled them in near the trees. The big animals halted, and the wagon was blessedly still, the swaying halted, the creaking silenced. Ki leaned down to wrap the reins around the brake handle. She put both her hands on the small of her back and arched, taking the ache out of her spine. Vandien rolled his shoulders and started to rise from the plank seat when the boy pushed past him to jump from the wagon and run into the trees.

"Don't go too far!'' Ki called after him.

"Let him run,'' Vandien suggested. "He's been sitting still all day. And I'd just as soon be free of him for a while. He won't go far. Probably just has to relieve himself.''

"I hadn't thought of that,'' Ki admitted. "You and I are used to a long day. It would be harder for the boy, especially to ask a stranger to stop the wagon for him. Maybe we should make a point of stopping a few times tomorrow. To eat, and to rest the horses.''

"Whatever you think.'' Vandien dropped lightly to the ground. He stood stretching and rolling his shoulders. "But I don't think that boy would be embarrassed to say anything.'' He glanced over at Ki. "And I don't think your coaxing and patience will get anywhere with him. He acts like he's never had to be responsible for his own acts. Sometime during this trip, he's going to discover consequences.''

"He's just a boy, regardless of his size. You've realized that as much as I have." Ki groaned at her stiffness as she climbed down from the driving seat.

"He's a spoiled infant," Vandien said agreeably. "And I almost think it might be easier to humor him as such for this trip, instead of trying to grow him up along the way. Let his uncle worry about teaching him manners and discipline.''

"Perhaps," Ki conceded as her fingers worked at the heavy harness buckles. On his side of the team, Sigurd gave his habitual kick in Vandien's direction. Vandien sidestepped with the grace of long habit, and delivered the routine slap to the big horse's haunch. This ceremony out of the way, the unharnessing proceeded smoothly.

As they led the big horses out of the traces and toward the water, Ki wondered aloud, "Where's Goat gotten to now?"

A loud splashing answered her. She pushed hastily through the thick brush surrounding the spring. The spring was in a hollow, its bank built up by the tall grasses and bushes that throve on its moisture. Goat sat in the middle of the small spring, the water up to his chest. His discarded garments littered the bank. He grinned up at them. "Not a very big pool, but big enough to cool off in."

"You did get yourself a cool drink before stirring up the mud on the bottom, didn't you?" Vandien asked with heavy sarcasm.

"Of course. It wasn't very cold, but it was drinkable."

"Was it?" Vandien asked drily. He glanced over at Ki, then reached to put Sigurd's lead into her hands. "You explain it to the horses," he said. "I'm not sure they'd believe me." He turned and strode back through the trees to the wagon. Ki was left staring down at Goat. She forced herself to behave calmly. He had not been raised by the Romni. He could know nothing of the fastidious separation of water for drinking from water for bathing. He would know nothing of fetching first the water for the wagon, then watering the horses, and then bathing. Not only had he dirtied all the available water, his nakedness before her was offensive. Ki reminded herself that she was not among the Romni, that in her travels she had learned a tolerance for the strange ways of other folk. She reminded herself that she intended to be patient, but honest, with Goat. Even if it meant explaining these most obvious things.

He grinned at her and kicked his feet, stirring up streamers of mud. Sigurd and Sigmund, thirsty and not fussy, pulled free of her slack grip and went to the water. Their big muzzles dipped, making rings, and then they were sucking in long draughts. Ki wished she shared their indifference.

Goat ignored them. He smiled up at Ki. "Why don't you take your clothes off and come into the water?" he asked invitingly.

He was such a combination of offensive lewdness and juvenility that Ki couldn't decide whether to glare or laugh. She set her features firmly in indifference. "Get out of there and get dressed. I want to talk to you." She spoke in a normal voice.

"Why can't we talk in here?" he pressed. He smiled widely. "We don't even have to talk," he added in a confidential tone.

"If you were a man," she said evenly, "I'd feel angry. But you're only an ill-mannered little boy." She turned her back on him and strode away, trying to contain the fury that roiled through her.

"Ki!" His voice followed her. "Wait! Please!"

The change in his tone was so abrupt that she had to turn to it. "I'm sorry," he said softly, staring at her boots. His shoulders were bowed in toward his hairless chest. When he looked up at her, his eyes were very wide. "I do everything wrong, don't I?"

She didn't know what to say. The sudden vulnerability after all his boasting was too startling. She couldn't quite believe it.

"I just . . . I want to be like other people. To talk like they do, and be friends." The words were tumbling out of him. Ki couldn't look away. "To make jokes and tease. But when I say it, it doesn't come out funny. No one laughs, everyone gets mad at me. And then I . . . I'm sorry for what I said just now."

Ki stood still, thinking. She thought she had a glimpse of the boy's misunderstanding. "I understand. But those kinds of jokes take time. They're not funny from a stranger."

"I'm always the stranger. Strange Goat, with the yellow

eyes and teeth.'' Bitterness filled his voice. ''Vandien already
hates me. He won't change his mind. No one ever gives me a
second chance. And I never get it right the first time.''

''Maybe you don't give other people a second chance,'' Ki
said bluntly. ''You've already decided Vandien won't like
you. Why don't you change the way you behave? Try being
polite and helpful. Maybe by the end of this trip, he'll forget
how you first behaved.''

Goat looked up at her. She didn't know if his gaze was sly
or shy. ''Do you like me?''

''I don't know yet,'' she said coolly. Then, in a kinder
voice, she added, ''Why don't you get dried off and dressed
and come back to camp? Try being likeable and see what
happens.''

He looked down at the muddied water and nodded silently.
She turned away from him. Let him think for a while. She
took the leads from the horses and left them to graze by the
spring. They wouldn't stray; the wagon was all the home they
knew. As she pushed through the brush surrounding the
spring, she wondered if she should ask Vandien to talk to the
boy. Vandien was so good with people, he made friends so
effortlessly. Could he understand Goat's awkwardness? The
boy needed a friend, a man who accepted him. His father had
seemed a good man, but there were things a boy didn't learn
from his father. She paused a few moments at the edge of the
trees to find words, and found herself looking at Vandien.

He knelt on one knee, his back to her, kindling the night's
fire. The quilts were spread on the grass nearby; the kettle
waited beside them. As she stepped soundlessly closer, she
saw that his dark hair was dense and curly with moisture. He
had washed already, yes, and drawn a basin of water for her
as well, from the water casks strapped to the side of the
wagon. Sparks jumped between his hands; grass smouldered
and went out. He muttered what was probably a curse in a
language she didn't know. She stepped closer, put one hand
on his shoulder and stooped to kiss the nape of his neck. He
almost flinched, but not quite.

''I knew you were there,'' he said matter-of-factly, striking
another shower of sparks. This time the tinder caught and a
tiny pale flame leaped up.

''No, you didn't,'' she contradicted. She watched over his
shoulder as he fed twigs and bits of dry grass to the infant

flame. Idly she twined one of his damp curls around her finger. It bared the birthmark on the back of his neck, an odd patch shaped vaguely like spread wings. She traced it with a fingertip. "Vandien?" she began cautiously.

"Sshh!" he warned suddenly, but she had already heard it. Hoofbeats; a horse being ridden hard. As one they moved to the end of the wagon, to peer down the road. Goat's comments on how the Duke felt about Romni had put Ki's nerves on edge.

A great roan horse with a thick mane and tail galloped heavily toward them. The pale grey of the evening sky and the wide empty plain was behind it; it was the only moving thing on the face of the world. Its hooves were falling clumsily, as if it were too weary for grace, and lather outlined the planes of the animal's muscles, but for all that it had beauty. Atop it were two girls, their heavy hair spilling black and red and moving with the horse's stride. Their faces were flushed and bright beneath a haze of road dust. Their loose robes had been hiked up so they could straddle the big roan, and their bare legs and sandaled feet gripped the barrel of his body. Ki watched them come silently, seized by their beauty and vitality.

"It looks like the two girls from the hiring mart," Vandien murmured by her ear. She could hear the smile in his voice. "I guess the red-haired one is running off to her sweetheart after all."

Then: "Halloo, the wagon!" A clear voice rose in the twilight. Vandien stepped out from the wagon and lifted a hand in greeting. The two girls flashed wide grins as they saw him, and then the sweating horse was pulled from the road, and came toward them over the coarse turf. The girl in front pulled in on the reins. The roan tucked his head stubbornly, and then perked his ears to her voice. He halted obediently, but tossed his head as if to show her he obeyed only because he wanted to.

"Lovely," Ki muttered to herself, caught up in his clean lines and proud head.

"Aren't they?" Vandien said as the girls slid from the roan's back.

She had to nod to that, too. She guessed their ages fell somewhere between fifteen and eighteen years, but could not say which was the older. They were like enough in height and limb to be twins, but there the resemblance ended. The dark-haired girl with the startlingly blue eyes would have been a beauty anywhere, but her beauty would not have been enough to keep anyone's eyes from her sister. The other girl's hair gleamed between bright copper and rust. Her mismatched eyes, set wide above a straight nose, met Ki's frankly; it made what might have been a fault into a flashing attraction. Where her sister was olive, she was pale. Freckles bridged her nose irresistibly. When she smiled, her teeth were very white. She glanced from Ki to her sister, and then to Vandien. "I'm so glad we caught up with you!" she said breathlessly. "We didn't hear you'd left until after noon. If Elyssen hadn't been able to borrow this horse, I'd never have been able to catch you!"

"Borrow!" Elyssen exclaimed. "And I'd better have Rud back before morning, or Tomi's master will have hard words for him."

"Ssh!" the red-haired girl chided her sister, but amusement leaped between them like sparks. They both turned hopeful faces to Vandien. Silence hovered.

"Come to the fire and tell us why you needed to catch us," Vandien suggested. "We can offer you a cup of tea after your long ride, if nothing else," he added.

Dark was falling rapidly on the open plain. The tiny fire was like a beacon now as Ki and Vandien led the way to it. The girls came behind them, whispering to one another.

"Did you notice the bundle tied to Rud's saddle-cloth?" Ki asked softly.

Vandien nodded. "I told them we couldn't take passengers."

"But then you did!" It was the red-haired girl, stretching her legs to catch up with them. "We heard in Keddi that you were taking Goat to Villena. So we knew you'd changed your mind, and because Tekum's right on your road . . ." Her hand settled on Vandien's arm, forcing him to meet her hopeful eyes.

"We don't take passengers," Ki said gently. Going to the fire, she set the kettle of water to simmer.

"But if you're taking Goat to Villena, why can't you take Willow to Tekum?" Elyssen objected. "If he's a passenger, why can't she be one? We've money to pay for her passage."

"Because no angry father is going to come tracking him down. Brin sent Gotheris with us." Vandien's voice was firm, but Ki heard the reluctance that tinged it. Willow's wide eyes suddenly brightened.

"But that isn't how it is! You can ask Elyssen if you don't believe me. Papa doesn't mind me marrying Kellich. It's only that Papa hasn't much money right now."

"Yes, and too much pride to tell Kellich so," Elyssen cut in. "So when Kellich asked Willow to come away with him, Papa forbade her. Because he couldn't give her those things that every woman should take with her when she goes with a man."

"Perhaps a cup of tea would make all this clearer," Vandien suggested. Ki gestured that they should seat themselves on the quilt near the fire. As she moved to take mugs from the dish-chest strapped to the wagon, she wondered what she was going to say. She had never taken passengers before. She hadn't been enthused about taking Goat. She did not adapt easily to the pressures of sharing her life with other folk. Even Vandien had at first seemed more of a nuisance and an intrusion than a companion. She had saddled herself with Gotheris for two weeks, and already regretted it. Now this Willow was asking to ride along as far as Tekum. The worst part was that Ki could not think of any excuse to say no. Could two riders be any worse than one? And there was the money to think of, at a time when money was hard to come by. She glanced back at them, at Vandien nodding intently to the girl's story. She didn't have to ask his opinion. She added tea herbs to the kettle.

". . . so it happens all the time. When the girl's family has no joining gifts to give her, or the boy's family cannot afford to start him in a home, they run away together. Then both families say what wretched scamps their children are. But as soon as the first grandchild is born, the couple comes back and asks for forgiveness, and of course they're forgiven, and everything is fine again." Willow spoke fervently, while Elyssen nodded eagerly.

"It's so, Vandien! I swear it! Papa won't be angry. When Kellich went away, Willow cried for days and days, and Papa was horribly upset."

"You needn't tell him I cried!" Willow broke in, nettled.

"But you did! And Papa was angry, just as he always is when one of us is sad and he cannot change it."

"Are you sure he isn't angry because Willow won't give

way to his will?'' Ki asked. She passed out mugs, and then took the tea from the embers where it had been brewing. She filled the mugs they held out.

Elyssen dimpled with merriment. ''Then why would he give her coins, all he could spare, and tell her to forget that worthless Kellich and buy the horse she's always wanted?''

''He knew that if I had owned a horse, I would have followed Kellich as soon as he left. But the money wasn't enough for a horse. I know, for I tried to buy one. But I thought it might be enough for my passage. See?'' Willow untied the little cloth pocket from her sash, and before Ki could speak, she had upended it onto the quilt. A heavy crescent coin and a brief shower of copper and silver bits spilled from it. She looked up from Ki to Vandien, her mismatched eyes innocent and hopeful. ''Is it enough to pay for my passage to Tekum?''

''It's enough to get your throat cut, if you're foolish enough to show it to strangers on the road,'' Vandien growled.

Willow's eyes grew wide, and Elyssen leaped to her feet.

''Oh, sit down,'' Ki told them both. ''Vandien was trying to warn you, not threaten you.''

Ki met Vandien's eyes, read his silent comment. ''They'd only try to buy passage with someone else if we told them no,'' she said.

His dark eyes lit. ''I suppose,'' he agreed. He turned to Willow, who still stared at him anxiously. ''That's Ki's way of saying you can ride with us.''

''Oh, Willow!'' Elyssen sighed, while Willow began to scoop up the money and thrust it at Vandien, as if she feared he would change his mind at any instant.

''Thank you. Oh, thank you. I promise I won't be any trouble to you. I promise. Oh, I can't believe I'm really going. Elyssen said I'd never get older people like you to understand how much I need to be with Kellich and how much he needs me!''

Willow looked into her sister's face, and saw Elyssen's dark eyes mirroring her own joy. She flung herself at her sister, hugged her wildly. ''I'll never forget how you helped me, Elyssen, never! And when your time comes . . .''

Elyssen squeezed her tight, her eyes near closed, her face between laughter and tears. Suddenly her dark eyes flew open. ''Goat,'' breathed Elyssen.

Willow broke from her arms. She followed her sister's stare, and a strange silence fell. Ki and Vandien exchanged glances, puzzled at the sudden dampening of the girls' spirits. They were poised as if a wild beast threatened them.

Goat stood at the outer edge of the fire's light. His arms were laden with something. His expression was something between delight and disbelief. He came on haltingly, as if uncertain of his footing. He glanced from face to face, searching for an answer to whatever question was in his mind.

"Oh, Willow," Elyssen breathed in dismay.

"I'll be all right," Willow said in a soft, fierce voice. "I told you I would. I know how to take care of myself, Elyssen."

"Be careful anyway!" Elyssen whispered. She stood, saying hastily, "Well, all is settled, except for Rud and me. I promised Tomi I'd have him back in plenty of time to be rubbed down and rested before morning. Good-bye, all!"

"Wait, Elyssen!" Willow called, and hurried off after her sister into the darkness.

Goat came on, first glancing after the girls and then back to Ki. His arms were heavy with small, fuzzy brown objects. He carried them to the edge of the quilt, where Vandien and Ki sat. Stooping down, he asked in a hoarse whisper, "What did she say about me?"

Ki met Vandien's puzzled glance. "Nothing, Goat. Only that she had heard you were going with us to Villena, and she wanted to know if we'd mind another passenger."

Goat's eyes widened. "She wants to go to Villena with me?"

"No. Only as far as Tekum. I understand her lover is there, and she goes to join him."

"Kellich." A wealth of disdain was in his voice. And disappointment? Ki couldn't be sure.

"What's that you have?" Vandien asked the boy.

"Burr-fruit. From the Gwigi trees. You know." Goat seemed subdued, almost shy. He glanced to where the two girls stood, heads bowed together. Willow had taken her bundle from Rud's back. The two sisters hugged suddenly, tightly.

"No, I don't." Vandien reached and took one from the boy's armload. He turned it curiously in his hands. "I've never seen one before. Are they edible?"

Goat started at Vandien's question, as if he didn't remember they had been talking. He glanced at the burr-fruit in

Vandien's hands. "After you singe them in a fire, you can crack them open. They're sweet inside. I picked them to share." Rud's retreating hoofbeats drew his attention away again. He stared at Willow, who stood in the semi-darkness watching her sister ride away.

"One might almost guess you were trying to make up for the way you behaved earlier," Vandien observed heartlessly.

The boy's eyes jerked back to Vandien. "I suppose," he muttered. He glanced from the approaching Willow back to Vandien's set face. He didn't want to be rebuked in front of her.

"Good. I was afraid I'd have to reason with you about it later tonight." Vandien's tone made it clear to Ki that his "reasoning" might not be conversational, but the inference went right past Goat. Worry furrowed his brow as his eyes darted surreptitiously toward Willow and then veered away. Vandien looked at the approaching girl. "We won't say anything more about it now. But I'm better impressed with you. A boy who can apologize when he's been wrong isn't that far from being a man."

The note of approval in Vandien's voice suddenly had Goat's full attention. His face lit up, not into his fool's grin, but a tentative smile. "There's enough here for all of us. Even Willow," he added cautiously. "I'll show you how to cook them," he offered, speaking more to the girl than to Ki and Vandien.

She stared at him across the fire. Her eyes were as unreadable as a cat's. Then she came smoothly into the circle of the firelight, flowing like water. She resumed her place on the quilt, took up her mug of tea and sipped from it. The slight was obvious, and Ki winced at it. Goat blushed deeply.

"So how do you cook them?" Vandien asked curiously, as if he hadn't noticed anything amiss. But he had, Ki would wager. Probably only she could detect the sympathy in his voice.

"You just . . . put them close to the embers of . . . the fire and leave them in there awhile." The boy's voice kept hitching.

"Well, while you two are doing that, I'll get the main part of the meal going." Ki filled in the silence with her voice.

"Let me help," Willow volunteered instantly, her voice as disarming as her smile.

"I can manage," Ki told her coolly.

"Please let me, I love to cook," she begged, her face so innocent that Ki wondered if she was unaware of how she had humiliated Goat. Willow's fingers were quick and her smile easy as she sliced dried meat into chunks that simmered separately from the pot of vegetables and roots that Ki prepared. She exclaimed about the tidiness of the wagon when she put her bundle inside, and was generally so charmed and charming that Ki could not hold a grudge against her. Together they set out bowls and travelling bread while Willow told her ingenuously of her Kellich. He was, Ki heard, an excellent trainer and handler of horses, and had been offered a fine position with a wealthy man in Tekum. He was, she told Ki, a young man who was handsome, witty, chivalrous, and merry, a graceful dancer and a skilled swordsman. He was also, Ki surmised from the way she spoke, a bit of a dandy and apt to be quick-tempered. But Willow plainly considered those facets of his characters as virtues. Ki smiled to herself.

"Food's done!" Vandien announced, taking the pots from the fire. The savory smell filled the night. Ki poured more tea while he ladled out a generous serving into each bowl. Conversation lagged as the four became aware of their hunger. They ate, spoons rapping softly against bowls. "Tastes funny," Goat said once, and then hastily amended his words to, "I mean different from what I'm used to." Vandien dipped his head to hide a small smile, and Ki nodded. But Willow stopped eating and stared at him for a long moment.

They were wiping the gravy out of their bowls with travelling bread when Goat suddenly stood. "These should be done," he told Vandien, and, picking up a small stick, he coaxed each burr fruit from the fire. Small cracks showed in their furry rinds. After a moment of cooling, Goat picked one up and broke it open. The exposed pulp was between pink and red. Juice ran over his fingers, and a sweet smell filled the air. Vandien tossed one to Ki, who tasted it gingerly. The texture was like a baked apple, the flavor not quite peaches nor strawberries.

"No." Willow spoke flatly, then softened it with a "Thank you" to Vandien.

"If you're sure." He shrugged, withdrawing the offered fruit. "Goat gathered plenty of these things."

"They're good," Goat added timidly.

She shifted her gaze to him, and her face lost its charming smile. Her eyes hardened with an unreadable emotion. With disdain in her voice she said, "You know I wouldn't eat anything you'd touched, Goat. You know that."

A long silence fell over the group. The boy, embarrassed, knelt by the fire. He looked at Vandien. Ki raked Willow with her eyes, shocked by the casual cruelty of the girl's voice and words.

"These grow on Gwigi trees?" Vandien asked. His tone suggested that Willow's words were unworthy of notice. He knelt by the boy, only interest in his face, but Ki sensed his annoyance with Willow.

Goat's hand shook slightly as he batted another burr-fruit from the fire's embers. He nodded silently, his head down.

"And if you're smart, you won't eat them either." Willow pushed, her voice cold. Her sudden anger grew. "Nor sleep too careless around him. Because while you're dreaming, he'll sneak and steal . . ."

"That's not true, Willow!" Goat flared. But his voice was more scared than threatening.

"Isn't it?" Her words cut savagely. "I know better. But they don't, do they, little sneak-thief? I didn't think Brin would admit what cargo he'd given them."

"Enough!" Vandien's low voice cut through the argument. "I don't know what grudge you two share. But whatever it is, leave it behind, or keep it private."

Willow stared at him, her eyes as wide as if he'd slapped her. "Vandien's right," Ki cut in before she could speak. "We four will be travelling together for a while. If you two have old differences, forget them. Or ignore them and be civil to one another. The wagon is too small a place for bickering."

"But you don't understand," Willow began earnestly.

"Nor do I want to," Ki interjected firmly. "I don't want to hear charges of thief or liar thrown about. It matters little enough in the short time we shall be together. If something of yours is stolen on this trip, Willow, I shall make good its value for you. And that is all I wish to say about it."

Ki felt her heart hammering. Gods, how she hated a scene like this. This was why she and Vandien moved alone and apart from others. The bickering and quarrels, the useless anger, and always, always, people seeking someone to blame.

Willow stared at her. Her cheeks were reddened with more

than the fire's heat, her eyes bright. The girl was either very angry, or on the verge of tears. Both, Ki suspected. She did not look as if she were accustomed to not getting her own way. When she spoke again, her voice was tight. "Very well, Ki the teamster. Had I any other way to Kellich, I would have taken it, as you well know. I had thought you would wish to know what all the village knows about Goat. But as you do not, I will say no more about it. But I shall not sleep at night. And you will regret, very soon, that you did not let me say what I know is true."

"Goat. Time for us to check the horses." Vandien rose hastily, threatened by the possibility of Willow's tears.

"I don't want to . . ." Goat began, obviously fascinated and unsettled by the scene between Ki and Willow.

"Time to check the horses," Vandien repeated firmly, catching the boy by the collar and tugging him to his feet. They disappeared into the darkness. Ki smiled at his use of the Romni euphemism. Going to check the horses meant a man was going to relieve himself, or wanted a little privacy. Goat would soon learn it, she supposed. At any rate, Vandien had decided the boy was worth an effort. Leaving her with Willow.

Ki cast a sideways glance at her. Her cheeks still glowed. "Well, we'd better tidy up for the night," Ki suggested in a neutral voice. Willow met Ki's look with a sullen stare, but began gathering the dishes. She pointedly ignored Goat's bowl. With a sigh, Ki picked it up herself.

The awkward silence held as the dishes were cleaned and packed away. When Willow broke it, it was with another dilemma. "Where am I supposed to rest tonight?" she asked coldly.

"Wherever you wish," Ki replied politely. She would not rise to the girl's avoidance of the word "sleep."

"Where's Goat going to sleep?" she demanded next.

Ki sighed. "I hadn't thought about it. By the fire, I suppose."

"Then I'll sleep in the wagon."

"Vandien and I usually sleep in the wagon," Ki pointed out. She could feel her control slip and wondered with a sudden anger just where the hell Vandien was. Let him come back and manage his wonderfully charming young girl.

"I don't mind," Willow said smoothly.

"Did you ever consider that I might?" Ki asked, dropping all pretense of civility.

"No. I didn't. You couldn't possibly expect me to sleep near Goat, even if he weren't . . . what he is. Among my people that isn't done," she added primly.

Ki closed her eyes for an instant, got a grip on her rising anger. "I see." She gave a sigh, tried to breathe her irritation away. "Then why don't you sleep in the wagon, and Vandien and I will sleep outside? That should keep everyone's propriety intact."

"Near Goat? You're going to sleep near Goat?" The distaste in the girl's voice was not feigned. For whatever reason she disliked Goat, it was not a pretense.

"Vandien will protect my virtue," Ki assured her with heavy sarcasm, but the girl considered her words gravely. Her eyes were wide as she met Ki's gaze.

"I do not think even he could protect you from one such as Goat. Are you sure you wouldn't rather sleep in the wagon also?"

"Quite sure," Ki assured her. Willow's eyes darted to a rustling in the thicket that presaged Vandien and Goat's return.

"I'm going to bed now. Good night. And take care!"

The last she whispered as she turned and fled to the shelter of the wagon.

When Goat and Vandien appeared, their arms were laden with dead branches for firewood. Ki nodded her approval. Already the night was cool, denying the heat of the day. "Where's Willow?" Goat demanded of her.

"Gone to bed," Ki told him smoothly. "As we all should, if we are to get an early start tomorrow."

"Where?" he repeated.

"Where what?" she asked, feigning puzzlement.

"Where is Willow sleeping?" Goat demanded. Vandien winced at the boy's unconcealed interest.

"In the wagon." Ki kept her voice unconcerned. "Where the night insects will not bother her."

"We're all going to sleep in the wagon?" Goat asked eagerly. Without waiting for an answer, he started toward the steps.

"No, it would be far too crowded and stuffy. Ki and I will sleep under the wagon, and you can sleep by the fire."

"But . . ." Goat began, and then caught Vandien's look.

Ki could not imagine what he had said to the boy, but Goat suddenly closed his lips. He kept his words in check, but not the sulky look that claimed his face. Snatching up a good portion of the scattered quilts and blankets, he began to make up a bed by the fire.

Vandien refused to acknowledge his pique. "Good night, Goat," he told the boy affably. He gathered the remaining quilts and cushions and made up their bed beneath the wagon while Ki belatedly washed the road dust from her face and smoothed her tangled hair. He was already settled when she came to join him.

"Why under the wagon instead of next to the fire?" she demanded as she crawled in beside him. She knew the answer, and he knew it, but he spoke anyway. His voice was sleepy. "Feeling of shelter, keeps the rain off. And makes it harder for anyone to attack while we're sleeping."

"Like sleeping in a coffin," Ki grumbled. She dragged off her boots, blouse and trousers so that she was clad in loose cotton drawers and chemise. Shivering, she burrowed into the quilts and settled against Vandien. He was warm. She curled her body around his, her belly to his back. She could smell his hair and the warm skin of his neck.

"These children," he said softly, "make me feel old."

"Um," Ki agreed. She kissed the nape of his neck experimentally.

He sighed. "Very old. Ki, did you hear me earlier? Dictating, chastising, directing, warning. I sounded just like my uncle when I was a child."

"Your guardian?" she asked. With the tip of one finger, she wrote her name on the warm skin of his back.

"Yes. He was always directing me, never letting me do anything on my own. Not even choose which women I'd bed." Vandien's voice trailed off as his mind went back to those painful times, to his futile efforts to sire an heir for his line. He moved slightly apart from Ki, and she, knowing his old pain, let him. He wouldn't want to be touched just now. Damn. Well, that's how it was, then. She closed her eyes, sought sleep. "I'd hate to think I had grown to be just like him," Vandien said suddenly. "Ki, did you hear what Willow said earlier? That she didn't think any one as old as I am could understand why she'd run away to her lover? Do I look that old to you? Old enough to be her father?"

''Depends on how young you started,'' Ki replied sleepily. Then, ''Sorry. Not to me, Vandien. Only to somone as young as Willow.''

He rolled onto his back and stared up at the bottom of the wagon. ''How old do I look to you?'' he asked quietly.

The weariness of the day had suddenly found Ki. ''I don't know,'' she sighed. She opened her eyes a slit, stared at him. He was serious. Traces of lines at the corners of his mouth. A few hints of grey in the dark curls, mostly from old scars. Weathered skin that was more the work of sun and wind than years. She thought, as she had the first time she saw him, that it was not a bad way for a man to look. She'd rather die than tell him that. ''Old enough to be smarter than you act most of the time. Young enough to worry about foolish things.''

''Mph.'' He rolled to face her, dragging her covers away. ''That's not a very satisfactory answer.''

She tugged at the covers, opened her eyes. His face was inches from her own, his hand on the curve of her waist. ''Not a satisfactory answer?''

He shook his head, the curve of his smile beneath his moustache barely visible in the dwindling light from the fire.

''Then let me put it another way.'' She seized the curls at the nape of his neck and pulled his face to hers.

FOUR

In the coolness before dawn, Ki's strangely vivid dreams broke and dragged against her like cobwebs. Gently she drew away from Vandien and pulled on her clothes. The camp was silent; Gotheris slumbered deeply by the dead ashes of the fire, his arms flung wide in sleep. Ki took the kettle and water bucket and headed for the spring. She considered waking Vandien to share the quiet with her but decided against it. She needed this solitude; the rest of the day would offer her little enough.

On her way back to camp she passed Vandien. His hair was tousled, his eyes vague with sleep. He greeted her silently and moved on toward the spring. In camp, she found a few embers buried in the ash and coaxed them into blossom. She set the dripping kettle atop the small fire and mounted the wagon step.

The door was jammed. She tugged at it futilely several times before she realized that Willow had latched it. Suddenly irritated that anyone could lock her out of her own wagon, she pounded on the door. There was no response. "Willow!" she shouted. "Unlock this door!" Goat rolled over and opened his eyes.

There was a muffled reply, but Ki fumed on the step for several moments longer before a yawning Willow slid the door open. "What's the matter?" she asked sleepily.

"Why didn't you open the door?" Ki demanded, pushing in past her. "And why was it locked at all?"

"I wasn't dressed." Willow sat down on the tousled bedding. "And you know why I locked it. Because he's out there."

Ki glared at the girl, who sulked back at her. The silence was thick as Ki shrugged into a fresh tunic. Ki gathered up travelling bread and cheese from the food bins. Willow was still pouting on the bed when Ki left the wagon. The door slammed and latched behind her. Almost she turned back; but she set her teeth and let it pass. Foolish, to make a fuss over a latched door. But she hated its assumption, that the wagon space was Willow's, and Ki could be locked out of it. Forget it. Ki made a conscious effort to loosen the muscles in her shoulders and set her irritation aside.

She set the bread and cheese on a wooden platter from the dish-chest, and had just found the tea when an arm fell across her shoulders. "I'm hungry!" Gotheris announced in her ear. The sack of tea leaped from her hand as she startled.

"You spilled it all over!" he exclaimed, pushing forward to gaze at the wrinkled balls of leaves and herbs littered across the jumbled dishes.

Ki's hands were fists at her sides. She spoke each word separately. "Don't creep up behind me and grab me like that."

"I didn't!" Goat protested. "I only . . ."

A thudding of many hooves interrupted him. Ki held up a hand for silence while her eyes grew wide. Stepping around the tail of the wagon, she stared up the long flat road. Her heart leaped painfully, then began to hammer in her chest so that she could hear nothing else. Rousters.

There were six—no, seven—Brurjans, and two stout, ugly Humans, all mounted on great black horses with scarlet hooves. She gripped the corner of her wagon, watching them come, knowing there was no place to flee to, no place to hide. Childhood memories flooded her mind, of wagons set ablaze in the dark night, of Romni women fleeing with their children caught up in their arms, of men struck down by flying hooves as they stood, not in hopes of defending their lives, but only to buy their families time to escape. Rousters, come by nightfall or in the bright day, to put the Romni trash on the road again, to steal their bits of things and drive them away.

The Brurjans rode high and catlike on their peculiar saddles. Their huge jaws were wide with their hissing laughter, and their myriad pointed teeth flashed in the new sun that stroked their glossy hides. Their quilled crests were high. They did not pull up as they approached the camp, but rode full tilt into it, great hooves tramping Goat's bedding and the small fire, and sending the hissing kettle flying. Vandien emerged from the trees, a strangely small figure before the tall horses with their massive riders. The riders milled through the camp. Ki could not speak. Goat was plastered up against the wagon, his eyes wide, his mouth hanging open. The world tilted around Ki. One of the Humans rode close to her, sneered down at her disdainfully. Let Willow remain silent within the wagon, she begged the Moon. Her beauty was too fresh for one such as that to resist bruising.

One of the Brurjans snarled something, and the sea of rousters and horses was suddenly still. All eyes went to him, a great black-pelted creature with deep-set black eyes. His battle harness was scarlet and black leather, broken by threads of silver. A red cloak spilled down his furred back. His black-nailed hands gripped his mount's reins lightly. His horse had wicked eyes, and its ears were tilted back toward its master, waiting for a command to lash out with hooves or teeth.

Like a stray cat strolling insolently into a strange butcher shop came Vandien. He slipped between two great horses fully as large as plow beasts, unmindful of their restive scarlet hooves. Ki wondered what magic kept him safe as he moved boldly through the rousters to confront their leader. He took up his stance, arms crossed on his chest, slightly to the left of the horse's head. He looked up, raising his chin as he struck eyes with the Brurjan. His brow was unlined as he said, "Good morning."

"Is it?" the Brurjan asked with callous humor. His Common was thickly accented.

"Isn't it?" Vandien asked calmly. Ki winced. Three Vandiens rolled together might make up the bulk of one of the Brurjans. His rapier, she realized belatedly, was in its sheath on a hook in the wagon. The Brurjan stared down at him.

"You Romni?" one of the Human rousters suddenly demanded.

For a second Vandien didn't move. His gaze remained

locked with the leader's. He didn't even turn to the Human as he asked contemptuously, "Do I look Romni?" Vandien paused, then asked the leader coldly, "Did you want something of us?"

The Human broke in. "They aren't the ones we want, but it don't mean we shouldn't shake them down. Woman there looks Romni, Allikata. I've seen her kind before, up North. Duke doesn't want Romni coming into his holdings."

The leader's eyes flickered briefly to his man. Then he stared at Ki as he asked Vandien, "Papers?"

"Ki. Fetch the papers." Vandien didn't look at her, didn't move from where he stood.

Ki turned to the wagon, stepped up on the step and tugged at the door. It jarred against the latch. A trickle of icy sweat ran down Ki's ribs. If Willow would unlatch it, she could step in, grab the papers, and step out without the rousters even knowing Willow existed. But if she didn't open the door . . . Ki rattled the door against the lock softly, hoping the girl would unlatch it. There was no sound from within the wagon.

"While you're here, can you tell us if the road is good as far as Villena? We're taking our boy to visit kin there. We'd heard rumors of thieves, but then someone said the Duke's roadguard had cleared them out. That would be you, wouldn't it?"

Vandien was speaking more rapidly than he usually did, trying to keep their attention away from Ki. It wasn't working. Ki could feel the silence as the rousters stared at her.

"Fine tack," Vandien observed. "Good leather like that's hard to come by." Reaching up, he took a sudden grip on the bridle of Allikata's horse. Ki gasped, knowing as well as he did what would happen. The battle-horse screamed angrily, struck out with front hooves and teeth. All eyes jerked to Vandien as the great beast lifted him clear of the ground and with a shake flung him aside. He landed, rolling, near another horse, which immediately struck out at him. She knew why he had done it, and didn't waste her dare. Ki turned her back on him, and with a muscle-ripping wrench tore the door open.

She pushed past the dangling hook and snatched up a roll of papers from a shelf. Of Willow the only sign was a slipper peeping out from beneath an untidy heap of bedclothes. Someone cursed loudly in Brurjan, and a Human laughed sadistically. Ki leaped from the wagon, the papers held aloft. "Here they are!" she called loudly, and strode between the dancing horses of the two nearest rousters.

Vandien got up slowly, one arm wrapping his ribs. As Ki approached he slowly folded his arms across his chest. She didn't look at him, but walked straight up to Allikata and thrust the papers up at him. He unrolled them carelessly, glanced at them, and tossed them back. "It says two travelling. There's three of you."

Ki opened her mouth, but Goat answered, his voice cracking with excitment. "Maybe. But there must be twenty-five of those filthy Tamshin in the caravan that passed us yesterday. They're who you're supposed to be after. For those horses! I bet those horses were stolen! I knew that big roan stallion was too fine a beast to belong to Tamshin!"

"The white mares!" A Brurjan suddenly demanded gutturally. "They still had the white mares?"

"Yes!" Goat answered happily. "They passed us just before dusk. They couldn't be far away; maybe at a place with more water, and trees for shade." Goat's face had taken on a dreamy expression, as if he could see the place he was describing. The faces of the patrol lit up evilly. Vandien looked ill.

"No, Goat, you're mistaken. The Tamshin passed us before noon, moving north and fast. They are long gone by now. The wine merchants passed us just before nightfall."

Ki's voice rang clear, but no one turned to it. Allikata only laughed, a short fierce sound. His tongue was red behind his white teeth.

"If we hurry, they'll just be rousing from sleep," a Human added appreciatively. Allikata gave a shout, and the horses wheeled suddenly and left the camp at a gallop. One rider's boot caught Ki's shoulder as he passed, shoving her nearly into the path of another horse. Then they were gone, the thunder of their hooves fading, and only the trampled camp to show that they had been there at all.

She scrabbled to her feet. In two steps she was beside Vandien. "That was stupid," she said tersely.

"You're welcome," he gasped. He let his arms hang at his sides and she tugged his shirt free of his belt, to lift it carefully. He flinched as her fingers gently prodded. "Bruised," she said in a tight voice. "Maybe cracked, but not broken."

"Same ones," he said, trying to make his voice light, but she could hear the effort it took for him to speak. "And that was a Brurjan, too. You remember that tavern in Silva?"

"Where I had to pay for the hole in the wall?" Ki asked.

"Yes. Guess I just don't make a good impression with Brurjans."

"No. You should stick to walls. You made a hell of an impression on that one."

He made a vague effort to tuck in his shirt, then gave it up with a twisted smile. Ki touched his face, and when he lifted his eyes to hers, she kissed him softly. He caught her hand.

"That's twice," he said, his voice still breathy with pain. "Twice in two days that you've kissed me. I remember a time when if you kissed me twice in a month, it was remarkable."

Ki shook her head at him silently, finding no words for her thoughts.

"What about me?" Goat demanded suddenly. "Isn't anyone going to thank me? If I hadn't sent them after those Tamshin, they'd have wrecked this place. And probably killed Vandien and raped you and Willow."

Ki rounded on him. "And what do you think they'll do to the Tamshin? What you did was cold and disgusting." She choked into silence, unable to speak her anger.

Vandien's eyes were hard and black as he stared at the boy. "We were handling it fine, until you stepped in. If there's ever a next time, you remember that Ki and I handle things, while you keep silent and unobtrusive. Understand me, boy?"

There was a whip's edge to his final question. Goat both flinched and bristled. "Oh, yes," he spat bitterly. "I'll remember. I'll keep silent and unobtrusive while they kick the snot out of you, I will, and with pleasure, and when they . . ."

"Fine. That would be wonderful. I'm pleased we understand one another." Vandien's voice was cool, every trace of anger gone from it. He turned from the boy's ranting as if it were the humming of a mosquito. "What was wrong with the door?"

"Willow latched it," Ki said tersely.

"Willow!" Vandien exclaimed, remembering the girl. "She must have been terrified. Is she all right?"

Ki looked disgusted. "Willow!" she called. "You can come out now. They've gone."

In an instant the disheveled girl appeared in the door of the wagon. She raced across the trampled earth to fling herself into Vandien's arms. He exclaimed with pain, but didn't push her away. "I was so scared, I was so scared!" she sobbed into his shoulder. "All I could think of was to hide."

"Are the Duke's patrols always so threatening?" Ki asked. "I would rather have faced the robbers."

"She doesn't have travelling papers," Goat guessed suddenly. "You thought they were after you, didn't you, Willow?" His voice was snidely speculative. "Why would the Duke's patrol be interested in a little girl running away to her lover? Or is Kellich starting to take his big talk seriously?"

"Shut up! Shut up!" Willow screeched savagely, and Vandien held her firmly to keep her from going after the boy.

"Quiet!" Ki bellowed, her voice cracking on the word. Silence fell. Vandien looked astounded at the command. Ki took a breath, feeling her throat's rawness. "Now. Quietly," she said. "Tell me. I knew Vandien and I needed papers because we had the wagon and were doing business with it. I thought it was sort of like a trade permit. It seems I was wrong. Are you two supposed to have travelling papers, just to go from town to town?"

"Of course," Goat answered. "Or how would the Duke know where anyone was? How could they tell good citizens from rebel scum? I have *my* papers. My father got them the morning we left. I have no reason to sneak from town to town. Not like some."

"Willow?" Ki asked.

The girl buried her face against Vandien's shoulder. "I didn't have time! I didn't have enough money!" she wept. "If I'd waited for the papers, you'd have gone. And I needed the money to pay you to take me. I didn't think anyone would stop us or check us. What are you doing to do?" She lifted red-rimmed eyes to gaze into Vandien's face. "Are you going to leave me here? Do you know what they'd do to me if they caught me, alone on the road, with no papers?" She was shaking.

"They might think you were a rebel," Goat observed heartlessly. "Or a sympathizer, carrying information. Or maybe just a roadside whore and . . ."

Ki's look shut him up.

Vandien put steadying hands on Willow's shoulders. "No one's leaving you," he said softly. "But don't you see the danger you put us all in? If you'd told Ki and me, we would have been prepared. It's not like the Romni don't know how to handle harassment. Ki knows a dozen tricks, and I have a few of my own. But we need to know what we're up against. We're strangers to your Duke's holdings."

His voice was calm, reasonable. Willow lifted her tear-stained face. "The Duke's patrol," she faltered, "keeps the roads clear. Of robbers, and Tamshin, and such . . . those without papers. Rebels, they call them. Rebels. As if just being too poor to afford papers, or not wanting to account for every step of your life, should be a crime. And the Duke lets—if they find anyone without papers—they can take what they wish from them. Even their lives. It's how they're paid. Oh, the Duke pays them some, but that's how he keeps them eager. If you don't have papers, you're game for the patrol."

"Eager." Ki said the word flatly. She looked at Goat. "You knew that?"

The boy shrugged carelessly. "Everyone knows that."

"And you still put them after the Tamshin." There was disbelief in her voice.

"They're only Tamshin!" he protested hotly, while Willow cut in with, "You'd rather they had me?"

"I'd rather they had no one. I'd rather I'd never heard of your Duke or Loveran." She turned away and picked up the battered kettle. She examined it to see if it would still hold water. For a moment Vandien watched her, then took Willow's shoulders and gently pushed her aside from him to walk over to the trampled quilts. Cautiously he bent down, his hand against his sore ribs. He picked up a quilt and shook it.

"It's mendable," he said, and began to fold it up.

"Most things are," Ki agreed. "But not all."

He knew what she meant. "They're young, both of them. It's easy to forget that."

"Especially when they nearly kill you because of it. Vandien, I am full of an evil feeling. A foreboding."

He nodded slowly. "This Duke of Loveran . . . This doesn't seem a good place for folk like us, does it?"

"My mother was a full-blooded Romni, even if Aethan

wasn't. It shows in my face. The next patrol won't be so easily fooled.''

He sighed. ''Maybe not. What do you want to do? Take Willow and Goat back to Keddi, give the money back, and get away from Loveran and its Duke?''

''And go where?'' She squared her shoulders, took the quilt from him. ''No. We'll go on. There can't be many patrols, or there'd be no Tamshin at all. Maybe we won't meet any more. And if we do . . . well, the Tamshin survive. We will, too.''

''Maybe,'' he said. He touched her, but she pulled away, too upset to share her fears. He sighed and let her go. Still cradling his ribs, he turned, to find Willow and Goat staring at them. The scrutiny suddenly annoyed him.

''Can't you see there's work to do?'' he demanded. ''Willow, go in the wagon and put together something we can eat. Goat, tidy up the camp. I'm going for the horses. The sooner we're on the road, the better.''

Both young faces clouded with rebellion, but they grudgingly moved to their chores. Vandien ignored them as he got the grain sack and went after the team. Sigmund stopped cropping the grasses and lifted his great head as soon as Vandien appeared. Sigurd only swung his body so that his broad rump was toward him. Vandien wasn't fooled. He shook the grain sack once. Sigmund came eagerly, his muzzle nudging Vandien's shoulder, and Sigurd trailed reluctantly behind him.

A new quarrel had already broken out at the wagon. Willow's face was pink, while Goat glowed with satisfaction. Ki stood between them, fists on hips. ''The wagon seat holds three people. Someone has to ride inside. That's all. You two work it out.''

Vandien skirted the group, moving the horses into their traces. Ki turned her back on Willow as she indignantly exclaimed, ''But why should I have to ride inside the stuffy old wagon all day? Why can't we take turns, or Goat walk beside the wagon or something?''

''My father paid for me to travel comfortably,'' Goat was saying at the same time.

Vandien parceled out grain to the team as Ki lifted the heavy harness into place. ''Maybe,'' Vandien said softly, "we could put them both into the wagon, and shut the door behind the seat so we didn't have to listen to them."

"Somehow I think we'd still hear them." Ki tightened the last strap. "But I know someone who'd better ride inside. You."

"Me?"

"Yes. You look green. Does it hurt much?"

"Enough to make me want to puke, but I know that would hurt even more."

Ki started to laugh, stopped abruptly. He knew what she was thinking. "Not a damn thing we could do for them. The rousters' horses are twice as fast as Sigurd and Sigmund. And even if you could have warned them, where could they hide? Don't let it poison you."

Ki shook her head, not looking at him. He put his hand on her shoulder and leaned on her as they went to the wagon's door.

Goat sat firmly on the wagon seat. Willow glowered up at him. Neither Vandien nor Ki said a word as they passed.

"It's not fair!" Willow burst out suddenly, and then fell silent as she watched Vandien clamber slowly up the wagon step and inside. "Is he going to ride in there?" she suddenly demanded.

"Yes," Ki admitted. "So I suppose you can both ride up front with me. I'll sit in the middle so you don't have to look at one another."

"No. I'll keep Vandien company, I guess."

Willow's sudden capitulation startled Ki, but it was a relief, too. The idea of spending the day seated between two squabbling children hadn't been pleasant. But as she mounted the wagon, she considered that spending the day alone with Goat was not a happy alternative. He was already holding the reins.

"I'm driving now, all right?" he said as she seated herself beside him.

"No." Ki tugged the reins from his grasp and kicked the brake off. She shook the reins and the greys stepped out. The wagon lurched from the turfy roadside back up onto the roadbed. After the shade by the spring, the sun was very bright. Ki squinted down the long, empty road.

After a long stretch of boring prairie, Goat asked suddenly, "Are you so mad you aren't going to talk to me all day?"

Ki considered it. "Perhaps."

"Because of the Tamshin?"

"Yes."

A whimper came into Goat's voice. "But I thought I was helping. It saved your life, you know that. Those Brurjans were about to make porridge of Vandien."

Ki felt no mercy for him. "You know that, do you?" she asked sarcastically. "You know so much of Brurjans, do you? I'd have said they were just about to ask us for a bribe."

"And you'd have been wrong!" Goat broke in suddenly. There was no whimper to his voice now, only a boy's wild anger. "Allikata had decided it would be interesting to break Vandien up slowly, to see how much pain he could take. And one of the Humans, it was his turn to be first at the women, and he was wondering if you'd fight or weep."

There was a savage satisfaction in his voice that chilled Ki. Against her will she turned to meet his pale eyes, more yellow than brown. She did not like to admit her disgust was tinged with fear.

"Believe your own wild stories if you like," she began in a shaky voice.

"I believe what I know, and I know more than you like. More than anyone likes, and so they hate me. Would you like to hate me more? Then I'll warn you that it isn't wise to leave Vandien and Willow alone in the wagon together. Not when she is wondering if he would protect her if the Brurjans came again, and he is wondering if he is as old as he feels. Young enough to worry over foolish things . . . isn't that what you told him?"

For an instant Ki was confused. Then a killing fury gripped her. So the boy had been awake last night, and listening to them. Blood suffused her face suddenly. And watching them, too? The team tossed their heads, baffled by the trembling that came down the reins to them. She would not strike him. She would force herself to remember that he was only a boy. But . . .

"If ever . . ." Anger made her voice crack. "If ever you spy upon us like that again, I shall . . ."

"Shall what?" Gotheris demanded spitefully. He stared at her. "What can you do to me? You already hate me. Every time you think of me, you are filled with annoyance and irritation. But you'll keep your contract, you'll take me safely to Villena. No matter how horrid I am, you'll give me to my uncle. No matter how nice I am, either.''

A different note entered the boy's voice on his final words. For a long time Ki drove in silence. There were more trees now, in scattered groves set back from the road. Perhaps the remains of failed farming efforts. When she trusted herself to speak, she said, ''I don't think I hate you, Gotheris. Much of what you do makes me angry, but . . . what's that?''

''That'' was something in the distance, a scatter of objects beside and upon the road. They moved erratically. Ki settled back on the seat. ''Looks like someone's herd of swine loose in the road. Rolling in the dust.''

''Close enough,'' Gotheris observed heartlessly. ''Tamshin.''

At his words Ki stood, to peer ahead, and then startled the team with a cry. She slapped the reins on the grey backs, and the horses broke into a ponderous trot and then a heavy canter. She drove them standing, swaying with their rhythm. The entry to the caravan slid open behind her. Willow peered out. ''What's the matter?'' she demanded. Ki didn't answer. The road stretched ever longer before her, making it seem as though she would never arrive.

When she did get there, she was too late. She pulled the team in to keep them from trampling the first of the bodies. From the way they lay, it was apparent the Tamshin had been moving when the rousters caught up with them. These were the stragglers, who had fallen as they fled, the first victims of the scarlet hooves and blades.

Ki stood frozen, staring down at them. Too vivid were the memories they stirred, of other bodies on a dusty road, of a man and two children she had called hers. Behind her she heard Willow's rising pants, the beginning of hysteria. Beside her, Goat stirred restively and complained, ''I smell shit.''

''Shut up.'' Ki's voice was dispassionate. ''Willow. Close the door. And don't waken Vandien. He doesn't need this.''

She booted the brake on, wrapped the reins about its handle. Slowly she dismounted and walked over to the first body. The bloodstains on the pale robe were already turning brown in the heat of the sun. There was no need to check for signs of life. Flies buzzed angrily as she turned the body over. She refused to look into the face. With averted eyes, she lifted the shoulders and dragged the body from the road some little distance to the paltry shade of a dying oak. Beyond it was a scorched area where long ago a house might once have stood. She was too heartsick to be curious about it. Slowly she walked back to the road, went to the next body. A child. Unmindful of the blood and feces that fouled his little body, she picked him up and carried him to place him by the other. Goat watched her avidly from the wagon, silent but absorbed in her actions. She paid no attention to him.

She had moved the wagon forward and started to lift the shoulders of a third corpse when the woman came to meet her. She was Tamshin, tall and willowy, but the grace was gone from her movements. Her face was bruised to blackness, and blood had clotted in her long hair. Her thick accent and swollen lips made her hard to understand.

"Stop. Stop, please. Leave them. Leave us and go away."

Ki lifted her eyes to meet the woman's, but she turned her head aside, refusing the communion of grief.

"I would help you," Ki offered softly. "With the dead and with the injured. I have food, water, and bandages."

A boy came up to stand beside the woman. His eyes were wide and empty. Ki glanced up the road, saw other survivors busy among the dead. They made not a sound.

"No." The woman spoke with difficulty, swayed and put a hand on the boy's shoulder. He stood steady beneath her weight. "No. Go away. We are Tamshin, our dead are Tamshin. Go away."

"Please," Ki said. "There are so many . . ."

"You are . . ." The woman searched for the word. "Unclean. You must not touch our dead. Go away."

"I understand." Ki backed slowly away and stood at the side of the road as the woman and boy bent over the body of an old man. With difficulty they dragged him from the road.

"Your way is clear now," the woman said. "Go."

"May I leave you water?"

"Unclean. Unclean! Go away!" The woman screamed the last words, and suddenly began to sob.

Ki spun away from her and fled toward the wagon. As she reached it Vandien stepped out suddenly and caught her in his arms. He held her close. "You should have called me," he said into her hair.

"I didn't want you to . . . They don't want our help. We desecrate their dead. They want us to go."

"Then we'll go. It's the only thing we can do for them, Ki."

She nodded slowly. He followed her up onto the wagon's high seat, moved Goat over with a glance. He took up the reins and kicked off the brake. For once Ki said nothing about his driving. Only Goat dared to speak. Leaning forward to peer up into Ki's striken face, he said, "You see how they are? Ungrateful. And filthy. You smell terrible."

"Shut up, Goat," said Vandien.

FIVE

"Don't touch that."

Goat slowly drew his hand back from the whip in its socket. "All you do is boss me around," he complained.

"Right."

It's like being shut in a box, thought Ki, while someone keeps hammering on the top. Goat's nagging and Vandien's sotto voice replies counterpointed the annoying chirring of the night insects. She moved closer to Vandien, and despite the muggy evening, took comfort in his warmth. He should have stopped for the night hours ago. Perhaps Vandien was trying to make up for the time lost this morning. Perhaps he dreaded the necessary conversation and expected squabbles. Soon they would have to; the big horses needed their rest. Sigurd tossed his head in annoyance, feeling for more slack in the reins.

"You don't have to keep the reins so firm; they know what they're doing," she chided Vandien.

He roused at the first words she had spoken in hours. "Feeling better?" he asked.

"No. Just more numb. I hate what happened, but there's no way to undo it."

"Vandien?" Goat started in again.

"No," Vandien replied pleasantly.

The boy turned his face from them, tightness in every muscle of his back. Something in the way he bowed his head touched Ki. She took pity on him. "What is it, Goat?"

He cleared his throat but his voice still choked. "So what should I have done? I thought they would kill us all."

Vandien answered, his deep voice soft. "Kept silent. Waited. I know it would have been hard. But it's better to hold back your top stakes until you know what your enemy is betting against it."

"If they had been going to kill us . . . if you had known they were . . . would you have told them about the Tamshin?"

"I don't know." Raw honesty from Vandien. "It's hard to say what I'd do if faced with death, especially painful death. Even harder to say what I'd do if I knew I could keep my friends from death by betraying strangers. I'd like to say I'd go down fighting and take a few with me. But from what I know of Brurjans, I wouldn't have much of a chance." He glanced past Ki to the boy, trying to see if his words were making any impact. "It's sort of like trying to say what you wouldn't eat if you were starving. If you're hungry enough, rotten cabbage and dead rat aren't that bad."

Ki didn't ask how he knew.

"But they were going to kill us," Goat insisted.

Vandien sighed. "Let it go, Goat. It's done. But if there's a next time, keep silent and still. Look to Ki or me to see what you should do. No matter what you think. Or know." The last words he added grudgingly. But they eased the tension, and a sort of peace settled over the gently rocking wagon. The cuddy door behind the seat slid open.

"Aren't we ever going to stop?" Willow asked plaintively.

Vandien didn't answer, but pulled the team off the road. There was nothing to recommend the spot, but there was nothing better in sight either. The grass desert stretched in all directions, gently swelling and ebbing, but neverly sharply enough to be a valley or a hill. The grazing lands of yesterday and the abandoned farms of this morning had given way to brushy patches of coarse grasses interspersed with sandy stretches. The horses would get sparse grazing tonight. They'd need more grain.

The team halted and Goat leaped off, nimble as his namesake. Ki followed him, and then glanced back up at Vandien. He was moving as slowly as an arthritic old dog. A pang of guilt singed Ki. How could she have forgotten about his ribs?

"Take it slow," she cautioned him. "I'll do the unharnessing and get camp set up. Then I want to take a look at your ribs."

"Any excuse to get my clothes off," he muttered, but could not quite bring up a grin. Ki shook her head.

The horses were glad to be rid of their harnesses, but not enthused with the scruffy grey-green grass she led them to. Both greedily sucked up the measure of water she poured into their drinking tub. After they had drunk she grained them and rubbed the sweat from the rough grey coats. There was a festering sore on Sigurd's neck. She got salve to treat it, noticing that Vandien was directing Goat and Willow in setting up a camp. He sent her a quick smile from where he leaned against a quilt folded over a wagon wheel. Goat knelt beside a smouldering fire while Willow poured water from the cask into the kettle.

The sore on Sigurd's neck was a nasty thing that finally expelled the squirming grub of some parasitic fly. Ki washed it and then smeared salve over it. Sigurd, whiffling after the last of the spilled grain, paid no attention to her. Ki sighed and wiped her sticky hands down her tunic. Maybe tomorrow night they'd find a river where she could do a wash. Vandien would love that; he could use his bruised ribs as an excuse for her to pound out his laundry as well as her own.

The little fire seemed very bright after working in the semi-darkness. She stood a moment, letting her eyes adjust. And then a moment longer, to adjust to something else.

Willow knelt beside Vandien, dragging his shirt gently off over his head. She dropped it to the ground, said something softly. As Vandien held his arms up slightly, Willow moistened a rag in water and held it against his side. The bruise was purple where the horse had scored, fading to pinks and greens at the edges. Willow was smiliing as she sponged his skin. Goat's words, which she had earlier dismissed as juvenile vindictiveness, came suddenly to her mind.

She strode into camp. The kettle was already on, the stew starting to bubble. All done neatly and well. Nothing to complain about, nothing to question. They had it all under control. She crouched by the water cask at the tail of the wagon, to run water into the basin to wash her face and hands. Goat came out of the wagon with a platter of travelling bread and cheese. Ki still hadn't thought of anything to say.

Goat looked from her to Vandien and Willow. "Food's ready," he said loudly. "We can eat as soon as you can get your hands off him, Willow."

Willow laughed. "Don't you wish it were you, Goat?" she asked snidely, but as she looked past him she saw Ki. Their eyes met, and for a moment Willow looked scared. But Ki said nothing, and after that instant, Willow's face changed. She smiled, a little cat smile. "Vandien will tell me when he's had enough," she said. Ki wondered if she were speaking to Goat at all.

"Enough," said Vandien. "It's not helping. I wish I could take just one deep breath." He lifted his eyes to Ki, and there was nothing in them but weariness.

"Did you use warm water or cool?" she asked him.

"Cool," he said briefly.

Ki nodded to herself. "After we eat, let's try warm, with some Cara buds crumbled into it."

Willow bristled. "My mother always used cool water on things like that. To keep the swelling down."

"That makes sense," Ki agreed smoothly. "But sometimes warm will loosen a pain." She met Willow's eyes, sensed a challenge in them. Ki didn't want to play. She turned away from the look, to take dishes from the chest and shake loose tea from them. Enough tea had lodged in a cup to brew tonight's pot; she'd have to buy more in Algona.

"Vandien?" she asked over her shoulder. "How far to Algona now, do you guess?"

"Two days?" he hazarded.

"More like three," Willow corrected him. "We haven't made very good time."

Ki said nothing, but dished the food and poured the tea. When she finally filled her own plate and turned around, Willow was ensconced beside Vandien. I would never sit that close to a man not mine, Ki thought. She watched the way Willow spoke to him over the food, tilting her head and smiling at his brief answers, speaking softly as if someone might overhear. She felt stubbornness rise in her. If Vandien did not object to it, she wouldn't. A small cold voice in her asked her if she were trusting Vandien's judgement or testing him. She didn't answer it, but took her plate and sat down by the fire. Goat gazed at her across the flames. There was a dab of soup on his chin.

"How long have you been together?" he asked her suddenly.

"What?" Ki glanced up from her bowl.

"You and Vandien. How long have you been together?"

Ki reckoned back with difficulty. Some years were much like the others, and others had been so eventful that they seemed to be more than one year. "Maybe five or six years. Or closer to seven, I guess. It's hard to say, Goat. We are not always together, like this. Sometimes he rides his own paths and I take mine, knowing we will meet somewhere down the road. Sometimes he goes back to visit the place of his childhood, to see those of his family who remember him. Sometimes, when the haul is simple and dreary, he rides ahead and rejoins me when I arrive."

"Doesn't sound very loyal," the boy observed.

Ki snorted lightly. "To speak of it coldly, perhaps not. But in the ways that are important, we are loyal."

"And other women? Does he have other women, while you are separated, and you have other men?"

Ki stared at him across the fire. "That is scarcely a polite question."

He met her gaze coolly. "I knew you wouldn't answer. Because you don't know."

She glared at him, thinking she should let this conversation die but instead said, "If you mean, do I ask him to account for every moment he is away from me, I do not. Nor does he ask me."

"I see," Goat snickered. "Like they say. 'Two can't get on, and one can't hurt it.' " He sniggered again, a nasty child's laugh.

Ki's voice was flat. "Goat. Why do you behave this way? You have manners when you want them. Why must you be so rude, when you can be pleasant?"

"That's the answer, then, that I don't want to be nice, right? And why should I be polite to people who either scold me or ignore me?"

"Goat," Ki began, feeling horribly weary. But Willow was suddenly at her shoulder.

"Vandien wants tea. And I'll heat water for his ribs."

There was a smug assumption in her voice that Ki wouldn't let herself react to. "The Cara buds are in a clay pot with a cork stopper, on the shelf over the window," she told the girl. "Don't put them in until after the water is steaming."

Her instructions took Willow by surprise. She bobbed a quick nod of assent and withdrew. Ki turned to Goat. "Help me gather up the supper things and put them away."

"But . . ."

"Now, Goat."

He obeyed her, copying the way she gathered the cups and bowls and scrubbed them out with sand and rinsed them sparingly with water. There were a few brief words as Willow refused to let Goat touch either her bowl or cup. Ki didn't intervene. Let them settle their own squabbles; she was sick of them. And tired. By the Moon, she had never known she could be this tired and still stand. And Vandien looked no better than she felt. His head was tipped forward on his chest, the steaming cup of tea at his side nearly upset. She crouched beside him to right it, touched his wrist in passing. No fever, only weariness. He didn't stir as she rose and went to check the horses.

When she came back into the circle of firelight, Vandien was stretched out on his back while Willow carefully arranged a steaming cloth on his ribs. The aromatic Cara flavored the air of the camp. Goat crouched by the fire still, watching them like a hungry dog. Ki ignored him and walked directly to Vandien. His dark eyes turned to her as she crouched down beside him.

"Any better?" she asked him.

"Some. Not a lot."

"Um." Ignoring Willow, she lifted the cloth, ran her fingers lightly over his flesh. She heard him catch his breath as she touched the imprint of the hoof. "You'd better sleep inside the caravan tonight. Hard earth and a chilly night is the last thing you need."

"And I don't mind at all," Willow put in prettily.

"It wouldn't matter if you did," Ki observed. She put the cloth back in place. Something gripped her ankle lightly for a second. She glanced down and Vandien looked up at her gravely. Then his face lit up with the wickedest grin she had ever seen him wear. "I should stave in the rest of your ribs," she told him quietly, but could not down an answering grin. Damn the man. Someday she'd figure out a way to stay angry at him.

She clambered into the caravan and straightened the rumpled bedding on the sleeping platform. With iron control, she made up a bed for Willow on the floor beside it. She knew better than to ask the girl to sleep under the wagon. She gathered up other bedding for Goat. "Only twelve more days," she muttered, consoling herself.

She paused on the steps.

"And then what happened?" Willow was asking Vandien.

"And so we met again in Firbanks." His words were edged with pain. "We found we did better together than we did apart. Ki had a new wagon built, and when she moved on, so did I."

"Enough stories," Ki interrupted, her voice sharper than she had intended it to be. Who was this girl, to be asking how they had met and come together? She let Goat's bedding thump to the ground beside the fire, and turned back to Vandien. "You need rest. Let's get you to bed."

"I won't argue," Vandien promised, reaching up a hand to her. She stooped so he could get a grip on her shoulder and eased him to his feet. He leaned on her, yawning cautiously.

Goat stood looking at the bedding. "There's only one cushion here, and if Willow's going to sleep out here we'll need two."

"Willow can sleep inside on the floor. That's all for you, Goat."

"But I can't sleep out here all by myself! What if the Brurjans come back?"

"They won't. You'll be fine."

"But, Ki! You don't know that for sure. It's too scary. Why can't I sleep inside with the rest of you?"

"He's not sleeping anywhere near me!" Willow objected loudly.

Ki sighed. Vandien said, "It wouldn't kill me to sleep outside," but she shook her head vigorously. Her voice was as sharp as a knife. "This is ridiculous. All these quarrels are ridiculous. You are going to sleep inside where you can get some decent rest. Willow, you can sleep inside just so I don't have to listen to you two quarrel. Goat, I will sleep outside so you don't have to be afraid. Is everyone satisfied?"

A silence followed her words. The two youngsters were merely quelled, but Vandien looked shocked. Ki felt embarrassed. Willow stepped out of her way as she helped Vandien up the high step into the caravan. He sat down heavily on the bed and looked up at her. "Ki? Are you all right?"

"Yes," she snapped, then sighed. "I'm just tired, and . . . I don't have a word for it. What I saw today, and knowing I am partially responsible . . . I don't know. And all the squabbling. And now Goat has me wondering if they won't come back, looking for easy prey."

"Try not to be so tense," he advised her.

"How should I be?" she demanded.

He shrugged, then winced. "I'll be better tomorrow. I can take more of it off you."

She tried to soften toward him. "I'll be better, too," she offered awkwardly.

He caught at her hand, but Ki was too aware of Willow standing in the door, watching them. She squeezed his hand, then pulled free. She gathered a few odd pieces of bedding, leaving him the lion's share. She didn't think she'd be sleeping tonight anyway. Willow took a very long time to move out of her way, but Ki stifled an urge to push past the girl.

Outside there was no easing of tension. Goat was waiting for her. "Are we going to sleep by the fire?" he demanded instantly. "Or shall we sleep under the wagon?"

"You can sleep anywhere you wish. I'm sitting up and keeping watch for awhile."

"Shall I keep you company?" he offered hopefully.

She heard the caravan door shut and Willow scrabbling at what was left of the latch. That's another thing I'll have to fix, Ki thought, but not for a while. The thought gave her a small satisfaction. Goat was still watching her. The light was behind him. He stood with his shoulders bowed in toward his chest, and the details of his face were shadowed. He clutched his trailing bedding, like a child frightened from sleep by the bogies. Being angry suddenly took too much effort.

"If you want," she conceded. "Or you can sleep. Just don't expect me to be good company. I'm too tired, and there's too much on my mind."

"If you want—" Goat swallowed audibly, and his voice was very soft. "I could rub your head. It would make your headache go away, and you could rest."

Ki became suddenly aware of how her temples were throbbing. Before, the pain had seemed a part of her anger. She could imagine, with sudden lethargy, how good it would feel to have someone massage that tension away.

"It's a thing my mother taught me, when I was very little," Goat added shyly. "Something she said every healer should be able to do. It feels nice."

"I—thank you, Goat, but no," she replied wearily. "No, I think I shall just sit quietly and look at the night and keep watch. But that was a kind offer."

"You don't want me to touch you." His voice was petulant.

She was too tired for this. "Yes," she admitted. "That's true. I wouldn't be comfortable."

"Why?"

Ki was arranging her bedding. She leaned a cushion against one of the tall wheels of the caravan, and then sat down against it, dragging a quilt over her lap. She looked at Goat.

"Why?" he repeated.

"Why don't you go to bed?" she responded.

"I'm not sleepy yet. Why wouldn't you be comfortable with me touching you?"

Ki sighed. The strength of her anger had forsaken her. "Because you're still a stranger, and I'm not comfortable being touched by strangers."

"How long would it take before I wasn't a stranger?"

The note was in his voice again, suave lechery with a runny nose. She wondered where he had picked up the lines and the inflections. It sounded like something a tinker might say to a tavern whore. She shut her eyes.

"How long did it take before Vandien wasn't a stranger?" Ki didn't open her eyes. "Why don't you ask him?"

"Why don't you tell me?" Earthy, suggestive tone.

"Goat." Ki shifted slightly. "Why are you being an ass?"

"Why are you?" His voice was full of sudden hurt. "How can you let them sleep together while you sleep out here?"

She opened her eyes, recognized his jealousy and understood his adolescent reasoning. If Vandien was sleeping with a girl Goat wanted, Goat would retaliate by seducing Vandien's woman. It was too silly for comment. Yet he needed an answer. She tried to think of one that wouldn't prompt any more questions. "Goat, don't worry about it. Vandien is probably sound asleep by now. And even if he weren't, and even if he were inclined toward Willow and she were receptive, his ribs would keep him from acting on the impulse. So no one has anything to worry about. Now, please, go to sleep?"

"You don't know Willow," he replied sulkily. He tossed his bedding to the ground and dropped onto it, curling up like a dog.

And he does know Willow, Ki thought to herself. How? It isn't likely that girl would take up with an odd boy like Goat. Yet there's been something between them, to account for all the hostility and jealousy. Let it go, it's late and I'm tired.

For a time she sat listening to the night. The insects chirred incessantly, and there was the comfortable sound of Sigurd's and Sigmund's great hooves shifting as they dozed. A soft whicker of owl's wings as the predator passed overhead. No hoofbeats. Nothing to fear. She drew up her knees, set her forehead against them and let herself doze.

"Vandien?" Willow whispered.

"What?" he asked grudgingly.

"I'm scared. Can I come up there beside you?"

He sighed silently. Earlier, Willow's machinations to make Ki jealous had seemed mildly humorous. But this . . . "How would you be any safer up here?" he asked wearily.

A brief silence. He sensed her sudden uncertainty when he didn't respond as she expected. "Because . . . I'm afraid I'll fall asleep, I'm so tired. So I thought I could come up there and talk to you and stay awake. So Goat can't bother me." She was sitting up, leaning her elbows on the edge of the bed. He turned his head to look at her.

"Willow, I'm really tired, and my ribs hurt. I don't want to stay awake and talk. Now be a good girl and let me go to sleep." His avuncular tone was deliberate.

"But . . ." She was flustered. Evidently, this wasn't going as intended. What had she intended, he suddenly wondered. He heard the rustle of the straw mattress, opened his eyes again. She had edged farther onto the bed. "You don't understand about Goat. At all. Or you wouldn't be going to sleep, either."

"Oh? Well, why don't you sit on the floor, then, and keep yourself awake by telling me about him?"

"All right," she agreed quickly, and clambered up to sit on the bed beside him. He opened his eyes again. In the dimness of the cuddy, she looked very young. Very, very young. "Goat has Jore blood," she began. "Do you know what that means?"

"I suppose it means one of his ancestors wasn't Human. His father mentioned it to us; I didn't think it was especially important."

"It isn't . . . usually. There's a lot of mixed blood in this part of Loveran. You see a lot of half-Brurjan, especially in their garrison towns. And . . . other crosses. But not many Jore crosses, and hardly ever one with Human body and Jore eyes."

"So?"

She edged closer to him. "So, it means he can see . . . everything." She lifted her hand in an encompassing gesture, let it fall so it brushed his thigh. "Everything anyone dreams, he can spy on."

Vandien shifted in the darkness, hitching himself away from her accidental touch. By the Moon, his ribs ached. But he was intrigued now, whether he wanted to admit it or not. "So Goat can tell what you dream. Why should that worry you?"

He could feel her eyes on him in the darkness. "Because he uses what he learns from dreams to hurt people. To make fun of their secret longings, or expose their mistakes, and take advantage of their fears. Once he's been inside your dreams, he can change how you feel about them." Overcome by the enormity of the thought, Willow melted beside him. She lay on her side, facing him, her jaw propped on her hand.

"He can change how you feel about your dreams."

"Yes."

"And why is that so important?"

"Don't you see? He can take your secrets and use them against you. He can make your dreams go where he will. Nothing you have ever thought is safe from his spying. And everything he learns spills out of his mouth. He has no honor." She spoke bitterly, as one betrayed. Vandien sensed himself very close to the heart of the puzzle, and held his tongue.

The silence lengthened. Willow wiggled closer to him. She wore a scent, like ginger and oranges. He could hear her breathing, but he waited her out.

"Once," she breathed, "I trusted him."

He didn't let himself smile. "Oh?"

"And he betrayed not only me, but my friends."

"By telling what he knew you had dreamed?"

Willow shook her head impatiently, and he felt the brush of her hair. "I asked him to . . . find out a thing for me. A thing that would be useful for me to know. And he did. But instead of telling only me, he told it all about, bragging of what he knew. So it wasn't any use at all to me and my friends."

The rebels. Ah. "I imagine you were very angry with him." Vandien wondered if she were so naive she thought she was being clever, or if her childish intrigue was a mask.

He could feel the warmth of her young body crossing the distance between them. But he could also sense the calculation as she contrived to let her leg brush his. The uneasiness that stirred in him now was not what she was seeking to arouse.

"Of course I was angry! We were all angry, he put us all in danger. And Kellich had to . . ."

"Leave," Vandien filled in for her.

"Yes." Her voice was very low. "It was all Goat's fault, because he couldn't keep his stupid mouth shut. Kellich says there is no strength in a man who cannot keep a secret, nor honor in one who breaks faith with others for personal gain or glory."

"Mmm." He had dozens of questions, but he knew that not talking much was the best way to encourage confidences. When she leaned over and put her hand lightly on his upper arm, he didn't move away from it. Her fingers moved, probing the muscles there.

"You're strong," she whispered. "Stronger than you look. And brave. What you did today, to buy Ki time—that took courage. And quick wit to think of it." She shifted her body closer on the bed. "Strong men, with the courage and the wits to put their strength to use, are rare. And we need them so desperately."

Her breath was against his cheek. "Did you make the same speech to Goat when you asked a favor of him?" Vandien asked innocently.

She jerked back as if he had slapped her. "And does Kellich know how you recruit for your cause?" he continued. "Or did he teach you, perhaps, how to win a man to do your work for you?" Her silence was an audible tension. "And what would you have done if I had tried to accept the bribe first, and then do whatever it is that you've been building up to ask for?"

"I'd have put a knee in your sore ribs, you . . ." she sputtered, at a loss for a name bad enough to call him. She moved then, suddenly, and he blocked it, covering his injured ribs, but it was not an attack. She sat up suddenly, her face in her hands. He heard her draw in a shuddering breath, but he cooled his quick sympathy. Tears might simply be the ploy one used when seduction failed.

"You don't know what it's like," she said thickly.

"I might, if someone explained it instead of . . ."

"It's horrible!" she burst out. "This Duke and his Brurjan guards and his travel passes and his endless quarrels with everyone. Loveran has not a single border-neighbor that trusts us. He has cheated the Windsingers until they no longer hear the pleas of the farmers. Look around you as we travel—do you think it was always grass desert here? When the Duchess was in power, these were the grain fields of Loveran, the pastures thick with fat cattle and white sheep. Now our whole land is dying. Dying! And Kellich says unless we bring back . . ."

"The Duchess. And throw down the Duke. I heard the talk in Keddi. I can sympathize, if what you say is true. But to send you out to bring back men for his cause . . ."

"Kellich hates it as much as I do. But he says it's like a test. You were staying loyal to Ki—I could feel it. And that's a thing to watch for, for Kellich says that a man true to his own cause can be true to a greater cause. And he says that if I pick the men carefully that I approach, that the . . . offer will never have to be paid. For once they've been with us, they see the right of it, and don't ask for anything more than to do what is right. . . ."

"Oh, shit," Vandien breathed softly, but she heard him.

"It's not how you think it is at all!" she said angrily. "No man but Kellich has ever touched me. Nor ever will. It is only a thing one does because one has to . . . like the smuggling. Because one has to do it to keep the cause alive, to survive."

"Sort of like sacrificing those Tamshin today?"

Willow swallowed. "Goat did that, not I," she muttered after a moment. "But, yes, if it were for the cause. Even the Tamshin, such as they are, aid us. They've been willing to die for us. I'm not saying I like what Goat did. And don't you think he did it to save me or anything foolish like that. He did it for the reason he does anything. To show off what he knows. But, yes, we expect that kind of sacrifice. That our friends will die for our cause."

"Yes, I'm sure that little boy had strong political convictions," Vandien said sourly. "Must have been really sustaining for him when the horses trampled him."

"We can't think in terms of one person, even if the person is a child," Willow whispered fiercely. "Kellich says the cause must be our family, the child or mate or parent that we could die for. For the land is our begetter, and if we suffer the land to fail and die under the tyranny of the Duke, then we have betrayed ourselves and our children to the end of all generations.''

''For the life that is the land,'' Vandien muttered to himself, recalling a boy, an oath, and a sacrifice made long ago. He was tired of hearing Willow repeat what ''Kellich said,'' and he doubted she understood half of what she mouthed. But he did, much better than her youthfulness could encompass, and her words stirred a pain he thought had scarred over long ago.

Ki dreamed. The dreams engulfed her as water engulfs a diver; they pulled her down and under. She flickered through images bright with color and soft with shadows. Landscapes, horses, Romni wagons, laughing children. Ki stood back from her dreams in a dark place, regarding their passing with equanimity. There were folk she knew, Big Oscar and Rifa, not as they were now, but young as they had been when she was a child, and there was Aethan's wagon, and the first team of horses she remembered, Boris and Nag. A glimpse of each and then on, shuffling memories that filled her eyes but didn't touch her. Here was Aethan, older, starting to stoop, and there was Sven, her first glimpse of him, so boyish that she could scarcely reconcile the image with her memory of him as a man. The flicker of memories slowed suddenly, let her regard him as she once had, running her eyes over his blue eyes and fair skin, over his wide shoulders and silky blond hair that flowed down his back. The unbound hair of an unclaimed male of his people.

Ki felt something in her quicken at the thought, and the airs of her dream seemed suddenly charged. She sensed a passing of time that followed Sven through her memories. Here he was on a spring day when the caravan of Romni had passed through Harper's Ford; there he was, his cheeks ruddy with the kiss of winter wind, when she and Aethan had returned that way later in the year. The dreams skipped forward frantically, searching, searching, pausing whenever Sven had come into her life, and then hastening on again. And here Sven was older, and his shirt hung open and his fair, wide chest was slick with sweat. And here—ah, yes. The dreams stopped. It had arrived.

The wooden planks of wagon floor were pale new wood, and sticky yet with sap. She lifted her eyes to where Sven stood before her, shirtless, his back to the new bed with the new blankets on it. Ki couldn't breathe. She was shaking. Sven's face was very solemn. He was waiting. Waiting for her. She took a step closer to him. She smelled the smell of his sweat, male and young, and the smell of her own nervousness. He put out a hand and his fingers brushed her jaw. She felt the tremble in them. He was no more experienced than she, and but a year or two older. And yet they had made their promises to one another, and now they were free, to touch and be together. If they could find their courage. She looked at his hair, bound back in a long tail now. A taken man, a man claimed by a woman. Claimed by Ki. His hand fell to her shoulder, and before he could draw her near, she stepped closer to him. The instant of hesitation melted, and her skin was suddenly alive, aware of every brush of skin or cloth against it, and the smell and taste of his skin filled her mouth and nose. He was so strong, so wise in his maleness, so sure.

Clothing fell, and the wooden edge of the bed bruised the back of her thighs as she tumbled across it. She pulled her eyes up and looked only at his face. His eyes closed to slits as he positioned himself. He was gentle, slow, careful, and yet his mere touch was a jolt against inexperienced flesh. Ki cried aloud. Sven's mouth closed over hers, swallowing her cries, and his body descended upon hers. . . .

Somewhere an older Ki watched their uncertain finish, witnessed the sudden awkwardness of their first parting, and then the confidence with which they came together a second time. She saw much she had not remembered until now; how he had bruised his head against the wall, the circle of red dents her teeth left in his shoulder, his hair unbound and lying across her eyes and mouth. Somewhere an older Ki smiled sadly in the darkness, shared the hunger of their young passion but not its fulfillment. She could only witness and remember. Remember so clearly that she almost felt Sven's hands upon her. . . .

Ki jerked her head up, found a tangling darkness like wet nets, floundered and struggled and suddenly opened her eyes. She was breathing as hard as if she had run a footrace; her tunic clung damply to her back. Slowly the darkness parted, shadows re-formed as recognizable shapes.

The fire was a shamble of coals with the ends of sticks littering its edges. The wagon wheel was solid behind her, digging into her back through the cushion. That huddle to the left of the fire was Goat, sleeping in a tangle of blankets. He lay very still, his face turned away from her. His shoulders looked tight and hunched, as if expecting a blow. He had taken his anger to bed with him, Ki decided. She drew a deeper breath and came to herself. A nightmare. Well, like a nightmare in its intensity. She plucked her clothing free of her sweaty skin.

Sven. The love of her childhood, her husband, the father of her children. Dead. She wished suddenly that Vandien were beside her, that she could turn and touch him and console herself with the goodness of her present life instead of regretting the sweetness she had lost. But he wasn't, and it would be days and miles before she was alone with him again. Once more she let her head settle to her knees.

Why, after all these years, dream of Sven? And why of that particular time? Was she remembering when she was as young and callow as Willow? She shook her head against her knees. Young, callow, and ignorant, yes. But not as nasty, never as sly. At least she didn't remember herself that way. She wondered how others had seen her.

Murmuring voices from the wagon behind her. Willow's low voice, intense, unmistakable. A savage curiosity beset Ki, but she held herself still. What were they talking about, those two? And had she dreamed of the man she'd lost because she feared she'd lose this one, too? Foolish. She knew him too well. Whatever else he might be or might have been, he had honor. Polished, she thought, to a brighter sheen than her own. She need fear no betrayal from Vandien. "My love," she breathed softly, speaking the word he seldom heard from her. Then, "My friend," she added, taking strength from the thought. The voices went on a long time. But Ki slept long before they were silent.

SIX

"Goat, why don't you get down and walk for a while? Stretch your legs," Vandien suggested pleasantly.

Goat gave him a yellow smile. "Why don't you?"

Ki closed her eyes for one long moment, then opened them again and fixed them on the road ahead. All morning the two had been exchanging small barbs, but Goat was getting a little too brave now. Vandien smiled at him in silence. Ki could feel his muscles gathering. "Ki," Vandien said in a very soft voice. "Pull the horses up."

"Vandien." She said no more than that, putting all her meaning into the name. Not a cautioning, but a plea. Vandien sighed audibly and leaned back. The clopping of the team's hooves filled the silence. The long straight road stretched flat before them. It seemed to Ki that the sandy soil they passed today was yellower. And that was the only difference from yesterday. Algona. She mouthed the word silently to herself. First leg of the journey, a measuring point, a way of saying, well, that much is done. There was a dark smudge on the far horizon. It might be Algona, or it might be stunted foothills. Either would be welcome, the hills for the change in terrain, the town for the marking point in their journey.

Vandien closed his throat. "Willow told me a lot of things last night."

Goat snickered nastily. "I'll bet she did."

"I'm talking to Ki," Vandien said icily. "Be quiet, or I'll make you quiet." Goat's eyes grew larger and his lips tightened. "I couldn't sleep much, for the pain. And she said she

76

preferred to sleep during the day while we traveled anyway. So we talked. Or she did, and I listened. Mostly about her lover, but later she got into other things. The politics of Loveran are fascinating; we've wandered into a hornet's nest, just waiting to be stirred.''

"This Duke of theirs seems to keep things tightly controlled.'' Worry tinged Ki's words.

"Perhaps. But remember what Trelira said, about the Duke's Brurjan patrols keeping the roads free of robbers and rebels? Willow says the emphasis is more on rebels than robbers. And who the rebels are, the Brurjans determine.''

Ki hissed speculatively. "Tamshin, for instance?''

"Or Romni. Or anyone else with too fat a caravan, or too high-stepping a horse. The merchants are getting tired of it.''

"Turning into real rebels, perhaps?'' Ki surmised.

Vandien nodded at her past Goat's bowed head. The boy was dozing in the sun, eyes closed, mouth slightly ajar. "From what I heard in Keddi, they've found a focus. The Duchess. The Duke's mother. She held all the power until he came of age and packed her off to a new life with a 'contemplative order.' I understand she finally escaped her meditations and bonds, and would like to have her duchy back. If what Willow tells me is true, it wouldn't be a bad thing. This grass desert used to be grazing lands and farms, before the Duke came to power and started quarreling with the Windsingers. You know how they are; no percentage for the Windsingers, no decent weather. No rain at planting time, no cooling breezes for seedlings, no . . .''

"Um. Yes. I know how they are. So?''

He knew what the "so" meant: How does all this relate to us? Politics to Ki were a nebulous thing, consisting of petty officials to be outwitted and trade laws to be circumvented.

"So that's what all these travel permits are about. The Duke reasons that if he can keep all his subjects where they belong, except for those with a good economic reason for moving around, he can prevent the massing of supporters for the Duchess, and cut down the flow of information among the rebels. He controls the Brurjan guard. He disbanded the Duchess's troops, so there's no other standing force of any kind. By keeping everyone busy accounting for where they are, the Duke prevents the gathering of any force loyal to her.''

"Willow has no travel permit." Ki was slowly grasping it. "Therefore, if we are stopped by the Brurjans, and she can show no papers, we are automatically rebels."

"Right. And in her sympathies at least, they'd be right about Willow being a rebel. Or, at least Kellich sympathizes with their cause. When Willow talks, it's 'Kellich says this,' and 'Kellich says that.' I don't think she's given much thought to it on her own." Between them, Goat nodded with the gentle jolting of the wagon, his lips vaguely smiling at some childish dream. Vandien glanced over at Ki. Her green eyes were fixed on the distance, her dusty lashes unblinking. Impassive, he thought, to the news that she could be beaten and robbed, raped and killed, in fine legality. She looked ahead, believing that somehow she could cope, she would survive, and that tomorrow would find her in a better place than this. The Romni dream. And was it so different from his own attitude?

"Vandien." Ki's voice made him realize he was staring at her. "It doesn't change much. Rousters have always been able to do whatever they wished to Romni. It's nothing new."

"I suppose it isn't. To you. But I thought you'd want to know about it."

"Yes. It's better to know, I suppose." Ki waved at a fat blue fly that had found her. "And it's obvious that these rebels have already gained your sympathies. But you and I, we can't afford to be pulled into a thing like this. Look what happened to us the last time we got involved with Windsinger politics. We lost. Remember? That's why we're here." She paused, thinking, while Vandien frowned down the road. "I wonder. Is Willow . . ."

"TWISTED BEAST!" The scream of anger and outrage came from within the wagon, in a voice Vandien would never have recognized as Willow's. Between them on the seat, Goat jolted to wakefulness. He sat up very straight, staring.

"Nightmare," Ki said mildly. "She's having a nightmare. Wake her and . . ."

But before she could complete the sentence, they heard the wild scrabbling of nails against the cuddy door. As it scraped open on its tracks, Vandien asked, "Willow?"

She came through the door like an infuriated cat, all claws and wide red mouth and tangled hair. One hand gripped

Goat's hair on the back of his skull, while the other raked down his face. She was shrieking wordlessly, and Goat added his cries of pain. The pair thrashed wildly on the seat as Goat grabbed at her wrist while she dragged his head back and down by her grip on his hair while pushing her knee into the small of his back. The struggle jostled Ki, who was trying to keep control of the spooked team, while Vandien made vague and cautious efforts to intervene with one hand while shielding his damaged ribs with the other.

The chaos lasted but a moment before Ki had hauled in the team and kicked on the brake. Her eyes lit with sudden green fury. Vandien's eyes widened at the set of her face, and he was already moving before she bellowed, "Get clear!" Still Vandien barely clambered out of the way before she stood, gripped the doorframe for purchase, and, setting her boot to the struggling adolescents, gave a firm push that tumbled them both from the high seat to the dusty earth.

Willow gave a muffled shriek as she fell atop Goat, and the breath rushed out of the boy with an audible gasp. For an instant they both were stunned, and then Willow took advantage of her perch, setting one knee down hard on Goat's shoulder, and raining blows on his face and chest. Vandien, clinging to the side of the wagon, watched in horror as the boy turned his head, dragged up one arm to shield himself, and then sank his teeth into Willow's lower thigh.

"Sit down," Ki warned Vandien, and before he could, she shook the reins. He half-fell onto the seat, gripping the edge as Ki stirred the team into a ragged trot. The sounds of the combat fell away behind them, to be replaced by more distant cries of "Come back!" and "You can't leave us here!" and "My father paid good money. . . ."

Then even those sounds faded as Ki shook the reins, urging the horses to more speed. Vandien glanced back, to see both Willow and Goat pelting after the wagon. Willow was holding her torn blouse closed as she ran. Blood streamed from Goat's nose.

"Don't even look at them!" Ki hissed, and he jerked himself around. The cold set of her lips as she stared down the road startled him. Her eyes were hard as jade when she glanced at him. For a long moment he said nothing. Then he began to laugh, softly at first, then trying in vain to shield his ribs from the paroxysms of his belly muscles. Ki glared at him, looking so like an outraged Puhkin idol that he roared with helpless laughter, and then gasped at the pain it cost him.

"Ki," he wheezed when he could. "We've come a good ways. You can't really intend to leave them."

"Can't I?" she snarled. "Can't I? Watch this!" Leaning forward, she rattled the whip in its socket, and the team lurched into a sudden gallop. But the day was hot, and Ki's swift anger was already being replaced by shame. Vandien saw the reins slip through her fingers, watching the greys toss tentative questions back down the lines to her, and, reading her disinterest, begin to slow to their preferred leisurely pace. A cautious peek back revealed Goat trotting doggedly after them, while farther back Willow plodded along disconsolately. She was weeping and Goat cursing. He leaned back on the seat. Ki was sitting very still, her gaze focused far down the road. He slid the cuddy door shut and moved over to sit beside her on the seat.

"The worst thing about children," Ki observed, speaking in a very small voice, "is that they require one to act like an adult while provoking one to act like a spoiled brat."

"I was just about to say that I couldn't have handled it better myself," Vandien mused. He looked at her carefully. She didn't meet his glance. "Ki, the walk will do them good. And the message that you have had enough of their squabbling was long overdue. Besides, I wanted to talk to you alone."

Ki lifted an inquiring eyebrow.

"You might have noticed that I was trying to get Goat to walk and let me speak with you alone. I think I can explain what just happened."

"Besides two spoiled brats getting into a scuffle?"

"Well, there's a little more to it than that." Vandien smiled briefly. "Or there is, to Willow's mind. Have you ever heard of a jutan?"

Ki shrugged. "Some kind of a demon, isn't it?"

"Not quite. As I understood it, it was a stealer of dreams. A jutan has the power to steal your dreams."

"So you sleep without dreams? Doesn't sound all that bad."

"No. But it's similar to what Willow was telling me about Goat last night. Only she was attributing it to his Jore blood and strange eyes. According to her, there's a lot of folks in Loveran that aren't as Human as they look. Jore blood doesn't always show, there's Brurjan crosses, and others she was more vague about. But anyway, Goat has Jore blood and odd eyes, so he can dream-steal. Willow says Goat can listen in on your dreams. He can send nightmares or visions of paradise. Also, he can use what he steals from your dreams, to trick you or shame you.''

''I don't get it.''

''Like a married man dreaming of a secret lover, or a servant dreaming of stealing from his master. Goat might threaten to tell your dreams. A person with Jore eyes can make your dreams go where he chooses, so he can discover any secrets you have.''

''Sounds like a bogey tale,'' Ki complained.

''Only if you don't believe it. To Willow, it's a very scary idea. Especially since she seduced Goat into finding something out for her rebels. Only when the time came for him to collect his reward, she refused. So he made the information public knowledge instead. She feels he betrayed her.''

''Oh. And he feels she used him. That's what this is all about?''

Vandien nodded. ''She's been sleeping in the wagon by day because she's afraid to go to sleep while Goat's sleeping. She was full of tales of things Goat is supposed to have done. She says it started when he was small; he'd tattle about the things he had seen in people's dreams. The things didn't have to be real; just that someone had dreamed of her sister's husband in her own bed, or that some skinny little wretch had dreamed of being a bold warrior that every maiden swooned over. Things to make folk laugh. It wasn't so bad, before he found out that people would give him things if he promised not to say what he had seen in their dreams.''

''Do you believe any of this?'' Ki demanded. She glanced around the corner of the wagon. Goat was about three wagon lengths behind them, plodding along at a speed that just kept pace with the greys. His chest was heaving, and she guessed he was too winded to catch up. Willow trailed him by another wagon length, her face set in icy anger.

''Willow believes it. And so did a lot of folk in Keddi, if what she says is true. Keddi is a stronghold for the rebels. When word was put out that Goat had betrayed the cause, well, I think that's why his father is apprenticing the boy. Maybe to keep him alive. The feeling was strong enough that none of the merchant caravans wanted to take Goat to Villena. Which is why we've got him.''

''And why the tavernkeeper was willing to pay extra for us to take him. Wonder what she thought he had seen in her dreams?''

''Who knows?'' Vandien shrugged.

''And who cares? It sounds to me like a trick . . . something that would work very well against someone with a guilty conscience. It's like telling someone's fortune. All you have to do is hold the hand firmly and keep track of the pulse and sweat to know if you're saying what he wants to hear.''

''No!'' Vandien feigned astonishment. ''Would the Romni, holders of mystical powers for generations, practice such a deceit?''

''Practice? Hell, who needs practice? We're already perfect at it.''

She glanced briefly away from her driving, grinning at him with a feeling close to their usual easy companionship.

''Stop . . . please.'' Willow panted the words, stumbling alongside the wagon.

Ki sighed silently, and pulled the team in. The girl gripped the seat with one hand, the other holding closed her torn blouse. She was panting and disheveled, clothes and skin dusty save for where tears had smeared across her face. Looking down at her, Ki was suddenly ashamed of herself. ''Willow,'' she began gently.

''Bitch!'' Willow hissed, and Ki's shame evaporated. ''You left me back there with him.'' Willow choked on an angry sob. ''Alone with him, not caring how he attacked me!''

Vandien's voice was bland and helpful. ''Actually, Willow, we left Goat alone back there with you, not caring how you attacked him.''

Ki glared at him, then back to the girl, who was glowering at them. ''Actually,'' Ki added coldly, ''my personal feeling was that I didn't much care how either of you attacked the other, as long as you didn't do it on my wagon. A sentiment I still feel. Do you understand me?''

''But . . . but he came into my dreams. I felt him. And then—look, he bit me! Here, look!'' She tugged up her draggled skirts to show a neat circle of red dents in her lower thigh. "He bit me!" she repeated, disgust evident in her voice.

"It might have been more difficult for him if you hadn't been sitting on his chest," Ki observed. "I've never understood the logic of one person attacking another, and then being offended when the other person fights back."

"But . . ." Willow stammered in her outrage. "But he's a boy, and I'm a woman. He should have more respect!"

"Yes," Ki agreed smoothly. "As should you. More respect for yourself than to get into a squabble in the first place."

"Yes!" Goat's voice sounded in vehement agreement. He had come up on the opposite side of the wagon and was clambering up onto the seat. "We should leave you right here, you simpering sow! Let you walk to Tekum and your precious Kellich!" He moaned the name abandonedly. "Leave you for the Brurjans to find. I wonder how Kellich would like you after a herd of Brurjans had been through you . . . or how well you'd like him? Maybe you'd like their hairiness even more than his!"

Vandien stood slowly. He placed his boot carefully in the center of Goat's chest and pushed. The boy flew backward, landing on his rump in the road with a thud that made the dust billow. He was too astonished to make a sound.

"Works well," Vandien observed to Ki. "I see why you used it before. Perhaps they need another little trot before they're going to give us any peace."

"No!" Willow clutched desperately at the wagon. "Please!" she added in a different tone as she looked up at Ki's set face. "I . . . I won't fight with him anymore . . . if he doesn't start it first!"

Ki swung her gaze to Goat. He was still sitting in the road. Slowly he got to his feet, rubbing his buttocks. "I'll leave her alone," he grudgingly promised. Willow was already clambering in the side door of the wagon. As Goat climbed up on the seat, he muttered, "Not that I ever did anything in the first place. I was just sitting here when she jumped me . . ."

"Liar!" Willow hissed from within the cuddy. "You came nosing into my dreams . . ."

"Shut up!" Vandien bellowed, in a voice so unlike his normal tones that Sigurd jerked sideways in the harness while Ki recoiled from the blast by her ear. She stared at him in amazement. "Now," he went on hoarsely, "I don't want either of you to say a word to each other for the rest of the day. Or *about* each other," he added as Goat's mouth opened to speak.

Goat closed his mouth. An instant later he opened it to complain, "But that will be boring!"

Ki started the team and Goat settled with a lurch into his seat. "Peaceful is the word you're looking for," she informed him. "Boring is walking behind the wagon in the horses' dust."

He fell silent, but his yellow eyes brimmed with reproachful tears. The wagon trundled on, the silence it bore getting thicker and stiffer with every step the horses took. Ki was aware of Willow's muffled sobs within the cuddy, could picture her leaned up against the plank walls listening to be sure no ill was spoken of her. Ki stole a glance at Vandien, saw his dark eyes mirror her own discomfort. Puppies, she thought. One going to be married, one going to be apprenticed, but no more than puppies after all. She couldn't stand it.

"Vandien," she ventured into the choking silence. "How did that story end?"

"What?" he asked in confusion.

"'The Pot of Jam and The Bird of Life.' You started telling it to me at the inn that night, and never finished it."

A slight smile touched his lips as he recalled what had interrupted the telling. "I don't remember where I left off."

"Nor do I." Ki wouldn't look at him. "Just begin again at the beginning."

"Very well." Vandien nodded, suddenly seeing her intent. Reaching to his throat, he lifted a loop of worn green string from around his neck. He settled it onto his fingers, preparing to weave the story-symbols of his people as he spoke. "It's almost worn out," he said softly.

Ki glanced away from the road to look at the fine string. "Guess you'll have to make another trip home for a new one," she suggested cautiously. On his infrequent trips to visit his family, he always returned with a new story-string. Yet of all the stories he told Ki, very few were about his people or what he did on his visits home.

Vandien was silent, settling the fine twine around his fingers. His hands moved, tossing and looping the thread into the familiar symbols for his name. He looked at the twin webs he had made, one on each hand, joined between. He sighed suddenly. "No," he decided abruptly. "I think I'd better just find something else to use. It's hard to find the right kind of string, though. It has to be tough, but flexible, and a little bit stretchy. It can't be too thick . . ."

"What about the jam pot and the bird of life?" Goat interrupted suddenly.

Vandien freed a hand from the string, smoothed his moustache over his smile. Ki knew the boy's attention pleased him. "Better than coins, almost," Vandien had once told her, "is when you're telling the story, and no one even sneezes."

" 'The Pot of Jam and The Bird of Life.' " Vandien announced the story formally. The string lifted, looped, and fell over his fingers into an elaborate star, the beginning of a story. "Once there was a rich farmer, with many acres of fine crops growing in black soil by a brown river. While he was alive and healthy, all his family lived very richly, but one day the farmer sensed that his time was coming for dying. So he called before him all his sons and daughters, and they were as many as there are purple-and-white turnips in a good garden, for this farmer had plowed and sown energetically for all his years."

Behind them, the cuddy door slid open a crack. Willow, very pink about her mismatched eyes, peered out.

"I wanted to see the pictures," she excused herself hoarsely.

"Of course." Vandien slid the door open further, turned sideways and wedged his back against the jamb so that his hands were visible to Willow as well as Goat. "Well, as each son or daughter came before the old man, he gave generously to each one, according to the child's interest. To one son who had tended the pigs in rain and cold, he gave a herd of fat swine. To a daughter who had pruned and tied the grapes even in the heat of the sun, he gave a hillside vineyard. To the daughter who cooked fat fish for his table, he gave the fish-trap in the river. And on and on, until all was given away, and the old farmer thought he could die in peace. But just as he lay down on his fat feather-bed and prepared to let out his last breath, his youngest daughter came to him. He had forgotten all about her, for all day she had been where she always spent her days—out in the forest, harvesting what she had not sown, reaping what she had not planted. A basket of wild berries was on her arm, and her lips were red with the juice of those she had eaten. The old farmer looked at her. He did not love her as well as he loved his other children, for he could not understand one who did not plant the seed and tend it. But he could see that she was still his true daughter, and because of that he owed her some pittance to keep her alive. Her eyes, green as moss under old oaks, were reddened where she had been weeping, and her hair, smooth and brown as autumn acorns, was wild on her shoulders where she had clawed it in her grief at his dying. 'Daughter,' he said, 'little have I left to give you.'

" 'Father,' she said, 'little that matters to me, and I will tell you that I would gladly give up whatever you gift me with, if it would buy you but one more day of life.'

"Then her father felt shamed, for in truth all he had for the girl was a little pot of jam. And that was of no use to anyone, for the jam was sour and full of pits, while the pot had such a long and narrow neck that no spoon would fit down it, even if the jam had been fit to eat. This, you see, was why he still had it to give, for no one else had ever wanted it."

Ki stole a glance at the group. Goat had curled forward, his elbows on his knees, and for once his face was empty of any slyness or malice. He was a boy listening to a story, and Willow might have been his sister. Her red hair was loose upon her shoulders, and she twined it soothingly around one index finger as she listened, her odd eyes watching the play of the string on Vandien's fingers. A smile even touched her lips as Vandien drew the loop of string out in a long, long neck to show how foolishly the little pot had been turned.

Ki let the reins go slack in her fingers, trusting the greys to follow their noses down the monotonous road. As Vandien spoke, she watched, not his fingers, but his face, the dark of his eyes that sparked with his enjoyment of the tale, his features that mirrored each character in turn. She wondered, again, what had brought him into her life, and what made him stay.

Then her interest was caught in the story, and she forgot to wonder as the horses drew them, step by steady step, closer to Algona.

SEVEN

The rising sun cast a pink glow over wagon, sleepers and browsing horses. Ki lay still a moment longer, savoring the peace. Vandien lay beside her, burrowed deep in their blankets. Only his dark curling hair and the back of his neck was visible. Sleepily she took a curl between her fingers, drew it out and watched it spring back. He mumbled something, but did not move.

Last night had been more peaceful than any since the trip began. Vandien had filled Willow and Goat with tales all the afternoon, stories made more fascinating by Vandien's skills as a teller. There had been only one brief squabble, when Willow had asked to be taught to make symbols on the string, and Goat had quickly insisted that he be included. With unusual patience, Vandien had suggested they take turns, and changed their jealousy over his attention into a sort of competition. Willow had even grudgingly conceded that Goat was the quicker to learn the finger twists. Her brusque compliment had won her a look of such worship that Ki wondered how she could be blind to the boy's feelings. When it was time to make camp that evening, Goat had been willing and helpful, responding to Willow's snubs and criticisms as if they were helpful suggestions.

After they had eaten, the story-string had come out again, and Vandien spun out the long tale of the tailor's twelve sons. By the time the twelfth son had completed his dozen tasks and won the admiration of the Huntswoman of the Green

Woods, the moon was high and the night blossomed to full blackness.

All had been ready to sleep; even Willow was nodding. But when Goat wished them all sweet dreams, Willow snarled, "As one who does not sleep at night, I expect no dreams at all, Goat. None!" She had slammed the cuddy door behind her, then opened it a moment later to expel a fall of blankets and quilts. Vandien had stared in astonishment, but when he had opened his mouth to speak, Ki touched his arm. "Ignore it," she suggested. "Let's just go to sleep. Algona is just down the rise from here, and Tekum but a few days beyond it."

"Thank the Moon for that," Vandien muttered. He took a wad of blankets from her arms and settled into them, sinking into sleep so rapidly that Ki realized how much pain his ribs were actually giving him. When she took blankets to Goat, she found him sitting by the fire, his eyes already closed. She shook him gently by the shoulder, and he roused slowly.

"Algona is not far from here," he whispered. A peculiar smile touched his lips. "Not even as far as Keddi was from my father's house. We will be there before noon tomorrow. It is full of people and their lives, brimming with their stories. Like a cup waiting to be drunk."

Ki smiled, taking pleasure in the boy's sleepy imaginings. Vandien's tales often had that effect on children. She had seen the street children in a market continue to sit, dreamy-eyed, in a circle around Vandien long after his story was finished. Goat had glimpsed the wideness of the world in Vandien's stories today. She pushed his bedding into his hands, and he curled into it like a sleepy pup. As she arranged herself carefully down Vandien's back, she reflected that the man and his stories might do more toward growing the boy up than he could ever imagine.

Ki had risen, washed, and put the kettle on before the rest began to stir. Willow looked bedraggled and grouchy after her sleepless night, but Ki and Vandien scarcely noticed her. Both exchanged silent glances over Goat, who folded his blankets and stacked them beside the wagon before offering to fetch and harness the horses.

"Go ahead. Watch out for Sigurd, though. He doesn't think he's off to a proper start in the morning unless he's stepped on your foot or nipped you," Vandien warned him.

"Oh, he won't bother me. I'll have them harnessed before you can gather up the dishes." He ran off in happy anticipation.

Ki stared after him. Then Vandien gave her a grin of vaguely paternal pride. "Boy's coming around," he observed, and stiffly rose to load the blankets into the wagon while Ki gathered dishes. Willow sat by the fire, dragging a comb through her hair and occasionally sipping at a mug of cooling tea.

The great horses came to harness docilely. They stood quietly in their places, enduring Goat's fumbling efforts with the harness and buckles until Ki came to help him. Then, indeed, they were ready to go, and Goat was the first to scramble up onto the seat. Willow entered the cuddy, but opened the door that led onto the seat so that she was included in the group. "Are you still in that much pain?" she asked curiously as Vandien slowly mounted the wagon.

He didn't answer, but sat breathing quietly as Ki climbed up behind him. She took up the reins and the horses left the small meadow where they had spent the night. The greys stepped out briskly as if they, too, had spent a peaceful night and were eager for the road. Their ears were up and pricked forward as they started down the road into Algona.

The town was in a slight depression in the wide plain, perhaps for the sake of water. They were passing outlying farms now, fields that had already been harvested and looked strangely shaven with their stubble still standing. Algona spread out before them. Ki considered it in the morning's pale light. Most of the buildings were mud brick, and the streets were laid out in concentric circles around a more impressive stone building. People and animals moved soundlessly in the distant streets. She watched them dreamily as Vandien began telling one of the ornate T'cherian fables that were his favorites. Ki found them obscure.

He had only reached the first moral of the five-part tale when the wagon gave a lurch. Ki had halted the wagon in the rutted trail.

"Something wrong?" he asked, and she gestured.

Down the road, two wagons and a man leading three camels were queued up in the road. Their way was blocked by a flimsy wooden barricade. Behind the barricade were five Brurjans. One was perched sideways on his horse overseeing the other four as they burrowed through the contents of a wagon. The man who held the horses' reins was very still, his head bowed. He did not watch the Brurjans rifling through his possesions.

"Smuggling check!" Goat announced, bouncing on the seat.

"For what kind of contraband?" Vandien asked uneasily.

Goat shrugged. "Perfume, gems, weapons, writings of the Seven False Prophets. Anything the Duke has forbidden to the common people. Some goods require a special permit and an extra tax to carry."

"And some goods the Brurjans want for themselves. Some traders carry a few knives with fancy hilts for the Brurjans to confiscate so they won't look too closely at anything else. And they'll be checking travel permits." Willow's voice shook.

"We'll get you through," Vandien assured her, but his voice was less confident than usual.

"I don't have a damn thing to bribe them with," Ki muttered to herself.

Vandien opened his mouth to remind her of the Windsinger's gold, then shut it. No use arguing that cause. Another worry struck him. "What about my rapier? Will they try to take that?"

Goat shook his head. "Too old and plain. Just wear it and they probably won't even mention it. The Duke doesn't mind a person having one knife or a sword. But a wagonload of weapons might be going to the rebels. That he wouldn't like."

"Besides, if you hide it, they'd just think there was something more to look for," Ki pointed out. Her voice held the weariness of long experience with petty border officials. "They'll know we wouldn't travel far without a weapon of some kind. Wear it so they can see it, or they'll wonder where it is and what's with it." Unconsciously she touched her belt knife. "Besides, that's not the problem. . . ." Her voice trailed off.

Abruptly she shoved the reins into Vandien's hands and clambered awkwardly back into the cuddy. She pushed Vandien's rapier in its worn sheath out to him. He had scarcely buckled its belt around himself before she was pushing their travelling papers into his hands. She dug Goat's paper's from his bag, tossed them to him. Vandien twisted around to watch her rummaging through the cupboards.

Ki churned strong cheese and vinegar in a bowl, then added a handful of grain and a corner off a block of bean paste. She ordered Willow to creep into the cupboard where they usually stored potatoes and other tubers. She closed the door firmly and turned the catch, muffling the girl's complaints. Then Ki heaped a couple of quilts in front of the cupboard. A quick slosh splashed the mixture over the two quilts and down the cupboard door. Vandien turned away, wrinkling his nose in distaste.

"Think it'll work?" he asked as Ki resumed her seat.

She shrugged.

The Brurjan guards were searching the second wagon, tossing bales of something to the dusty road to see what lay beneath them. The driver sat stiff on the wagon seat, staring straight ahead. "Could we go around Algona?" Vandien suggested softly.

Ki shook her head. "Road doesn't go that way. The second we pulled off the road, they'd know we're hiding something. They already noticed our stopping. They'll have questions, but I've got answers." She turned to Goat. "Remember that, Gotheris. I've got the answers. If they ask you anything, just shake your head and look sick. Let me handle everything else. In fact, start looking sick right now."

Sudden comprehension dawned on Goat's face. He slid the cuddy door shut and leaned back against it, his arms crossed over his belly. He stared down at his feet, a puckered look on his face, as Ki put the wagon into motion.

"The boy's a natural," Vandien observed in approval. Goat flashed him a brief smile, then curled over his belly again.

Ki pulled up well back of the camels, but the team still snorted their disapproval. She took a firm grip on the reins to keep them steady while Vandien climbed down and threw open the side door of the wagon. He stood casually beside the open door, waiting, while the Brurjans finished their inspection of the camels. He watched them surreptitiously and was relieved when he didn't recognize any of them. He had feared they might be part of the group who had killed the Tamshin. He didn't think Ki's control could stand up to a chance meeting with them. He was sweating. He wished they'd had more of a chance to rehearse with Goat. One false move on the boy's part, and Willow was finished.

The Brurjans approached, their incongruously small boots making puffs of dust with every step. They moved with feline ease, yet resembled great cats no more than they did Humans. They were Brurjan, of a kind to themselves with their great toothy maws and soft pelts, their muscular bodies and black clawed hands. Vandien looked up into cold black eyes. He tried not to think of how easily this creature could rip his arms from his body. Instead he nodded casually.

"Papers!" the one on horseback demanded. Vandien heard Ki's polite mutter as she turned them over. "We're taking the boy to be apprenticed to his uncle in Villena," Ki volunteered. "He's to be a healer. Can you believe that of so sickly a boy?" Her voice carried clearly to Vandien, and he nodded to himself. So they were going to play it almost truthful. Well, it was a surprise, coming from Ki, but it might be easier.

"Hmm." The black clawed hands rifled quickly through the papers. He glanced at Ki, his black eyes hard and evaluating. "The boy's papers are okay. Yours don't even mention Villena. This is just a general travel permit. See, this stamp is only good within three days of Keddi."

"That's not what we were told," Ki replied, wondering if he were fishing for a bribe.

"Well, it's what I'm telling you now. See the clerk in the Ducal Office. Hauling anything else?" The voice was hard with no effort at politeness. Liar, it called Ki, and expected no truthful answer to its questions.

"Nothing but our travelling supplies," Ki replied.

The Brurjan by Vandien wrinkled his tawny nose as he leaned into the cuddy. "Goddam stinking Humans," he muttered as he mounted the step. The wagon creaked dangerously under his weight. Vandien let him get well within, said nothing as he opened the bedding cabinet and tumbled the quilts to the floor to search behind them. He dragged his clawed hand through the bins of flour and grain, searching for hidden trinkets or weapons. Ki's clothing and then Vandien's joined the heap on the floor. Vandien kept his lips sealed as the Brurjan filched an enameled brass bracelet, slipping it into his pouch. He remembered the street girl he had bought it from, choosing it from her tray of bracelets and feathered earrings as Ki stood by his shoulder, protesting and laughing as he insisted on trying every bracelet against her browned wrist. He looked away as the bracelet vanished forever, along with a handful of coppers he had forgotten in his other vest.

It was only when the Brurjan stooped by the tuber cupboard that Vandien spoke. "Sorry about the vomit. The boy was sick all over in here. Mind you, don't get any on you. I hope Algona has a public well, so we can clean things up in here."

The Brurjan dropped the quilt and straightened abruptly, knocking his head against the cuddy ceiling. He glared at Vandien, sniffed his dripping fingers, and then growled his outrage. As he left the cuddy, he slapped his hand clean down the front of Vandien's shirt. Vandien grunted with the impact, but forced himself to stand still and accept it. Willow, he reminded himself firmly. Willow.

"They clean?" the Brurjan on the horse demanded.

"No," snarled the searcher. "But there's nothing worth taking, either."

"Go on, then," the leader ordered, and turned aside from the wagon. Goat belched loudly and spit a mouthful of saliva into the road dust, earning him a glare from the searcher. But a shepherd with some ratty sheep was approaching, and the leader was gesturing for him to perform his search.

Ki shook the reins and the wagon lurched forward. Vandien caught the doorframe, swung himself up inside the caravan and pulled the door closed behind him. He crouched by the potato cupboard. "Just a little longer," he muttered. "We're past the guards, but stay hidden until Ki tells you to come out." He straightened slowly, and began unbuttoning his soiled shirt.

Algona was a dusty little town, built of mud bricks, paved with mud bricks, a place constructed from its own dust and the infrequent rains. The water well seemed to be the sole reason for the town's existence. All the caravans stopped here for water and a day of rest, so the Ducal Offices were here to collect fees and issue papers, and the Brurjan troops were quartered here to enforce the Duke's will. There was very little else for Brurjans to do in Algona, which accounted for their unusually sullen temperaments, and their sour outlook on the drab little town accounted for the beaten and furtive attitudes of the folk they encountered. Or so Ki reasoned as she pulled a sopping shirt from the wooden bucket. She

wrung it carefully over the bucket, conserving water out of
long habit. The shoulder seam was torn out of this one. Ki
clicked her tongue. Vandien would mutter over mending it.
His own fault, though. Why couldn't the damn man practice
his fencing without a shirt on, instead of tearing out shoulder
seams with extended lunges?

"When is he going to get back?"

Goat's whine was so in tune with Ki's own thoughts that it
didn't even annoy her.

"Soon. I hope. As soon as he gets our papers fixed." Ki
rocked back on her heels and looked around. The public well
was no more than a wide depression in the earth, paved with
stone blocks. The water welled up somewhere in the center of
the depression and filled it before the overflow was channeled
away to the gardens surrounding the Ducal Offices. Surrounding the well was a great open courtyard. In it, children played
while women bent over tubs and garments. No one spoke to
Ki, but the bright wagon and the big horses were objects of
curiosity. Mothers repeatedly called children away from them,
while studiously ignoring both Goat and Ki. Ki wrung out the
last garment and tossed it into a basket beside her.

"Maybe he went to a tavern and got drunk and forgot all
about us," Goat suggested sourly.

"I doubt it." Ki looked at the basket of wet laundry,
wondering how to dry it. The bricks of the courtyard were
coated with dust. Senseless to spread clean wet clothes out on
them. Maybe tonight they'd camp by trees, or at least near
clean grass. She hoped the clothes wouldn't sour before then.
And she hoped Vandien had enough coin to pay for the
papers they'd need to get out of this town. Goat's papers were
good all the way to Villena. Damn this Duke and his rules.
She suspected they were being overcharged for their travel
permits by officials who sensed they were strangers to the
routine. Well, there was little she could do about that. Except
to get out of this Duke's territory as swiftly as she could . . .
after she had dropped off Goat, of course.

"Want me to go look for him?" Goat offered hopefully.

"No. Just stay where you are. As soon as Vandien's back,
we're leaving. I don't like the feel of this town; we're too
obviously strangers, and the Brurjans are too bored."

"They can't be any more bored than I am," Goat grumbled. "Can't I just get down and walk around a little? What's

the harm in that? There are so many people here, so different from people I've known before. I want to see everything.''

"Look around. This is it." Ki tapped, then opened the side door of the wagon, and pushed the basket of laundry in before her. It was stifling inside the cuddy, but she shut the door behind her. The door of the potato bin swung open. Willow peeked out, then crawled out. Her red hair clung damply to her face and neck. "Are we leaving?" she asked hopefully.

"Talk softly. No. Vandien isn't back yet. You must be patient. And try to be more still. Twice I heard the wagon creak behind me while I was doing the laundry. Luckily Goat was up on the bench fidgeting, or anyone could have guessed someone was inside. We have to be careful, Willow. This whole town feels like a storm cloud. The townfolk would like a chance to peck instead of being pecked; the Brurjans would love a new kind of prey. So. Be still, be silent, and as soon as Vandien gets back with the papers, we'll be on our way. Do you understand?''

Willow was poking through the laundry. "Did the tea stain come out of my red skirt?" she asked anxiously. "It's Kellich's favorite.''

Ki drew the skirt out of the basket and shook it out for Willow's inspection. The girl studied it, then nodded and smiled. "I want to wear that, the day after tomorrow when he meets me. I want to walk into the Two Ducks with that skirt swirling around my legs and my hair loose on my shoulders.''

There was something in the girl's wistful voice that no woman could have denied. Ki found herself answering her smile. "The Two Ducks? Is that an inn?''

Willow nodded happily. "It's on the edge of Tekum, not far from the land and house of the man Kellich works for. He said he would meet me there.''

"He did?" Something seemed slightly odd to Ki, but she couldn't put her finger on it. Ki refolded the red skirt and set it atop the basket of laundry. "Be still and be silent, then, and we'll get to the Two Ducks by the day after tomorrow. Are you hungry?''

Willow shook her head. "Two hot to eat anything.''

"Then sleep if you're bored. No, in the cupboard, Willow, I'm afraid. Just in case anyone peeks in the window.''

The girl gave Ki a martyred look, but obediently crawled into the cupboard and drew the door almost closed. With a sigh for the heat, Ki tugged the cuddy door open onto the seat.

"Any sign of Vandien?" she asked Goat.

There was no reply. There was no Goat, not on the seat, nor in the shade of the wagon, nor anywhere in the plaza that Ki could see. She filled her lungs for a shout, then expelled it silently. No use calling. He'd known she didn't want him to leave. Her calling wouldn't bring him back. Damn boy! Didn't he realize how serious the situation was, how important it was to get back on the road and out of this fortified town? No, he must have known. And either not cared or . . . well, she hoped he had gone to find Vandien. He'd latch onto Goat and drag him back.

Nothing to do but sit on the seat and wait, and be both bored and edgy. She dared not leave the wagon to look for him. She'd seen how curiously the children watched the wagon. The instant she was gone, they'd be into it. And with the catch broken on the cuddy door, there was no way to prevent it. She settled back on the plank seat, squinting her eyes against the brightness of the sun. The wide blankness of the plaza seemed to double its dazzle and throw it all in her eyes.

That dazzle had died and afternoon edged toward evening before she saw Vandien coming. His rapier swung with his stride and he looked jauntier than he had in many days. The stiffness was gone from his body, and as soon as he caught her eye she saw the white flash of his smile. Full of himself, and satisfied too, she'd wager. While she did the scrubbing and minded Willow. And lost Goat, she added angrily to herself.

"Pull their noses up and let's be gone," he suggested as soon as he was within range. From his shirt he pulled a rolled paper tied with a scrap of orange ribbon. "We're clear all the way to Villena," he added smugly.

"Took you long enough," she grumbled. "Vandien, I've . . ."

"I know, hot and waiting and nervous, but it takes a bit of talk to get a petty official in a backwater town to relax. I knew I was in luck when I saw he was Human, not Brurjan. At least this Duke has that much sense. So we swapped a few tales, and I listened to him lie about how pleasant his job was and how fiercely he'd competed to get it. And then we rolled, double or nothing, for papers to Tekum. And I lost. . . ."

Ki's jaw dropped and her face lost color.

"So then I got angry, and said, let's do it again, for papers as far as Rivercross. And again I lost."

Ki's mouth closed slowly. She looked ill.

"And then I said, 'Well, by the Moon, let's make it papers as far as Villena,' and we rolled again, double or nothing. And I won."

"How could you?" she asked faintly.

"Easy. The bones love me, child. Fortune's favorite child, that's me, though she sometimes takes a while to remember it. I did have to fluster and fuss between rolls, and complain how someone with such gorgeous robes and such a richly appointed room and a serving maid like a young goddess could take advantage of a poor peddler like me. When he lost at last, Ki, that man was positively gracious about it. I don't think anyone has ever flattered him so much in one afternoon." His excited voice paused, waiting for her amazement.

"Goat's gone." She spoke into the pause, watched his dark eyes widen as the news sank in.

"How long?" His eyes were hard black now, all business. It boded no good for Goat when he was found.

Ki hated to shrug. "Hours. I took the wash into the wagon, and came out. He was gone. He'd been restless all morning, complaining about all the people he'd never get to meet . . . typical village boy come to town, so sure it's going to be different from where he grew up."

"Damn." Vandien put an infinity of meaning into the one brief word. "Any idea where he'd go?"

"No. Well, he did mention that perhaps you'd gone into a tavern and forgotten us, and that maybe he could find you. So."

"So that's quickly checked. There aren't more than six in this town, and all within a quick walk of the Ducal Offices." His eyes went far; his tongue ran hastily over his upper lip. "None of them looked like a place that would welcome a stranger's trade, let alone a mouthy boy like Goat. Perhaps . . ."

"Go ahead," Ki urged him as he hesitated.

"You go ahead. Take the wagon and team and go at a walk, as if they're exhausted or sick. Very slowly. Head

toward the gates, but don't go out of them. I'll be along with
Goat as swiftly as I can. I have a notion that it will be better
if we're already on our way when I catch up with that boy.''

Ki nodded tersely. It was as good a plan as any. Vandien
gave her a quick nod and a flash of teeth that wasn't really a
smile but was reassuring anyway. He set off at a trot across
the plaza, one steadying hand resting on the hilt of his rapier
as he ran. She watched until he was out of sight, then
gathered up the team's water bucket and grain trough. Putting
their bits in and checking the harness took but a few moments
more. Then she climbed up on the seat, and with a few
muttered words that could have been a prayer or a curse, set
the team in motion.

''Damn kid. Stupid. Just plain stupid.'' Vandien slowed to
a walk. His muttering was attracting the stares of passersby;
he shut his jaw firmly. But inside his head, the promises went
on. When he got hold of that boy . . . He shook his head,
baffled. The boy had behaved so well this morning . . . and
now this. After he and Ki had agreed to do everything
possible to be inconspicuous, right down to avoiding a cool
drink in a local tavern, that fool boy had to do this.

Well, there was no sense being inconspicuous now. He'd
wager Goat hadn't been. His eyes roved as he hurried up the
streets, and he checked each alley he passed. Earlier he had
found the architecture of this town boring; squat square buildings set out on gently curving, if narrow, streets. Now it was
to his advantage. If Goat were outside, he'd be visible for
blocks.

He set his teeth as he came to the first tavern. The doorway
was a black gap in the mud brick wall. Vandien felt like a
target as he stepped in and peered around the dim interior.
The place had seen better days—at least, he hoped it had; it
was depressing to think that it might always have suffered
these cobbled-together tables and benches, these bleary, sod-
den men. The place stank of oppression and despair. The two
women in the room swiveled toward him like windvanes
feeling a favorable breeze. One leered invitingly, and Vandien
gave her a polite nod as he turned toward the door. Goat
wasn't here, and Vandien suddenly decided that asking if
anyone here had seen him would consume more time than it
was worth. Not even the innman, endlessly wiping a mug on

his greasy apron, looked as if he could put three words together without effort.

One of the women called something rude after him, and was rewarded with a low wave of laughter. He hurried on, trying not to look as if he hurried. Ki was probably halfway to the gate by now. He'd checked it out earlier; it was a proper gate in the crumbling remains of the city wall of the inevitable mud brick. Manned by Brurjan troops, too. They'd best all be on the wagon with their proper papers to present when they went through.

The next tavern was of better quality, but no more welcoming. The innman regarded Vandien suspiciously despite the small piece of silver he rolled up and down the table. A boy? Yes, there had been a strange boy in here, telling lies about riding with the Romni and facing down a whole patrol of Brurjan troops. They needed none of that kind of talk around here. This was a peaceful tavern, and folk left their troubles outside the door. No, he didn't know where the boy had gone, and didn't care, either. Strangers were nothing but trouble, what with half of them being thieves and the other half rebel spies a man could get hung just for talking to. Less this innman saw of strangers, the better he liked it. He liked his local trade, yes he did, and the Brurjan troops who dropped in for blood and milk at the turn of their shifts, which was pretty soon, yes, and he'd be glad to see them as he always was. . . .

Vandien took the hint, but let the coin fall flat and stay. He didn't like the way the local patrons gazed after him as he left. They were burly working men, with one small group of wiry-locked Callistri in one corner. None of them lifted their gazes from the drink-ringed tables, but there wouldn't be one of them who wouldn't be able to describe him to anyone who asked.

Clear of the tavern, he turned the corner and hastened through the yard of a livery stable. The next tavern was only a few blocks away, if he remembered correctly, and . . .

A bray of laughter, followed by a girl's giggle, stopped him in his tracks. He turned slowly, but saw nothing. Yet that laugh, he was sure, was Goat's. The stable was an open affair, not much more than a thatched roof held up by dark beams. A pair of oxen chewed their cuds and regarded him with calm brown eyes. In the next stall an old mule dozed, its

muzzle nearly touching the ground. Beyond him was a rick of
bleached yellow straw, straw that suddenly shifted with another giggle.

"Goat!" Vandien barked with sudden certainty.

The boy's head popped up from the straw. His cheeks were
very red, and his mouth was wet. The girl's head appeared
more slowly. Her eyes were round and wide. As she met
Vandien's stare, a blush rosed her cheeks. But Goat grinned
delightedly as if an audience had been all that had been
lacking to complete his pleasure. "Pretty little poppet, isn't
she?" he asked Vandien roguishly as he emerged from the
straw, dragging his conquest with him. He began to refasten
his loosened clothing. "I'll bet you wish you had done as
well today."

Vandien looked aside, disappointment so sharp in him it
made him feel sick. Goat shamed him. He'd believed better
of him. There was an innocent eagerness in the girl's eyes.
She was pretty only with the fleeting beauty every girl has on
the brink of womanhood. Her narrow nose and chin would
seem sharp when lines came into her face, and the generous
young breasts she was now struggling to hide would soon
hang like pouches on her chest. Vandien had seen thousands
like her; it struck him as tragic that she had spent the brief
wonder of her virginity on Goat.

"It's time to leave," he told Goat in a tight-lipped voice.
"I've been looking for you. Ki's waiting on us."

But Goat was still strutting too high to hear the anger in
Vandien's voice. He gave a theatrical sigh. "So, my little
love, then it must be over. Remember me well." He gave a
dirty little laugh. "I'll certainly remember you!"

Vandien glanced up in time to see the girl's face shatter. In
that one brief instant her prettiness popped like a fragile
bubble. "But . . ." she stammered. "But I'm going with
you. I dreamed it, last night. First this, and then how we
would ride out of the city together, on the tall white
mares. . . ." She saw the truth in Vandien's agonized embar-
rassment. "You came in my dreams," she whispered in
horror. "It has to be true!"

"Ah, well!" Goat's voice was bluff and hearty as a tavern
boaster's. "That's the way it is, missy. A man has to have
what a man must have. And certainly you seemed willing to
give it! Vandien, old man, you've never had a gallop like

that! It's a thing no man could resist! I'm sorry if you were deceived, little love, but a man can scarcely refuse . . .''

"Not a man." Vandien's voice was cold. "A goat. I'm sorry, miss." He fumbled an instant at his belt, then saw her eyes and stopped. A gift of coin could only make it worse. He had nothing else to give her, except a look of sympathy.

"There, there, let this brighten your face, then," Goat said in a masterful way. Vandien glimpsed the handful of coppers he was ready to scatter, and something in him broke. He backhanded the boy, heard the coppers ring on the wooden planked floor at the same instant that Goat stuck it with a thud.

Vandien hauled the dazed boy to his feet. As he dragged him from the stable, Goat came to life. His eyes flashed with green glints of anger. He jerked free of Vandien's grip and stood independent. A thin trickle of blood was starting at the corner of his mouth. "Who do you think you are?" he demanded shrilly. "You can't treat me this way! You're nothing but a hired carter, paid to take me where I want to go! And I'll say when we leave! Me! I'm the one who paid for this trip! And if you ever treat me so again, you'll be very sorry. Very, very sorry! Think what could happen to you and your precious Ki if I told the Brurjan guards what I know! You'd be very sorry, but it would be too late! So watch your step, man, or . . .''

Vandien had his weight behind it, and it was his fist this time, not his open hand. Goat dropped solidly. The boy was heavy, but there was a lot of satisfaction in dragging him by his collar. He only wished his ribs didn't ache so. And that his heart didn't ache for the sobbing girl.

EIGHT

The stars were very bright and more numerous than Vandien had ever seen. His head was pillowed on a bundled quilt and the earth beneath him was warm. Satisfaction flowed through him as comfortingly as his own blood. He listened to the crackling of the fire and the horses' teeth grinding the rough dry grass. Laundry draped on the low-growing bushes made friendly ghosts in the night.

Ki's silhouette came between him and the firelight. "It was stupid," she informed him. Her knees cracked as she squatted down beside him. He took her mug of tea and stole a sip from it.

"Necessary." He felt too lazy to even make complete sentences. The long tension of the day had taken its toll. Now that it was finally eased, he felt both incredibly sleepy and very smug. Too smug to trade words with Ki. Besides, the argument was already old.

"Stupid. If I hadn't stopped and pretended to be taking a stone out of Sigmund's hoof, you would never have caught up with us. Dragging him like a sack of potatoes. You couldn't have attracted more attention if you'd been blowing a horn."

"A diversion," he said lazily. "Carefully planned. The Brurjans at the gate were too busy asking me why the boy was unconscious to wonder what might be inside the wagon. No smuggler in his right mind would go out of the gate like that."

"Hmm." Ki sipped at her mug. "I put a poultice of cold

tea leaves on it, but his face is going to be purple. We'll be lucky if the bruises fade before we get to Villena.''

"I'm truly distressed to hear that," Vandien said laconically.

"You should be. What if he had come to at the gate and made good on his threats? Or what if a patrol stops us again? He's still furious. He's full of low names for you. He must have told me two dozens times that you were going to be very sorry you'd treated him that way. I was glad to get out of the wagon and leave him there. You should see his jaw. It's a wonder he can talk at all.''

"Breaks my heart." Vandien smiled briefly. "I knew he wasn't going to come to at the gate." He made a show of massaging his knuckles.

"You get that much satisfaction out of hitting a little boy?" Ki asked acidly.

Vandien wasn't fooled. "More. Infinitely more. You can't imagine how good it felt.''

"I'm ashamed to say, I can," she admitted with a small smile. She settled comfortably beside him.

"Willow's asleep?" Vandien asked after a moment.

Ki nodded to the dark. "Under the wagon. I think she's exhausted from the tension, and couldn't stay awake any longer, no matter what she believes about Goat." Her voice faded into the silence between them.

"And what do you believe?" Vandien finally asked her.

"I don't know," Ki admitted. "I haven't been sleeping too well since we took on Goat, but my waking hours haven't been pleasant, either. That girl said she'd dreamed of him?''

"Yes." A more serious look came over his face. "I think that's what upset me the most. Not a boy and girl in the straw, but the deception he used to get her there. The lack of honor.''

"Honor is so important?''

His dark eyes pinned hers. "Yes. A man's honor is what he is.''

Neither spoke for a long time. Ki sat up, arranged the quilts and Vandien's arm more to her liking, and settled into them again, pillowing her head on his shoulder and upper chest. She spoke softly. "I like the sound of your heart beating.''

"Me, too. I'd be very annoyed if it stopped. Ki, what do you believe about Goat?''

She sighed, and he knew she didn't want to talk about it. But she would. "Everything, and nothing," she said. "Yesterday, and this morning, he was like a different boy. Helpful, kind. But this afternoon . . ." She paused, took a breath. "I suppose I believe that we should be careful. Knowing that he might be capable of such a thing negates it, doesn't it? It's kind of like finding out a man's a liar. He doesn't deceive you easily after that. I won't be swayed by anything I dream."

"But you aren't going to give up sleeping?" Vandien filled in.

"Oh, I'll sleep, all right." Ki lifted her head, slowly scanned the camp. Willow was a motionless huddle under the wagon, and the door of the cuddy was shut as tight as Goat could slam it. She ducked her head and brushed her lips down Vandien's face to his ear. "I'll sleep if there's nothing better to do."

"Um." He settled more comfortably. "You're warm. Feels good on my ribs. Well. So, what are we going to do after we drop Goat in Villena?"

She lifted her mouth from his neck. "If you're too tired, just say so."

"I'm not too tired. I just enjoy being persuaded. And it brought to mind what I heard in town today. About a week from now, there's going to be a festival in Tekum. The Duke will be there, with all his retainers, and there will be jugglers and street musicians and wrestling on the village green. . . ."

"And so?" Ki asked, loosening the lacing of his shirt.

"And so I thought we might want to stay and enjoy it."

"Not a good idea," Ki said decisively. "Does this tickle?"

"Not exactly, but it's nice. Why not the festival?"

Ki paused to answer him. "Timing's all wrong. We should be nearly to Villena by then. Because the Duke will be there, and if the Duke will be there, then his Brurjans will be there, and if the Brurjans are there, then we don't want to be there."

"But we'd be part of a crowd, hardly noticeable in the throng. There'd be a lot to see and do, and maybe we could pick up some freighting that will take us out of Loveran. Even if we don't, the man who issued our papers today said that Tekum boasts a number of good swordsmen, and that the Duke always offers a purse for the . . . hey! Be careful of my ribs, will you?"

"I hate this damn belt buckle. Next town we come to, I'm buying you a different one."

"It works fine if one doesn't get in a rush about it, Ki." His hands moved lazily to her assitance. "But you could buy me a new one at the Duke's festival in Tekum if you want. Staying for it would delay us a few days at most."

"Delays are one thing that I have no tolerance for," Ki said pointedly.

"And you say I'm impatient and impulsive." He sighed theatrically as he reached for her.

Ki awoke to darkness. Vandien's elbow was in her ribs; sleepily she shifted away from it and resettled herself in the quilts. Then she heard again the sound that had wakened her. Willow drew another shuddering breath, sniffed again. For long moments Ki listened to her weeping, trying to imagine what could be wrong with her. At last she rose and went to her. The dry earth was warm beneath her bare feet. She crouched by the wagon, gripping a spoke of one of the wagon's wheels. "Willow?" she whispered gently.

The prone figure of the girl twitched. She buried her face deeper into her crossed arms. "Go away," she said in a small, muffled voice.

"All right, if that's what you want." Ki knew that some kinds of grief did not bear sharing. But others did. "I'll go away, Willow. But if you change your mind and want to talk to someone, or just have someone sit up with you, let me know. I'm not hard to wake."

Willow took in a gasping breath and suddenly lifted her face to stare at Ki. In the deep shadows under the wagon, her eyes were two smudges in her pale face. "That's wonderful." She spat out the words. "Now you'd like to listen to me. Now, when it's too late! Well, there's nothing to tell you, Ki. Nothing's left. Unless you want to hear about a bad dream I had. Unless you want to share my nightmare with me!" The last she all but shrieked at Ki. Ki stood and backed stiff-legged from the wagon, repulsed not so much by Willow's words, but by the low chuckle that echoed them; a laugh she would swear came from within her wagon.

She sensed Vandien's wakefulness even before she touched him. She snugged her body against his, belly to back, feeling chilled despite the warmth of the night, and shrugged the covers up.

"What happened?" he asked softly.

"I don't know. I heard Willow crying and went to see what was wrong. She said . . ."

"I heard. Goat?"

"I think so. I think he got into her dreams somehow and gave her a nightmare."

"Or maybe she just had a nightmare about him."

"I hope so," Ki muttered against his neck. "But somehow I don't think so."

Morning came muted in grey. The bright blue skies that had shimmered over them for days were suddenly robed with clouds. The air was muggy, the team restless in the charged atmosphere. Rain, Ki thought to herself, and thunder. She breathed deeply of the heavy air but it didn't satisfy her lungs. She rolled from the blankets and staggered upright.

Vandien sat cross-legged by a tiny fire, a mug of tea balanced on one knee. He raised his brows at her as she rubbed her face. "Why didn't you wake me?" she demanded.

"I thought we could all use a little extra rest."

She drew water from the cask on the wagon and sloshed it over her face. She ducked to peer under the wagon. "Where's Willow?" she asked, turning to accept a mug of tea from him.

"Sleeping . . ." His voice faded as he stooped to poke at her empty blankets. The eyes he raised to Ki were anxious. "She's gone," he said needlessly.

"How long?" Ki wondered, "and where to?"

He shrugged. "I've been up about an hour. I thought she was still sleeping."

"Goat!" They said the word simultaneously, but it was Ki who dragged the wagon door open. The boy was there, lying on his back with one arm flung out. A foolish smile was on his swollen face. As the light touched his eyes, they opened. He turned his head to squint at them. The smile faded.

"Oh. Good morning." There was heavy sarcasm in his voice. Ki ignored it.

"Do you know anything about Willow?" she asked anxiously.

The fatuous smile returned. "Oh, yes,' he replied leisurely. "I know lots about Willow. More than she knows herself," he added, a giggle in his voice.

"Where's she gone?" Vandien demanded impatiently. "There's bound to be patrols along this stretch of road, and if she's spotted alone, with no papers . . ."

"Gone?" The word came out of Goat as if it were a rock he'd discovered in his mouth. "Willow's gone?"

"Yes," Ki told him angrily. "And if you know where, you'd better say now."

"She can't be gone." Goat sat up, frowned, then winced and put his hand to his jaw. "My face hurts still, you pile of sheep dung," he told Vandien angrily. In the next breath he muttered, "She wouldn't dare be gone. She can't be gone." He glared at them as if he suspected a trick. "She's probably off peeing in the bushes."

"Sure she is. Since dawn," Vandien agreed sarcastically. He turned to Ki. "Now what do we do?"

She shrugged. "We can wait for her to come back. But we aren't sure that she'll do that. Or we can look for her. Damn. I should have stayed with her last night, made her tell me what she was crying about."

"I should have tried to talk to her," Vandien added guiltily. "But I was just so tired."

Ki shook her head. "None of this does us any good now. There's no good in worrying about what we should have done. The question is, What do we do now?" She turned aside from them, climbed up to the top of the wagon itself. "Willow!" she called. But the heavy air of the gathering storm muffled her shout. Ki turned slowly, scanning the prairie in every direction. Its seeming flatness was a deception. The tall dry grass and low growing brush were moving in the winds of the rising storm like the waves stirred by a storm over water. Any of a hundred rises and dips could be hiding Willow, even if she were walking back toward them. And if she were deliberately hiding, lying flat in a swale of grass, they could look for days and never see her.

"Where did she go, Goat?" Vandien's voice was flat. "And why did she go?"

"How would I know?" Goat demanded angrily. "I was sleeping in the wagon, stupid. It wasn't my job to watch her."

"Goat." Ki cut into the argument. "Did you get into Willow's dreams last night?"

He scrambled out of the wagon. He suddenly struck her as ridiculous, his clothes awry and his hair wild from sleep, his pale eyes huge in his swollen face. Her question hung in the air between them, and as she looked at his childish stance, his arms crossed stubbornly over his narrow chest, her own words seemed silly. This spoiled and pouting brat the nefarious dream-thief of the old legends?

"That's stupid," he echoed her thought. "Willow tells you a lot of gossip about me, and then, just because she runs away, you think it's true. You're stupid, both of you. Just as stupid as that dumb Willow."

"The girl in Algona," Vandien said, his voice soft and fanged. "Was she stupid, too? Or was she lying when she said she had dreamed about you?"

Goat looked flustered. "I don't know!" he sputtered. "Some stupid girl says something . . . who cares what the stupid little wench said . . . she just wanted to make an excuse, because she let me mate her. She wanted to make it my fault that she couldn't keep her legs together."

Vandien lifted his hand suddenly and Goat instantly shrank in on himself, throwing his arms up to cover his face.

"Hitting him won't get anything out of him," Ki observed pragmatically, but disgust was in her voice. "Leave him alone, Van." She climbed down from the wagon to stand in front of the boy. Vandien gave a huff of frustrated anger and turned away from them. Going to the fire, he began to kick dirt over it.

Goat peered out anxiously from the shelter of his arms. Seeing that Vandien was a safe distance away, he dropped his arms. "It wasn't my fault," he told Ki earnestly. "None of it was my fault."

"Whatever." She dismissed the earlier quarrel. "What I need to ask is this. Where do you think Willow might be?" As the boy opened his mouth to protest, she quickly filled in, "I know, you said you don't know. I'm only asking you what you guess, where you suppose she would go if she felt very upset. You know her better than Vandien and I do; maybe you can guess what she might do."

The calmness of Ki's words reached the boy. He stood scuffing his foot in the dust. He finally looked up at Ki guilelessly. "She'd probably go on to Tekum. To her precious Kellich!" There was a wealth of distaste in his words suddenly. "Yes," he added, staring off down the road. "She'd hurry ahead to Kellich, to try to explain."

"Explain what?" Ki prodded gently. But Goat was wary again.

"Whatever was troubling her," he said sweetly. "That would be just Willow's way. Run ahead and tell all her troubles to big, brave Kellich. Big brave Kellich can make everything all better. Or so she thinks." The sneer in his voice was unmistakable now.

"Vandien!" Ki called, but he was already putting the big horses to harness.

When the rain broke it came down in sheets of grey water that shut down the world around them and set Goat scuttling inside the wagon. Lightning flashed in the distance, and cleared a space of silence in which Ki and Vandien listened to the creak and rumble of the wagon and the damp clopping of the horses' hooves in the now wet road. He reached and put his hand on her leg as the thunder reached them, filling their ears with its threat. Ki took one wet hand from the reins and set it atop his.

"You're worried," he said, sliding closer to her.

She nodded into the rain, blinking against the heavy drops. "I feel responsible," she admitted.

"Me, too." The rain was not cold, but it was constant, drenching them and running down their faces. It soaked Vandien's hair to his skull, making his curls lie flat on his forehead and drip in his eyes. "I always wondered what it would be like to have children." He paused. "It's a pain in the ass."

"When they're your own, it's even worse," Ki told him. "Except for the times when it's wonderful." They rode a long ways in silence. The rain stained the grey backs of the horses to a deeper charcoal. The road became both sticky and slick. The horses began to steam. But despite Ki's anxiety for Willow, the storm brought a strange peace with it. The drumming of the rain on the wagon became a noise so constant it was a different kind of silence. She and Vandien were alone on the box, rocking together to the sway of the wagon. The annoyance of the rain trickling down her collar and running a wet finger between her breasts seemed minor.

"A few weeks ago, I'd have said this was miserable weather." Vandien echoed her thoughts. "Now it seems peaceful."

She nodded into the rain, blinking away the blinding drops. "I've missed you," she said, and laughed aloud at how senseless her words seemed. But he understood. He lifted his hand from her leg and put his arm across her shoulders.

It was nearly noon before they came upon Willow. "She must have slipped away right after I talked to her, to get this far," Ki observed. Vandien nodded silently, and stared at the small figure plodding ahead of them. Her clothing was drenched, and her long skirt clung to her. Mud weighted the hem; her slippers were a ruin. Her hair was plastered down flat. But her spine was straight and she did not look back, even thought she must have heard them coming. Ki glanced over at Vandien and slowed the big horses. Vandien stood, then agilely swung down from the moving wagon. His boots threw up clods of mud as he ran.

When he reached the girl he slowed to keep pace with her. Ki watched them walk together, the girl's back straight and angry at first, and then starting to hunch in misery. Vandien, she knew, probably wasn't saying a word. As a storyteller, he excelled, but his ability to listen, to nod and be understanding, had earned him more meals. She watched him listen, saw Willow wave her arms wildly and even caught the sound of her angry words as she ranted at Vandien. Then suddenly the girl turned and butted into him, burrowing her face into his shoulder and clinging to him as she stood crying in the rain.

Ki let the team come up on them and pulled them to a halt. She sat silent on the seat, feeling the wind of the storm buffet the side of the wagon as it drove the rain suddenly against it. Vandien was patting Willow's back. He looked up at Ki, a resigned expression on his face. "Come on," he told the girl softly. "Let's get up on the wagon. You'll get there a lot sooner that way, you know."

"I guess." She lifted her face from Vandien's shoulder, but did not look at him or Ki as she clambered up on the seat. She sat on the farthest edge of it, curled over her clenched fists and shivering. Vandien had to climb over her to regain his seat by Ki. As soon as he was settled, she started the team. They rode on, the silence as thick as the rain that pelted them.

"Willow?" Ki ventured finally.

Immediately the girl sat up. "I don't want to talk about it!" she flared. "I told you what he was, but no one believed me. No, everyone thought I was some stupid little twit, full of wild fancies. Well, now he has ruined me. And there's nothing anyone can do. So I don't want to listen to a lot of stupid apologies." Willow sniffed angrily.

Ki sighed, but said nothing. The pelting rain slowly changed to a pattering, and then ceased. As suddenly as it had begun the storm was gone, blowing off into the distance. Before them, the sky opened in a wide streak of blue, and light poured down like a gush of white wine, flooding the landscape before them. Ki pulled the team in for a moment to stare at it.

The land was obviously sloping away from them now. It was a very gradual slope, but in the far distance there was the silver glint of an immense river winding through the valley. There was an edging of dark green along it; trees, Ki decided. On the far side were the green and yellow shapes of tilled fields. The unnatural clarity of the light after the storm made it seem closer than it was. Rivercross would be on that water, she decided, and Villena not far beyond it. If only it were as close as it seemed, and both these annoying children delivered.

"Tekum?" Vandien asked, pointing, and she followed the direction of his finger. Yes, it was there, a pattern of fields and beyond them, enough buildings to make a respectable town. This, at least, was attainable.

"We'll be there sometime tomorrow," Ki estimated. It looked like a pretty, restful place. There were trees there, too, perhaps orchards on the outskirts of the town.

"That low building at the beginning of the town. That's the inn where Kellich said he'd meet me. Those orchards belong to his master. And the meadows beyond." There was childish pride in Willow's voice as she spoke of her lover.

All were startled as the cuddy door slid open. Goat thrust his head out. "What are we stopping for . . . Oh!" He stared at Willow and the atmosphere around the wagon was suddenly as charged as it had been before the storm. She stared at him, hatred shining in her eyes. Ki held herself ready for another tussle. But Willow turned her head away from Goat. Her lips were a hard line as she stared out over the wide river valley.

The wagon started with a lurch. Goat bumped his head on the side of the door. "Close the door, Goat," Vandien suggested. Goat looked from Willow's stiff spine to Vandien's cold eyes.

"I didn't do anything to her," Goat said suddenly. "But you'll never believe that, will you? No matter what she says, you always believe her, and you always think I'm lying. I didn't do a single thing to her. . . ."

"Did so!" Willow hissed angrily. She whirled suddenly to confront him. "Lying won't change it, Goat. I know what you are, they know what you are, everyone knows what you are! You think you can run away from it, but you can't. When we get to Tekum, Kellich will know. Kellich and the whole inn! No matter where you go, people will find out. . . ."

"Oh?" Goat's voice was suddenly cold. "And you're going to tell Kellich all about it, aren't you, Willow? In every little detail? Well, then, let's share what I know. Your pretty little Willow, Vandien, with the mismatched eyes? You think her so sweet and naive, running off to find her true love. I think you should know more about her. She isn't what she appears, neither she nor Kellich. Willow is never what she pretends to be. I'm not the only one around here with mixed blood. Mine just shows. Did you know that when she was twelve or so, four of the old women in her village went to the Ducal adjutant there and swore she was a witch? Cost her papa a lot to get those charges dropped, it did. Of course, that was before he moved his two daughters to Keddi; Willow thought no one would ever know that about her. Didn't you, Williow? Now it's your turn. Go ahead, tell a secret you know."

Willow had gone white except for two red spots on the points of her cheeks. She stared at Goat, and then swayed as if she would fall from the wagon. "Keshna!" she invoked wildly. Vandien put out a hand to steady her, but as he touched her she stiffened. Drawing herself up straight, she took a deep breath. The wagon jolted on. Ki's grim face stared out over the ears of her team. Goat sat quite still, smiling at Willow's back. The sound of her ragged breathing was louder than the creak of the wagon. Twice she drew breath for speech, and Vandien kept his hand on her shoulder, braced for whatever she might say.

She took a sudden deep breath. She turned to him. Tears

had tracked down her face and shone still in the brightness of the sun after the storm. But she no longer wept. Her eyes were open, but shallow; her soul was walled up behind them. He sensed that a decision had been made, and wondered what it was. But when she spoke, her calm words took him by surprise.

"Won't you tell us another story, Vandien, to pass the time?"

NINE

The day's travel had been long, and neither the cheeriness of the sun flooding the damp landscape with light and warmth nor Vandien's tales had been able to make it shorter. Ki had found a good campsite, with deep grass and a grove of trees. Goat and Willow had kept the peace, by exchanging no words at all. But Ki felt strung as tightly as a harp string. Prickly with tension, she waited for some new outburst.

Vandien felt it, too. She had sensed it in the way he told his tales today, choosing the most innocuous ones, tales more fit for lap-size children than two who bordered on adulthood. He had told them well, but with none of his usual embroidery. Now he was grooming Sigurd with a maddening thoroughness that had the beast stomping with impatience. He and Vandien regarded each other with affectionate malice in the best of times; the last thing she needed was to have them get into a spat tonight.

She dashed the dregs of her tea into the sputtering fire and crossed the camp. She took the currycomb firmly from Vandien's grip and gave Sigurd a nudge that told him he was free to go. The great beast stepped out sedately for two paces, and then suddenly gave a wild curvet that brought him down just short of Vandien's toes. Even as Vandien roared, Sigurd leaped away, dancing out of reach. "Let him go," Ki counseled him, touching his wrist lightly. Sigurd, for his part, dropped ponderously to the earth and rolled, destroying Vandien's grooming efforts.

"That damn horse," Vandien snorted, torn between anger and laughter.

The easing of the tension was so marked that Ki hated to bring it back. But she had to. "What did Willow tell you, earlier?" she asked him.

"When we were walking?"

Ki nodded.

He shook his head. "Nothing, really. Mostly how much she hated Goat, and it was all our fault she was ruined and no one would ever trust her again."

"But she didn't say what Goat had done?"

"No. Well, she said something I don't understand. He had spoiled her memories. Something like that."

Ki stood still, thinking it through. Finally, she sighed. "I think I understand what she meant. I had a strange dream, shortly after we took Goat on." She paused, and found herself unwilling to tell Vandien exactly what the dream had been. "It was like someone was sifting through all my memories," she said reluctantly. "And looking in on the most personal ones."

Vandien winced, and looked away from her. "I thought I was getting somewhere with that boy," he muttered, and then burst out, "Why didn't you say something to me?"

"What could you do about it? Besides, I thought it was only a dream. Now that I know what it was . . . I don't know what I'm feeling. Anger. And violation." She glared over at Goat, recalling what she had dreamed. The blush that reddened her face was not shame, but fury. Fury that was suddenly engulfed by puzzlement. "I'd like to kill him, Van. But that doesn't help me understand what's happening now."

"Vandien," he corrected her automatically. Then, "What do you mean?"

Ki jerked her head, and Vandien glanced past her. Willow finished refilling Goat's cup with spiced tea. Goat was grinning delightedly as Willow waited on him, but it was the look on Willow's face that was unsettling. She was not smiling, nor glaring. Her face was carefully bland, almost blank.

"She looks like a very polite guest who smells something terrible in the soup, but is so well mannered she will eat it anyway," Vandien observed.

"She wants something," Ki said, suddenly sure of it.

"But what?"

"Revenge," Ki guessed. "Vandien, I'd like to kill him. But I know I won't. If a grown person had spied on me that way, I'd have to kill. But I look at him, and I see a wayward, very spoiled child."

"To me, that makes his dream-stealing more offensive, not less," Vandien observed. "I'll kill him for you."

She looked at the set cold anger in his dark eyes. "Would you?" she queried softly. "How? Beat him to death while he cried and screamed for mercy? Run him through with your rapier, after you had chased him down? Strangle him in his sleep?"

A shudder ran over Vandien, and she felt the sudden tension run out of his body. "No." His voice sounded old. "No. You're right. I couldn't."

She touched his hand. "I know. If you could, I couldn't feel about you as I do."

Amusement flickered across his face. "Why don't you ever admit you love me?"

For an instant their eyes locked. Ki squirmed in discomfort. "Good friends are too hard to come by," she said at last, and he laughed.

"That they are," he agreed, and squeezed her hand. "So. To get back to the subject. What do we do about Goat and Willow?"

"I don't know," Ki admitted. She watched Willow get up to put some wood on the fire. When she sat down again, she was closer to Goat. Not sitting beside him, but closer.

"She's stalking him," Vandien said. "But perhaps we should do nothing . . . unless we have to. We'll be in Tekum by tomorrow afternoon. We leave Willow there, and that's an end to it. Then on to Villena, to get rid of Goat. Then . . ." He let the sentence dangle, looking quizzically at Ki.

"Then we go north, away from this damn Duke and his Brurjans and his papers and checkpoints." She spoke defiantly, expecting an argument. Instead Vandien nodded.

"I think you're right. I don't like the feel of this land, or its folk. Always watched and watching. But I say we bear north and east, away from both this Duke and the Windsingers."

"North. We can go east after I've gotten a new wagon."

"We'll see." Vandien's capitulation was uttered in so distracted a tone that Ki turned to see what he was watching. A shiver of dread snaked up her spine. Willow had not moved. But Goat had. He sat at her feet beside the stone she perched on. His head was leaned against her knee. As Ki stared, her pale hand lifted, settled on his hair, stroked it. Like a fondled kitten, Goat nestled his head closer against her knee.

Without hesitation, Ki turned and strode back to the fire. She didn't break stride as she gripped Goat by the collar and hauled him to his feet. Willow gasped and Ki saw sparks of anger in those blue and green eyes. Ki's anger met them.

"What was it to be, Willow? A little silver pin driven up behind his ear? Or a quick bit of knife across his throat?"

But the glitter was already erased from Willow's eyes. The face she turned to Ki was passive and empty. "What do you mean?" she asked slowly.

"I'm talking about Goat's head on your knee, and your hatred of him. They don't go together, Willow, not unless you're getting him in close enough to kill. I won't have that. I've been paid to take him to Villena. And I'll get him there. I don't condone what he did to you." She glanced at the boy, still half-strangled in her grip. Disgust filled her face, and her sudden push sent him staggering. "If it's any comfort, you weren't his only victim. But much as I hate what he's done, I won't have bloodshed. You can't undo what's happened, Willow." Ki was almost whispering now, and the girl's face was still. "Leave it behind you and go on from here, forget it and take up the rest of your life. Think of Kellich, and take comfort in him."

At the mention of his name, life passed briefly over Willow's face. And agony. "I do think of him," she murmured. "I do." With those words, her face closed again, her eyes going as empty. "I meant no harm to Goat," she said calmly.

"Let me go, you ass! Mind your own business!" Ki turned from Willow, to find that Vandien had a firm grip on Goat and was easily dealing with the boy's efforts to shake him off.

"Let him go, Vandien." Willow's request came just as Goat gave a violent lunge away from Vandien. Vandien released him, letting the boy's own momentum carry him away. Goat plunged into the dust at Willow's feet. He scrambled up angrily.

"Leave us alone!" He stared from Ki's face to Vandien's. "Is it so hard to believe she likes me? Yes, she likes me, and

she asked me to sit beside her because she was lonely. You
don't believe it, do you? But it's true!''

Vandien opened his mouth to speak, but Willow interrupted. ''It's true,'' she said. She reached out a hand to Goat,
and he took it as he sat down beside her. He stared up
defiantly.

''You see,'' he said. ''She likes me.''

''I give up,'' Vandien muttered. He snagged Ki's hand and
drew her along. Together they walked off into the evening.
The night was fragrant and soft around them, and overhead a
myriad of stars shone. But Ki could not surrender herself to
the peace.

''I don't understand.'' There was pain in her voice, for
Willow.

''I don't either. Look.'' He tugged her up a small rise of
earth. He pointed down the long gentle slope before them. The
distant lights shone warm and yellow. ''Tekum,'' he said
softly. He stood behind her, his arms around her, his mouth
by her ear. ''Tomorrow it will end. Willow will go her way,
and we will take Goat on to Villena. Do you think the team
could stand longer days? I'd be willing to drive evenings, to
get us there sooner.''

''Maybe.'' Ki sighed, and turned in his embrace. She held
him close, smelling his smell, a scent like herbs and grasses
damp in the morning. She felt the strength in his arms, in the
muscles that ran across the flat of his back. Her strong fingers
kneaded the flesh of his back and he groaned with pleasure.
''You know,'' she said in his ear, ''there are Brurjans and
checkpoints and papers and cracked axles and thrown shoes
waiting for us down every road. Why do we keep on wandering the way we do?''

He shrugged, and his fingers tracked her aching spine. ''If
we stayed in one spot, we'd just have to wait for them to
come to us,'' he observed. ''But I'll be glad to see the end of
this run. Very glad.''

''Me, too.''

They walked slowly back to the camp, savoring the light
wind that carried the moisture-laden air through the night.
Habit made them both gather a few dry sticks as they walked.
In the camp, Ki poked them carefully into the fire, then lifted
the kettle. ''Shall I make more tea?''

He didn't reply, and when she looked at him, his face

combined disbelief and disgust. Ki stared at him; then her
ears, too, picked up the muffled sounds coming from the
wagon.

Their eyes met. Vandien stepped toward the wagon, but Ki
flowed up from her crouch by the fire, to step in front of him.

"No." She kept her voice low.

"But . . ."

"Leave it. There's nothing you can say or do. She has to
make her own mistakes and learn from them."

"But why? She despises the boy, and what he feels for her
is only what a bull feels for a cow in springtime. . . ."

"I know. I don't understand why, Vandien. But interfering
now would not save anyone anything, and would only embar-
rass us all." She drew him back, beyond the fire and away
from the sounds emanating from the wagon. She brought him
a mug of tea when it brewed, and found him stretched out on
his back, staring up at the stars. Ki sat beside him, cross-
legged. She held her own mug and set his within easy reach.

"What are you thinking?" she asked softly.

He took a long time to answer. "I'm thinking that if I had
it all to do over again, it would be different."

Ki sipped her tea and nodded. "Yes. We'd have paid more
heed to her, and kept them separated. Or never taken on
passengers at all. I'd have done better to go vagabonding with
you. Or gone back north to Firbanks for a new wagon."

"Yes. That, too."

Something in his voice silenced her. He continued looking
up at the stars, ignoring his tea. When he spoke, she wasn't
sure if it was to her. "Perspectives change, when you look
back on things. I told you once that I ran away from my
family, after I couldn't sire an heir for my parents' line. I was
their only child; when they died, I was the only one carrying
their name. I couldn't inherit until I proved that I could carry
on my line. I was young, but my uncle urged me to father a
child immediately."

Ki nodded in the dark. Her fingernails were biting into her
palms. He seldom spoke of these things.

"He found women for me. 'Suitable women,' he called
them. Older women who had already borne children. Big-
breasted, heavy-hipped women who would never miscarry or
be taxed by childbirth. Women that filled me with awe."
Vandien swallowed. Ki listened to his long silence. When he

went on, there was a falsely light note in his voice that cut her. "My own mother had died when I was an infant. I didn't remember her at all. I'd been raised by my uncle, and been watched over by Dworkin, his man. I knew nothing of women, save what I'd heard whispered about. But I tried. By the Moon, how I tried. At first I could at least bed them, though I couldn't make one pregnant. But later, as I failed time after time, and the pressure from my uncle grew greater and the disdain of the women more obvious . . ."

"Vandien." Ki couldn't listen to any more.

He stopped. For a long time, all was silent. She reached out to him, but stopped herself before she touched him. He lay so still, staring up at the sky. He took a deep breath. "Then my cousin got a village girl pregnant. A wild, fey little thing, slim as a willow with big dark eyes. It seemed to take no effort at all for him. I saw then how deeply I had failed. And I did the only logical thing. I left my cousin to inherit, for we shared many ancestral names. And I took the names of my parents, Van and Dien, and ran away. My only regret is that I didn't run away sooner. I think I knew, even before I tried, that I would fail. Weak son of a weak line. My parents had produced only one child. With me, the line failed entirely. I was glad to disappear, and take my shame with me."

"I'll bet your cousin was glad to inherit."

Vandien rolled his head toward her. "Of course he was. Don't think I haven't come to see that. I didn't when I was a boy, but in my years of wandering, my eyes have opened. The sooner I failed, the sooner my cousin could be made heir, to my father's lands as well as his father's and mother's. It turned his comfortable holdings into something just short of magnificent. A prize stroke of fate for him."

"And did you never think that your uncle had a hand in that fate? How old were you, Vandien? Twelve? Thirteen? A young stallion is not the most reliable stud, but that doesn't mean he never will be. A bullock, if too young, will not . . ."

"I'm not that young anymore, Ki." The smile he gave her was pensive, and affectionate. "If I were able to father a child, I imagine you'd have a few by now."

"I don't want any."

"Liar." Vandien sighed and took her hand. She let him

hold it, but could think of no reply. "It bothers me," he said suddenly, "what Goat does. That girl back there in Algona. Willow tonight. He takes something from them, Ki, and they may never even know they have lost it. That girl and Willow . . . they will have memories that will intrude at times, spoiling a tender moment, stealing the shine from a precious thing. . . ."

"Like you have," Ki said slowly.

He nodded. "I should have run away sooner. But I didn't. And I can't stop what Goat does. I had started to like him, Ki. To think I could give him something he needed. And then, that girl . . . Keep him out of my path until we get to Villena. I won't be able to tolerate him after this."

"I'll keep him out of your way. But I don't feel much differently myself." Ki eased down beside Vandien. The night was mild and the earth warm. She lay beside him, not quite touching him, and the open night seemed cleaner and more wholesome than the camp beside the creaking wagon. She closed her eyes, thinking of Firbanks and the wainwright there. She slept.

"But you promised!" Willow's wail split the morning. It jerked Ki awake. She sat up with a start, then groaned, feeling she had torn loose every stiff muscle in her body. Dew had settled on her and chilled her. The crushed grasses beside her were the only sign of where Vandien had slept.

She clambered to her feet and stumbled toward the wagon. She splashed water from the cask over her face and hands, and then tried to make sense of the scene that presented itself.

Willow, her hair a tousled gleam in the new sun, was pouting prettily at a rumpled Goat. He was crouched by the fire, putting bits of twigs on the coals. Obviously they hadn't been awake much longer than Ki. "You promised it to me," Willow repeated, her voice husky with rebuke, and something warmer. Goat looked up at her and grinned. He spotted Ki and the grin grew wider as he rejoiced in his audience.

"I'll give it back to you," he said in the sticky sweet voice one might use to a spoiled child. Willow brightened. "But not just yet," he teased for Ki's benefit.

"Goat," Willow cajoled, and moved closer. A sly smile stole over his face as he stared at the fire.

"All right," he told her. "Close your eyes, then."

He stood, dusting off his knees. He leered genially at Ki, but her attention was on Willow's face. Beneath the closed eyes, the mouth was a finely drawn line; above them, the brow was smooth. Like a sculpture, Ki thought, purged of human emotions and thoughts. Like an empty thing of stone.

Then Goat swooped his face in and kissed her. Willow's eyes flew open, and for an instant Ki read her face. Outrage, disgust, and horror. And then nothing. The face smoothed over as a mason wipes a trowel over damp mortar, smooths and seals it. Then, a smile, as empty as a limp wineskin. "Oh, Goat, stop teasing me! You promised you'd give it back." There was a purr beneath the whine that made Ki's stomach tighten.

"I will," Goat promised her indulgently. "But later, Willow. Later." He hooked his arm around her and tugged her close. He turned his smile on Ki and she felt sick to be watching them. "I see you're finally up, Ki. Well, I hope you and Vandien had as good a night as we did. Though I won't say we got a lot of sleep!" He cackled and hugged the girl closer. Willow's body went to his as if it were a sack of old clothing, neither resisting nor aiding the hug. Her face was empty and her eyes were careful.

The silence grew too long. There was nothing Ki could ask or say. Finally, she simply observed, "We'd better get on the road if we want to be in Tekum today." A ripple of despair washed over Willow's face and was gone, like a wave spending itself on a sandy beach.

No one seemed hungry, and Ki didn't bother with food that morning. She loaded the wagon, gathering the scattered mugs and the kettle, stowing it all neatly as Goat giggled and pawed at the passive Willow. Ki wondered what had become of Vandien, but she did not call. He knew where she was, and that the wagon must leave soon. Let him have this time to himself. He needed it so.

Then, as she brought the big grey horses up to harness, he was suddenly there. His cream shirt was sweated to his body, and his sheathed rapier was in his hand. Fencing with shadows, she guessed, slaying all the dark things that menaced him from his dreams. He moved Sigmund into the traces, pulling straps and fastening buckles. Their eyes met briefly across the wide backs. "Hello," he offered apologetically.

"You know we can't go to that festival in Tekum."

"I know. I'm just keeping the skills sharp. In case."

"Hmph," she agreed skeptically. Then she turned at the sound of the wagon door shutting. She heard the ghost of Goat's high giggle, and knew Willow was inside with him.

"Shit," said Vandien, with great feeling. Then he followed her up onto the high plank seat. She took up the reins as he settled beside her.

"We'll be in Tekum soon," she promised him.

"Better late than never," he conceded. Then he leaned back on the wagon and seemed to go to sleep. Ki started the team.

TEN

Some wise great-grandfather had planted saplings along the main street of Tekum. They were great grey-trunked trees now, offering shade and relief to eyes wearied by endless eddying prairie. Ki wondered if anyone remembered the name of the tree-planter, or even gave a thought to the man who had greened what was otherwise an unremarkable-looking town.

"There's the inn," Vandien observed.

Ki nodded. The signboard hung from rusted chains. Two Ducks. Ki clicked to the greys as she turned their heads into the innyard. It didn't look busy. A team of mules hitched to a buckboard dozed in the afternoon sun. An old dog lay flat on the baked earth. His tail flopped lazily at the wagon's approach, but he didn't bother to lift his head.

Ki halted the team. Silence. A fly buzzing. She looked at Vandien, and their eyes met. He looked miserable. Ki lifted her hand slowly, knocked on the cuddy door. "Willow," she called softly. "We're here. The Two Ducks."

For another moment, silence reigned. Then, "Oh, no!" Willow moaned. "Not so soon!"

Goat muttered something in a salacious tone. Willow made no reply that Ki could hear, but she was trying not to listen. She felt the girl's movements in the cuddy. "Probably gathering up her things," Vandien muttered. Ki didn't add, "and getting dressed and brushing her hair." It took a very long time for Willow to open the side door of the wagon and climb out.

She looked awful. The clothing she wore was rumpled, the shining copper hair a tangled nest. She dropped her single bag of possessions at her feet. Goat leaned out the door of the wagon. Ki glanced back, to see Willow smiling tenuously up at him. "Now?" she asked. "You did promise," she added, her smile getting shakier.

For a moment Goat smiled down at her. Then his look grew cagier. "Ride with me to Villena," he offered. "Then I'll tell you."

Willow's face crumbled. "I cannot!" she begged.

"Then I cannot." Goat shrugged. His smile grew wider.

And Willow's face changed. Green and blue eyes blazed with anger. The snarl that contorted her face seemed almost reptilian. Ki expected venom to shoot from her lips, while Goat recoiled in horror. "I hate you!" Willow hissed. "I hate you and I have always hated you! Your touch is like the touch of a slug, of offal smeared against the skin! You stink, and your breath is foul. You are the poorest of males, and your body . . ."

"You liked it well enough last night," ventured Goat, but there was no courage in his taunt. It sounded like a plea.

"I hate you!" Willow shrieked, and sprang toward the wagon, clawing.

Goat slammed the door shut. Ki picked up the reins.

"I hate you all!" Willow screamed after the wagon. "All of you! You brought me to this, you ruined me!"

Willow sank slowly down to sit atop her bag. Her shoulders shook with her sobbing. Ki glanced across at Vandien. His face was grey, his mouth a flat line. "I feel," he said softly, "as if we have done a great evil, all unwares. And I feel accursed, as if there is yet a debt to be paid."

"You sound like a old tale." Ki could not keep the awe from her voice. She, too, felt the wrongness of what they drove away from. If a curse felt like a weight draping her shoulders and a black net closing around her heart, then Ki felt cursed.

The cuddy door behind them jerked open. "Aren't we going to stop at all?" Goat complained. "I want to see a bit of Tekum before we . . ."

"Not here," Ki said tersely. "The next inn, perhaps. But not here."

"But—"

Vandien reached back and slammed the door. His hands clenched the edge of the seat. Ki glanced at his white knuckles, then fixed her gaze on the road. The tree-lined street was quiet; most trade closed down for the heat of early afternoon.

"I don't know if I can stand it," Vandien said in a strangled voice. "Having that thing in there."

Ki nodded. Suddenly Goat did seem more of a thing than a person. "What do you suggest?" she asked softly.

Vandien shook his head wearily. "We can't just leave him here."

"He'd only find his way back to Willow." Ki paused, then observed, "Like rotten meat. You hate to carry it with you, because of the stench, but you fear to throw it aside lest you poison some poor beast."

"His uncle in Villena." Vandien's voice was unenthusiastic. "I hope that poor bastard knows how to deal with him. I don't."

"I wish we didn't have to stop here at all. But we're low on salt and tea, and I want to ask the smithy if he has anything for ticks and fleas. This damn warm weather . . .'"

Ki let the sentence dangle, and she could feel Vandien make the journey north with her, back to the cool lands. What was a snow-blocked pass or ice on the harness buckles compared to endless heat and bugs and guards and papers?

They were almost outside the town before she spotted an inn that suited her. It was set back from the road and there were few animals in the yard, and none of them looked capable of bearing a Brurjan's weight. From somewhere close by she heard the clang of hammer against anvil. Sigurd and Sigmund drew the wagon obediently into the yard. They stopped and stood, waiting for water.

The hostler who came from the stables frowned briefly at the garish wagon, but seemed to know his business as he moved surely around the horses.

"Water, and grain for them. Take their bits out, but don't unharness them; we won't be staying that long," Ki told him.

He nodded to her words, then gave a puzzled frown. "Aren't you come for the festival? Not far off, now. Folks already getting ready for it."

She shook her head, then transferred her attention to Vandien. "I'll buy you a beer," she offered.

He astonished her by shaking his head. "No. Let's just get

our errands done and be moving on. I've no urge to explore this town or spend any time here.''

The cuddy door slid open. "But I do!" Goat protested. "I want to look around before we move on. I want . . .''

"No." Vandien's voice was flat. Goat glared at him for a moment, then turned to Ki.

"I can at least walk around with you while you do your errands. We need more honey, and I want . . .''

"I'll be walking around with Ki while she does her errands. You'll be staying here and watching the wagon. I don't want you to leave it, and I don't want you talking to anyone. Some inngirls have fathers, Goat, or brothers, or sweethearts. Try your tricks here, and you'll be lucky if it's only my fist you feel. Do we understand one another?''

Goat glared at him in outrage, and then slammed the door. Ki had remained silent throughout their exchange. Now she asked Vandien worriedly, "Do you think it's safe to leave him alone?''

"He'll be a lot safer alone than if I have to stay here with him," Vandien promised her blackly. He grinned at her then, suddenly and disarmingly, but there was an edge to his smile that she had never seen before, and it did nothing to disarm his threat about Goat. She took his arm and walked him away from the wagon, feeling the tension that was thrumming through him. Ki sighed, and wished she could lose the image of the distraught Willow glaring after the wagon.

They brought the tea first, and a small earthenware pot of honey sealed with yellow wax. Ki tried to get him interested in the leather goods in a small open-fronted shop, but the usually gregarious Vandien was withdrawn. He was as charming as ever, and the leatherworker eager to show him her wares, but there was something missing from his manner. Warmth, Ki thought, and caring. Usually he could make every person he talked with feel as if he were the most fascinating character Vandien had ever met. Today he was distracted, as if he were listening to something else. "No, no, I'm content with what I have," he explained, running his hand down the worn sheath of his rapier. "It's old, but she draws easily from this, and it keeps her safe. Anything fancier would only attract attention." He looked up at the leatherworker as if seeing her for the first time. "Work as fine as yours for a simple traveller like myself? Would only make the Brurjan guards think there was more about me than there really is. But I thank you for showing us your goods."

The leatherworker warmed toward him. "The Duke's Brurjans seem to think that of anyone they meet, these days," she confided to them. "Such a sifting of travellers as they have done of late. There are rumors of a rebel spy travelling to the Duchess. It is said that he has knowledge of the Duke's troops, and the strength and fortifications of Masterhold itself. The Brurjan that lays claws on him first is to be richly rewarded, with seven black mares and a white stallion from the Duke's own stables."

"All the more reason for us to remain unobtrusive," Ki filled in. Vandien had wandered back to the street and was watching the traffic. A haunted look was on his face. He was right, Ki decided. Finish the errands quickly and leave.

She thanked the girl, and they made their way to the smithy and found he had herbs which, rubbed against the horses' sweaty hides, would stave off the worst of the fleas and ticks. He also had a paste for worming, one he assured Ki was necessary in this part of the world as a monthly tonic. Vandien stood bored as she listened to the smithy, and did not even join in on bargaining him down to a price she thought fair. Her arms were full as they left the smithy's barn, and Vandien carried the tea and honey, so she could not take his arm as she longed to.

"Sure you don't want just one quick beer?" she offered again as they approached the wagon.

"Well . . . no. No, let's get on our way to Villena. Goat! Open the cuddy door, my hands are full. Goat!"

No answer. No creak of motion from the wagon. The horses shifted in their harness as Vandien waited. Then he turned, stacked his goods into Ki's arms, and jerked the door opened himself. "Goat!" he roared, as the door came open.

There was no reply, and the look he turned on Ki was unreadable. "He's gone," he told her, and jumped down from the wagon step. She struggled laden up the step to dump their purchases on the bed. She came out of the wagon to see Vandien coming out of the inn.

"Not there," he said tersely. They looked at each other in silence.

"Want me to check the other shops around here?" Ki offered, but Vandien shook his head, his expression suddenly savage.

"You know where he's gone as well as I do. Damn Goat, can't leave anything alone. It was bad enough as it was, and now to go back into it, to have to see her face again."

He moved as he ranted, placing the bits in the horses' mouths, setting aside the water buckets the hostler had left for them. "Let me just pay the innkeeper, then," Ki suggested.

He was holding the reins when she came out, and for once she said nothing about his driving. The team felt his tension down the reins, for they stepped out smartly and Sigurd, for once, tried no tricks with him. Back they went, the shade of the great trees flickering across the greys' backs and changing them to silvers and whites and almost blacks as the light changed.

He turned the wagon into the dusty yard of the Two Ducks Inn, and pulling up the team, set the brake and jumped down from the seat. Ki followed him, hoping they would find Goat, hoping that they wouldn't find him with Willow, hoping desperately that nothing was going to happen, but feeling, just as instinctively as Vandien had all day, that something had already happened, that all that was left was to make a salvage attempt.

The quiet of the innyard had been deceptive. Ki and Vandien stepped into a dream standing motionless, like a play waiting for an audience. Guests of the inn stood in a white-faced circle about a grouping of three. Willow, sitting at a stained wooden table, her face cradled in her arms, her glossy hair a spreading copper against the table's dull surface, while Goat, his face a frozen mask of fear, plucked desperately at her sleeve, begging, "Willow, make him stop! Tell him you wanted to!" The man with the drawn blade had to be Kellich. Ki would have known him anywhere. This was who Willow loved, and rightly so. This man in the loose shirt of scarlet silk and black trousers tucked neatly into shining black boots. This man, slender as his blade and as flexible, with a graven face an idol might have envied as the setting for eyes that were darker azure than an August sky. But Willow could not have loved the pain and anger in those eyes, the humiliation that whitened his tanned skin to sallowness.

"Come to your death, whelp!" Kellich invited Goat.

"No!" Goat wailed, and stepped once again into the shelter of Willow's body as Kellich moved around the table. "Willow! Make him stop it! You wanted to be with me, you know you did! I felt it, you wanted me. Tell him! Tell him to let us go!''

Willow lifted her head suddenly. Nothing of youth was left in her face. Hopelessness and hatred had blended to leave her green and blue eyes scarcely human. She turned a killing look on Goat. ''I wanted what you stole from me!'' Her voice was low, gravelly, but carried well. ''So I put in my mind what you wanted to see. Did you think I wouldn't know how to do that, you, who know so much about me? When you stole all my life from me, made my memories a mockery, didn't you stop to think that I might hate you for it, but know how to hide that hate?''

Goat's eyes bugged out, yellower with terror and outrage than Ki had ever seen them. ''Bitch!'' His shriek broke on the word. ''Bitch, copper-haired bitch! You made me think you liked me, you made me think you cared for me!''

Willow shook her head slowly, her red mane sweeping her shoulders. Her face was harder and colder than ice. ''I hated you. Your touch on me was like rats scampering over my body. I loathed it. I loathed it!'' Willow screamed the last words, and Goat cowered. She looked desperately into Kellich's face then, but his eyes did not change. He was not a man with deep wells of forgiveness within him. Her first error was to be her last.

Willow saw it as surely as Ki did. She rose with a ponderous heaviness, slapped away Goat's clutching hands. She moved away from him, into the circled watchers. ''Kill him,'' she said to Kellich in passing. ''It will not save anything for us, but it may save the next person he meets. Have no pity for him.''

''I'll have no blood on my floor!'' the innkeeper interjected suddenly. His ruddy face was already dripping sweat. ''I'll call the guard, I will! Duelling's forbidden, and I'll not have the Duke's guards saying I sanctioned it here! I'm warning you, Kellich! Much as I like you, I'll call the guards.''

Kellich's eyes had never left Goat. ''Call away,'' he told the man. ''It won't be a duel here, Geoff. It's an execution; no, an extermination. Not for myself, not for my own pride or honor, though.'' He turned suddenly on Goat. ''Give it back to her,'' he said softly. ''And I might let you live.''

For a long instant Goat stared at him. Then his face crumpled, and tears brimmed his Jore eyes. ''No. I can feel the lie! You're going to kill me, no matter what I do.'' His lower lip suddenly jutted, trembled. ''None of you . . . ever . . . liked me at all!'' The last was the wail of a betrayed child. Then he threw his head up, suddenly defiant. ''When the guards get here, I'm telling. I'm telling them everything, Kellich. Your head will be carried on a pole at the front of the Duke's procession, this festival.''

The boy had judged wrong. His threat did not cow Kellich, nor the crowd. Ki felt the whole room grow colder, felt all the people at the inn suddenly accept the necessity of Kellich's killing Goat. No mercy for him. And if Kellich did not kill him, the mob would. Goat had touched a nerve.

''Oh, damn!'' Vandien breathed beside Ki. ''Damn, damn, damn, why can't I just let it happen!'' Then, before she could react to his words, he was stepping forward, his hand light on the hilt of his rapier, calling out, ''Hold, Kellich! Hold!''

Ki stood transfixed as the man swung his attention to Vandien. ''You're free with my name, for a stranger,'' he observed. His blue eyes darted to Vandien's hand on the rapier hilt, swiftly measured the man against himself.

''I feel I know you, from all that Willow has said about you,'' Vandien began, but Kellich interrupted with a strained laugh.

''My sweet Willow seems to have found much time to speak of me, to other men!''

''You do her an injustice.'' Vandien was trying to keep his voice level. ''The girl loves you. No one else. What happened between her and Goat is a thing I cannot explain. But perhaps she could, if you would give her a chance. And hearing her out would reflect better on your honor than killing an unarmed boy. No matter how revulsive we might find him, Kellich, he is a boy. No good can come of your killing him. Let me take him out of here, away from this town and out of your lives forever. Don't let him spoil what you have with Willow.''

Uncertainty danced in Kellich's blue eyes. His gaze went past Vandien, found Willow. Ki saw a spark of life and hope come to Willow's face. ''It's true, Kellich!'' she cried out desperately. ''All of it's true. I love only you, and if you would listen, I could make you understand what happened.'' Her voice grew suddenly stronger. ''In only one thing is he wrong. You have to kill Goat. Not for me or what he has done to us. But for . . . for a greater good, one we both hold dear.'' Her voice faltered, as if fearing she spoke too much.

Kellich's face changed. Ki could not tell if he would heed her earlier plea, to listen to her. But she knew he would fulfill Willow's other request. He would kill Goat. Unless Vandien stopped him.

All knew it. Goat pressed himself against the wall behind the table, whimpering. The circle of folk shifted, tightened. ''I'm sending for the guard right now, Kellich!'' the landlord threatened, but Kellich did not hear. Like a witch's water stick seeking moisture, his blade lifted, wavered, pointed accusingly at Goat. ''Will you be killed like a rat in a corner?'' he asked Goat. ''Come out at least, to meet your death.''

''Kill him, Vandien! Kill him!'' Goat shrieked, already skewered with terror.

Metal whispered against leather as Vandien's rapier came clear of its worn sheath. Ki saw him change, this drawing of weapon doing something to his body. Quicker and more lithe he became, inspired by snakes and cats and all things that live by quick wits and sinuosity. Her blood quickened. This was a different Vandien, one she had seen but once or twice before. This was not the man who drew his blade and led her through the exercises of fencing, who had endlessly and patiently corrected her until she had become a foil fit for him to practice his skills against. No. This was someone different. ''By all that is green and growing,'' Ki prayed, but her voice would not come past her lips. She could only watch, stay out of his way, and protect his back. Her mouth was dry.

Vandien's rapier leapt out, not to pierce, but to tap Kellich twice on the shoulder in quick succession. ''Turn, man,'' Vandien told him softly. ''Face me.''

And Kellich turned, his blade leaping up to meet Vandien's in a screaming steel kiss that held them both.

''Let's not do this,'' Vandien proposed in a soft voice. ''We've no quarrel, you and I. Let me take the boy and go. I promise I shall take him far from here. I've no more love for him than you have, but his blood would shame your blade.''

There was no compromise in Kellich's face. ''Just go away,'' Kellich suggested. ''Let me get this done quickly.''

Vandien shook his head slowly. Ki wondered if anyone

else could see the strength the two men pitted against each other as their rapiers held that touch, could see the measuring of skill that was taking place. She could. And she could see suddenly that Kellich was good, and more than good. And he was young, with the fire that burns so hot in youths before experience comes to bank it.

She looked at Vandien suddenly with new eyes. When they had first met, the same fires that blazed in Kellich now had been hot in Vandien. He had changed, Ki realized abruptly. His body was not the svelte body of a youth, but had the heavier set of a man, the dart of impetuosity replaced with the deliberate movement of experience. She had seen him draw blade many times, most often for the joy of the contest, but sometimes in anger or danger. As the coldness swept from her belly, she knew this was the first time when she had seriously wondered if he would win.

"I can't just leave," Vandien said. The tip of his rapier darted away from Kellich's, was pressing his blade from the other side almost before Kellich could respond. Almost.

"Vandien? That's the name?" he asked. The tendons in the back of his hand stood out.

Vandien nodded silently.

"It's good to know the name of a man, before your blade wears his blood."

It began in that instant, too swift for Ki's eyes to follow. The whicker and whisper of metal against metal, the swift taps and challenges, the deceptive feints that measured the opponent, the bold attacks and the lightning ripostes. Boots moved against the wooden floor and Vandien's shirt began to stick to his back. Ki tried, but could not see the struggle. Her eyes hung on foolish things, on a loose thread dangling from Kellich's sleeve, on the dark ring Vandien wore on the hand he held high behind him. Kellich's blade darted in, was trapped and spun aside by Vandien's blade, and for an instant the men sprang apart. She heard Vandien suck in breath, thought of his ribs and felt ice track down her spine.

"You're good," Vandien breathed.

"And you," Kellich conceded grudgingly.

"This doesn't have to be," Vandien reminded him.

Kellich shook his sweat-damped hair, and his rapier rose once more.

"So be it, then," Vandien said, and his voice chilled Ki.

Not because it was cold, or tired, but because it was hot with
excitement, full of the lust of the fight. She saw the man
move in, knew that what had gone before had been but
preliminaries. He had taken Kellich's measure, and found it
good. Admiration for the boy shone in Vandien's eyes, and
the impetuosity she thought he had outgrown flamed suddenly
in him. He took the challenge home to Kellich, and she saw
the youth's eyes widen in shock as he was suddenly put on
the defensive. But then his blue eyes sparked suddenly, as if
they met the joy in fencing that drove Vandien now, and were
ignited by it. They moved like dancers, like a paired team of
pacing horses, matching and swaying to one another's
movements.

There comes a place, Ki thought, or perhaps it is only a
moment. A time when youth and experience may meet and
cancel one another. When Kellich would thrust, or weave
lithely aside, or dart in impetuously, her heart would clench
in terror for Vandien. But the boy's moves were met by the
man's sure hand, with concise movements of a blade that
wasted no energy, shifted not one whit more than was necessary to deflect Kellich's attacks. Vandien was a center that
the youth orbited, the pillar of the maypole dance the boy's
rapier wove around him.

The room was almost silent, all caught up in the contest.
Occasionally a man grunted with effort, or made the twitching of muscles that betrayed how closely he followed the
contest. Willow was a frozen statue, her eyes so wide they
seemed unseeing. Goat had not moved from where he was
stuck to the wall; only his lower lip trembled as he watched
the fight that would decide his fate. Ki felt the sweat that ran
down her back, and she prayed it would end, but did not want
it to end, for fear it would end in the death of one of them.
There was a gasp as, without warning, Vandien's rapier
licked in to dab scarlet on the point of Kellich's shoulder.
"First blood!" someone called out, but at the instant it was
uttered, the tip of Kellich's blade shot past the guard of
Vandien's rapier to open a shallow gash in the back of his
forearm. Both fenced on, as if there were no such thing as
pain. Ki watched the blood run and then drip from Vandien's
arm, outlining in scarlet the muscles that stood out in his
forearm. She felt dizzy, as if it were her own blood leaking
out.

A murmur from the crowd drew Ki's eyes up to Vandien's face. He was smiling—no, grinning, as demented as a demon. Even more incredible, the smile was matched by the one on Kellich's face. She could have sworn that both men had forgotten their quarrel entirely, were fencing for the pure joy of matching their skills against an equal. Both their chests were pumping like bellows, and a streak of darker scarlet marred the crimson of Kellich's sleeve. She saw Vandien put into play moves she had seen him practice against his shadow in the bright darkness of the full moon. He was pushing himself now, bringing out every trick he had ever learned or tried, dancing and darting in ways as unpredictable as a cat's play with a mouse; and Kellich was standing up to him, putting aside his attacks, but only just, and then riposting and being turned himself. They were both winded now, gasping with sounds almost like laughter, blue eyes and black shining in mutual concession of skill. Relief washed through Ki's heart. She knew suddenly, as clearly as she had known anything, that no one would die here, or even be badly injured. In another moment they would put up their blades and bow to one another, would share a drink or five, and that Vandien would find a way to make peace between Kellich and Willow.

Vandien was pushing him again, in a final series of thrusts that Kellich turned at the last possible moment. The laughter was plain in their gasping now, and all the circle was grinning. Save one. Ki saw his face suddenly behind Kellich, contorted with anger and hate and fear. She cried out aloud, but it was too late, for Goat had already stepped in, had already given Kellich the one push from behind that was all it took. His rapier went wide; the staggering step he took to try to regain his balance carried him wildly forward. Amazement widened his eyes and his mouth opened silently.

It was Vandien who cried aloud as his thrust, unchecked, sank his rapier deep into Kellich's chest.

ELEVEN

As Kellich fell, the supple blade of Vandien's rapier ripped free of his chest, flinging a bright spray of red droplets. They freckled the faces of bystanders, who cried out in horror and recoiled as if sprayed with poison. But above their sounds rang out Goat's high-pitched victorious shriek. "He's dead! He's dead! He's dead!"

Vandien's rapier clattered to the floor. He dropped to his knees by the youth. Unbelieving, his fingers reached, touched the spreading stain where Kellich's life was pumping out in fainter and fainter gouts. He pressed to hold back the flood that poured past his fingers. "Kellich?" he asked. But the youth's eyes were open, wide and blue as the empty sky. His mouth was ajar still, as if he would never get over the surprise of his death. "Oh, Kellich," Vandien whispered. He touched the boy's cheek, the hand that still gripped his weapon. "I'm sorry." His voice broke on the words, and his head sagged onto his chest. His shoulders drooped, and his hand went up to cover his mouth. Ki heard the ragged breath he drew through his bloody fingers.

From without the inn, a shout. "Guards coming! Guards coming!"

Within the inn, instant mayhem. No one wanted to be at the scene of a duel, let alone one that had ended in death. Frantic customers shouldered past Ki, sending her staggering as she fought her way toward Vandien. "Not in my inn, oh no, not in my inn!" the tavernkeeper was wailing.

And above the curses and shouts as folk fought their ways

toward doors and windows, Ki heard Willow's voice ring out. ". . . nothing left for me! Nothing! Because of you! May you never know a moment's peace or rest for all your days to come! I curse you and all that care for you and any children you father! May you know loss such as mine! May you never forget what you have done. Never!"

Vandien was still on his knees beside the body, his face raised to Willow as if she had blessed him. Blood welled in the tracks of her nails down his face, and as Ki moved in, she slapped him again. He didn't move. Ki wasn't sure if he even knew she was there. She shoved Willow aside, and the girl sprawled by Kellich's body, clutching at him and sobbing wordlessly.

Ki gripped Vandien's arm. "We have to get out of here. The guards are coming." He didn't respond. She shook his shoulder, then tried to drag him to his feet. "Please, Vandien. Get up. We have to get out of here."

He looked up at her blankly. "I didn't mean to kill him," he said softly. Tears suddenly brimmed his dark eyes. "It's like I killed myself . . ."

She snatched up his rapier from the floor, got under his arm and levered him to his feet. He tottered as if he were drunk. "It's going to be okay," she told him as she guided him to the back door. "It's going to be all right." They reached the wagon and she pushed him up onto the seat. She took the kerchief from her throat and wiped the blood from his face, then wrapped it hastily around his still-dripping forearm. He sat still and dumb under her touch. She opened the cuddy door, tossed his rapier inside, slammed it shut. Kicking off the wheel brake, she started the team at a careful walk and held them there despite her hammering heart. Mustn't look like we're in a hurry, she told herself. From the front innyard, she could hear the shouts of the Brurjan guards and the screams of those being questioned by them. She guided the team down the narrow alley between the stables and the manure piles and out into another street. "Willow knows who we are and where we're going," she reminded herself. "She has no reason to keep still about it. Except that she has no travelling papers; maybe she'll be hiding herself . . ." But Ki knew she couldn't count on that. At the next corner, she turned randomly.

Vandien looked bad. He was swaying with the wagon, and

his face was dead. She pushed the cuddy door open, grabbed
the wineskin off its hook and pushed it at him. It held cheap
wine, good only for washing the road dust from a dry throat.
"Drink some," she told him, and he obeyed her mindlessly.
She left him holding the skin and swaying stupidly with every
jolt of the wagon; if he looked drunk, maybe the guard
wouldn't stop them for questioning. For now, she had to find
shelter for them and the wagon, and give the turmoil at the
inn time to subside.

Some hours she passed in a run-down wainwright's on the
far side of the town bargaining for axle grease, linchpins and
other trivial supplies. The man didn't object to making money,
and her wagon was all but invisible in his yard full of rotting
hulks of other wagons and rigs. Vandien remained sitting,
drinking the sour wine and staring at his hands. Ki left him
alone. She couldn't think of anything she could do for him.
He needed to think through what had happened. It was hard
to leave him alone, but he had to make his own sense of
Kellich's death. She tried to keep herself and the wainwright
busy with small talk.

Early evening brought a soft, forgiving darkness and a
little-used north road that would take them out of town. Or so
the wainwright assured her; she hoped he was right. It wasn't
unusual for folk to know little of the roads that led away from
the towns they had been born and raised in.

The horses snorted occasionally, complaining of the dark
road and the annoying ruts that crumbled under their heavy
hooves, but Ki kept them to their pace. The town fell away
behind them, and then the cultivated fields. They finally
entered the endless swell of the prairie. Vandien still hadn't
spoken. She slid closer to him on the seat. Hooking one arm
around his waist, she pulled him tight against her. He sighed
suddenly, and put his arm across her shoulders. She didn't
mind the weight. Turning her head, she brushed a kiss across
his stubbled cheek. She waited.

"Ki," he said, and stopped. For a long time, he said
nothing. She moved her hand up his back, rubbed the tight
muscles in the back of his neck. He didn't relax.

"He was one of the best swordsmen I've ever faced."

She nodded into the dark.

"I think we could have been friends."

She nodded again.

"Oh, gods!" he cried suddenly. "I killed that boy!"

"You didn't mean to," she whispered. She let go of the reins to hold him, and the team, free to do its own will, immediately halted. Around them was only the empty night, the chirring of insects and the smell of the earth as the dew settled. Ki held him, wishing he would cry or curse, anything but hunch and hold his pain inside him. She ran her hands up and down his back, then hugged him suddenly, kissing the side of his face fiercely, trying to make him feel less alone.

He moved then, capturing her wrists and gently setting her away from him. "The horses need to be unharnessed."

"Yes. And I'll make a fire. You'll feel better when you've had a cup of tea and something to eat." Her own words sounded inane, but it was all she could manage. She let him unharness the team while she found straw and twigs and bits of scrubby brush to build a fire. The small light in the darkness was cheering; she took courage from it. She filled the kettle from the cask and set it over the flames, then climbed the wagon step to get the new bag of tea.

It was dark within the wagon, and she groped over the bed where she had earlier tossed the sack of tea. Something warm stirred under her hands.

"Ki? Have we stopped finally?"

She stumbled backward down the steps, fleeing as if confronted by a nightmare. Goat followed her out, rubbing his eyes and blinking after his long sleep. She couldn't make a sound, could only stare at him. She didn't remember thinking of him since they left Tekum, but now she knew a part of her had deliberately decided to leave the boy behind. That same part was both horrified and enraged to see him emerge from the wagon. He walked toward the fire, holding his hands out toward it.

"DAMN YOU!"

It was the pain in Vandien's voice more than the anger that froze her for the instant that it took him to get to the boy. Goat went down under him, and Vandien's hands tightened on his throat before she could reach them. Stupid details imprinted themselves on her mind as she flung herself into the struggle: that the cut on Vandien's forearm had opened and was leaking darkly in the firelight; that Goat had not changed his shirt and there were great rings of sweat under his arms; that the boy looked like a dying rodent as his drawn-back lips bared his long yellow teeth. Then she was in the middle of it, wedging her shoulder against Vandien's chest and up, kneeling on Goat's chest as she levered the man off him, and then springing up to fling her arms around Vandien as Goat raced, howling, for the shelter of the wagon. Vandien flung her off with a curse and sprang after the boy, but he already had the door shut. She heard a thud and then the clatter of overturned pans as he piled things against it. Vandien turned to the other door, but she got to the seat before he did. She sat, her back to the other cuddy door, and looked down on him.

"Don't!" she warned him as he started up.

"Get out of my way." He spoke as if she were a stranger, one he would not mind bloodying. It shocked her.

"Listen to me." Her voice was shaking. "Wait a minute." He didn't. He was coming up onto the seat. She planted her hands on his shoulders, held him back. She wondered if he would throw her aside, knew that his anger made him far stronger than she, wondered what she would do if he did. He didn't, but all of her weight was insufficient to keep him on the ground. He was on the wagon seat. She plastered herself against the door.

"Vandien. Listen. If you touch him right now, you'll kill him. It won't stop at a beating. You'll kill him!"

"That's right." His voice indicated he would enjoy it.

"I can't let you." Her voice was even shakier, but truth rang in her words. Vandien pulled his eyes up to meet hers. She was drawing a line. No compromise. He'd have to hurt her to get her away from that door. She watched him think about it, and it hurt that he had to think about it, but she knew him well enough to understand it. "Please," she said, and she knew she was begging him, and that was another thing that had never been between them. It got through his anger.

For a long time, all was still. When he finally spoke, his voice was thick with heavy emotions. "Get rid of him."

The evenness of her tone surprised her. "I will. In Villena."

"Now. I can't be around him, Ki. I can't tolerate him anywhere near me. Get rid of him now, or I'll kill him."

"I can't."

He stared at her, and she sensed how hard it was for him to hold back. She forced her words out quickly, trying to make him see.

"If I toss him out here, there's only one place for him to

go. Tekum. And he's hurt Willow enough already. I feel responsible for part of that hurt. I won't be responsible for letting him back into her life.''

She saw those words penetrating his anger, saw the barest hint of a nod, a concession. ''I have to take him to Villena,'' she said quickly, and saw Vandien's anger begin to rise again. ''Because,'' she pushed on, ''he's not the sort of thing you leave running about on its own. Someone has to take charge of him. His uncle's expecting him. So that's where he goes. I can't turn him loose on unsuspecting people in Rivercross, or just throw him out on the road to attach himself to travellers. You can see that, can't you? Vandien?''

He pulled back from her. He stood clear of the wagon, and in the gleam of the tiny fire his face held only a few planes of light. He seemed far away, and when he spoke, his voice was even more distant. ''Keep him away from me.'' A pause. ''I don't want to see him, I don't want to hear him. I don't want to smell him. Or I'll kill him, Ki. I'll kill him.''

''It wasn't my fault!'' came Goat's wild caterwauling from within the wagon. Ki saw Vandien's eyes widen, and she pounded a fist angrily against the cuddy door.

''Shut up!'' she commanded him. The boy was silent again. ''I'll keep him away from you, Vandien. But I have to take him to Villena and turn him over to his uncle. You understand that, don't you?''

''All I understand is that he made me kill a man worth ten of him. A hundred of him. Made me kill him unfairly, made his death too quick . . .'' He turned aside abruptly, shaking his head fiercely. He walked away quickly, almost running, and she lost his silhouette in the blackness.

She hugged herself, held in her trembling. A wave of dizziness swept over her, and she suddenly felt how hard her heart was beating. But it was over, she told herself. For now. She took a great breath. ''Open the door, Goat,'' she heard herself say. ''He's gone. Open the door, and listen to what I tell you, if you want to get to Villena alive.''

He walked into the darkness, feeling the wagon dwindle behind him, losing the small light of the tiny fire. On across the dark prairie, feeling the sparse dry grasses whisper against his boots, like the whisper of drawn steel. . . .

''If I hadn't been showing off,'' he said to the empty night.

"If I hadn't been pressing the boy, showing him how good I was. If I hadn't been making death thrusts, and trusting his skill to parry them . . ." His voice faded. But so had the boy been pressing him; had he dropped his own guard for even an instant, it would have been Kellich's steel in his chest, in his eye, laying open his flesh. He tried the justification on. It didn't fit. Instead he found himself thinking of how preferable that would have been. A quick death in a fair fight—yes, but what if, like Kellich, he had been pushed from behind? It would change everything; it had changed everything, he had seen it change everything in that fraction of a second before Kellich fell. Kellich had believed that he was in league with Goat. Dying, Kellich had taken a piece of Vandien's honor with him. It was gone, never to be redeemed.

He fingered the back of his forearm, tracing the line of Kellich's rip. Absently he prodded it, searching for pain. There wasn't any, at least not the sharp pain he had expected. It had closed already, a thick, ragged seam on his arm. The pain it gave him was only a deep aching, as if the bone of his arm were frozen. But maybe even that was just a reflection of the deep cold ache inside himself.

Vandien sighed, but the heaviness didn't lift from his chest. He stopped walking, forcing himself to face the decision. Was he going back to Ki's wagon and the boy it sheltered? What if, instead, he kept on walking? He could, he knew that. He had faced the world on his own before, with less. In many ways, it would be the easier thing to do. If he turned around now and went back, it would be a commitment, of sorts. Not only to taking the boy on to Villena, alive, but to living with what he had lost. Living with what his rapier had done.

He thought of watching his father oil that blade by firelight, never trusting it to a servant, but always doing it himself, sitting in the quiet of the very late evening on the warm bricks of the great hearth, polishing the blade, then lifting it and watching the light run up and down its length. Sometimes he would trust it to Vandien's grip, kneel by his son and set it in the small boy's hand and counsel him as to stance and posture until the boy's shoulder and wrist ached despite his father's supporting hands. "This blade," he had said to his son, more than once, "has never drawn blood in an unjust cause. That is its honor, and your honor, too." And he would trace for his son the ancient, stylized talons on the grip, worn almost beyond recognition, and the spread wings and pinions of the hawk that made up its guard. . . . Vandien found himself fingering the back of his neck, touching the spread wings of the birthmark there. He jerked his hand away. "Yes. And he told me that as long as that blade remained in the family, our honor and line would never fail. Wrong on both counts, Papa." No heirs and no honor. And the fabled luck that was supposed to go with his birthmark seemed in remarkably short supply. Or perhaps it was as Ki had said, only luck, and no one had stipulated good or bad. He sighed again, but could not breathe out the heaviness that had filled his lungs ever since he had knelt over Kellich's body and listened to Willow curse him. Well.

He stood a moment longer, listening to the night. He had never felt so alone. In his killing of Kellich, something else had been severed as well. A link to his past. A rapier. Such a minor thing, a blade, a weapon, a tool. He had never thought before how firmly it anchored him. He had carried it, he knew now, to remind himself that wherever his roving with Ki might take him, he was still his father's son. Another might sit at the head of his table, his cousin might wear the necklace of his holdings and mind the borders of his lands. But while he carried his father's sword, he had known he had still his father's and mother's names, and their honor.

So he had thought.

Slowly he turned and began to walk back to Ki's wagon.

TWELVE

By late afternoon, Ki wasn't sure if she was going mad or if everyone else was.

Goat stayed in the wagon. She had convinced him that to let Vandien see him was to commit suicide. He had not doubted Vandien's animosity; the difficult part had been convincing him that she not only could not, but would not, stop Vandien. The boy had been rabid in his anger. "I saw him in danger, and I tried to help him. I did help him! If it hadn't been for me, Kellich would have tricked him into stopping the fight! And then he would have killed him!"

"They were both ready to down swords, you idiot!" Ki told him angrily. "Any fool could see that!"

Goat's eyes had gone very wide and far. "I know what I felt," he said distantly. "I felt it!" His odd eyes suddenly flooded with tears. "And I didn't want to see Vandien die!" He threw himself onto the bed, his face to the wall. Ki had left him, shaking her head. The boy was crazy. He had slept in the wagon, eaten in the wagon and now he rode in its rumbling belly. Ki neither saw nor heard him. That she was grateful for that almost shamed her. Almost.

But if Goat was isolated, so was Ki. Ki drove. Vandien sat. He sat in a silence that was neither cold nor angry. He was indifferent to her, caught up in some inner debate of his own. Still. She had waited up for him last night. When he finally came back to the camp, she had been ready to listen to anything he might say. What she had not expected was his withdrawal from her. Her few efforts at conversation were not

144

noticed by him. The food she prepared was eaten in silence. He slept beside her but apart, and his dreams had rocked and tossed him. She had tried to shake him awake, and when that failed to rouse him, she had wrapped her arms around his sweaty body and tried to calm him with her embrace. His arm, where Kellich had ripped it, was the only cool part of his body. She had sandwiched the arm between them, trying to warm it. He had quieted as she held him, but toward morning awakened her with a shudder and a shout. "Are you all right?" she had asked, but he had only stared at her, his dark hair wild, his eyes shot with blood.

She had stood his silence through the harnessing up, enduring it all morning. But now, for the fourteenth time, he sighed, a sigh that did nothing to relieve the tension she felt thrumming through him. She put her hand suddenly and firmly on top of his thigh, making him jump. "Talk to me," she urged him.

He shuddered and rubbed his face. "About what?" he asked thickly.

"Anything."

She waited but the silence only grew. She cleared her voice determinedly. "I hung up your rapier. You should clean and oil it tonight."

He stared at her, his eyes growing darker.

"Or do you want me to clean it for you?" she pressed deliberately.

"No." He struggled a moment. "I'll clean it . . . soon."

"It was an accident. You didn't mean to do it, and I'm tired of you moping about it."

"It's not that simple, Ki."

"In the name of the Moon, why not? If he had fallen the other way, you would have missed, and you certainly wouldn't be thinking now about your thrust that hit the wall. That the boy's chest was there and unguarded was not your doing. . ."

Vandien squeezed his eyes shut. "It was. Can't you see it as I must? What was I doing? I was trying to kill Kellich, seeing how hard I could press him and still have him turn my steel aside." He cradled his injured arm against his chest, his fingers running up the ridge of the rip. "And why? To keep him from killing one of the most disgusting human beings I've encountered in my whole life. I killed him, Ki. And it's changed the way I see myself."

Ki hissed in annoyance. "Vandien, don't torment yourself this way. There was a terrible accident. It hasn't changed you. Take it from someone who's seen you through some rather strange times. You're a good man. Nothing's changed."

Silence consumed her words. Then, "Honor," he said. He let the word stand by itself.

"Honor?" Ki asked at last.

"I've lost . . . honor."

"Vandien." Ki's voice was pragmatic. "You intended no unfairness in that fight. What if he'd caught his foot on a loose nail and tripped? Isn't it the same?"

"No. This . . . feels different. Dishonest."

"Dishonest!" Ki exclaimed. "Vandien, I've heard you tell enormous lies to people eager to believe them. I've seen you drive bargains so sharp they border on theft. And I seem to recall that your first attempt at horse theft was what brought us together. . . ." She couldn't keep the amusement from her voice.

His face didn't echo it. "Equal weapons and the outcome determined by skill alone," Vandien muttered.

"What?"

He cleared his throat. " 'In an honorable fight, gentlemen employ equal weapons and the contest is determined by skill alone. No gentleman seeks nor uses an unfair advantage. No skilled swordsman needs one.' "

"Where did you learn that?" Ki asked curiously.

"An old fencing master beat it into me," he muttered.

Ki snorted. "With those rules of conduct, it's a wonder he lived to be old."

The look he gave her said he didn't see any humor in her comment. She changed the subject. "Even with last night's detour, we can't be more than a couple of days from Rivercross," she offered. "And then Villena and then . . ."

Hoofbeats.

She pushed the reins into his hands, scrabbled up to peer back over the wagon's roof. Misfortune rode six black horses, and their scarlet hooves flashed in the sun.

She dropped back down to the seat. "Road patrol. Six Brurjans." For the first time since the fight at the inn, she saw a flash of spirit in his eyes.

"Can't outrun them," he pointed out. "Play innocent or fight?"

"Play innocent," Ki said slowly. "Then fight if we have to. Want your rapier?"

"They wearing armor?"

"Light stuff. Mostly leather . . . I didn't take that good a look."

"Knives, then. If we look too ready for them, they'll never believe we're innocent."

"Right."

It was all a sham, a play of words to pretend it wasn't hopeless, that if it came to fighting they'd have a chance. Ki took the reins back. Six Brurjans, armed, in light armor on battle-trained horses. If she took down one and Vandien took down one . . .

"There'll only be four left to kill us," Vandien pointed out.

"I've been living with you too long," Ki mumbled. She kept her hands steady on the reins. The hoofbeats were close now, and then Sigurd snaked his head up and gave a sudden whinny. "Steady," Ki whispered, to herself as much as the team. She kept them to their walk.

The Brurjans hit them like a wind full of dust, swirling around the wagon, making the greys go back on their haunches and bare their teeth. "Pull up!" called one. His black coat was streaked with grey, his harness and his horse's were red trimmed with silver. His battle teeth had grown so long he could no longer close his mouth over them. "Oh, shit," Vandien breathed. No Brurjan grew old being honorable. Ki stopped her team. She and Vandien sat silently regarding the ring of riders.

"Kirilikin?" The grizzled old Brurjan wasn't addressing them.

One of his men rode closer to peer at Vandien. He shrugged, a strangely human gesture of his massive brown shoulders under the brass-studded leather. "Probably him," he grunted. "He's got the scar."

"Bring him." The grizzled one wheeled his mount. "Duke wants him killed in the village square."

Kirilikin leaned over to grip Vandien by the back of his collar, but he was already in motion. Vandien launched himself at the Brurjan, using the momentum of his whole body to punch his blade through the thinner, more flexible leather that shielded Kirilikin's throat. A great gout of blood followed the knife as he withdrew it and Kirilikin groped at his throat in surprise. It had happened in less than a heartbeat.

Ki slapped the reins on the greys, and the big horses surged toward, but not through, the equally large black horses that blocked their way. A black-pelted Brurjan leaned from his mount to seize the reins and got the back of his hairy arm laid open to the ridged bones by Ki's short blade. He roared in anger, his crest rising, his maw gaping wide to expose his battle teeth, but drew back, disabled for the moment.

That short instant was as close to victory as they came. Ki never knew how Vandien was thrown to the ground, but he was there before she was, for she landed atop him, then rolled onto her bad shoulder, awakening that old injury. She started to get up, but something whacked her across the small of her back, and she went flat on her face in the dust. She felt split open like a stepped-on crab. Pain was all she knew, her body screaming at her to be still, that she was dying. Vandien was seized, dragged to his feet. She heard a roar that ended in a shriek, then coarse gibing, and the short, terrible sound of flesh struck very hard. She lifted her head.

Vandien had scored again, but paid for it. A Brurjan crouched in the road, her black-nailed hands over her belly. Red leaked between her short fingers and she was cursing, while two of her fellows sat their mounts, pointing at the entrails that bulged from the slash and laughing. Vandien lay face down in the road. Scarlet streamed from the back of his head and slid down the angle of his jaw. He didn't move.

Beyond him, a Brurjan had dismounted and was checking Kirilikin. He looked up from him, shrugged at their leader, and began methodically stripping the body. Someone else had already caught his horse.

Ki let her head fall back onto her arms. Her legs didn't belong to her anymore. She stared at Vandien's body, lying in the sunny road, and the sight of it echoed through her soul. The Brurjan finished stripping Kirilikin's body. He moved to Vandien's, rolled him over with a boot. "It's nearly dead."

"Damn!" The grizzled leader turned in his saddle and struck suddenly at one of the men behind him. The blow left four trails of blood down the guard's jowl. "That's for being too quick with your demi. Duke's orders are that duellers are to be killed in the square, not out on some road where no one sees it. Something like this makes us all look bad." The

chastised soldier looked down at his pommel, his teeth slightly
bared. The leader turned back to the Brurjan by Vandien.
"Bring it anyway. It's better than nothing."

The crouching Brurjan nodded, grabbed the front of
Vandien's shirt. Ki saw his bloodied features twitch slightly.

"No!" It was a prayer, not begging, but it drew the
Brurjan leader's eyes. His look was flat. He jabbed his demi
at the soldier he had earlier rebuked.

"Only the one that duelled needs to be publicly killed. Put
her in the wagon and burn it. Then bring the team. They look
old, but they're well matched. We'll get something for them."

The soldier looked displeased. "But, Vashikii," he began
to object, but the leader leaned over and jolted his demi into
the soldier's ribs. He bared his huge battle fangs and his
spiked crest rose as he spoke.

"Do it, scum. If you miss the execution, it's your own
damn fault. Way you hit him, we'll be lucky if he's alive to
execute. So you do the dirty work here, and no complaining,
Satatavi."

The female Brurjan dropped suddenly to her side. Her
hands fell away, and her entrails spilled from her body into
the dust. She hadn't made a sound. Vashikii shrugged.
"Satatavi. Put her and Kirilikin in the wagon also. And bring
her gear and horse."

It all seemed very far away. The rushing noise inside Ki's
ears was so loud that she could barely make out the words they
were saying. Words. Funny to think of words issuing from
those brutish mouths, of sentences and thoughts being pushed
out by red and black tongues past wickedly pointed teeth. As
well expect poetry from a serpent, song from a vulture. A
Brurjan gripped Vandien's shirt as Ki might heft a sack
of flour. The Brurjan stood and Vandien's feet dangled clear of
the ground. He looked small in the creature's grip, yet he'd
been able to kill two of them before they took him down.

She tried to anchor her thoughts in reality but they flowed
away from her. The time left was so short that none of it
really mattered. She and Vandien were already dead, the
wagon already cold ashes, Sigurd and Sigmund pulling a
plow through a farmer's field. She hoped they'd get good
care. "Good horses," she said dimly. Vandien's body went
over the back of Kirilikin's horse, was lashed to the high,
narrow saddle the animal wore. Blood dripped from his hair,

red drops that became black when they met the dust. She could not take her eyes from him, watched the lurch of his body as the slack was taken up suddenly in the horse's lead rope, watched the rhythmic jolting of his head as the troop moved off at a hard trot, stared after him through the masking yellow dust the scarlet hooves stirred up.

Then he was gone, her view blocked by her wagon. She heard Satatavi grunt as he hoisted Kirilikin's body to his shoulder and lugged it toward the wagon. There was a coppery taste in Ki's mouth, and the roaring in her ears grew louder. Independent of her command, her hands scrabbled at the dust, closed once more on her belt-knife. They hadn't bothered disarming the Humans once they had felled them. Vandien had taught them their error once; she would reinforce it. Her back felt severed. Her legs responded only feebly to her. There weren't going to be any lightning leaps to her feet. No. Concentrating, she began to draw one leg up under her.

"Gold."

Goat's voice was soft but clear. Satatavi dropped Kirilikin's body and pulled his demi from the thong that secured it to his battle harness. Then he stood, staring at the boy, his great jaws slightly ajar as if in surprise.

Ki suddenly felt woozier than ever. The ever-present singing of the insects had suddenly moved inside her skull, and the day seemed warmer, sleepier. Her eyes sagged and it was difficult to think of anything except Goat's voice.

"We have gold. And we will give it all to you, if you let us go. All that gold, and you need share it with no one."

Satatavi stood frozen, staring at the boy who had materialized in the door of the wagon. Goat's yellow eyes locked with the Brurjan's black ones. "Gold," he whispered again, seductively. "Just take the gold and leave. Tell them you did as you were ordered."

The Brurjan's narrow red tongue spilled out between his teeth, curled to moisten his lips. He swayed slightly, and abruptly his eyes narrowed. He shook his head violently. "No!" he said, his voice thick. "I'll take the gold, and burn the wagon! No reason to do just one or the other!"

In two steps he had seized the boy and held him inches from his fangs. "Where's the gold?" he demanded gutturally.

Goat squirmed frantically in his grip, trying to lean away from the teeth and rank breath that burned his face. "I don't know!"

The Brurjan flung the boy aside, whipping him past his shoulder as if he were a rag. Goat met the ground hard and sprawled there. Ki watched the Brurjan enter the wagon. A moment later she heard the sounds of breaking crockery and rent wood as he began his search. It wouldn't take him long. The small cupboard set under the mattress was neither that small nor that secret. Objects began to hail out of the wagon around Goat—the floor keg split on the ground, followed by a shower of dried beans as the Brurjan shook out the sack in search of the hidden trove. Goat lifted his head, looked at Ki. "Tell me what to do," he begged.

She got her other knee under her, pushed up slowly from the ground. The pain rode her, injecting her with agony and sucking out her strength. She tried to fix her mind elsewhere, to find anger as she listened to her home being ransacked, to find a killing urge toward this Brurjan who had sent Vandien to his death. But all she could fix on was the foolishness of the creature. Vashikii would never have left two enemies alive while he searched for plunder. He would have methodically eliminated all danger before looting the wagon. He would have secured the black war-horse, which danced nervously in the dust as an armload of quilts were thrown out of the wagon. Vashikii had lived long, and his battle fangs had grown thick and yellow because he had not taken chances. Just as Ki promised herself she would live a little longer than this one who had killed her friend. She leaned, panting silently, against the side of the wagon, and waited. Goat had found Vandien's fallen knife. He picked it up, looked at Ki, and stepped around the tail of the wagon.

It didn't take long. She heard his muffled *Hmph!* of triumph, heard the pale clink of the yellow coins against one another as he hefted the small but heavy sack. The plank floor creaked under his weight. He was heavier than two Humans, and too tall. The wagon had not been built for his kind. He had to duck to exit, and his jaws led the way as he leaned out, his throat stretched long and unprotected as he blinked once in the sunlight.

The same sunlight winked on the brief glint of Ki's blade, and then only the small blackened haft that stuck out from the side of his throat like an arcane handle. A cry bubbled out of him, sprinkling red, and he batted savagely at Ki. The blade had gone into the big artery on the side of a Brurjan's throat, and they both knew he was dead.

His blow took her on the side of the head and she fell, then scrabbled out of his reach. He reached up and pulled Ki's knife from his throat. He came after her. They both knew she would die with him. She lay on her belly in the dust, watching him with green lizard eyes.

Goat leaped from the top of the wagon. His weight staggered the Brurjan, but the creature did not fall. Goat's knife rose and fell, scoring the Brurjan's leather harness and inflicting one slight flesh wound before a hairy arm swept the boy into the dust. But the delay had been enough. He sank beside the boy, fell across him, and the last of his blood pumped out over Goat's chest. The boy shuddered and lay still.

Ki let her head fall forward onto her arms. Blood and dust and death. She had killed again, taken the life of another sentient being as she had sworn she would never do again. It distressed her, briefly, that she could find no remorse. Only surprise at how easy it had been. How simple it was to kill, when one was properly motivated. Then the day greyed briefly, and she sank into that soft greyness.

"Vandien," she said softly into the road, tasting dust with his name. The sound of her own voice roused her. How long had she been lying here, how long had he been gone? She knew that he was already dead; but some part of her demanded that she see the body and touch its final stillness. It was this least logical part of herself that pushed her body up. She staggered upright. This emotional part, grown stronger than she had ever recognized.

"He's dead." It was Goat's voice, full of awe, coming from beneath the body.

"Maybe not," she croaked, but already grief was tightening her throat.

"No." Goat whispered it. His narrow hands rose slowly, to clutch at his own throat as he stared at the dead Brurjan atop him. His yellow eyes seemed to spin and spark like the eyes of a Harpy. "I felt him go. It was nothing like an animal . . . one moment he was there, wishing you dead, and the next he was . . . bigger. And getting bigger, and bigger, looming over you, ready to snuff you out like a palm over a candle flame. And then . . ." Goat's voice sank even softer. "And then he went somewhere else. And I nearly followed him there!'' Fear shook the boy, making his teeth chatter. ''I nearly followed him there!''

He scrabbled out from under the Brurjan's body frantically and then crawled to Ki, as if rising were beyond him. He sat at her feet for an instant, staring up at her. Then he suddenly hugged her knees, burying his face against her skirt and shaking her with his trembling. ''Oh, Ki! It's what Vandien felt, when he killed Kellich. It was too big, too real!'' He clung to her, weeping as a much younger child might, and she found herself patting his shoulders, telling him that it would be all right, all right, all right.

A long time passed very slowly as she stood there. At last the boy's trembling subsided and he slowly drooped away from her. He looked terrible, as if he had been through some wasting illness. She found herslef pushing the hair back from his face. He looked up at her and she stared down into his face. Purified. Sanctified. Something. Like metal passed through the cleansing fire. ''I killed the Tamshin. When I told the Brurjans about them. And I killed Kellich there. But Kellich went hating me, and when he was gone it was like a pain in my mind that stopped. I didn't care. Because I didn't really understand . . .'' He groped for words, found none. There was a comprehension in his face that was more terrible than any grief, that Ki sensed surpassed her own understanding of what had come to pass.

''Goat. It's going to be all right,'' she said, lying, but having to say something to the boy. It wasn't right for a child to be filled with whatever now possessed this boy. But he shook his head at her, refusing false comfort.

''Ki, we have to go after them. After Vandien. And we have to hurry.''

''Yes,'' she said softly, and the boy jumped up. He started toward the wagon, then stopped. ''What do we do about them?''

She looked at the crumpled bodies. Flies were gathering. ''Leave them,'' she suggested.

''And the horse?''

''It will eventually go back to wherever they've been stabled. It wouldn't let us get near it, anyway.''

''Should we try to . . . cover them, or something?''

''No. I'm too tired to care. And they're too dead. It doesn't really matter, Goat. No matter what we do to them, they'd still be dead.'' She paused, breathing. If she closed her eyes, the pain from her back was red and blotted out all thought. She tried to find some order in her mind. "Goat. I can't. You'll have to sort things. Anything that's still useful, toss back in the wagon.'' She looked again at the crumpled Brurjan. "Nothing with blood on it,'' she added quietly. Goat nodded silently, his eyes still full of pain.

She clambered slowly up onto the seat. She sat down carefully, took up the reins. The pain from her back was a living thing, sucking the strength from her body.

Goat clambered up beside her. He took the reins gently from her hands. "I think it's finally my turn to drive,'' he said.

She nodded, leaned back on the seat and felt the world slide into deep blues and blacks around her. The wagon started with a sickening jolt, and she found it was all she could do to keep a grip on the seat and ride along.

Cooking meat. The smell taunted her. I don't eat meat anymore, Ki reminded herself. I'm too closely linked with all things that move to want to feed on their flesh. But suddenly it seemed a silly resolution, a child's fantasy that by abstaining from meat she could somehow break the cycle of feeding and being fed upon. With or without her it went on. She had killed today, and she did not have to eat of Sativa's flesh to have preyed upon him. She suddenly perceived that eating meat or not eating meat changed nothing. She could not abstain from being Human, nor deny the position Humans held in the slow wheel of life. So she had stopped eating meat. It meant nothing. If she walked about with her eyes closed, would the colors go out of the world?

Her eyes were closed, and had been for a long time. Slowly she opened them. It was evening, the curtains of night fluttering over the world before closing completely. A pall of smoke along the road made the light dimmer and stung her eyes. Burning meat. And hair. And blood spilled new in the dust.

Goat's eyes were fixed on the road, holding the reins as carefully as if they were gossamer. She followed his gaze to where a dim red glow marked a fire by the roadside. Neither one spoke as they slowly approached it. Both sensed there was something momentous about to be revealed; both were too weary to guess what it might be, or to be eager for it.

The scene that greeted them seemed like the ghastly balancing of an earlier one, the counterweight to the scattered Tamshin under the bright sun. The backdrop was the darkening sky and the beginning of stars, the ruddy touching of the firelight upon the still forms. The toppled bodies of the four Brurjans had been stripped of harness and armor, and ignominiously heaped to one side. Their gear burned with the bodies of those who had fallen killing them. They burned with the flare of spilled oil and the tenacity of piled brushwood. No one would ever be able to identify who had fallen bringing the Brurjan guards down. The horses and weapons had been taken.

She got down slowly, walked toward the fire. The Brurjans, she noticed, had been killed thoroughly, several times over. The chest of one had been stabbed so repeatedly that the yellowish shards of its ribs glinted through the mangled flesh. Red sockets gaped where Vashikii's battle fangs had been pulled. The savagery of it bespoke a hatred she did not like to consider.

She drew closer to the fire, wrinkling her nose against the smell, unwilling but compelled. The heat of it scorched her face, and she knew her hair would be full of the smell tonight. She circled it slowly, peering into its depths. Little was left, only the scanty outlines of bodies; two, perhaps three of them. One was clearly too tall; another wore sandals, the leather straps visible against the charred flesh. The third was under the other two, face down, indistinguishable save that he was Human. She stared at the roasting body. About the right height, about the right build . . . She knelt by the fire, staring at him, willing herself to notice some grisly clue that would prove her wrong. Goat kept silent. She knelt until her face felt scorched by the nearness of the flames and the burning flesh was an unbearable stench in her nostrils, knowing, but denying.

Something was digging into her knee. She shifted her weight, glanced down. All heat went out of the fire, all living warmth from her body. A horn button. She had knelt on it, and it had dug into her knee. It was still sewn firmly to the scorched cuff that was the sole remainder of a cream-colored shirt. Finely woven stuff, that fabric. Woven by the tiny-fingered Kerugi folk, and it had cost her a shameful amount of coin, but she had loved the way it had felt under her hands when his body heat was seeping through it and her fingers traced the muscles of his back beneath it.

"Vandien," she said, calmly.

"It was a rebel fighter." Goat contradicted her. "They always burn the bodies of their dead. Ever since the Duke ordered some bodies exhumed, and then crucified them . . . the bodies, and the families of the bodies. Because the bodies showed the marks of Brurjan weaponry, and he knew they had risen up against his Brurjan guard."

There was a nervous disorganization to Goat's words. Ki drew back from the fire, stared at him. He was hugging himself as if chilled to death. His eyes were very big. He looked, she thought, as if he had lost everything. Strange that he should feel so much and she should feel so very little. "Don't believe he's dead," he pleaded. "Don't. It's not him. The rebels wouldn't have burned his body. They'd have dumped it with the Brurjans. Vandien wasn't one of their own, they wouldn't care what became of his body or his family. They care only for their own."

"It's his cuff." Her throat cracked on the words.

"But it's not him!" Goat insisted desperately.

"Then where is he?" Ki demanded of the night. The darkness pressed close to the fire and filled in the eyes of the swollen dead. "He was almost dead when the Brurjans took him. If he lived this far, being jolted like that, it would be a minor miracle. But if he did, where is he? What would the rebels want with an injured stranger, a casualty that could only slow them down?"

Goat looked away from her. Something in his posture made her demand again, "What would they want with him, a stranger and wounded to the death?"

"Not an injured stranger to them," Goat said haltingly. "Kellich's killer. The man they probably came after. The one who brought down their plan to assassinate the Duke."

THIRTEEN

Burning down, the bodies melding, becoming indistinguishable from one another. Little would be left. Whoever had built this fire had known well how to do it. Practice? She supposed.

"Ki?"

"What?"

"Shouldn't we push on, try to catch up with them?"

She pulled her eyes from the fire, saw the boy's genuine concern. "No, Goat. It's . . . too dark now. And the horses need to rest."

"Here?" he asked in horror.

Where else? she wanted to ask. She couldn't imagine moving on, leaving him here to burn alone. But she watched the boy's eyes go spooking back to the Brurjan bodies, saw how he shivered with dread, not of the imaginary things, but of the final truth he had glimpsed today. The bodies crumpled beneath their burden of burning brushwood. A dragon's tail of sparks whooshed into the air and Ki's eyes followed it, saw the bright bits wink out into nothingness.

She had left Vandien there, finally, got back up on the wagon and left. Pushing on, pretending for Goat that Vandien was not dead and that they were hurrying after him. What should I have done? she asked herself. Waited until the fire died, tried to sort which charred bones had been dear to me?

"There's not much that's fit to eat." Goat spoke from inside the cuddy through the open door.

"I'm not hungry anyway," Ki observed, keeping her eyes on the road. The lights of Tekum were yellow sparks. "Just fix something for yourself, Goat."

"He sure made a mess of the wagon."

"Brurjans are like that." Ki heard the abrupt anger in her voice, tried to modify it. "Goat, I don't feel much like talking just now. Okay?"

"All right. You're worried about Vandien, right?"

"Right." Close enough to the truth, anyway.

"They'll keep him alive, if they can." Goat's voice was cautiously reassuring. "They'll take decent care of him. They need him."

So did she. But she didn't have him any more than they did. No one had him. Her soul fell into a black gulf.

"He's good with a sword. That's important to them." Goat's voice was hesitant, wary. Asking to be asked. She complied.

"Why?"

Goat clambered back onto the seat. She couldn't really see his face in the dark, but he still stared off into the night. "What I took from Willow," he said softly. "What she wanted back so badly that she was . . . kind to me . . . was a part of a plan. I don't know everything—no one rebel ever knows everything about a plan, except the Duchess. I didn't understand it all, because Willow didn't. But Willow was to be the one to make the contact with the Brurjan that could be bribed not to look for poison on Kellich's blade." Goat's voice fell away. "Only I took the name of the Brurjan out of her dream."

"Moon's light," breathed Ki. She stared at Goat, disbelief warring with enlightenment. "You can do things like that." When she said the words, they came out as a statement.

"With some people," Goat conceded slowly. "Willow has Jore blood, too, though it doesn't show in the same way as mine. Nor would she admit it. But I know it. It makes the link easier for me. But she can't . . . reach into someone like I can. She is just . . . very persuasive. Her talent doesn't have the strength of mine. It's part of why she hates me, I think."

"I see," Ki said slowly. How much jealousy had Willow felt, knowing this boy could offer the rebellion so much more than she could? Had she deliberately alienated him from her friends, to eliminate him as competition? Competition for what? For respect and honor? For Kellich's attention? Would Kellich not have needed her if Goat had been recruited?

Reality broke over Ki like a cold wave. And she had been taking the boy back into the middle of that quarrel? Insanity. Vandien was gone; nothing could be served by following the tracks of the rebels. Senseless. Better to get the boy out of here, to deliver him to Villena as she had promised. Then would be the time to take revenge for Vandein's death. Perhaps by then she would know who to blame for it.

"Don't move. We don't want to hurt anyone. Unless we have to."

One moment the night had been a quiet and empty place around them. Now hooded figures ghosted up from the grass, flowed into the road. Sigurd whinnied in sudden alarm and threw his head back. Reflex made Ki pull them in even as someone gripped the edge of her wagon, swung easily up onto the box beside her. A knife touched her throat. Her eyes flickered over the highwaymen. Seven, eight of them. Humans. But those were only the ones she could see. Were there others behind the wagon, more still lying flat in the grass? Goat was twisting his shirt front in his hands. She put out a hand to his shoulder, gripped the boy to steady him. He quivered under her touch.

"What do you want from us?" Ki asked quietly.

No one answered her. They were already moving around the wagon. She heard the side door open, felt the weight of an intruder rock the wagon. "Just follow the plan," one of them reminded the others. "Everyone knows his own part."

"Rebels!" Goat breathed.

"Quiet!" the leader barked again. At least Ki assumed he was the leader. He was the only one who had spoken, and he held the knife at her throat. In their flowing brown robes and hoods, they all looked remarkably alike. His shapeless hood had a slash for his eyes. She saw their glitter, but could not tell what color they were, nor anything else about the man. "Climb down," he ordered gruffly. "And put your hands in front of you."

"Take whatever you wish and leave us in peace," Ki suggested. "We won't report this to anyone. We were just leaving this area anyway. There will be no trouble from us. We have business that takes us far from here."

"Your business has become our business," the man said sternly. The knife pressed more firmly, and she became aware of the figure holding a blade to Goat's throat. She rose carefully, clambered down in the shadow of the knife-wielder. They walked Goat over to stand beside her. "Clasp your hands together, palm to palm," the leader directed.

Ki glanced at Goat. The boy's trembling hands were clutched before him. His face was drawn. She copied him, joining her hands together and holding them in front of her. The hooded man bound her wrists with a strange, flat rope that only tightened when she flexed her muscles against it. Goat was already bound. Behind her someone mounted the box of her wagon, took up the reins. Then a bag came down over her head.

The sack smelled of grain, and she nearly choked on loose chaff that shook free from its rough weave. The hands that seized her elbows were not rough, but neither were they gentle. She was hurried forward, sent stumbling through the dry grass and rocks for a good distance. She heard Goat cry out, the sound cut off short. "Goat?" she called out, and a hand slapped hard against her belly, making her lose her breath. She was pushed up against a large, warm animal.

"Mount it," an unfamiliar voice ordered, and as she struggled to do so, someone large caught her around the waist and heaved her up on the animal. The only harness she could find was a rough blanket strapped over the horse's back. She gripped the edge of it, wrapped her legs around its barrel body. It started forward without any warning and she lurched backward, nearly losing her seat. "Hold on," a gruff voice warned her, and then the beast was jerked into a jolting canter, and her ears were filled with the sound of moving horses around her. If she slipped down, she'd be trampled.

Blind and powerless to control her fate, she was carried forward in a nightmare journey. She gripped the edge of the horse's banket tightly, using every bit of strength in her legs to keep a firm seat. She drew a deep breath, imposed an artificial order on her mind. One thing at a time, she decided. These horses couldn't keep up this pace for long. They were farm plugs, not warriors' horses. So they couldn't be going far. Once they arrived, she might have an opportunity to free Goat and herself. It was the best plan she could think of now.

She gripped the thought and hung onto it, pushing all else out of her mind.

"What is this place?" Goat's voice was eerie in the darkness.

"I don't know. Some kind of a root cellar, maybe?" Ki put her hand on the boy's shoulder and patted it. She could feel him vibrating with nervousness.

She wondered what time of day it was. She had no idea of how long they had ridden, blinded and bound, nor how long it had taken her to work free of her bonds and get the bag off her head. It hadn't helped much. It was as dark without the sack as it had been with it.

The smell of earth was all around them. She had already discovered that the ceiling of rough slab wood was but a handspan over her head, and that to touch it brought down a shower of soil. The chamber itself was small, no longer than a tall man lying down, and about half again as wide. Her jaws ached from chewing the rope from her wrists, and her wrists were chafed raw where the bonds had worked against them.

"I'm thirsty," Goat said suddenly.

"Not much we can do about it," Ki observed quietly. She was groping her way along the wall. There had to be a door, but if there was, she kept missing it. All her hands found were earth and occasional tangles of roots. Once she stepped in something that might have been vegetables gone bad. She certainly hoped that's what it was. And around the fourth corner and down that wall again. And here it was at last. The door. She had missed it before because she hadn't remembered how her head had been forced down before she'd been pushed in. It was a very short door, no more than waist high. She groped for a handle, found none, pushed on it. It didn't yield at all. Probably barred from the outside. She sat down slowly, put her back against it.

"What are they going to do with us?" Goat sounded even shakier than he had earlier.

"I don't know." Ki pulled her knees up, rested her forehead against them. "I don't even know what they want with us. If they just wanted to rob us, they should have taken the wagon and gone. Or killed us then. What are they keeping us locked up for? I can't think of any way we're useful to them."

Goat had been coming toward the sound of her voice. Now he stumbled over her feet, crying out as he fell.

"Careful," Ki warned him, and heard him scrabble up and crawl over to sit beside her. His shoulder pressed against hers. He was shaking. "Why are you so afraid?" she asked him quietly.

"I could feel it . . . how much they hated me. When they were tying me up and putting me on that horse."

"Maybe you were just imagining it," Ki said comfortingly. "They seemed efficient to me. Like they were moving us somewhere, but didn't particularly want to hurt us."

"You still don't get it, do you?" Goat asked her. "Ki, I can feel what other people feel. The pity you feel for me now, the hatred those people felt for me. The way the Brurjan felt as he was dying. That was the awfulest it's ever been. Because Brurjans are so open anyway, like animals, it's like they're always shouting at you what they think of you . . ." His voice trailed off. When he spoke again, it seemed to come from a great distance. "When I was little, I didn't understand. I couldn't separate what I felt from what other people around me felt. People acted one way when they really felt a different way. I felt everything, for everyone . . . and then when I got older and more sensitive, it was even worse. At night. When everyone was dreaming into my mind. When people sleep, they drop all the guards, most of them. They just yell it all out, over and over again. We moved away from town after it got so bad, to where I didn't hear as much of it. But some always got through. Dreams are strange. I don't understand how people think of them, how they make them up. I've never been able to dream that way . . . not to make up one of my own. The closest I could do was to find ones that I liked, to listen to them the closest and try to ignore the others."

Goat had stopped talking. Ki had no idea how long the silence had lasted. Or was it silence, for Goat? Was it ever silent? Not a dream-thief, not an eavesdropper. An unwilling participant in others' lives, like a guest forced to listen to his hosts' quarreling through a thin wall. She tried to imagine a small child sharing his parents' emotions, an adolescent subjected to the unfiltered imaginings of the village's night minds.

"Don't feel guilty, please," Goat begged. "Guilty is the worst. When people are kind to me because they think they've hurt me. I wish . . ."

"What?" Ki asked.

"No." Goat spoke the word slowly. "If you ask someone to feel a certain way, and they do it because you've asked them to, it's not the same thing as if they just did it because they wanted to. Do you know what I mean?"

"I think I do. If you have to say to somone, 'Please kiss me,' there's not much point to the kiss."

To have someone be kind to you because they liked you, Ki thought to herself. Is that so much for a boy to long for? She leaned back against the door. And waited.

Goat broke the silence with a whisper. "Someone's coming."

Ki strained her ears but heard nothing. But of course Goat had not heard footsteps, but had felt the approach of the other person's emotions. "Someone friendly?" she asked hopefully.

"No." Goat's voice pinched with anxiety. "Someone very wary. Don't be too near the door. She's frightened enough to hurt you if you startle her."

Ki didn't argue. Daylight was a blinding whiteness after the eternal dark of the root cellar. Ki's eyes had no time to adjust. The sack of food was tossed in, the door slammed again before she had any chance to see what was outside. Her jailor had been no more than a dark silhouette against the brightness. She listened to the bars of the door being dropped into place. One, two, three of them. "They aren't taking any chances on us getting out," Ki grumbled to herself.

"They're afraid," Goat explained needlessly. "Mostly of me. They hate me, too. For you, this one felt guilt . . ." His voice trailed off uneasily. He was holding something back.

"You can hear their exact thoughts?" Ki asked as she rummaged in the sack.

"No. More their feelings." He paused. When he continued, strain made his voice higher. "I felt . . . they were thinking of killing us."

Ki came to her feet. "Are they coming back now?" Fear brought her back to life. The boy's voice was so certain of the threat.

"No. They're both gone now. I think they're afraid to stay too close to the cellar. For fear of what I might be able to do, I suppose." He paused thoughtfully. "They must be riding horses, to get so far away so fast. I can't feel anyone at all out there now. Only you."

"Oh." Ki wondered what impressions he was receiving

from her, then buried the thought. There were some apples in the sack, a skin of water, some round meal cakes. That was all. "Apple?" she asked, proffering it to the darkness, and felt Goat take it from her hand.

She heard him bite into it, chew, then ask, with his mouth full, "I've been so hungry. How long do you think we've been here?"

"I don't know," she answered softly. She wasn't really concerned with how long they had been here so much as how much longer they would be kept here. Already the small room stank of sweat and wastes. And why were they being kept at all?

"About what you felt . . . just now. Are you certain of it? Maybe they were just . . ." She couldn't think of what else they might be thinking.

"I've felt it before," Goat said. The pause grew very long. "It's the same as what Kellich felt for Vandien. What Satatavi felt for us. It's like a way of classifying how much to feel. Animal. Rock. Tree. Soon-to-be-dead-person. They didn't want to feel too much about us."

Ki pressed the apple she still held against her cheek, felt the coolness of its smooth skin. She bit into it, chewed methodically. Soon-to-be-dead-person. She was not hungry, but if they had given them food, then she probably should be hungry. What was it Vandien was always saying? "If there's nothing else you can do in a tight spot, it's always a good idea to eat or sleep. To be full and rested for when there is something you can do." But there wasn't going to be anything she could do, and he wasn't going to turn up to help her. Not this time.

Vandien. She tried to call up his face against the darkness, but only got the image of him as she had last seen him, thrown over the horse like a meal sack, the blood drops falling swift from his hair. He was dead. She knew it. She eased down to her haunches, her back braced against the sandy wall. She forced herself to think about it, very carefully. He was dead. She was soon-to-be-dead. Then everything would be gone, not even someone left to remember it. There would be no touch of his hand on her face, no warm breath on her shoulder in the darkness. No deep voice spinning long tales in the evening by the fire. His scent would fade from the coverlets on her bed. It wouldn't matter. Strangers would use those blankets, and never think of the way his lips moved against hers. Gone and ended.

"Ki?" Goat asked cautiously.

She lifted her head. "What?"

"I . . . I couldn't feel you. It was like you were . . . gone. Like the Brurjan."

"No. I'm here." But she felt the truth of his words. She was gone. Her life hung limp as an empty sail. She tried to convince herself that there were important things to be done. She and Goat must escape, she must regain her horses and wagon, she must get the boy to his uncle in Villena. "And then what?" some sardonic voice within her kept asking. And then resume her life, she told herself. Find a cargo, deliver it, get paid. Why? So she could eat, rest and find a cargo, deliver it and get paid. The triviality of it overwhelmed her. A purposeless round, like a song sung endlessly over and over. Until it stopped. It had no more meaning than sitting in a root cellar and waiting for someone to kill you. But sitting in the cellar was easier. Until it stopped. Just as Vandien had stopped.

It was not, she suddenly knew, that Vandien was gone from her life. She could have lived with that, if he had ridden away, let his life lead him elsewhere. She did not love him that selfishly. She would have known that somewhere he existed, that somewhere he continued. That was all she wanted of the world. To know that somewhere in it, he existed. He didn't have to be hers, had never really been hers at all. But even when he had not been by her side, she had known that he was somewhere, and it had pleased her to think of him riding through the rain on his horse somewhere, or telling tales by an inn-fire, even standing on a hillside looking over the lands that should have been his but were not. He had ended. Nothing more of him, ever. His line had ended with him; no child carried his precious names. He was gone as completely as the song is gone when the singer closes his mouth. She suddenly comprehended the void.

She sank completely to the floor, pressed her eyes to her knees. She opened her mouth, tried to breathe but could not. Grief and anger filled her. The truth rounded on her. Damn it, it did matter! He'd left her, damn him. Died and left her howling in the dark for him. The fabric of her life was torn across, and she hated herself for ever letting Vandien became a part of it. She'd always known it would come to this. Her eyes burned but tears would not come.

"Stop!" Goat begged her. "Please stop!"

"I can't," she whispered.

"Please," he whimpered, and then she heard him break. Horrible choking sobs ripped his throat. He cried as only children can, giving way to hopeless, inconsolable sadness. She listened to the fury of her grief shake the boy, close his throat and reduce his voice to a helpless keening. She sat panting in the darkness, knowing she should go to him, comfort him somehow. But she had no comfort, not for herself and not for him. There was only this suffocating grief that filled the cellar like a palpable thing. Goat became her grief, gave tongue to it with his hiccuping wails, gave form to it as he thrashed on the floor.

Ki drifted. Somewhere a cellar was filled with a grief so abiding that a boy convulsed in its grip while a woman crouched numbly. An ending was coming, bringing peace.

There were noises, a terrible light. A man stood before her, dragged her to her feet. "Stop it!" he cried, and shook her wildly. Ki was dragged from the cellar, thrown onto the rough sod outside it. The man vanished, reappeared a moment later with the jerking boy in his arms. Then Brin lowered the boy carefully to the earth, and spun on Ki. "Stop it!" he roared. "You're killing him!" Ki saw the raised hand, knew the blow was coming, but could not recall why that should be important.

FOURTEEN

Blood was slick in her mouth. She coughed, spat it out and sat up slowly. The sky slowly cartwheeled around her head and then settled. Gradually she took in her surroundings. There was the gaping black door of the root cellar. Over there, the mounded remains of a sod hut that had fallen in and grown over. In the skinny shade of a dying tree, Brin knelt over Goat.

No. Not Brin. This man was more weathered than Brin, more muscular. Even looking at his back, she could feel the difference in his temperament. Leather-tough and capable, she gauged him. She stood up silently, cast about for a stick or a rock. She didn't know why he was angry with her, but she didn't want to face him without a weapon.

"It's all right." He didn't turn to face her, and at first she didn't realize that he was speaking to her, not Goat. "I didn't want to stun you. But it was the only way to force you back inside yourself. Before Gotheris died under your onslaught."

She hadn't found a weapon, and as he turned slowly to face her, she decided she probably wouldn't need one. There was something about his face that was calming. The man seemed to radiate a soothing kindness. She relaxed.

"I'm Dellin, Brin's brother. I came looking for you."

Ki felt suddenly woozy. She sat down, drew her knees up, folded her arms atop them and leaned her chin on her arms. Her thoughts seemed sluggish and numbed. She asked, "How did you find us?"

Dellin made a sound between a cough and a grunt. "As

well ask a Human mother how she knew where her screaming child was. Brin had sent me word that the boy would come to me sometime this season. His message stank of distress; I suspected then that something was wrong. Then I heard from Tamshin that some of their folk had seen a Jore-eyed boy on a wagon coming toward Tekum. So, suspecting trouble, I came to meet you. Once I got past Rivercross, it was not hard to find you.'' Dellin shook his head slowly. ''The boy has been taught no shielding at all. What was Brin thinking of, to keep him so long? I should have had him ten years ago.''

''Is Goat . . . Gotheris all right?'' The boy lay unnaturally still. His arms were folded on his chest, his legs drawn out straight. Composed like a corpse, she thought, and she shivered in the sunlight.

''I have him asleep, for now. And I've pushed him back mostly inside himself. Poor boy couldn't understand what I was doing, and fought me. Strength such as I never faced before; luckily, he is untrained, and I know tricks he doesn't even suspect. Still . . .'' Dellin's voice trailed off as his eyes met Ki's. Jore eyes, like Goat's, but more comfortably dark, more Human.

''You're confused. I'm sorry. So Brin didn't even see fit to make sure you understood the nature of boy. You're not from around these parts, are you?''

''We . . . I come from the lands north of here.''

Dellin nodded slowly. ''Then you know nothing of Jores, do you? Never even seen a full-blooded one, I suppose, for they don't willingly come around Humans anymore, even here.''

''Why is that?''

''Humans kill them.'' He fixed Ki with a stare that made her feel uncomfortable, almost guilty. ''They always say they don't mean to. But they do it anyway. Humans feel things so strongly, so intensely, and when those feelings become too strong and there is a Jore nearby, they simply empty their pain, or joy, or lust into the Jore.''

''Is that . . . is that what I was doing to Gotheris?'' Ki asked faintly.

His eyes met hers. ''We were not meant to experience such intensity of emotion. It kills us.''

Ki realized abruptly that this man in his Human form did not recognize himself as Human. He was as different from her as a Brurjan or a T'cheria. As he looked at her she realized the depth of his alienness. The very familiarity of his Human shape suddenly seemed monstrous, a mask of clay and twine to deceive the unwary. She felt herself draw back from him.

"Yes," he agreed. "And Gotheris is just as foreign to you as I am, but the poor child does not even know that yet. What Brin was thinking of to keep him, to let him be raised by a Human mother, I do not know. The boy . . ." Dellin's voice faltered. His inhuman eyes bored into Ki's, seeking her understanding. "The boy has no sense of self. He has no personal identity, no idea of where he stops and others begin. He has grown up exposed to a constant flood of emotion. There is no place I can touch him that has not already been scarred over, like a piece of glass abraded by sand until it is opaque." Dellin's voice became strained. "He no longer believes what he senses others feeling. You Humans so often act one way when you feel another. He has tried to copy that, and only hurt himself more. Sometimes he ignores what others feel and thus responds incorrectly. And offensively." Dellin's eyes bored into Ki's as if seeing all she remembered. "But most often he becomes whatever he is near, greeting anger with anger, distrust with distrust . . ."

Ki suddenly had an image of colors spilled from paint pots, of their edges merging, of yellow meeting blue and becoming green, and then red leaching into it, and purple, until all bled into murkiness and no true color was left. Goat. His fickle moods, his suddenly strange behavior as he tried to become acceptable by adopting whatever behavior and personality seemed successful. Wanting to be liked for himself, but not even sure who or what that self was. "Didn't Brin know?" she asked helplessly.

Dellin shook his head slowly. "I am more Jore than he, even through we are brothers. The Human blood flowed more surely in his veins. He felt no discomfort with his Human mate. When the boy was small, I sensed he would be strongly Jore. I asked for Gotheris then, but they denied me." Dellin squeezed his eyes shut, opened them again. "It was the mother more than my brother, I believe. Even then she was abusing the child, loving him with no moderation, giving him no chance to develop his own feelings. I could not stand to watch it, and it caused many quarrels between Brin and me.

Finally, he drove me from his home. And I let my own anger persuade me to do a cruel thing; I left Gotheris there.'' His voice suddenly deepened. ''This is as much my fault as theirs.''

Ki rose carefully, found she was steady on her legs. The inside of her cheek still leaked blood into her mouth, but it seemed a trifling hurt in light of what Dellin had told her. She moved to stand over Goat. The boy's face was unlined, his eyes closed. She stooped closer to see the rise and fall of his breast. He seemed so like to dead that she put out a hand to touch him.

''Don't!'' warned Dellin. ''I have quenched your emotions for you, and pushed him back inside himself. But you have been too long together, and touch strengthens any link. You'd kill him.''

Ki drew back. She sat still a moment, wondering why her own thoughts seemed so slow to her. ''Quenched my emotions?'' she said aloud. She groped within herself, seeking for some difference. Vandien was dead. That was sad, horribly sad. She knew it was tragic, but could not feel it. It was an intellectual grieving she felt now, a keen-edged inventory of her pain that somehow did not cut her. She was very still, considering it.

''Muffled, perhaps, is a better word. It is a thing we Jore can do for Humans. A kind of healing, for those whose emotions threaten to overwhelm them. Sometimes a Human feels so intensely that he retreats too far from himself, and cannot find his way out again. Then we Jore can enter him, can deaden his pain and bring him out, or erase the memory that is too painful to live with. It is the Jore healing. Surely you have heard of this?''

Ki shook her head. She lifted her eyes to Dellin. ''What will you do now?''

''Take the boy to Villena with me. Start the training that should have begun when he was a baby. I will have to keep him insulated from others at first, until he learns to shield himself, but after that, he will be fine. I hope.'' His strange eyes seemed to pin her confusion down like it was a wriggling insect. ''What will you do?''

''I don't know.'' Ki cleared her throat, made a firm decision not to sound so feeble. ''Find my wagon and team and reclaim it. I can't make a living without it. Go back north, I suppose, where I understand the folk and know the roads. Start again.''

"You're lying to yourself. You have no desire to do that."

She felt her eyes go flat, knew their green had gone grey. "Nevertheless," she said quietly.

"What about the man? This Vandien?"

She stared at him, feeling plundered. He read her again. "What I know comes from Gotheris; the poisons I had to bleed from him before I could induce him to sleep. He was full of your images of this man, of your sharings. You have a bond to Vandien, one not easily severed. If he bleeds, you feel the pain, and he takes joy in your triumphs. You will abandon him?"

She touched her tongue to the laceration inside her cheek. Pain. When she spoke, she formed the words carefully. "He has abandoned me. He's dead."

Dellin stared at her long. She felt him probing her feelings. I should feel invaded, she thought to herself. I should probably feel outraged and angry. But she could not summon the energy to feel anything. So she stood quietly before his penetrating gaze, which fixed not on her, but on somewhere infinitely beyond her. His touch on her mind was light and oddly soothing, reminding her of Vandien stroking her hair. Vandien. For a second she felt her grief, vibrating like the plucked wire of a harp. Vandien. Echoing off into the distance.

"No." Dellin spoke conversationally. "He's not dead."

Ki felt no patience with his attempt to falsely comfort her. "I saw the body," she said in a cold voice. "Look. This was his." And from her pocket she drew the singed cuff with the familiar button.

Stepping to her, he took it lightly from her hand. She felt a part of herself go with it. "Yes. Yes, this was his, his imprint is upon it. But why do you say he is dead?" Dellin fixed her with one of his odd stares. Abruptly his eyes narrowed. "I suppose it can be so, then." He spoke softly to himself, almost meditatively. "It is a thing I have never completely believed before, but now I must. As intensely as you Humans feel, as strongly as you bond, out of sight is still out of awareness. This, then, is what his mother feared. This . . . severance from her child. This gap."

His eyes left Ki, strayed to Gotheris sleeping still. Dellin lifted his head, stared across the plains. Moments dripped

away. Ki was still, content to watch him stare. She felt
heavy, filled with the weariness that usually came only from
hours of physical labor. Too tired to sleep, she told herself,
but needing the stillness to let the body slowly relax. She
leaned against the spindly tree that sheltered Goat, her eyes
starting to droop. And jerked alert as she felt Dellin's mind
brush hers.

"Not even Brin," he said aloud, sadly. "For all his Jore
blood, Brin has no more awareness of his child than the
mother does. I can find no thread between them. To them,
Gotheris is as absent as the dead." He met her eyes again.
The smile that touched his face now was pitying.

"He's alive," he told her. When Ki only stared, he repeated himself. "He's alive. Vandien. Tired and ill and
anxious, but alive. I tested the bond that links you. He's
alive."

Ki sat down. For a long time she said and thought nothing.
Her mouth was slightly ajar, and as she breathed she tasted
the day upon her tongue. So. Another breath. And so. Vandien
was alive. Did she dare to believe it? Something surged
within her, and she knew she didn't dare to disbelieve it. He
was alive. "And so am I," she said, and felt the wonder of
it. A desire to continue being alive reawakened and jolted
through her.

"We have to get out of here," she told Dellin suddenly.
"Goat . . . felt . . . that the people holding us were going to
kill us. How did he put it? That they thought of us as
'soon-to-be-dead' people."

There was a slight smile on Dellin's face. "Isn't that how
you were thinking of yourself?"

Ki shrugged. "Perhaps. But not anymore. And I don't
want to stay around here to find how they feel about it. We
have to get Goat out of here, especially. He seemed to be the
main object of their hate." She narrowed her eyes at Dellin,
considering him. "Can you use this 'bond' I have with
Vandien to help me find him?"

Dellin laughed softly. "It is not like a piece of string
stretched between you, with him at the other end. It is more
like a dream you share, and I can feel that he is still dreaming
his part of it. More than that I cannot explain to a Human.
You feel it without knowing you feel it. That was one reason
you were so taxing for Goat to be near these last days. You

were feeling one thing and believing another, while saying to him that you believed that what he felt and knew was true. . . . Do you understand?''

Ki shook her head slowly. ''Days?'' she asked, seizing the only part she could grasp.

''By my estimate, about two.''

''How far is Tekum from here?''

He shrugged. ''For my mule and I, perhaps a day.''

Ki nodded. ''They'll have taken Vandien there. And maybe my team and wagon. You'll come with me?''

''Of course.'' Dellin looked surprised that she would ask. ''You still owe the boy the rest of the trip to Villena.'' His eyes grew troubled. ''And he must be shown what the wrong use of his Jore blood can lead to.''

FIFTEEN

Voices. Talking right by him, pushing their sounds up against him. Shouting in his ears. He tried to turn away from them, but found he couldn't move. He was bound. No. Not bound. But every part of his body was too heavy to move. Just keeping his eyelids up was difficult enough. He tried to find himself in space and time, could not. He caught at the tattered edges of memories that unraveled beneath his scrutiny. Kellich falling, the ring of Brurjans closing on him, Goat's yellow teeth bared in terror . . . he could not put them into any sort of order, and the attempt to do so was making him dizzy and sick.

"You didn't give him enough," someone whispered.

"Shut up. I know what I'm doing." An angry woman.

"Do you? Or are you so hungry for revenge that you have lost sight of our true purpose?" This voice was older than the other two, mature and in command. Vandien instinctively turned his eyes toward it.

"He's awake." The man had a beard that fringed his jaw, a nose like a hawk's beak and dark eyes. He moved, coming closer, and Vandien found it hard to keep his eyes focused on him. He crouched by Vandien, and he felt the man's dry hands touch his face. The world seemed to suddenly flop over as Vandien got his true bearings. He was lying on his belly, cheek to a coarse pillow. The man's fingers probed the back of Vandien's head, pressing as if to check for a weakness in his skull. Vandien winced, spun away from the world for a long moment, and then came back to it, feeling like a swimmer surfacing to air and light. They were talking again.

". . . not enough time. It was a clear signal to the Duke that Tekum is not as quiet as he has been led to believe. Killing the Brurjans cost us three men and laid up five others. For what? For a half-dead stranger we can't put any trust in. It was a mistake."

"Perhaps." It was the older man's voice conceding that, placatingly. "But in any case, it's too late to worry about it. It's done. We have to go on with whatever tools we have. It's too late to change the whole plan."

"It's never too late for caution. I think we should try a whole different approach. An ambush of the Duke's party . . ."

"No." The older man again. "It's too late for a sudden change like that. We'll never get an opportunity like this again. Everything is in place. In two days the Duke will be here for the festival. The plans of Masterhold have fallen to us. When he goes down, our friends move on Masterhold. It falls to the Duchess." The man paused. His voice became graver. "But only if the Duke falls. We have two days to reestablish contact with our inside friend. Two days to get this man on his feet and convince him of the justice of our cause. Two days to show him there is only one way to redeem his honor."

"Redeem his honor?" A youth's voice, angry and incredulous. "He has none. You won't reach him that way, Lacey, with talk of honor and right. Say rather that we have two days to convince him that he can do what we say and depart with coins, or die."

The older voice again. "He doesn't look like a man who greatly fears death. I do not think he will be swayed by threats. I think we must appeal to his sense of justice . . ."

"It would be a further waste of time to do so, and we have little enough as it is," a woman broke in. "No, Lacey. I've another way, one I've already set in motion, one that . . ."

"Willow," Vandien gasped, finally placing the voice.

He watched the heads turn to him. Willow's eyes were flat, and she was dressed in a severe robe that was the color of parched grasslands. Hatred burned in her, but did not illuminate her. She cloaked it from all but him, and he felt it strike and burn into him like a pitch arrow. His eyes met Willow's and he knew he was looking at his death. The coldness of that death washed over him suddenly, and he gave himself up to it.

"Get up."

Vandien opened his eyes. "Me?" His voice was thick; his tongue wanted to stick to the roof of his mouth.

"Who else?" The speaker was a young man with a tangle of blond hair and grey, almost colorless eyes. His sullen frown looked vaguely familiar. Vandien thought perhaps he had been one of the onlookers when he fought Kellich. Kellich. He winced from the memory and started to close his eyes. The youth kicked the edge of his bed, sending a painful jolt from the back of his skull throughout his whole body. "Don't close your eyes when I'm talking to you, damn you! Get up!"

He got up, moving faster than either he or the startled youth had believed he could. He paid for it in acid pain that exploded from his skull and drenched his body, but it fueled his sudden anger, and he found his hands about the boy's throat, heard the back of the boy's head bounce off the rough wall. "Please!" the boy gasped, scrabbling at Vandien's wrists.

"Please what?' he asked savagely. He found himself fully awake, totally confused but angry. He channelled the anger into meanness, thudding the boy again against the wall.

"Please . . . let me . . . go! Please!"

Vandien was still deciding when he felt the knife prod his lower back. "Let him down," a voice suggested pleasantly. An older, mature voice. The leader. The conversation he had dreamed suddenly came back to him. But there were still gaps in his recent memory and they angered him. Other people were entering the room.

"I could break his neck before you killed me," he observed.

"Then there would be two of you dead, and nothing achieved by it. Why not let him down and hear what I have to say before you kill anyone?"

Vandien stared into the boy's face. Terror stared back at him. The unfocused anger he felt was like a fog around him, driving him to violence. He wanted to hurt someone, to make someone pay for the pain and confusion he was experiencing.

"Come now." The warmth of the man's voice was like a

friendly hand on his shoulder. "You're overwrought, man. Don't do a foolish thing on an impulse. You've done too many foolish things lately." He felt the pressure of the knife ease.

"I want to know what's going on," Vandien said harshly. "I want to know how I got here. I want to know . . ." He stopped himself before he mentioned Ki and his need to know where and how she was. If they did not know of her, he wouldn't drag her into his trouble.

"And you will. If you let us tell you. Come. Let the boy go, sit down, have something to eat. We're willing to answer all your questions. Just give us a chance."

An instant longer he held the boy; then he slowly took his hands away, let him slide gasping to the floor. He turned slowly, trying not to jar himself. The pain from his skull had not abated, and the slightest movement sent out waves of agony. But he hid it as he turned to face his captors and assess his prison.

It was a fairly large place, with walls of mud brick and dirt floors. No windows, and only one door. It was poorly lit and shadows haunted it. Sacks of something were piled in one corner. In addition to the cot he had rested on, there was a worn chair, a plank table, an old saddle frame, and a tangle of leather harness straps dangling from pegs. A storage place of some kind? His attention went quickly to the folk that filled the place. About a dozen of them, he guessed, and all dressed in brown robes. A few had their hoods thrown back, but most gazed at him from deep within shadowy cowls. Willow did, but he spotted her anyway, almost instantly. She returned his gaze with a flat look of dislike unsettling in its intensity. He shifted his eyes away, appraised the others. Farmers and tradesmen, he thought to himself, studying the sturdy muddy boots that peeped out from under the robes, the muscled hands that clutched at the fronts of their garments. None of them had the bearing of soldiers. Nor the discipline, he observed, as one man demanded, "Who put you in charge, Lacey?"

"Who said I wasn't? This is my place, and I'm the one taking all the chances. So we run it my way." Lacey looked slowly around the assemblage. Few met his gaze, but Willow did, staring her cold defiance. Vandien noted that Lacey's eyes moved away from hers, breaking free of that challenge.

No one else disputed his authority, so Lacey cleared his throat and said, "One of you bring him some food. The rest of you . . . if you must stay, sit down instead of milling around like sheep."

As the others moved slowly to his suggestion, Lacey turned to Vandien. "Come, man, sit down. Over here." He gestured toward the rickety table and old chair. Vandien followed him slowly, carefully aware of the way the folk parted to let him pass. Lacey indicated he should sit, while he himself leaned up against the wall. Vandien sat, and as he did so he became aware of what an effort it had been to stand. He pressed his feet against the floor to still the shaking of his legs. Damn poor time to be feeling this weak.

Lacey appeared to be studying him. Vandien stared back. Dark eyes, jutting nose . . . Lacey suddenly became the man from his dream, and the dream suddenly became an earlier awakening. The realization further disoriented him. He sat, staring silently at the man. Someone clomped a tureen of soup down before him; the greyish gravy slopped over the lip and puddled on the table. A slab of bread and a wooden spoon were tossed down beside it. Vandien made no sign of noticing it or the server.

"Go ahead and eat," Lacey said gently. "It's been a day and a half. You must be hungry."

The displacement in time made him feel suddenly shaky, or perhaps it was the greasy aroma of the soup. His hunger suddenly superceded all things, and he tore a piece off the slab of bread, sopped it in the soup and filled his mouth. It was not the flavor of the soup, which was greasy and strongly spiced, which swamped his senses, but rather the physical act of eating. The jarring headache that had become a part of him lessened in intensity, and he suddenly felt more inclined to be rational. He glanced up at Lacey, found him watching him closely. For that matter, every eye in the place seemed to be fixed on him as he ate. He swallowed. "So?" he asked Lacey.

"You killed Kellich." A statement, not an accusation.

Vandien nodded silently. He wouldn't tell them he hadn't intended to; to Kellich's friends it could only sound like an excuse. For an instant their eyes met. Vandien turned his attention back to the food, uncertain of what he'd read in Lacey's eyes.

"Kellich was our best. Our hopes were pinned on him. You know that Festival starts two days from now, here in Tekum?" He paused to harvest a brief nod from Vandien.

"And that the Duke will be here, to collect the high-summer shares from the farmers."

A shrug from Vandien. He continued eating, trying not to betray his intense curiosity. What was the man leading up to? It was obviously not vengeance for Kellich's death; he could have killed Vandien at any time in the past day or so, or just left him to the Brurjans to execute. So what was it?

"The Duke enjoys many sports, most of them of the bloodier varieties. But his especial favorite is swordplay. He always watches the matches during Festival, and awards a medallion bearing his image to the man he judges the best. We had planned on Kellich winning that medal. We had even taken steps to insure that there would be no competitor even close to his skill level."

Vandien scraped the last spoonful of soup from the bowl. The noise seemed loud in the silence of the room. What the hell could be so important to them about winning a medallion for swordplay? He doubted that town pride could be so important in a place where even the merchants looked badgered. He glanced briefly at the assembled folk, saw how they watched him as Lacey spoke. Waiting for his reaction, dangling after a word from him. He cheated them of it, simply staring at Lacey and waiting.

Lacey sighed. "After Kellich had won the medallion, the Duke would be likely to invite him to dine with him, in his private rooms, probably the ones over the Byroad Inn. And after a meal and a few glasses of wine, the Duke would invite him to a friendly match of the blades."

Vandien allowed himself to speak. "What makes you think so? Every nobleman I've ever had to do with was unusually cautious about exposing himself to an enemy's blade. Or do you think he'd have believed Kellich was his loyal subject?"

Lacey's eyes fell to the scarred tabletop. A spasm of pain crossed his face, then vanished. "We think he would do so, because he has done so every Festival for the last four years. Always he dines with the winner of the medallion, always he offers to pit his blade against the winner's." Lacey's voice grew suddenly hoarse. "He is a very fine swordsman, our

Duke. And knows it. Always he kills the winner of the medallion. . . .''

Vandien was wiping his bowl out with the rind of the bread. ''And fools keep on trying to win it?'' he asked scathingly.

Lacey stared at him. Another man spoke, a hooded man seated on one of the sacks stacked against the wall. ''It is not like a tournament where there is one final winner. The Duke watches all the matches, but there is no one final match. There is simply a time when he says, 'Enough!' Or he may ask two chosen men to fence against one another. Then, to those who have pleased him, he gives gold, a heavy pouchful, enough to take a man and his family through the year. And to the one who has fought the best, in his own private judgement, he gives the medallion.''

Vandien nodded sourly to himself. Sadistic bastard. He'd wager that times had been bad enough in Loveran that many men were willing to bet their lives against a sack of gold. The challenge probably seemed easy to most of them: fight well enough to win often, but not well enough to be the best. He sighed. ''Kellich thought he was good enough to win the medallion. And then what? Good enough to fight the Duke and kill him?''

''No,'' Lacey said softly. ''No one thought Kellich was good enough to win against the Duke. But Kellich's blade was to carry a slow poison. Kellich was willing to make a sacrificial reach to get past the Duke's guard and bloody him.''

''No!'' Willow cried suddenly, wildly. ''That wasn't what he planned. Not to die! Never to die! He told me he was good enough, that he was sure he could wound the Duke and still win the match. That he would come away from it alive and we would be married, that we would live together many long years. . . .'' Her face had gone very pale beneath the shadowing hood, her eyes two bright coals of witchfire.

Lacey shook his head slowly. ''No, Willow. So he told you, to give you courage. But he knew he would have to die, would have to stop caring about his own guard to get in past the Duke's. We all knew Kellich would have to die to win.''

''No!'' Willow staggered forward from where she had been leaning against the wall. She pushed her hood back, revealing how she had shorn her coppery hair for grief. It stood up in wild licks from her skull, making her look pathetically vulnerable.

"Believe me, child," Lacey whispered. "None of us wanted it that way. But we knew . . . and you must have seen that even if Kellich could outfight the Duke, even if he could wound him and somehow win the match, that the Duke would never let him leave those chambers alive. Even if he had been sure of a killing thrust, the Brurjan guards would have killed Kellich within moments. That was the reason for the poison, and finding a Brurjan who could be bribed not to find Kellich's blade tainted." Lacey sighed. "But now it has all gone to ruin. Goat stole from you the names of the guards who could be bribed. And Vandien killed Kellich."

"No." Willow spoke the word in a sullen child's voice, as if she had been instructed to fetch water or go to bed early. "No. Kellich wouldn't have gone along with that. He loved me."

"Willow." Lacey's voice stopped hers. "It was Kellich's plan. He brought it to us, and we refused it. Until he made us see it was our only chance."

"No! You're making that up, you're lying to me!"

No one was contradicting her. No one had to. Eyes gazed at the floor, at the ceiling, at Vandien's chair, at anything but Willow. No one moved to comfort her. Vandien suddenly had the perception of her being alone in the room, set apart from all the others. She had been a tool for their politics, her love for Kellich turned to the good of the rebellion. And now she was a tool that had failed, had lost its edge and usefulness. She had not needed to know the true plan, had been more useful in her ignorance. Their letting her perceive the whole thing now could have only one meaning: that she was no longer of any use to them at all. Vandien felt a chill in his belly as he wondered how thorough they were about tidying up loose ends. Willow stood where she was, hugging herself. She was not weeping; it sounded as if all her strength was consumed by breathing. Her shoulders rose and fell with every rasping breath she took.

"It was a stupid plan from the start," he observed, breaking the silence. "Full of holes. Any plan where you don't expect to survive is inherently bad. To think that because a Brurjan took your bribe he would actually do what you paid him for is ignorance. Rather he'd turn around and betray you

for the extra his master would pay him for it. And slow
poison . . . where's the sense in that? So the Duke would
have plenty of time to torment Kellich and make him betray
the rest of you?''

''Kellich wouldn't betray anyone!'' Lacey declared firmly.
''Our cause was sacred to him, his highest purpose in life.
And the slow poison did have a reason; it was to give us time
to negotiate with the Duke. Once he sickened, we'd let him
believe we had a cure for it. A cure he could buy only by a
gradual surrender of power. Our first demand would be that
he disband his Brurjans. Next we would ask that the Duchess
assume control while he recovered. Then we would . . .''

''Idiocy.'' Vandien spoke softly, then glanced around the
room, shaking his head. Farmers and tradesmen, artisans and
tavernkeepers. It was all wrong. Where was the authority
behind the rebellion, the shrewd political players guiding it?
Lacey couldn't even assume he had authority here. It was
wrong, all wrong. ''Look,'' he said gently. ''Everything I've
seen about your Duke and his reign makes your plan laugh-
able. If he thinks he's dying, he's not going to negotiate.
He's going to start a bloodbath in hopes of taking you with
him. What would he have to lose? He'd figure he could
capture one of you and wring the antidote out of him. And the
Brurjans? They have a saying: 'Only a vulture is friends with
the dying.' There'd be no restraints on what they'd do,
disbanded or not. You'd plunge all of Loveran into a nightmare. It would gain you nothing. The Duke might die, but the
Brurjans would pick your bones clean.''

His eyes darted from face to face, hoping for some sign of
understanding, one gleam of enlightenment. There were none.
The rebels stared back at him, their eyes flat and disbelieving.

''It's too late for us to back out now,'' Lacey said softly.

Vandien leaned back, crossed his arms on his chest. ''That's
too bad,'' he said in an equally soft voice. ''Because I believe
it's never too late to avoid stupidity. Even if I believed in
your cause, even if I could go along with something as low as
a poisoned blade, I couldn't go along with the sheer foolishness of this plan. Find yourself another sword.''

''We're prepared to offer you . . .''

''Offer me the moon, I still won't go along with this. By
your own admission, win or lose, I die.''

"You won against Kellich. There's always the chance you could defeat the Duke and . . ."

"Face his Brurjans. No thanks."

"But if some of our men were willing to break in afterwards, help you with the Brurjans so you . . ." Lacey broke off suddenly, making a motion for silence. It wasn't necessary. Everyone had already frozen. From outside came the sound of hoofbeats. All heard the horse reined in outside the door. "Be still," Lacey breathed. He'd gone pale. Strain showed on every face. Except Willow's. There was something akin to a smile on her mouth as she rose, defying Lacey's command, and walked to the door. She eased it open a crack, then glanced back over her shoulder at them.

"It's all right," she said, and then slipped out the door.

"What the hell is that girl up to now?" demanded a rebel of Lacey. The man could only roll his eyes and shrug. But in a few moments Willow came slipping back into the room, bearing an angular object wrapped in a piece of coarse sacking. Her eyes met only Vandien's as she crossed the room. She stopped in front of him. "Are you absolutely certain you won't fight for us?" she asked, poisoned honey in her voice.

"I already told you, Willow." Vandien kept his voice level. "Find yourself another sword."

She swept the remains of his dinner to the floor. Even before the bowl had stopped rolling on the floor, she shook the sacking over the table.

The rapier fell with a clang and rolled toward him. He caught it up more by reflex than by thought, exclaiming with anger over her rough treatment of it. Then he stared at his hand gripping the hawk's hilt, ran his eyes up the blade that still bore traces of Kellich's blood.

"That's the only sword we'll need, Vandien." Willow was coldly sure of herself. "You'll kill the Duke for us. Not because you believe in our cause or for a handful of greasy coins. You'll do it for a chance to see Ki alive again."

He lunged his full measure, and the tip of his rapier found the precise center of the small x he had scratched on the plank wall. The metal of the blade bowed with the impact. A solid thrust that would have emerged from a man's back. Satisfactory sword work. Don't think about anything else, he instructed himself. The sword is all. Don't be distracted. Just practice. Don't wonder how you got from wherever you were before to wherever you are now.

After he had demanded proof that Ki was still alive, they had left him alone in the storage barn or whatever it was. Discordance had been his major impression of the group as they left. Lacey had not liked Willow's little surprise. She had taken control from his hands, but he could not publicly argue with someone who had given him the handle he needed on Vandien. And Vandien had lain down on the cot to ponder his situation. He must have dozed off.

And awakened here. Some kind of a loft, with a peaked ceiling and plank floor. No windows, but light leaking in between the boards. Terrible light for practicing. Tip to x again, blade bowed. Draw back. So they had moved him while he slept. That was all. Yes. Come in, picked him up, dragged him about, and left him here. He, who usually slept light as a cat, had slumbered through it all. Certainly. He lunged again, scored his mark perfectly. He would not be distracted.

He drew back, eyed the distance, tried a balestra. A quick spring from the balls of both feet carried him forward a short distance before he immediately launched into his lunge. It was a distance closing manuver. The tip of his rapier took the mark squarely as he extended his body to its full reach. But as the small jolt of impact reached his hand, his hilt jumped free of his fingers. A numbing cold seemed to streak up his arm, and he watched, incredulous, as his weapon clattered to the floor. He cradled his chilled arm against his belly, rubbing his fingers up and down the raised red welt that marked the passage of Kellich's blade. He bit his lower lip slightly, anticipating pain as he prodded the length of the injury.

Nothing. No feeling at all. He explored his hand, wondering if the hilt had somehow jarred against bone. He found no bruise. There was little sensation at all. He rubbed his arm gently, and with a sudden tingling like ants running over his flesh, it came back to life. Almost. There was still a cold along the bone, a terrible old ache. He was stooping to pick up his rapier when the trap door in the floor of the loft opened behind him. He spun to face it, his blade already challenging the intruder.

The tray emerged first, landed, and was pushed scrapingly along the floor. Willow followed it up, clambering awkwardly over the lip of the door. She glanced at Vandien, then stood and dropped the door into place behind her. Then she turned back to him and stared at him, waiting challengingly. He neither moved nor spoke. "That's your food," she said at last, pointing to the tray.

"And you came up here to tell me that. In case I might not guess it."

She reddened, ran a hand through her spiky red hair. "I came up here to make sure you fully understand the terms of our agreement."

"What is there to misunderstand? I kill the Duke. I die. Ki lives." He kept his voice flat, cold.

"That's right." Willow tried to copy his tone, failed.

"I do have one question. Suppose I refuse, or fail. Who gets to kill Ki?"

The girl looked suddenly rattled. "That . . . that hasn't been discussed. If you do as we say, it never will be."

"I just wondered. I thought that, as you had laid out this plan, you'd be the one to implement it. It obviously wasn't Lacey's doing. In fact, he didn't look pleased about it at all. But you had . . . persuaded Kellich's friends to help you with it, so what could he say? Turn against you and risk splitting his rebellion into factions? Besides, I know how much you hate both of us, after we treated you so badly, our deliberate cruelty to you and all. And I know how dearly you love this cause. I thought perhaps you'd claim the honor of killing Ki. By the way, how do you plan to do it? If I fail or refuse, I mean? Knife? Strangulation? Slow starvation?" He nudged the tray with his foot. "Poison?"

"You're disgusting." Her face was white, but she spoke without stirring.

"No. Your plan is disgusting. You're asking me to murder a man I've never seen before, by treachery, and lose my own life in the process. And that's if everything goes right for us. If it doesn't, I die anyway, and you cold-bloodedly murder my friend."

"The Duke is a tyrant," Willow flared back. "A cold-hearted beast! No method of death is too cruel for him, no treachery too underhanded. Our land groans under his cruelty, our farmers suffer and their children shiver in . . ."

"The harsh rains of the Windsingers. Is that something you have to memorize to join this club? Willow, all winter rain is cold down the back. Neither tyrants nor weather should be taken so personally. If it rains, build a shelter and get out of it. And if you are tyrannized, band together and refuse the tyranny. A consortium of lesser nobles, backed by landowners and merchants . . .''

"Would take too long! We must act now!"

"This land will be awash in blood, then. You have no plans after you kill the Duke. At the end of it, you will only discover that the most dull Brurjan can be a worse tyrant than the most dedicatedly depraved Human.''

"That's how you see it. After all, what do you care? You hitch up the horses and move on; you have no ideals, no dreams of freedom . . .''

"No wish to assassinate anyone. It's not my quarrel, Willow. Nor yours. You aren't in love with the cause, with this rebellion. You were in love with Kellich, and willing to aid the cause to please him. You don't have a stake in this any more than I do. You could walk away from this right now. Knock out the guard downstairs, help me find Ki and free her and we'll go across the border and be gone. Walk away from this whole thing.''

For an instant he thought he had carried her. Her eyes went wide and empty, as if visualizing the unwinding road that led to better places. But then her brows drew down in a frown. "You expect me to be a traitor to all Kellich believed in?" she demanded angrily.

"Why not?" Vandien exploded. "He betrayed everything you believed in! You believed in love, and marriage and children. Life. Kellich believed only in death.'' His voice became harsh. "He wanted to be the glorious hero, not the contented husband. You were just a prop in his pageant, Willow. The beautiful lover left behind to mourn the fallen patriot. To become a symbol of the revolution. And damn you, you're playing it out! He didn't have the courage to live for you, Willow. All he was looking for was an excuse to die!''

Halfway through his words, he regretted them, but they spilled out anyway. Her face went harder and colder, her mismatched eyes becoming the colors of glacier ice. "And you gave him that excuse, didn't you? You made sure of it for him.''

Cold jolted through him, and he didn't know if it came

from his arm or her eyes. He transferred his rapier to his other hand, cradled his injured arm against him. She watched him coldly. And in her eyes . . . what? Satisfaction? Before her eyes went empty again. A dreadful suspicion grew in his mind.

"You promised me proof that Ki is all right. I want to see her."

"No." For the first time he pinned down the uneasiness that had unnerved her. Whenever Ki's name came up, she sidestepped like a nervous filly.

"Why not?"

She hesitated too long. "We've decided it wouldn't be wise. Bringing her here would attract too much attention. We can't spare the men to do it, and . . ."

None of it sounded right. His mind made the leap. "You've already done it, haven't you?" His throat closed up on him suddenly. He felt a light-headedness that made him sway. "She's dead, isn't she?" Of course they'd already killed her. It made more sense. Tidier. Smarter. And soon he'd be dead, and the whole thing neatly wound up.

"No. No, she's fine, and she will be as long as you continue to do as we say." Willow spoke very rapidly. "But you can't see her just now. It's my decision, really. I've seen you two together. She draws strength from you, and would become more difficult to handle. We might have to hurt her. And you'd do any stupid thing for the sake of protecting her."

"Like killing a Duke," he said. His voice sounded distant. He could feel his heart beating in his chest. He knew his face had gone white.

"Eat." Her voice was expressionless, but her eyes betrayed some secret panic of her own. "You should eat that food right away." She crouched by the trap door, tapped on it. "And practice. You'll have to take my word that Ki is alive now. If you want Ki to still be alive tomorrow night, you'd better be at your best."

"I'm not hungry." His words were an empty reflex. Ki was dead. He could read it in Willow's hasty effort to leave, the way she resisted any further talk with him. Ki was dead already. His heartbeat thundered in his ears. Ki was dead, and . . . the last piece suddenly slipped into place. He'd been a fool. The cold emptiness that flooded his heart set off a glaring white light in his mind, mercilessly illuminating everything he had hidden from himself. The cold-blooded logic of their plan was suddenly revealed to him. Very tidy. No loose ends.

"Eat it anyway." She sounded worried.

"I don't like the flavor." He watched her face carefully as he added, "Every damn thing sent up here tastes the same, same herb or spice in the bread, the tea, the stew."

There it was, the tiny widening of her eyes. Her control of her face was good, but too late. "It's a strengthening herb, well known in this part of the world. I'm surprised you don't know of it. We're trying to give you every advantage we can."

He snorted, kept the suspicion from his voice. "Herb lore. Something to bemuse old women after their children have grown up. Three-fourths of it doesn't do what they say, anyway."

The trap door in the floor heaved upward, the closed face of the guard appearing briefly. He glared at the bared rapier in Vandien's hand, then drew back to allow Willow to descend.

"What's it called?" he asked as she reached a leg down for the ladder.

"What?"

"The strengthening herb. What's it called?"

"Oh." She paused—overlong, it seemed to him. "Thwartspite."

His heart sank, his belly went cold. But he kept his voice even. "Think about what I said," he called after her, with little hope that she would, knowing it could make no difference anyway. All things were fixed now, lashed into their courses.

"No. You think about what I said." Her voice floated back to him. "Festival starts tomorrow. The first matches will be just after noon."

He waited until the trap door was shut completely, heard the bolts securing it shot home. Then he allowed himself to sink slowly to the floor, still cradling his arm against himself. Not that it hurt. It felt fine, now.

"Bloodfriend," Ki had said, nudging the small, blue-flowered plant with the toe of her boot. "Cleans poisons from the system, some say." She had stooped to pinch off a handful of the small flowers, shaking her head. "Doesn't really. But it makes a sick animal feel healthy and strong, so it shows well enough to sell. Makes a good poultice for an infection is all I' use it for. Thwartspite, I've heard it called, too.'' He sat very still on the attic floor, remembering the angle of her jaw as she had looked up at him, the way her long hair swung forward of her shoulders, the easy way she flowed up from the ground to stand.

Gone. Everything. Ki was dead. He'd lost his honor in a fight against a fanatic with a poisoned blade. He looked down at the sword in his hand, at the blade that had betrayed him. He considered the puckered seam on his forearm. Not even Kellich had been what he believed. A poisoned blade. Vandien had even played the fool to him. And now, nothing was left. No family. No name. Only himself to think of. Only one last satisfaction to give himself.

''Fight the Duke and die,'' he mused aloud. ''Hell, I might as well. I'm dead already.'' He picked up the bowl of cold soup and sipped at it, tasting the antidote to the poison that already chilled his arm and moved through his body with every beat of his heart. Setting down the bowl, he lifted the mug of lukewarm tea in a mocking toast to the empty room. ''May you all go down with me!'' he declared, and grinned a smile Ki would not have recognized. ''You bastards.'' He drained the mug.

SIXTEEN

Festival time had come to Tekum. Sparkling shards of glass and tiny bells swung from the branches of trees that lined the main street. The sweet high ringing kept time with the light that flashed from the glass whenever the wind stirred their branches. Bright booths had mushroomed in the shade of the trees, selling everything from toys to tonics. The Human population of the town seemed to have increased fourfold, with here and there a T'cheria or a Dene to mark the contrast. The Brurjans, of course, were everywhere. They were not near as numerous as the Humans, but their hulking size and the near-visible violence that shivered around them made them the dominant element of the crowd. There was no uniformity to their battle harness or weapons, but they needed no badges to mark them as the Duke's. Vandien watched them moving effortlessly as the Human crowd parted to give them way, and wondered if the Duke knew what he was doing to give his safety into their hands. But instead he asked Lacey, "What's the occasion for this festival?"

Lacey snorted. "The Duke ordained it, twelve years back. It's to commemorate his coming to power."

"Why hold it in Tekum?"

Lacey's eyes squeezed shut briefly. "We had a militia, then. Stationed here, along the caravan route, to keep down robbers and such. Young fool in charge rallied to the Duchess's cause. Duke brought his Brurjans in. Didn't take long." Lacey nodded to the long line of trees. "Wasn't a tree here

190

that wasn't swinging a body, and a hell of a lot of them had two.''

The high singing of the bells became suddenly a mocking carillon to Vandien's ears. "So this is how he reminds you, every year, that you depend on his largesse to survive. And that even the best of you will never better him at swords.''

Lacey looked at him in bewilderment. "I never thought of it that way before,'' he muttered disgruntledly. "It's just a thing the Duke does. Very typical of him. Doesn't matter why he does it, anyway. It's our only chance at him, that's all that counts. Come on, now. The others will already be gathering. Duke always holds it on the threshing floor in Merp's barn.''

Vandien nodded curtly and followed him through the press of folk. He walked behind Lacey, letting the heavier man forge a pathway for them. As he passed through the crowd, eyes swung to him, held an instant, then darted away. Damn fools. Was there anyone in this town who wasn't in on the plot?

A manic grin settled on his face, and he took to meeting all eyes for the fun of watching them widen and then jerk aside. He felt good. The realization of that startled him for a moment, and then he felt the full impact of it. Damn, he felt great. These bastards had plundered his soul, had taken from him all that he had ever valued. He had nothing left to save. Not even his own life. Ki had gone, and her passing had left less than nothing within him. The gentler parts of his nature had died with her, leaving him only the hard and sharp to do with. The impulsiveness that had always characterized his decisions was now in complete control. It was a heady feeling.

He was totally aware of his body, his skin tingling and tightening at the slightest brush of a stranger's cloak. His heart was pumping steadily in his chest and he was cognizant of each surging beat, counting out the moments of his life's passing. He wondered if it were the poison affecting him so, or the stimulation of the Thwartspite. Perhaps it was only his knowledge that he could die today, that this blue sky might be the last he would walk under, that these smells of dust and sweat and food cooking might be the last ones he would breathe. How slow was the slow poison from Kellich's blade? Another handful of days? A few hours? He looked out over the crowd and wondered how many of these folk were also squandering their last day, blissfully unaware of it. For some, he'd make it certain.

He had not been paying attention to where they were going. The threshing barn loomed up before them. The structure was little more than a roof supported by massive timbers and a smoothly bricked floor. A gathering place as much as a threshing grounds, for dancing and village celebrations. Today it had been swept clear. At one end of the barn, a raised dais of new wood held a single massive chair. Nothing would block the Duke's view. Common spectators had spread their cloaks or mats on the ground and sat on them, eating and drinking and talking loudly to one another. Contestants were scattered over the smooth floor, some standing nervously or idly, others limbering muscles or showily practicing for the onlookers. Vandien ran practiced eyes over them. Only four struck him as competent, and two others as possibly dangerous. The others looked to be tavern louts and barnyard boasters, their weapons cheap bazaar blades or Grandfather's ancient shoulder-wrencher. He frowned slightly, knowing that going against them would be more like fighting with staves than true fencing. He turned to Lacey, speaking low.

"The man in green there; tell me about him."

Lacey glanced away. "Kurtis. One of ours. He'll make you look good. You needn't fear him. He's under orders not to be much of a challenge to you."

"He wouldn't be in any case. Look how he drags his feet. Those two, warming up together . . . are they yours also?"

"Yes. Students of Kellich's. Blume and Trask. Blume's the one with the lace. Again, you've nothing to worry about. They've both been instructed to lose in such a way as to make you look very good." Lacey spoke reassuringly.

"I wasn't worrying, Lacey. But the one in the boots should, if he always locks his elbow like that. The woman there, in the red silk blouse?"

"Another of ours. She's good, but she won't hurt you."

"She moves well, but without inspiration. Kellich taught her?"

"I believe so. Vandien, stop fretting. Everything has been arranged; you cannot lose."

A grin split Vandien's face, tugged at his scar. "Unless I win. Two more, Lacey, and then leave me alone. There's a man, standing quiet now, beside the third timber. Black beard, grey at his temples . . . see him?''

"Damn!" Lacey swore fervently. "He was warned away, several times. We told him there was bigger game afoot. But his wife is with child, again, and all his sheep went down this spring with the wobblies. Farrick's after a purse of gold, to get him through the winter; but he's more likely to go home to a smoking barn for not listening to us.''

"Leave him alone," Vandien warned him, and his voice was flat and ugly. His dark eyes burned into Lacey and the man flinched from their depth.

"All right," he said softly. "But be careful of him. He's good.''

"I know." This was one of the ones he had mentally marked as dangerous. Farrick moved with quiet control and beautiful balance. He was older than Vandien, and bigger. He'd have a longer reach, and a damn good reason to fence his best. One to be careful of. "And her?" Vandien asked, nodding toward the other contestant he had marked as dangerous. "What do you know about her?"

Lacey glared at the woman who was tucking her long pale braids up under a red cap. "She's as crazy as a rabid vixen. There's no reasoning with that girl. You may have to kill her to get past her. She's another one was warned away, but didn't choose to listen.''

"I'll decide that," Vandien said quietly. He was watching her face. She was nervous, but a fervent hate burned in her blue eyes. "Who is she?''

"Darnell. She used to fence with her brother.''

"And?''

"Last year was a hard one for their family. Just before harvest, their grainfield took the crust and had to be burned. Her brother came here to try his luck with the sword, to see if he could win gold from the Duke.''

"And?" Vandien prodded again.

"And he won the medallion instead. She's gone mad, Vandien. Darnell will do anything to get her own chance at the Duke.''

He nodded to Lacey, watching her. Darnell was small and whip-quick. Her face was too strong to be called pretty, and her eyes burned with an intensity that cleared the area around her. She glanced at him suddenly and their eyes locked.

Nothing left to lose, they agreed, and she sent him a quick smile. Dangerous.

He left Lacey then, striding out onto the threshing floor. It was as if the main actor had just stepped onto the stage for the play. The crowd's noises hushed briefly, and then rose in intensity. Vandien ignored them. He cleared his mind of them, and the world became an empty place. He might have been on a hillside beside Ki's old wagon as he saluted his shadow and began stretching out his muscles. He closed his eyes, and for a moment he smelled woodsmoke and tea and horses, felt the clean breeze on his face, and heard Ki exclaim, half in annoyance, half in admiration, as the bound point of his practice foil found her. For an instant the pain-loss jolted through him, and he wished he were wearing something of hers, some token . . . but no. He did not fight today as a man fought in honor of his lady, but as a man fights who has nothing left to defend, least of all honor. The only purpose of his blade today was to take as many with him as he could.

Then the silence in his heart was suddenly silence in his ears as well. He drew himself up, turned to see where all heads were turning.

Six Brurjans afoot, in black and silver battle harness, flanking a great black stallion whose mane and tail had been plaited with silver wire. Silver weighted the bridle on the horse's small savage head and silver winked on the light saddle. Black and silver was the man astride him. Of black silk were his garments, and the armor he wore was black leather and silver, styled after the Brurjan fashion but scaled down to a Human. His hair was black, and black his beard, but his eyes were silver grey in his weathered face.

The Duke stepped from his horse's back onto the dais. He stood a moment, looking out over the assembled folk. His eyes raked them over, discarding the spectators quickly before sorting the contestants before him. They lingered a moment on Darnell, sneered briefly at one posturing braggart, and then swept past Vandien. Too swiftly. Vandien felt the marking of their passage, knew then that the Duke already knew all, but would play out the charade for whatever reason. And so he drew his rapier, clasped the hawk's talons in his, and saluted the Duke formally with his blade. Others around him noticed, and copied his gesture, but did not realize the depth of its meaning. Vandien knew that his personal bout with this man had already begun.

They drew lots for their first matches. Vandien listened with only half an ear as someone shouted out the rules for the contest. Lacey had already told him. The Duke liked his blood-sports. A touch was a touch that drew blood. The Duke decided when a bout was complete, although a man could acknowledge himself beaten and completely retire from the contest. Other than that, the bout continued until the Duke said it could stop.

A man in a red sash examined the cube of wood in Vandien's palm, then gestured him toward a loutish youth with a skim of child's beard on his face. His first opponent. Other pairs were forming up, saluting the Duke, receiving his nod of consent, and saluting one another. Already two bouts were in progress.

Vandien moved to face his opponent on the strip allotted to them. The boy had a decent sword that he held as if it were a poker. He'd tire quickly, Vandien decided, and turned to face the Duke. He made the formal salute to him, tip of weapon toward the floor, then up with the guard almost touching his chin, then weapon extended at shoulder level. Vandien held the final stance until the Duke had acknowledged him with a nod, then turned and gave the same salute to his opponent. The boy, baffled, mimicked him awkwardly, grinning in an embarrassed way. "Begin," commanded the red-sashed man, and the boy leaped at Vandien, swinging his weapon as if it were a cudgel. Vandien caught the heavier blade on his own, diverted it, stepped in to dab the point of his rapier into the boy's chest and stepped out again. The boy looked startled. His weapon sagged to point at Vandien's knees as he clapped his free hand to his chest. He looked at his bloodied palm in amazement, then glanced up at Vandien as if for confirmation. Vandien shrugged lightly, the point of his rapier never wavering as it menaced the boy at eye level.

"I'm done," said the boy, and turned aside abruptly to push past the red-sashed man and out through the crowd that ringed the threshing-barn now. Vandien turned to find the Duke's eyes already on him. He could not read them at this distance. Pushing down a chill of foreboding, he shot the man an insolent grin. The Duke startled slightly, then leaned forward, spoke a word to a red-sashed man standing before

the dais. He in turn hurried forward to whisper to the red-
sashed man who had supervised Vandien's first bout, then
darted past him to signal to two fencers that their bout was
over. One contestant he tapped on the shoulder, and then
jerked his head toward Vandien.

As the man came toward him, Vandien recognized him as
one of Lacey's men. He had cast aside the green cloak that
had earlier distinguished him, but Kurtis was still dragging
his feet when he moved. He tipped Vandien a wink, then
mouthed the words, "Don't worry." Vandien felt something
within him grow harder and colder. Salute the Duke, receive
his nod, and turn. His lips smiled at Kurtis as he made him a
careful salute. "Begin," said Red-sash, and the two blades
met. The man was heavy with his blade as well as his feet,
and the condescending expression on his face told all that he
was holding back his skill to allow Vandien an easy win. His
weapon replied conservatively to Vandien's testing, as if he
were an instructor trying to encourage a sluggish student. For
a few movements Vandien pushed him, trying to win something more than a token response to his attacks. The man was
scarcely fencing at all, more like he was standing with a
broom, waiting to be stuck so he could concede. With a snort
of disgust, Vandien disengaged his blade, let the tip droop to
point at Kurtis's ankle, and hover there. Kurtis's eyes darted
to meet his in amazement and dismay. "So make me look
good," Vandien challenged him softly, and waited.

The blood drained from Kurtis's face, and Vandien suddenly understood. Kurtis was perfectly willing to be stuck, to
take an injury to make Vandien look good. He was not
willing to put forth any effort that might make himself look
good to the Duke. The last thing he wanted was to be a
contender for the Duke's medallion. He made a halfhearted
stab at Vandien, an attack that bragged more of nervousness
than skill. There wasn't going to be any real challenge from
this man, Vandien decided, and moved in with an effortless
parry and a riposte that removed the lobe of his left ear.
Before Kurtis could react, he was back in guard position. He
smiled at him.

Kurtis's free hand shot up to his ear. He winced at his own
touch, looked at his blood, and then glanced up at Vandien
with outrage in his eyes. Kurtis let out a bellow like a struck
bullock, thrust, and charged. His obvious intent was a flèche.

His objective was to move past Vandien, and as he passed in front of him, to take him with a chest thrust. He was not prepared for Vandien's blade to parry his neatly out of line and drop in to allow Kurtis to skewer himself on Vandien's blade. Arterial blood was drenching his shirt when Kurtis looked down. "I wasn't supposed to die," he said with surprised dismay. He fell, slipping free of Vandien's point. Vandien dropped to one knee beside him. "Neither was Ki," Vandien whispered coldly. He rose easily, paced away from the man and stood once more in readiness at the end of his strip.

He stood, watching the people who rushed forward to cluster about Kurtis, to lift him and carry him awkwardly away. He felt nothing. Not even satisfaction. So one of them was dead for Ki. It wasn't enough. He caught Lacey staring at him with burning eyes; he returned the look flatly, letting no sign of recognition cross his face. He glanced up at the Duke.

The Duke leaned forward in his chair; his chin was in his hand, and he was staring at Vandien. Perplexity rivaled amazement on his features. He gestured to a Human in a dark cloak, who drew near to hear the Duke's whisper. The man replied vigorously, shaking his head and insisting on something. The Duke waved him off with impatience. He was, Vandien decided, beginning to distrust his spies' reports. If Vandien was the rebellion's man, why had he killed his ally? The Duke looked back at him and for an instant their eyes locked. Vandien smiled, and cleaned the sharpened tip and edge of his rapier on his sleeve. When he glanced up again, Darnell stood at the opposite end of his strip.

He studied her, trying to be cold, but knowing he didn't want to fight her. Small, quick, and so full of anger. He saw the truth of Lacey's assessment. He might have to kill her to get past her. The sudden knowledge that he didn't want to kill her filled him, and even as they were making their salutes he racked his mind for alternatives. A meat wound wasn't going to stop this one, nor even a slash across the face. She'd fight as long as she could hold her blade. . . .

Red-sash nodded and she was on him, inside the reach of Vandien's blade and coming after him. Damn, she was quick! He found himself retreating, standing more upright and fighting her from the outside, reaching over and around as he tried to attain a more threatening position. With a clash of steel she beat his blade aside, was once more inside his range. As he brought his guard back down, he could almost see her decision cross her face. A coupe. Stupid. A harsh answer to his dilemma came to mind, and before he had time to weigh it, she was moving. Her blade lifted in an attempt to go over his and dart in. He closed his mind on the decision, let his own blade shoot in. His found flesh first, entering the back of her arm just above the wrist. He felt his point slip between the two bones of her arm, then emerge. He heard the clatter of her weapon on the bricks, hoped it was over. But no—with her free hand she groped after her weapon, her eyes full only of her fury. She hissed at him in her pain and hatred, making it seem he had spitted some small, savage animal on his rapier. Neither blood nor pain was going to stop this one. Disabling her was his only alternative to killing her, for the Duke was making no move to put an end to the match. So he would have to do it himself. The decision was made. It seemed to Vandien that it was someone else who levered his blade between the bones of her arm, bringing pressure down until he felt the clean snap of the smaller bone.

She screamed, pain driving the intensity of her hate from her face. She fell, jerking her arm free of his blade, forgetting her weapon as she clutched at her arm. She'd fence no more today. Perhaps never again. His stomach lurched within him as he turned, moved to the end of the strip. She never saw the grave salute he accorded her as someone helped her stand and guided her from the strip. But Lacey did. Vandien glanced away from the man's sickened face. He had set these wheels in motion, not Vandien. Let him live with what they crushed; at least the girl was alive.

He glanced to the Duke, who was again in consultation with a red-sashed official. Three other bouts were still in progress, one involving two young men who seemed bent on seeing how much noise they could make with their weapons. The Duke didn't spare them a glance, not even when one finally managed a shoulder-smashing hit on his fellow. Plainly he was content to let them battle it out until one conceded. Vandien watched them idly until Red-sash spoke behind him.

"This way, please," he said politely, and something in the way he avoided touching Vandien put him in mind of the crowd parting before the Brurjans. He wondered if he shim-

mered with violence and disdain as they did. Within, he felt
only the thundering of his own heart, and wondered if it was
the work of the poison or the antidote that held the poison at
bay. The rapidity of its beating pushed him on, hurrying him
to work as much destruction upon his destroyers as he could
before their poison stopped him. He followed Red-sash across
the threshing floor, felt the eyes of the Duke following him.
He didn't condescend to notice the Duke.

Red-sash gestured, and Vandien took his place opposite his
new opponent. He had a few moments to observe him; it was
another of Lacey's foils, the one in lace. He had noticed him
earlier, a dandyish, prancing man who obviously loved playing
to the crowd. He had reminded Vandien of a brightly feathered cockerel strutting through the barnyard.

He didn't look so jaunty now. He was not watching Vandien,
but staring across the floor to where someone was only now
retrieving Darnell's blade. He scratched his nose with the
back of one belaced wrist; not an elegant gesture. And when
Blume turned to face Vandien, he could almost see the sweat
pop out on the man's upper lip. He looked at Vandien as he
might look at a rabid street cur—something ordinarily despised had suddenly become dangerous. Vandien ignored him
as he saluted the Duke, marked the snide challenge on the
Duke's face; he kept his own expressionless. Blume's salute
to Vandien was sloppy, as if the man could not quite make
his blade stop where it should. Fear was spoiling his posturing. The tip of his weapon trembled as their blades met.

"Begin," said Red-sash, and Blume lunged, then jumped
back as if he had surprised himself. Vandien replied to his
attack, and the man parried wildly, his wagging blade reminding Vandien of an ecstatic hound's tail. He leaped back
as he did so, taking himself out of Vandien's reach. Vandien
paused where he was, brought his blade up to challenge and
stayed there. Obviously waiting for Blume to regain his nerve
and resume the bout. Blume stared at him, and a flush rose
over his face. Vanity warred with fear; he took a moment to
straighten his cuffs, shot a falsely bright smile to someone
among the spectators, and then brought his own blade up and
stepped back into the match. But Vandien's first feint was
met with another of his wild parries, and then a beat that
knocked his blade aside.

Blume charged in, meeting Vandien chest to chest. "Have

you gone mad, man? I'm one of Lacey's men! You don't have to . . .''

Vandien's free hand pushed him off, and as he went back he brought his rapier down to cut swiftly, opening a slash beside Blume's nose and down his upper lip. He saw a flash of teeth before the blood covered them. ''Keep your distance,'' he said coldly, and fell back on guard.

He watched the realizations follow one another swiftly as they crossed Blume's face: he was bleeding, it hurt, his face was ruined, this man wants to kill me. And Vandien was ready when Blume suddenly decided he had better end this quickly, even if it meant being noticed by the Duke. And the Duke was paying attention, leaning forward on his chair, his face both alarmed and puzzled. Every one of Vandien's acts had been done with intent to cause great injury. The reports he had received on this man had obviously left something out. The Duke did not like unknown factors. He scowled as Blume plunged back into the bout.

Blume was fighting energetically now, but without finesse. Blood had drenched the front of his shirt, soaking the lace but leaving the face above it more pale than the linen had been. Pain and dizzying fear were making him careless. He dashed in with a sloppy attempt at a doublé, attacking toward the back of Vandien's body. He dropped under Vandien's guard so that his blade could move in as Vandien parried. He got in under Vandien's blade and knew brief satisfaction as his weapon gouged a ragged cut over the top of Vandien's hip. But the satisfaction was cut short by the tip of Vandien's rapier slipping quietly into the soft spot at the base of his throat.

For an instant they stood frozen in tableau, Blume's terrified eyes meeting Vandien's cold ones over their blades. Then Vandien withdrew his tip as smoothly as he had entered it, and Blume fell backward, clutching at his throat as he screamed a fine spray of blood.

Vandien stood still for an instant, waiting to feel satisfaction. The moment passed and he still stood, waiting to feel anything. But there was nothing. Only the thundering of his heart in his ears, and now the pain, hot and sickening, flooding up from his hip. He felt himself sway. It took an effort to sheathe his rapier; the tip wavered and circled the opening of the sheath, and went in with a smear of Blume's blood on the leather. The hammering of his heart in his ears had become a constant sound like the rushing of wind. Darkness edged in on him, narrowing his vision of the world. He felt something bump against his thigh. He glanced down, watched his sword arm hanging by his side. With his good hand he lifted it to his chest, held it against himself. It was like holding a stick of kindling. No feeling left in it at all. Damn.

He forced his eyes to stay open, lifted his head. A cluster of people stood before him. They were lifting Blume to carry him away. He couldn't tell if the man was alive or dead. Suddenly Lacey broke free of the group, stood before him. ''Bastard's whelp by a she-cur!'' he grated.

Vandien forced a smile. ''Do you really think you should be talking to me? The Duke's watching.''

Lacey spun about, looked up. The Duke nodded congenially to them both. Lacey whitened, began to walk away.

''Not so fast.'' Vandien spoke softly, but he knew his voice carried. Lacey halted. ''I need more thwartspite. It's wearing off. Without it, I'll never get as far as the Duke. It will all have been for nothing.''

''Die in your tracks,'' said Lacey, and walked away.

So. He had gambled and lost. He had thought Lacey would be so attached to his cause that he would give him the thwartspite to keep him going, in spite of what he had done. He wouldn't. So. Vandien felt himself sway again. So get off the floor, or die here. Someone took his arm. It was hard to see in the darkness, and he didn't recognize her until he heard her speak to Red-sash. ''No. He's not withdrawing. We're just going to staunch the bleeding on his hip, and then he'll be back . . . with the Duke's permission.''

It must have been given by a nod or some other sign, for Willow knelt by him and pressed a flat pad of bandages to his hip. It sent a wave of red pain coursing through him, and the darkness became two shades blacker. ''Take what I give you. Chew it, but don't swallow it. Hold it in your cheek.'' She fumbled at his good hand, and he had to let go of his sword arm to take what she gave him. He felt his own arm fall and thud against him lifelessly. He received what felt like a rolled cylinder of leaves, tucked them into his mouth, bit down on them. Acridity flooded his mouth and his body responded with a wave of saliva. He swallowed with difficulty, tongued the package of herbs down between his cheek and gums. His eyes suddenly watered, and his vision cleared. He looked down to find Willow still kneeling beside him. The cloth she held to his hip was heavy with blood.

"Stabbed in the ass. How humiliating." The herbs in his cheek made him mumble.

"Worse for Blume, I imagine," she replied coldly.

"If he'd fought decently, I wouldn't have had to do it. Nor the other one. They were making a bloody farce of your plot."

"But you would have, anyway."

"Probably. For Ki."

She looked up at him curiously. "How did you know?"

"I just knew."

She refolded the pad, held a fresh spot to the gash on his hip. The bleeding was slowing. "It wasn't my idea," she said slowly. "I really meant to let her go, alive. But when I went out there with food, she was . . . gone. One of the others did it, Vandien. I swear. They were the only ones who knew where she was. I'm . . . I'm sorry. I know what she meant to you."

"No, you don't." He stepped clear of her, no longer able to abide her touch. Her lie rang too clearly in his ears. He remembered her curse when Kellich died: "May you know loss such as mine." He felt the now familiar tingling in his arm, flexed his fingers, rotated the wrist. A wave of euphoria and incredible energy washed through him, and he felt the tempo of his heart pick up. He took a deep breath, felt his head clear even more. He rolled his shoulders, felt no more than the heaviness of having fenced all afternoon. His spirits lifted, and he felt strong, skilled and arrogant. A tiny voice within him suddenly wondered if this were his true feelings, or only an effect of the thwartspite. He pushed the question aside, and instead asked Willow, "How much longer do I have?"

She got slowly to her feet. She didn't ask what he meant. "I don't know. It depends on too many things. And you've taken so much thwartspite, it changes everything. . . ."

"What do you guess, then?"

She looked aside from him. "Late tonight. Early tomorrow."

"Before noon tomorrow, though?"

She nodded stiffly. "I'm sorry. If I had it all to do over again, I wouldn't."

He shrugged, winced at the pull against his hip. Damn, that was going to hurt. But not for long.

"You'll still kill the Duke for us?" He couldn't tell if she was begging him to do it, or begging to know why he'd do it. He shrugged carefully. "Why not? I don't have anything else planned for the rest of my life. May as well keep busy."

He turned away from her before she could say anything more. As she left the threshing floor, he was surprised to notice that the red-sashes were ending all the bouts, were clearing all the contestants from the floor. Had the Duke already reached his decision? He glanced up to find the man watching him. For a few moments they regarded one another in silence. Vandien felt himself being measured, and held himself steady under the Duke's scrutiny. Then, with the slightest nod of his head, the Duke indicated another man standing quietly at the other end of the threshing floor. As they began the long walk toward one another, Vandien measured him.

Farrick. Mature. Good reason for wanting this fight, but not filled with anger or ideological passion. A cool man, a conservative man. Beautiful balance. A dangerous man. For a moment, Vandien tried to become his opponent. What did he want? Not to win, not to face the Duke's sword. Would he fence sloppily in this bout, deliberately lose to Vandien? Not likely, after he had seen Vandien killing and maiming today. No, Farrick must still fight his best if he wished to emerge from this bout unscathed. He'd have to fight his best, and still not try to win. For a moment Vandien pondered the man's dilemma, visualized what he would do in Farrick's place. And what does he think of me? Vandien speculated. Probably judges from what he's seen so far. I've been fighting like a tavern brawler, up against these culls from the hack-and-slash school of fencing. So Farrick would be expecting wild aggression and crude attacks. Vandien permitted himself a small smile. But Farrick did not know Vandien was already a dying man. Farrick would not be expecting Vandien to fight to win. So. Farrick might be in for a small surprise.

They saluted the Duke and then one another. Silence lowered itself over the throng. No one doubted that this match would decide; for one a purse, for one a medallion of death. They assumed the stance, and a red-sash said softly, "Begin."

They moved with the grace of dancers as they tested one

another, and Vandien saw Farrick's eyes widen briefly as he reappraised him. And Vandien, too, was having to do some reevaluating of his man. Improbably, almost impossibly, this man fought in the classic Harperian style, and somewhere, sometime, he had been instructed by a master. For an instant the room wavered around Vandien, and he was a skinny youth again, this same blade in his hand, and Fol was propelling him backward, his training foil making clean *tick, tick, ticks* against Vandien's defending rapier. No screaming of sawing metal, no wild parries, not a degree of motion more than was necessary in wrist or elbow. Vandien found himself smiling and responding to that memory, saw an answering twitch at the corner of Farrick's mouth.

So let them see, these stick-swingers and scythe-fencers, how a gentleman did it. Let them see the root from which the other schools of fencing had sprung. The rhythm was set, point control was absolute, and they moved through their opening challenges like two dancers in perfect grace and counterpoint. Vandien felt he was getting the man's measure; he would rely on finesse and maturity, would wait for Vandien to become overeager and make some childish error. Fol. How many times had he tried the youthful Vandien that way? Yes, and won that way, too, he reminded himself. He leashed his eagerness.

The Duke was watching. He could not spare a glance, but did not need to. He could feel the man on the edge of his seat, almost hear him muttering to himself. He had never seen the like of this before, and never will again. The old Harperian masters are dead and their students scattered to the winds. Yet here, in this most unlikely of places, two have come together, and blades move as they were meant to, in rhythm and timing, passing by no more than a whisper, the clean *tick, tick, tick* of their metal as they touch in conservative parries, the honest thrusts that are swiftly turned and pass their targets by no more than the wingspan of a fly. It is beauty, and his heart sings with it, living only in this now to perpetuate this pattern.

But it cannot last forever. Vandien's shoulder is burning, his arm is leaden, his blade has the weight of a pitchfork, and he feels the tiny twitching trembles of muscles forced to work too long. He sets his teeth, firming up his arm, and begins to continually press Farrick. The man is older, he must tire soon. But Farrick smiles a small smile and lies back, accepting everything that Vandien offers, forcing Vandien to initiate all attacks. Just like Fol, damn him, and for a moment he knows the same outraged frustration of his childhood. His hip hurts suddenly, almost blindingly, and he knows he has little time left, that he must force something. He begins to increase the tempo of his attacks, and Farrick's small smile widens as he reads Vandien. But Vandien can also see the sweat beading on Farrick's face, the strain that drags at his mouth, and his ripostes are wider of the mark. There is something . . . it itches in Vandien's mind. Something Fol showed him once, a long time ago, something he has not tried in ages, has never had to try. . . .

Vandien lunges full out, continues to fence. The new posture briefly confuses Farrick, but he adapts to it, and the exchanges continue. And every moment Vandien is testing, feeling, waiting—and there it is, a slight weakening of his opponent's wrist.

Vandien lunges to his full extent, and Farrick replies, thinking he has him, but Vandien is no longer there. His free hand drops to the floor and braces him, carrying his body off to the side, and at the same time he lifts his weapon and his blade rises up, the tip to Farrick's throat, not entering the skin but dimpling it, and there is plenty of thrust left in Vandien's arm to put it through if he desires. If he wants to kill.

There is a silence. They are frozen at the center of the universe, in this moment, in this place. Their eyes are locked. Farrick stands still, the tip of Vandien's rapier pressing his throat, and Vandien is motionless, his body suspended just off the floor, supported by one hand, one knee bent and the other leg straight as he looks up at him. Then Farrick speaks. "Fol's Thrust. My old master spoke of it, but I've never seen it done before." A slow smile splits his beard. "Damn me, I'm dead!" He puts his head back and laughs aloud.

And time began to have meaning once more. The tip of Farrick's blade slowly drooped to touch the floor. He stamped once, then drew himself erect. He stepped back, and gave Vandien time to stand, to step back. And then he accorded him the salute one gives to the victor, the meticulous lifting of the sword and the grave smile of acknowledgement. Farrick sheathed his blade, turned and began to walk away.

"Wait!" The Duke's voice rang out over the assemblage,

breaking the silence that had held so many so long. He was on his feet, standing at the edge of the dais. His face was flushed, his eyes wide in his face. His mouth was slightly ajar still. He looked, Vandien thought, for all the world like a child who had been delighted by the seemingly impossible antics of a hedge-wizard.

Farrick halted, turned to the Duke. "I concede the match."

"As is right." The Duke looked down at a red-sashed man who waited before the dais. "To that one, the purse." He lifted his eyes then, and they pierced Vandien with their anticipation and dread. "To the other, the medallion. And bring him to my chambers this evening. We dine together."

Vandien lifted his rapier in a slow salute that marked the second phase of their bout.

SEVENTEEN

They put Goat on Dellin's mule. Even after the boy awoke he seemed dazed, and sat blinking stupidly as a half-wit at anything that was said to him. His eyes didn't open all the way. His mouth hung slightly ajar and he stared at Ki's moving lips when she spoke to him, asking him if he felt all right.

"I . . . think so. I am not sure."

Even his words came slowly. Ki turned to Dellin. "Did I hurt him that badly?" she asked anxiously.

"No. What you see is not the result of what you did, but the result of what his parents did to him. He isn't accustomed to having to listen to words and sort out their meanings. He's grown up listening to feelings and responding to what people felt toward him rather than what they said. Now, he has to learn. And more than that, he has to learn to feel his own feelings about things, without leeching the feelings of those around him." The mule clopped steadily along between them, with Goat making no response to Dellin's comments about him. "Blinding him would have been a gentler thing for me to do to him," Dellin commented sourly.

Silence spun out between them as Ki tried to comprehend the emptiness that must surround Goat now. The boy was alone inside his skull for the first time in his life. She glanced up at him; his eyes were fixed on the far horizon, and they were as empty and placid as an infant's. She found herself going back in her mind, trying to remember not what she had said, but all that she had felt toward Goat in the time they had been together. She winced. And how had it been for him those days in the wagon when she had despised him and Vandien had wanted to kill him? The sudden shame she felt weighted her lungs.

"Useless to regret it," Dellin observed. "Better to forget it. I will never understand the penchant Humans have for dwelling on past unpleasantness, and letting it shape the course of their future lives."

"Do you always listen in on what people are feeling?" Ki asked, trying to keep annoyance out of her voice. Not that it would keep him from knowing she felt it.

"Only on those I regard as my patients," Dellin replied calmly.

"I don't regard myself as needing healing, of Jore or any other kind," Ki observed, and this time she let her voice carry her irritation. "The only thing I need from you is your help in finding Vandien."

"You don't wish to resolve this mixture of feelings you have for him, before you rejoin him? Don't you think you should examine why you feel so much anger with someone you care about so deeply? And what about the self-anger and denial you are constantly dealing with? Why does it distress you so much that you depend upon him, and why do you constantly battle to conceal from him and yourself the depths of your feelings for him?"

"No." Ki's voice was flat.

"No to what?" Dellin asked, and she was pleased to notice a note of surprise in his voice.

"No to all of it. I don't need to understand what I feel for him; I've lived with it for years, and it seems to work well for both of us. If it isn't broken, don't fix it, my father used to tell me. No, Dellin, the most I want from you is to know where he is, so I can catch up with him. And then I have to find my horses and wagon. And find a way to put my life back on a paying basis."

"Do you realize how you hide from yourself behind these prosaic worries? Listen to how you say you must find him before he gets into trouble. Aren't you really feeling that you must find him before you get into trouble you can't face without him?"

The damn mule was too slow. At the rate they were moving, it would be nightfall before they even got to the outskirts of Tekum. Then, even if Dellin could take her straight to Vandien, there she'd be, in a hostile town full of Brurjans without even enough coins for a meal, let alone a room for the night. And how the hell was she ever going to track down her team and wagon? She turned to Dellin to ask him if he had any ideas, only to find he was already looking at her, his dark eyes full of pity.

"Sooner or later, you will have to deal with your feelings."

"Then it will have to be later. Dellin, once we get into Tekum, is there any way you can trace my horses and . . ."

But he was already shaking his head before her sentence was half begun. "I can't go into Tekum with you," he said gently.

"Then how am I going to find . . ."

"You'll find him. If you just trust yourself, you'll probably go straight to him. But in any case, I can't take Goat into Tekum. It's Festival there, and the streets are full of noise and emotion, too much for me to handle, let alone an inexperienced and sensitive child like Gotheris."

"Then why are you bothering going this direction at all, if you aren't going to help me find him?" Ki demanded bitterly.

He shrugged. "Duty, perhaps. I hate to see a person as confused as you are go floundering off into a dangerous place alone. Gratitude that you managed to bring Gotheris to me, even if you still owe us the rest of the trip. But most probably, curiosity. I would meet this Vandien, to whom you bond so tightly and who has left such a deep impression upon Gotheris. When we get to the outskirts of Tekum, I will find a safe place for us and let you go on alone."

"Wonderful," Ki said sourly. "Thank you very much."

"I don't understand," Gotheris interrupted.

"You mean her words do not match her face?" Dellin suggested.

The boy nodded.

"Now you are beginning to learn," Dellin said, and smiled at him. And the smile that Gotheris returned him was finally the boy's own.

Dusk was falling when they reached the outskirts of Tekum. The scattered farms were beginning to be smaller and closer to one another. Darkness was gathering around them, but in the town ahead yellow torches lit the streets and the dim sounds of merrymaking reached Ki's ears. Ki could make out the tree-lined streets that she and Vandien had passed down what seemed like ages ago. Their branches seemed to sparkle. She rubbed her eyes. Dellin stopped and the mule halted beside them. He peered about in the darkness, then pointed and spoke.

"There is a shed over there. The boy and I will spend the night there. It doesn't feel as if anyone is at home in the house. You will come back to meet us here, in the morning?"

Ki shrugged, feeling tired, frustrated and angry. "I don't know. I suppose. Can't you give me any idea of where to look for Vandien?"

"I know no more than you know yourself, if you would only listen to yourself. He's here, somewhere. The link between you is not a thread that can be followed, but is more like the echo of your voice bouncing back to you. Go feeling for him; you'll find him."

"I suppose so." Ki tried to keep the skepticism out of her voice. She must be crazy to even believe this man at all. Maybe she was only going looking for Vandien because she so desperately wanted to believe he was alive. To keep the darkness at bay.

Dellin led the mule away, across the pasture. She listened to the animal's splayed hooves crunching through the dry grasses until their silhouettes merged with the darkness. Then she moved on. The night seemed blacker now that she walked alone, but she found herself keeping to the side of the road and listening for other footsteps. Yet when she did encounter other folk, they paid little mind to her. She had reached the tree-lined street by then, and could make out the shards of glass and tiny bells that caught the yellow light of the torches and shimmered with it. The people who moved through the streets behaved as if it were full daylight, and a market day at that. A suppressed excitement seemed to shiver through the night air. Folk spoke to one another in rushed whispers, interspersed with much laughter. Ki wondered what the energy flowing through the night portended, then pushed the thought from her mind. As long as it kept other folk busy, it was all to her good. She moved like a ghost through the streets, untouched by the hilarity of Festival, keeping to the shadows, seeking only a man with dark hair and dark eyes and a narrow, crooked smile that kept her heart alive.

She passed cooking stalls, smelled the tantalizing odors of

dough cooking in hot fat, of spiced meat and simmering gravy. Her stomach snapped at her throat angrily. Well, no help for it. She should have asked Dellin if he had any coins. She certainly didn't, not on her, and the wagon would certainly have been looted. She tried to worry about her destitute status, couldn't. Find the damn man first; after that, the other would fall into place. Or it wouldn't.

She found herself standing in the innyard of the Two Ducks. It was crowded tonight with wagons and carts. Riding animals, their bits slipped and grain spilled before them, were tethered at the rail. Light and noise came through the open door. It was as good a place as any to begin.

She slipped in the door, timing her entry to coincide with three men leaving, and sought the shadowed end of the room. The night was warm, but a fire still blazed on the hearth and meat was roasting over it. The room was chaotic. In one corner a handsome but mediocre harpist was playing for a rapt circle of mostly young girls. They did not seem to mind the shouted conversations that were being carried on behind them, or the sudden gusts of laughter or cursing that occasionally swept the room. Ki picked up a half-empty mug that someone had abandoned and leaned against the wall, trying to look as if she were paying attention to the harper while covertly eavesdropping on other conversations.

The harper couldn't sing very well, either. Ki listened in on a man telling the woman with him that she was going to have to tell Broderick she wouldn't see him anymore, and then to two farmers discussing whether the Windsingers would send rain right before haying time like they did last year. Three other men were hotly discussing the day's fencing contest, arguing about whether someone was justified in being as savage as he had been. A mixed group of young folk at the next table were playing a game that involved guessing whether the down sides of some tiles were red, black or blue. Just as Ki was going to abandon this tavern and try another, she heard a name she recognized.

"Kellich wouldn't have had to do it that way!" a man was saying. He was among the ones who had earlier been discussing the fencing. Ki edged closer, keeping her eyes on the warbling harper.

"Damn right about that!" agreed the short man in the group. "Kellich was a damn fine swordsman. He'd have won clean, made it clear he was the best without having to cut anybody up. That bastard was no more than a butcher . . . just a damn butcher. Blume isn't going to last the night. And he was just getting set to ask Aria to join with him.''

"No." The man speaking now was more soft-spoken than the other two. He pushed brown hair back from his eyes. "I'm no happier than you two are about Blume and Kurtis. And what he did to Darnell was a shameful thing to see. But he's a swordsman, through and through. He gave back to each what they offered him. Kurtis and Blume thought they'd have an easy time of it; they weren't even trying to look like they were fighting till he stung them. And Darnell, well, if there was another way to stop Darnell, I don't know what it is. But when he took on Farrick . . . Moon's breath, but that was something to see. That was bladework, and I'd swear not even Kellich had that kind of grace in him.''

"Horsedung!" The short man looked angry that anyone would dare disagree with him. He spoke as if he were several mugs ahead of his companions. "All that pausing and tapping blades and moving up and back . . . looked more like a spring dance than two men with swords. If you ask me, he and Farrick know each other from somewhere, otherwise how could they have moved together like that, like some kind of jugglers or acrobats or . . .''

"You damn dumb plow-pusher, that's Harperian fencing," Brown-hair laughed. "I saw it once before, when I travelled up north to the horse fair with my father. That's how it's done, though what I saw today made the horse-fair swordsmen look like sheepboys with sticks. It must be true what they say of Farrick, that his family had land and monies once and that he came south when . . .''

"Farrick ain't no better than the rest of us, I don't care what kind of manners he puts on. And this damn Harperian fencing you keep talking about is more dancing fit for maids and boys than a way to treat a sword. And Kellich could have put him down as jerky before he could have gotten near him, if he'd tried those fancy dance steps when he fought him.''

"Kellich couldn't even have touched blades with him if they'd been fencing Harperian!''

"Damn you, Yency, you saying that outlander was better than our own Kellich?" The short man picked up his mug with no intention of drinking from it. The third man intervened hastily.

"Settle down, settle down, no one's arguing with you, man. Yency was just saying he liked the man's style, that's all. And what's it to us, anyway? Tomorrow will tell." The peacemaker's voice sank suddenly to a near whisper that Ki strained to hear. "If the Duke's dead, we'll say the man was a good fencer. But in any case, the outlander will be dead. Got to admit, Yency, that when he fenced with Kellich, he fenced with death. Even if the poor bastard didn't know it. Buy us another round, Yency, and let's talk about something else."

Ki drank from the mug before she realized it wasn't really hers, then set it down quickly. Her mind was struggling to piece together what she had heard. None of it made sense. She'd been expecting to find Vandien held hostage somewhere, probably badly injured, perhaps barely alive. But who else could those men have been talking about? Who else had fenced Kellich lately and beaten him? By the way they had been talking, it sounded as if Vandien had been competing in the fencing exhibition today. And winning, very bloodily. But he wouldn't do that! He wouldn't kill as part of a bout. And if he'd been capable of moving around, he'd have been looking for her, not fencing in some contest.

She found her way to the door, paused in the shadows outside. Harperian fencing. That's what he'd taught her. He'd told her it was an old style, perhaps the oldest known, and becoming rarer in the world. But it couldn't have been Vandien. It must have been some other outlander come into town for the festival. She'd look and listen elsewhere. Where? She thought of the inn across town, where they had stopped before, for no other reason than that they had been there together once. Follow her feelings, Dellin had told her. She tried to still the turmoil inside her, tried to "feel" where Vandien might be in this frantic town. Nothing. Stupidity to even try. She thought briefly of going back inside the Two Ducks and trying to corner that Yency person and find out more about the fencing tournament today. But the Two Ducks seemed a bad place to call attention to herself; if they remembered Kellich's dying there, they'd remember the woman who'd been with his killer. She pushed herself away from the wall, started up the street.

She moved through the shadowed areas of the street, avoiding the torches on their poles and the folk that clustered around them, laughing and talking and swatting at the swarming insects. Once more she heard the day's fencing mentioned, though never Vandien's name, only that "The stranger and the Duke will make a fine pair of it, and who cares who comes out of it alive?" The folk gathered about the speaker generally laughed at that. She ventured a few steps closer, hoping to hear more, but was then distracted by a woman in a sere robe and hood hastening down the street. There was something naggingly familiar about her purposeful walk, and Ki trailed after her, scarcely daring to hope.

By the time she had passed three torch poles, Ki was sure of her. Keeping to the shadows, she increased her stride, her boots silent in the thick dust of the street. Then in the next stretch of darkness between torches, Ki was upon her, throwing a choking arm around her throat and dragging her struggling into the darkness between two buildings. The girl bit, sinking her teeth deeply, but the cloth of Ki's shirt was thick, and she surprised her captive by only forcing her forearm deeper into her mouth. Effectively gagged, she struggled, but her loose robe hampered her and Ki was very determined. At the end of the building there was a pile of straw, not very clean. Ki threw Willow to the ground atop it, and stood over her glaring.

"What . . . what do you want of me?" Willow asked in a quavering voice.

"Vandien. Where is he?"

"Ki!"

The note of dismay in the girl's voice as she recognized her threw Ki off stride. But she masked it, demanding again, "Where's Vandien, and my team and wagon? I know your damn rebellion took them, and I want them back. Or I go to the Duke and name names."

"I don't know!"

Willow had answered too quickly and there was too much panic in her voice. Ki grabbed a handful of the robe over her chest, dragged her back up to her feet. Her anger had a focus now, and brought with it such strength that Ki knew she could kill this girl with her hands.

"I want them back," she growled.

"Vintner!" Willow gasped out suddenly. "Vintner took the wagon and team."

"And Vandien?"

"I don't know! I swear I don't know, Ki! The others took him. It's how we are, no one person ever knows the whole plan. I swear, I haven't seen him!"

Ki shook her. "But you can find out?"

"I . . . maybe. I don't know, they won't want to tell me, but I'll try. I swear I'll try. Only you mustn't go to the Duke. It would ruin everything . . . if the Duke found us out now, he'd kill Vandien as well. Please, Ki. Please."

Ki believed her. There was no mistaking the genuine fear that filled her voice when she spoke of Ki going to the Duke. So, she had a handle on them where that was concerned. And what Willow said about no one person ever knowing the whole plan did fit in with what Goat had told her of the rebels. Ki eased her grip on Willow's robe.

"This is what we're going to do," Ki told her. "First, we're going after my team and wagon. Then you're going to your friends, and you'll make them understand that I want Vandien turned loose, intact, just outside town, on the road going toward Villena. And that if he isn't, the Duke is going to know not only everything I know, but everything Goat knows about your rebellion. What do you want to bet that the Two Ducks would be a smoking ruin before nightfall?"

"Goat's . . . alive, too?" Willow seemed suddenly baffled.

"Yes, Willow. He is. And Vandien had also better be alive, too. Or a lot of other people will be dead before tomorrow evening. Do you understand me?"

Willow's voice seemed steadier now. "I'll take you to Vintner's farm now," she said decisively. "He and his sons are probably here in town still, at Festival. But that's just as well; I don't think he'd willingly part with that team."

"Nor did I," Ki reminded her acidly. She kept a grip on Willow's sleeve as they left the alley. Ki smiled and nodded to her as they walked, two women enjoying the evening together.

Vintner's farm turned out to be on the other side of Tekum, on a road rutted worse than any Ki had yet seen. His name had been his fortune once, but now they walked past vines that drooped brown and trailing from their frames. Scrubby grasses and thistles were dying between the vines and along the sides of the road. Even in the cool of the night, the place smelled dusty and dead. No lights showed in the windows of the house, and the lone watchdog came forth with its bony back arched and its moth-eaten tail tucked between its legs. Ki patted it absently.

"In back," Willow whispered, as if the stillness of the place made talking sacrilegious.

She was right. The wagon was pulled up beside a shed that held wooden vats long bereft of fruit. Even in the darkness, a single glance inside was enough to tell Ki it had been plundered. She stepped back to the ground, rounded on Willow. "Where are my things?" she demanded coldly.

Willow shrugged eloquently. "Everywhere, by now. They were distributed to those in the most need."

"And my need for them wasn't considered?" Ki asked acidly.

Willow shrugged again, and even in the darkness, her eyes were pale and without feeling. "Soon-to-be-dead" folk needed nothing. Ki felt a sudden coldness up her back and in the base of her belly. "What I'd really like to know," she said conversationally, "is how to tell the difference between the Brurjan road patrols and the rebel freedom fighters. They both seem to share a gift for despoiling travellers."

Willow's eyes blazed suddenly. "You can say such things, who have no idea of the deprivations we have suffered in recent years. When a blanket for your child's bed becomes a luxury, or a bit of meat to flavor the soup is a thing to look forward to, or your mule throwing a shoe is a family tragedy. . ."

"Those folk at Festival tonight didn't seem very deprived. Poor folk don't pack themselves into taverns and spend coins on holiday breads and skewers of meat."

"Not usually. It isn't often like that. But it is tonight, because the rebellion has given them hope. For tonight, they believe things may get better, and they remember how things were when the Duchess kept the Windsingers kind to us, and this valley was prosperous, when all of Loveran was a green place."

Fervor filled her voice as she spoke. Pointless to argue, Ki decided. "And my team?" she asked. She wondered if she could extract coin as well as Vandien with her threat of going to the Duke, but decided not to bring it up to Willow just yet.

"There's an old stable up the hill. He probably put them there."

"Show me."

Both horses whuffed a greeting to her. There was a scattering of dry grass in the manger they shared, a skimming of slimy water in a trough. Ki ran a hand over Sigurd's shoulder, felt dust spiked with sweat. She'd wager they hadn't been clean since they'd been taken from her. "Vintner is so destitute, he could not even afford the time to groom them, I suppose."

Willow didn't reply. Ki turned back to her in time to hear the heavy door of the stable thud into place. Her shoulder crashed into it a scant portion of a second after Willow wrestled the bar into place. The ancient boards gave with the impact of Ki's body but didn't yield.

"Damn it, Willow, let me out!"

There was no reply, but Ki could feel her on the other side of the door, listening silently.

"This place won't hold me for long. There's tools in here, and I'll be out of here by morning. And then the Duke's going to hear everything I know, Willow. Every damn thing!"

"He'll be dead by then," Willow said calmly. She spoke in a conversational voice, as if she didn't really care if Ki could hear her or not. "By morning the rebellion will have been served. Vandien will have killed the Duke. It has to be, Ki. Otherwise, Kellich's death is totally without meaning. I hope you can see that."

"I'll see you in hell!" Ki roared, enraged beyond reason. But Willow was still talking, heedless of any noise Ki might make, and for the first time Ki noted the edge of madness in the girl's voice.

". . . blade was poisoned. So he would die anyway, that would be inevitable. At least this way his death serves a purpose. Even Vandien came to see that. Death can have a meaning, if it is offered up in service to a higher cause. He killed two men today, cut another and mutilated a young woman, but they were not wasted. Those deaths were needed, to put him in position to kill the Duke for us."

"I don't believe you!" Disgust filled Ki, and then a tickling fear that Willow might not be lying. "Let me out of here!"

Willow's voice was soft. "Vandien serves us now, filling Kellich's place. He came over readily enough, once he believed you were dead and accepted that he was dying. I think the knowledge of one's own death can bring out the higher nature in a man. Vandien will be remembered, Ki. Take comfort in that."

Willow stopped talking, but Ki could think of nothing to say. She was babbling nonsense anyway. It was only when the silence had stretched thin to breaking that she asked of the darkness, "Willow?" But there was no reply, not even the sound of breathing. She was gone.

Ki crouched down in the darkness and tried to think. But no matter how she put Willow's words together, they made no sense. For whatever reason, the girl was lying. Vandien wouldn't kill in a tournament bout. And even if he had developed sudden fervor for this rebellion's cause, she couldn't see him in the role of assassin. None of it made sense. Willow had to be lying. The man she knew was incapable of such carnage. But the other men she had overheard in the tavern . . . she suddenly felt quivery. It was true. Something inside her collapsed. She felt betrayed, not only by Vandien, but by herself. She'd loved a man, and never really known him at all. Anger warred with pain. She chose anger. She rose, and began to grope her way around the wall of the stable, searching for tools to pry the old boards loose.

EIGHTEEN

They had given him a room at the inn, and someone had sent him up a tub of bath water. Between the beaten metal tub of warm scented water, and the two Brurjans outside his door, he didn't know if he should consider himself an honored guest or a prisoner. He was still mulling it over after his bath as he sat on the edge of the bed calmly tearing up one of the linens to bandage his hip. The inn could charge the Duke for the missing sheet; he didn't plan to be around to pay for it. Someone hammered at the door, then threw it open. A Brurjan filled the opening, his tall crest brushing the top of the doorframe in spite of his stoop. "Clean clothes," he said, tossing a bundle toward him. "So you don't stink at table. And hurry it up." He slammed the door on his way out.

"So. The bath wasn't for my benefit at all," Vandien observed to himself. The pale blue shirt was loose and cool, woven of a soft fabric he didn't recognize. The brown trousers were of the same stuff in a heavier weave, and fit him well enough; he wondered idly who had guessed at his size. On the other hand, perhaps the Duke kept a full wardrobe in a range of sizes to fit the people he planned to kill. Vandien smiled crookedly as he tucked in his shirt and fastened his sword belt.

He crossed the room to where his own clothing lay in a heap on the floor. From them he retrieved a necklace, a small carved hawk on a fine chain. For a moment he stared at it cupped in the palm of his hand, then he looped it quickly around his neck. A tiny packet he tucked securely into his cuff. The last item he took up was a small ball of wax that Lacey had given him that morning. He stared at it for a long time, then set it carefully on the floor. He put his heel atop it, pressed down. It squashed soundlessly, the milky poison squirting out to stain the floorboards.

Vandien mentally hefted the silver candlesticks weighting the heavy cream-colored tablecloth. Probably enough there to buy Ki a new wagon, he thought idly, and then winced from the notion. It was, he reflected, an obsolete measurement of value anymore. Better to say it was heavy enough to break the battle fangs of the Brurjan that was running her black-clawed hands up the sides of his legs, searching for concealed weapons. She slapped the bandage on his hip, winning a muffled grunt from him, and then pointed wordlessly at the sheathed rapier.

"You'll have to excuse her suspicions," the Duke said smoothly. He sat at the head of the table already. His hands were spired together before him. A spill of lace draped from each of his cuffs; stupid shirt to wear if he truly expected to fence tonight. Vandien made no reply.

"You'd be quite astonished to know the depths to which some folk would sink in an effort to do away with me. Let her see your weapon, please."

Vandien drew it slowly, presented it to the Brurjan hilt first. She took it from him carefully, ran first her eyes, then her short fingers up the length of the blade. A second time, and then she sniffed the metal suspiciously. She turned puzzled eyes to the Duke. "No poison," she said.

"Such a subtle race, my Brurjans. Such social finesse. Halikira, be a sweet thing and cleanse the blade in spirits of wine anyway."

Vandien thought he had never seen such a look of contempt as Halikira afforded her master, but the Duke chose to ignore it. Or perhaps he was truly unaware of it. As he received his wiped blade back from her, their eyes met briefly. Her face pelt was lighter than most Brurjans', making her eyes seem darker. For a moment their dislike of the Duke was shared; her black lips lifted a trifle to bare more fang. Then her eyes were empty again, and he turned from her toward the table.

"Please, be seated. You are . . . Vandien, I am told. Do I have the name correctly?"

"Yes." He drew out a carved chair, sat in it carefully. His hip was stiffening.

"An unusual name. I understand you are not from around these parts."

"No." A simple parry to the Duke's thrust.

The soup was brought, served to them by the Brurjan, the white cloth a strange contrast to the scarred and hairy forearm it draped. Vandien smelled chicken and cream and tiny mild onions. He tasted it and was suddenly reminded that he had not eaten since breakfast. He ate, leaving the Duke to be conversational.

"Travelling alone now, are you?" the Duke pressed.

For a silent moment Vandien regarded him. The Duke's eyes were hard as cold silver as they held him. Did he know about Ki? Vandien wondered. And then it didn't matter. He picked up a soft brown roll of bread, split it open to reveal the creamy inside. As he spread butter thickly on it, he said, "The leader of the rebellion for this area seems to be a man named Lacey. But he is not in perfect control of his people, and they could easily split into factions. They already hold the plans to a place called Masterhold. Does that have significance to you?"

The Duke was pouring wine. He set down the bottle, tasted his glass, then picked up the bottle and reached across the table to fill Vandien's goblet. "Betraying them now can't spare you the bout," he said softly. "The example must be made."

"I agree." Vandien lifted his glass, tasted it. A damn sight better than the swill Trelira had served him so long ago. Maybe this was one of those southern vintages he had heard so much about. His eyes met the Duke's. "I don't expect to live to see the dawn," he said, quite truthfully. He smiled, the expression tugging at the old scar down his face. The scar he had taken saving Ki from a Harpy. "I intend to see that many of them share my fate." He returned to his soup.

The Duke was plainly unsettled, and his silence lengthened. Finally, he said, "Do you think I will offer you money for this information, or a quick death? What are you trying to buy?"

Vandien shrugged, set aside the soup to make room for a plate heaped with sliced rare meat. He saw the Brurjan server's nose twitch in distaste from the smell of cooked meat.

"Revenge, I suppose. I'm supposed to kill you with a poisoned blade tonight. In return, they promised to set free a
friend of mine they hold hostage." He sipped more wine to
clear his throat. "I know she is already dead."

"How careless of them," the Duke commiserated. He
smiled coldly. "The meat is from our plainsbuck. I shot this
one myself. It isn't too rare for you, is it? I'm afraid I've
come to share my Brurjans' habits where flesh is concerned."

"It's fine." Vandien's voice was steady. "The bloodier,
the better. Blume and Kurtis—the men I killed today—they
were a part of this rebellion. And the fencer named Trask is
one of theirs, as is the woman who wore the red silk blouse
today—I don't know her name, but someone will." Vandien
sliced into the meat, lifted a forkful. He appraised the Duke
carefully and was suddenly wary. His face was troubled, but
in the wrong way.

He passed him a dish of stewed spiced fruit. A strange
smile stretched his lips. "Earlier today, I mistook you for a
man of honor."

Vandien accepted the dish, served himself some. It was a
good accompaniment for the strong-flavored meat. He didn't
reply to the Duke, but went on eating. Silence would draw
him out.

"I was sure you had some secret grudge against me,
something that drove you to win a bout with me at all costs. I
almost admired you for it. And when I witnessed your final
display of swordsmanship, I said to myself, 'There is a
nobleman born and true to the old ways of honor.' I knew
you wouldn't be swerved from your resolve to kill me."

Vandien set down his wineglass. "And?"

"And I find I'm wrong. You cut through those men for a
chance to betray them. For revenge." The Duke permitted
himself a small smile. "You may be more useful to me alive
than dead. I'd have to mark you in some way, so folk would
not think I'd gone softly with you . . . perhaps a slash down
your face. One more scar should not matter to a man marked
as you are. Though I'd like to see the swordsman who put it
there."

Vandien kept his rising temper from showing in his face as
he sliced more meat. "Not a swordsman, Duke Loveran. A
Harpy's talons. Not that it matters to our previous discussion.
I am curious as to what use you would find for an 'honorless'

man like myself. Do you refer to what I could tell you of the rebellion?''

The Duke made a dismissing gesture with his hand that had nothing to do with the meat being cleared from the table. ''The rebellion. Pah. Frankly speaking, Vandien, there is very little you could tell me of them that I don't already know. No. When I said you might be useful to me, I was speaking of your skill with the sword. Archaic and obsolete as it is, I'd still love to learn Harperian fencing.''

Vandien let the last thrust slip by him. ''If your knowledge of the rebels is so complete,'' he asked slowly, ''why haven't you acted upon it?''

The Duke chose a pastry from a beaten silver platter set before them. ''I might say they amuse me. Surely, even you must have been amused by the childishness of their plottings. Try one of the raspberry cream ones; my cook has a special knack with them. I could tell you that it's easier to leave them intact and deal with their small treacheries as my informants make them known to me; if I crushed them here, I'd only have a dozen more such 'rebellions' popping up tomorrow. Sort of like a skin rash, Vandien. Scratching only spreads it.''

''And your real reason for not dealing with them?'' Vandien was eating the pastry calmly, forcing his face to stay neutral despite the slow chill that was spreading up his arm.

''They simply aren't that important, nor that powerful. If I moved against them, their movement would gain recruits and impetus. If I publicly ignore them, while privately making sure that all their plots come to nothing, I take their credibility away. Who joins them now? Younger offspring with no money and no hope of inheriting, old men whose families don't pay enough attention to them . . . no one I need fear.'' The Duke looked up at him calmly. ''I'm afraid I won't be the vehicle for your revenge, Vandien. You see, there's nothing in it for me.''

''I see.'' Vandien's hand slipped toward his cuff, where he had concealed the roll of thwartspite. He felt for it, then became desperate enough to look. It wasn't there. The Brurjan's search had been more thorough than he realized. He glanced at Halikira; she lifted her lips slightly, rolled something briefly between her short fingers. He glanced away. Damn her. He lowered his sword arm to his lap, pressed it against the warmth of his belly. The ache eased slightly.

"Don't be so disappointed, man. A hundred years from
now, it won't make one whit of difference to anyone. Here.
Try this wine with the pastries; I find it provides the perfect
contrast." The Duke was pouring from a different bottle into
fresh glasses.

Vandien watched him idly. He could think of nothing
significant to say. His day had suddenly caught up with him.
His poisoned arm ached like desolation itself, and every other
muscle in his body was protesting his earlier exertions. Even
sitting down, his hip pained him. And the hot bath followed
by a generous meal had done nothing to increase his alert-
ness. The false energy of the thwartspite had led him to
exceed himself. Even his mind felt muzzy. Not one whit of
difference a hundred years hence. So the Duke had said. And
probably true. What would remain of him a hundred years
hence? No child would carry his names. His body would be
long gone to good black soil. His sword, perhaps; it was
already older than a hundred years. Where would it be?
Hanging in a dim corner of the Duke's Masterhold? Or maybe
heaped on a table full of secondhand weapons in some
Loveranish marketplace? And what would its honor mean
then, or his? What had it ever meant to him, really? He tried
to think of a time when being an honorable man had given
him the advantage in a fight. He sipped absently at the wine
the Duke set before him. "Of what use is honor?"

"None at all," the Duke replied.

Vandien startled, surprised to find he had spoken his question aloud. "It has to be," he insisted, but couldn't think of
any arguments to support it. A less honorable man would
have let Kellich kill Goat. A little less honor would have kept
Ki alive.

"Honor's of no use at all," the Duke was saying. "In fact,
it's a handicap. Tonight, for instance. Keep your honor and I
kill you. Or renounce it, take a slash down the face, and live
on as my retainer. You can ask my Brurjans; I'm a generous
man with those who work for me."

"I don't know," Vandien said, but he was not answering
the Duke, but himself.

"You don't have to decide right now," the Duke told him.
"Even in the middle of the bout, you can change your
mind." The man was standing, gesturing to Halikira to bring
his weapon. It was a lovely blade. Another time Vandien

would have itched to examine it. Its swept hilt glistened with a myriad of tiny sparkling stones set into it. A true swordsman would have disdained them, lest others say he used them to distract his opponents. But there, again, that was the thought of a man concerned with his honor. The Duke disdained honor. And Vandien had none left. He couldn't bring down the rebellion that had killed Ki. He'd die on the Duke's sword, and it would all have been for nothing.

"I've fought all day. I've taken a sword-slash on my hip. I've had a hot bath, a heavy meal, and wine, and I've sat still long enough to stiffen up. Will you call this a fair match?"

"Fair is like honor. Of no real value. But take a moment or two to limber up if you must."

Vandien was silent as he drew his rapier, made a vain attempt to stretch out his muscles. They felt liked dried-up twisted leather strips. At his first tentative lunge, he felt the wound on his hip open up. The blood seemed hot enough to scald as it soaked through the bandages. Ironic, when his sword arm felt so cold. He knew he gripped his rapier's hilt, but he could not actually feel his fingers. He glanced over to where the Duke was limbering up. He stared for a moment, then suddenly saw. The fancy shirt with the lace at collar and cuffs was camouflage for chain mail. Light and fine as it must be, he could still see its betraying outline when the Duke lunged. Vandien's sparse chances suddenly shrank.

He would have been better off not to have eaten at all. His whole body felt heavy, and his mind was muzzy. He tried to consider his options. There didn't seem to be very many. He could fight the Duke and die on his sword. He could accept the Duke's offer of a position as fencing master, and take a slash down the face and die of the poison. He could refuse to fight the Duke . . . and the Duke, a man without honor, would kill him anyway. Funny. It all seemed to end with his death. Well, if all he could do was die, he'd die well. He wondered how high up the Duke's throat his mail went. Probably a good leather collar under the one of lace. Halikira was watching him with unreadable dark eyes. Brurjans. Whatever else you might say about them, they died well. He grinned at her, offered her a sketchy salute with his blade. Her black lips writhed up slightly, a shadow of the Brurjan smile-snarl. And inspiration struck Vandien.

His hand and sword arm were cold, his hip stiff. He

slammed his mind shut to pain, forced his body to respond as he limbered it up, rapidly and roughly. He turned to face the Duke. Two other Brurjans were lifting the laden table, setting it up against the wall. "Rules for this bout?" Vandien asked quietly.

"None," the Duke said in an equally soft voice. "What do rules mean to men without honor?"

"Nothing. Nothing at all," Vandien conceded.

Vandien drew himself up straight. The Duke matched him. Their blades were down. Then slowly the salute began, the guards brought up chin high, tips up, blades vertical. The jeweled hilt glinted into Vandien's eyes, but his face never changed expression. Then, as the Duke began to bring his blade down and around, out to the side in a standard salute, Vandien extended in a lightning thrust. The tip of his rapier leaped precisely into the Duke's eye socket, sank a good four inches. It was out again before the Duke even began to fall.

"Lesson one in Harperian fencing," Vandien heard himself say. "Precise point control is everything."

The Duke's body hit the carpet.

Vandien swayed where he stood. The chill was spreading. He caught the rapier in his off hand as his sword arm died and fell numb to his side. He turned to the Brurjan guards, lifted the rapier to guard position. He'd show them a Human could die well, too.

Halikira was making a peculiar sound, almost like a dog panting. Her great jaws were wide, baring her gleaming battle fangs and blue-spotted tongue. She clutched suddenly at her belly, and leaned against one of her companions, who abruptly joined her in panting noisily. Suddenly she raised her crest, the spiky swath of semi-hair that crowned a Brurjan and was usually erect only during battle or moments of great emotion. Vandien braced himself.

The third Brurjan guard crossed the room slowly. Vandien turned, keeping his rapier up and threatening. This one was an older male, grey mottling his black pelt. He squatted by the Duke, and he, too, began panting noisily. He leaned forward suddenly, and with a thumb gouged out the Duke's pierced eye. He held it up, dangling tissue clinging to his black-nailed thumb. "Pig's eye, anyone?" he offered raspily. Halikira yelped suddenly and slid to floor, her panting increasing in tempo as the black male popped the eyeball into his mouth and gravely crunched it.

The strength went suddenly out of Vandien's body. He staggered to a chair, sat. "I never heard a Brurjan laugh before," he admitted bewilderedly to no one in particular.

"Then it's even. I never saw a Human do anything funny before," Halikira replied.

This comment further convulsed all three Brurjans. Vandien sat in his chair, feeling the cold seeping from his arm into his chest. Strange, he thought, to die hearing the sound of Brurjan laughter. His own smile dawned as the room darkened around him. He clutched at the chair to keep from falling.

When his vision returned, the Brurjans were already stripping the body. "His stuff ought to fit you pretty well," Halikira observed. "Korioko! Get that fancy helm out of the chest; the one with the crest on it. Hurry up. In fact, get out the whole battle harness. Bet it looks better on this one than it did on old Pig-eyes." More of the dog-pant laughter. Halikira tossed the fine chain mail into Vandien's lap. With difficulty he sheathed his rapier, ran appreciative fingers over the fine intermeshed links. The metal was still warm from the Duke's body.

"Get it on!" Halikira ordered him impatiently. Then, peering at Vandien more closely, "What's wrong with your arm? Your hand's turning blue."

"Poison," he said absently, fingering the chain mail. "Kellich's blade was poisoned. I'm dying."

"Coward's weapon. No fighter should ever have to die of poison. Here, I'll help you," she said matter-of-factly, and Vandien sat quietly, expecting a quick knife slice across the throat. LastFriend, the Brurjans translated knife, and were rumored to carry special ones to dispatch their own wounded. But instead she hauled him to his feet and began wrestling him into the chain mail. The cold was squeezing his chest now. He had neither the strength to resist her, nor to help her. In a moment more Korioki was setting a crested helm crookedly atop his head, and the other Brurjan, addressed only as Tiyo, was buckling the Duke's jeweled sword onto his other hip. Their hot meaty breath enveloped him as they laughed their way through the task of arraying him in the Duke's personal battle dress, right down to the heavy purse the Duke had been carrying. Then Halikira stood back and nodded her satisfaction.

"Looks better," she said affably. "Always turned my gut to see Pig-eyes in Brurjan harness. Man should fight like a Brurjan before he wears Brurjan harness." She glanced around the room, then turned back to Vandien. "You want any of his other stuff?"

He stook his head slowly. His good arm cradled his numbed one to him. Cold, spreading cold. His answer seemed to astonish them. Avariciously happy snarls broke out on their faces. They looted like children, competing and squabbling and bragging, and occasionally bringing some special piece to him and offering it to him. He always refused it, and with each refusal, their respect for him seemed to grow. Korioko bared his yellowed teeth in a Brurjan smile, and commented, "So were the Old Ones, who fought only for blood and weapons. So we are, even today, when we have made a Great Kill. You honor the harness." He glanced to Halikira and Tiyo. "Let's drink with him."

Tiyo tucked his chin into his chest, a Brurjan gesture of surprise, but Halikira cuffed him roughly. "It's a good idea. We'll do it." She stuffed the last of the Duke's jewelry into her shoulder pouch, and stood.

When she dragged Vandien to his feet, he nearly blacked out. Dimly he heard her say something about "His ass is still bleeding," which seemed to occasion much merriment among the threesome. His vision cleared slightly to find they were walking him down the stairs. He wasn't sure if his boots were touching the steps or not. As they passed the doorway to the common room of the inn, Halikira paused and leaned in. "Duke's dead!" she announced to the Brurjan patrollers lounging there. "VandienScarface killed him." She paused a moment. "It'd sound better in Brurjan. KeklokitoVandien. Now there's a proper name. Keklokito will drink with us! He leaves the spoils of the Duke to such as want them. And he says the town is yours! Celebrate a Great Kill as befits it!"

The Brurjans dispersed like bees from a smashed hive. Vandien heard the racketing of feet up the stairs, but as Hailikira dragged him out into the cool night, it seemed an equal number of Brurjans had followed them. He was aware that they cut a swath of destruction through the town. Festival booths crashed down in their wakes, door leathers were casually torn from the ties and flapped out into the streets. He heard screams and harsh Human shouts that drowned in Brurjan roars and curses. He felt strangely untouched by all of it.

They were in an unfamiliar part of Tekum now. They passed a small corral of cattle and then entered a low-eaved building with no windows. Even Vandien had to duck to get inside, and the Brurjans dropped to their knees. But within, the building opened up to a peaked ceiling. The tables and stools were massive, making Vandien feel a child again in a world engineered for adults. And the smell was overpowering. Blood. Old blood, new blood, blood mixed with milk. Cutting even through the stench of the blood was another smell, abrasive and hot. He couldn't identify it. The floor was packed dark earth, and flies swarmed up from it as they entered. Light came from torches set in sconces on the wall and from fat candles on the tables. It did not illuminate the place very well, but Vandien did not mind. He had heard enough of Brurjan Bloodhalls that he didn't need to see more. He heard an animal scream briefly in an adjacent room. A Brurjan entered, a small animal clasped expertly under one arm. Blood pumped from its cut throat into the beaten silver vessel he held beneath it. He looked up in mild surprise at the throng of entering Brurjans. Glancing about, his eyes settled on Vandien. He pointed a black-nailed finger in his direction. "No pets!" he said sternly.

"Not a pet," Halikira contradicted him irritably. "Keklokito made a Great Kill tonight. The Duke fell to him, and he has ceded to us all that was his, save his armor and arms."

Her words penetrated a corner of Vandien's mind. Was that what he had done when he told them he wanted nothing else of the Duke's? Given it all, town and Dukedom, over to the Brurjans? He knew he should feel appalled but could only feel the deadly spread of the cold. He hitched himself up onto one of the massive stools, tried to sit so that his hip didn't pain him. Halikira was still talking. ". . . bull, or maybe two. We all drink with Keklokito tonight. Here!" She drew a gold neckpiece set with red gems from her shoulder pack, crashed it onto the table. "Let that pay for all! And don't be slow!" She drew up a stool next to Vandein's and sat down heavily.

The rest of the table filled up rapidly. Halikira began loudly telling the tale of Keklokito's Great Kill. Her words seemed to blend with the swirling darkness of the Bloodhall

and the muffled bellowing of a bull in the next chamber. The
table had dissolved in helpless panting laughter and Halikira
was struggling to add how Korioko had eaten the pig's eye
when the Bloodhall's master appeared with an enormous
basin. He set it atop the table, and a small red wave broke
over the lip of it. As if from a great distance Vandien watched
drinking horns set out, and then the master came again,
bearing a small metal bucket that steamed. The contents
appeared silvery as he upended it over the blood, and Vandien
caught again the hot, abrasive odor. The master swirled it
through the fresh blood and then stepped back from the table.
All grew suddenly still.

Halikira gave him a nudge that nearly knocked him off his
stool. "It's your kill; you fill your horn first," she told him.

Obeying seemed easier than arguing. His sword arm was
useless. Even in the dim light of the Bloodhall, its color was
appalling. With his off hand he picked up a drinking horn
from the table; it was a fancy one, spiraled, with hunting
scenes etched into it. He dipped it into the blood, and no
sooner had he lifted it than a dozen others were plunged in.

His cup was heavy with warm blood, his fingertips red and
wet with it. Whatever had been mixed with the blood made
swirls of silver through the redness. He looked into it, felt he
was falling into its depths. Halikira jogged him again.

"Drink it before the blood cakes," she advised him, and
when he looked vaguely reluctant, she reminded him, "Hells,
man, you're dying anyway! Look at your arm!" This evoked
another chorus of panting laughter, and Vandien found himself joining in it. And when it ended with the lifting of
drinking horns, his rose with the rest. And he drank.

He drank fire and sandstorms and curling whiplashes. The
drink ignored his throat and belly and cut its own scorching
passage through his guts. He couldn't even get the breath to
gasp, and the Brurjans howled admiringly at what they judged
his impassivity to their drink. His breath burned out through
his nostrils and mouth. He forgot all pain from his hip, all
coldness. He suddenly tasted the bull's blood in his mouth
and nostrils, and it was hot and wet and alive, like sparks
leaping on his tongue. His darkening arm on the table before
him was suddenly funny, almost as funny as the Duke's
eyeball. It didn't matter. None of it mattered. Being alive was
all that mattered, and using life up to the very last instant.

Blood was life and life was in him. He swayed slightly as he turned to Halikira.

"What the hell are we drinking?" he managed to ask.

"Bull's blood," she said simply.

He ripped the Duke's purse free of its strings, smashed it down on the table. "Blood man! Kill another bull!" he roared, and Halikira crushed him in a hug.

"I like this Human," she announced to the assembled folk. "I think he should live!"

Someone near him began a panting laugh, and others took it up. Vandien laughed with them, unsure of the joke but having a wonderful time nonetheless. More blood was brought, and he drank another hornful, and it burned its way down his scalded throat in an agonizingly delightful way. It seemed to him that the Brurjans began to get silly after that. One of them wanted the Duke's helm for a piss-pot, and Vandien gladly traded it away for a Brurjan one twice the size of his skull. It hung over his eyes most of the time so that he frequently was unsure who he was talking to, but after a while that didn't seem to matter either.

Someone else bought another bull sometime later, and it was later still that Halikira sat down beside him again. He was a little surprised to find she had been gone. He was in the middle of trying to learn a new song, made trickier by the fact that it was all in Brurjan and he wasn't sure what he was singing about. She had a leaf laden with an ugly, tarry substance, and she wanted him to eat it. He explained to her several times, amid much panting laughter from the rest of the table, that he never ate anything that particular shade of brown. Someone offered to bet a bull against the Duke's sword that he couldn't keep it down if he did eat it. Vandien won the bet and had a horn of the bull's blood. It seemed much later that he traded the Duke's sword for another bull, and later still when a swaying Korioko convinced him that it was bad luck to ever let a coward's mark remain on one's body. Korioko yelled for a LastFriend to be brought to him, and when it arrived, he heated the snake's-tongue blade over the table's candles. Vandien willingly pushed his darkened arm out onto the table, sat still as the searing blade was laid over the mark of Kellich's rip. He smelled scorching flesh, and then a far-off pain itched at his arm. Before he could respond to it, Korioko was lifting the blade away and exclaiming with pleasure at how cleanly outlined the scar from the pronged blade would be. Everyone joined in congratulating him on the new scar, and the master of the Bloodhall donated a bull to the table in a rare display of Brurjan fellowship.

He wasn't sure when or why they went outside. It wasn't dawn yet, but a strange light suffused the streets. Halikira was leaning on him and he was struggling valiantly to support her.

"Keklokito. Black or white?" Someone demanded.

"Take white. The black won't face a pikeman," Halikira hissed.

"White," Vandien answered.

Someone gave him a leg up, and when he pushed the helmet from his eyes, he was atop a large white horse trapped out with the Duke's black and silver harness. It felt strange to be up so high, but good. "Everything feels good," he observed to Halikira.

"It always does," she answered, "after a Great Kill. Ride well and may your fangs taste blood often."

He couldn't think of a reply to that, and when he lifted a hand and leaned forward to speak to her, the horse interpreted it as a signal to charge. He left Tekum at a gallop, noticing in passing that half of the town was ablaze. It seemed an odd way to end a festival, but then, he had never really understood what they were celebrating in the first place.

He tried to remember where he was supposed to be going. Home. That was it. That was fine. It was time he paid a visit home. When dawn began to break before him, he realized the horse had slowed to a nagging trot. He pulled it in to a walk, lifted his eyes to the sunrise. Ki came suddenly to his mind, and then the remembrance that he was dying. He had only moments for his grief. The physical pain hit him first, knocking him from the saddle before the first convulsion lashed him. When the fit finally passed, his vision seemed extraordinarily clear. His body gave him one last moment of stillness, a final glimpse of sunrise breaking over the green hills of his father's keep. The great cold uncurled inside him. "I've come home, Father," he said to the one waiting for him, and fell into the darkness.

NINETEEN

It wasn't a stone in his hoof; she could feel no heat or swelling. Damn and damn and damn. She'd have to hope it was only a bruise. She patted Sigurd's filthy shoulder and got back up on the box. So, they'd walk, then. Just when she needed speed, this had to happen. She stirred the team up, sat back and tried to calm herself. It didn't work. There was a marked hitch to Sigurd's stride that filled her with fury. She'd like to kill Willow and Vintner. And if that was dawn breaking over Tekum, then Goat and Dellin would be expecting her anytime now, and she wouldn't be there.

Dawn meant another thing as well, something she pushed to the back of her mind. Dawn meant Vandien was dead, from Kellich's poison or the Duke's sword. It didn't much matter which had killed him. Either way he was just as dead. As dead as everything they had shared. She found she could think of him calmly. Much of the anger and tears had been worked out with a double-bitted axe and the wall of Vintner's barn. A numbness had replaced it. He was dead by now. How could it matter whether he had died for the rebellion or thinking of her? He was still as dead. She was still as numb.

She rubbed her eyes with dirty hands, looked again. Yes, dawn was breaking, but not over Tekum. The rosy glow over the town had to be something else. Fire? Maybe, but who'd set half the town ablaze?

Actually, more than half the town was ablaze, and the flames were spreading. The long hot days had made anything burnable tinder-dry. Sparks leaped the narrow streets

233

in the winds of the fire's breath. She picked her way through the
town, turning often to avoid the fires. Even avoiding the streets
where the buildings still blazed, Ki choked in the smoke and
blowing ash. No one seemed to be doing much about the
fires. The fires must have been the final culmination to an
earlier uproar. She saw only one body, but the signs of earlier
violence were everywhere. Broken furniture was strewn through
the streets, and door leathers dangled and flapped in the fire's
wind. She saw very few folk, and the ones she did see were
either salvaging or looting; Ki wasn't sure which.

The tree-lined main street had taken the worst of whatever
had happened here. Ki guided the team between the wreckage
of Festival booths, past burned-out buildings and scorched
ones, between trees whose leaves hung blackened and lifeless
from the fire's heat. Perhaps it had started here; no buildings
along this strip were actively burning still. Mud brick walls,
cracked and crazed by the heat, gaped emptily, their thatched
or wooden roofs burned away. Ki saw a few street children
salvaging bits of food from the wrecked booths. They were
competing with crows, and both groups stopped their pecking
to watch Ki suspiciously.

At first she didn't recognize the two figures coming toward
her. The boy walked at the man's side, the man's hand on his
shoulder. As she came abreast of them, Dellin lifted a hand in
greeting. She halted the team. Goat immediately scrabbled
into the side door of the cuddy. Dellin shrugged, and awkwardly clambered up to share the seat.

"Do you know what happened?" Ki asked.

Dellin shook his head. "The Brurjans ran wild, looting and
wrecking. They took everything they wanted, and wrecked
the rest. Then they rode off toward Algona." He shook his
head again, as if trying to clear it. "Such emotions as those
creatures harbor! And no restraints on any of it last night. I
tried to shield the boy, but . . ." Again he shook his head.

"What happened to your mule? The Brurjans?"

"No. Someone set fire to the shed where we were resting.
No place was safe anymore, so I decided to come and find
you. But once we were on the road, we met a wave of folk
fleeing the town's destruction. A merchant with two heavy
bags and a knife demanded our mule. He was so full of greed
and fear that he would have killed us for it. The mule wasn't

worth it, so I let him take it. I was too busy trying to protect the boy's mind to physically shield him as well.''

''Isn't it wonderful,'' Ki observed bitterly, ''how adversity brings out the best in all of us? The Brurjans turn on the merchants, and the merchants turn on you. But what triggered it all?''

Dellin shrugged. ''A Brurjan went amok and killed the Duke, I think. At least, the Brurjans were shouting his name through the streets and saying he had given the town to them. Keklokito, it was.''

So even that plot had gone awry. She wondered where Vandien had fallen, and how. The team stood still in the street. Ki's eyes wandered over the wreckage. ''Where do I go?'' she asked the empty street.

Gotheris poked his head out of the cuddy door. ''You didn't find Vandien?'' he asked. She heard anxiety in his voice.

''No,'' she replied, and the word came out harder than she meant it. Dellin looked at her curiously, and she felt the probing she was powerless to stop.

''The bond is gone.''

She shrugged. ''He's dead.''

''The bond is gone. While it was there, I could tell he was alive. But now it's gone. He's let go. Or you have.''

''He's dead,'' Ki repeated dully. Simple sorrow would have been a relief. Why did she have to deal with anger and betrayal and probing questions from a nosy Jore? Was he reading her irritation with him? Then let him, and be damned. She glared at him.

Dellin only looked at her.

Goat's face was worse. The look of sleepy bafflement hadn't left his eyes. A deep furrow divided his brows as he looked from her to Dellin and back. ''Something . . . is wrong,'' he said. He struggled with words. ''It isn't like . . . you feel it is.''

She shook the reins. Useless to explain to the boy that she could not put her feelings into simple words. She didn't understand them herself. This was what all her hoping and searching came to. She felt cheated and betrayed. Worse, she felt foolish. Because she had known all along, not just for a day, but for years, that it would come to this. That she would someday reach for him, in need, and he would not be there.

Anger shook her like the storm that had battered her wagon days ago, and self-disgust filled her at the way she had let herself be beguiled into depending on him. She turned her back on them and covered her eyes, trying to find a way to be alone. Dellin had spoiled her numbness.

"I can't help you without letting you hurt the boy." Dellin's voice came dimly to her. "I'm sorry. You'll have to face this on your own."

On my own, thought Ki, and the words echoed stupidly through her mind, repeated endlessly. On my own. She felt herself reach out, and suddenly knew the truth of Dellin's words. There had been a bond, but now she reached and felt only a wall. No one reached back. He'd let go of her. Sometime yesterday, he'd chosen to follow the rebellion. And died for it. Her loneliness stretched endlessly and achingly into a void that held no answers, no return of warmth. It was a bleeding that could not be staunched. On her own.

"I cannot allow it, not so close to Gotheris!"

The halting of the wagon jarred her. She had not realized that Dellin had been driving the team. She opened her eyes but could see nothing at first. Then nothing turned into the fingers of her hands. She lifted her face slowly, uncoiled. Dellin had risen on the seat. "Stop that!" he cried commandingly. "Let her go!" Ki turned her head.

From one of the remaining trees, a noose dangled. A young boy had hold of it, holding it open. Perhaps fifteen or twenty people, more than Ki had yet seen today, clustered in the streets. They muttered angrily, like stirred bees, and their faces were avaricious with hate. Three young men were dragging a woman toward the tree. "She's one of those damned rebels," someone shouted to Dellin. "One of those what killed the Duke and turned the Brurjans loose on us all. Friends with the very one that done it!" Others in the crowd muttered an angry assent.

"Let her go!" Dellin roared. The men halted, looked up at him. Their eyes flamed with hate. The woman bucked against their grip, threw her whole body backward trying to break free of their relentless hold. Her hood flew back.

Willow had aged in the night. Her spikily shorn head made her look like the victim of some devastating illness. Her skin was grey, and black soot smudged the side of her nose. With her mismatched eyes wide and rolling, she looked like a battered doll, victim of some wicked child.

"Let them kill her," Ki said quietly.

Dellin looked down at her. "I thought I should stop them, for Gotheris's sake. Now I know I must stop them. For yours."

In the brief interval of his speaking, the crowd had lost interest in him. One of the men gripped Willow's short hair, lifted her nearly clear of the ground as they pushed and dragged her forward. The boy, his mouth ajar, held the noose open and waiting for her.

Dellin's eyes wandered gravely over the crowd. But if he had hoped to see any sign of them relenting, he was disappointed. "Stop." Dellin said the word this time, and a plea was in his voice. He did not speak loudly, nor did his voice carry. It was almost as if he mouthed it under his breath. It did no good. The men who gripped Willow were strong in their purpose. Ki could find no pity in her heart for the girl. She had cursed Ki too well and too truly. A few folk at the edge of the crowd, suddenly sickened by what was to come, turned and hastened away. She saw a woman put a pleading hand on her husband's arm, lean close to speak earnestly to him. Reluctantly he accompanied her as she turned away. No one paid any attention to their leaving.

"Don't do it!" Dellin breathed again. The boy holding the noose jerked as if stuck with a pin. His eyes focused suddenly on the struggling girl, on the savage faces of the men forcing her near. His eyes widened as if he had just glimpsed demons walking by daylight. He yelped like a kicked pup, and fled.

"Damn!" One of the men cursed, and had to take one hand from Willow to snatch after the swinging rope. She took full advantage of his distraction, ripping a hand free to batter frantically at the man who gripped her hair. Ki sat quietly, watching her. Behind her she heard a muffled whimper, turned to see Goat framed in the cuddy door. He clutched the seat as if he were drowning and it was the only bit of driftwood in the sea. On his face was the panicky look of a child who cannot breathe. In his eyes was horror such as Ki had never seen.

"It's wrong," sighed Dellin.

The crowd was thinning. The man trying to bring the noose and Willow's neck closer together looked abruptly and dis-

tinctly uncomfortable. It seemed to Ki he suddenly found his
central role in the drama distasteful. "You'll be punished,"
Dellin warned ominously.

"Get the damn noose on her!" one of the men holding
Willow ordered him. But the one gripping the noose was
instantly angered.

"You want it done, do it yourself!" he snarled, and flung
the dangling rope at his companion. He missed gripping it,
and the noose swung past him, and then pendulumed past him
again. Those standing in the streets now seemed suddenly
more witnesses than accomplices. The hate-energy had bled
out of the lynching.

But the one who gripped Willow's hair was immune to the
change in atmosphere. Even as the other two loosened their
grips on her, he drove his fist into her belly, doubling her
over and briefly stilling her struggles. He kept his grip on her
scalplocks as he reached wildly for the passing noose and
snagged it. The rough rope was in his fingers, and he was
pushing it down over Willow's head when Goat growled.

"Feel it yourself!"

And he did. The man fell, gasping, to his knees, his nails
clawing wildly at his throat as he mewled out the terror that
had muted Willow. She fell bonelessly, her chin slipping free
of the noose. She sprawled in the street, her legs and arms too
long and angular in conjunction with her cropped head. The
other two executioners boggled at their leader clutching at his
throat. Long strings of spittle were falling from his open
mouth, dangling and then darkening his shirt front. They
backed in disgust, then spun and walked off in different
directions, shoulders hunched, the one with his arms folded
tightly around his body. Of the lynch mob there was only the
victim lying in the street, and the executioner strangling in a
nonexistent noose.

"Stop that!" Dellin barked, and his long fingers cracked
like a whip as they struck Goat's fixed stare from his face.
Red and white streaks remained in their wake, and an astonished look in Goat's eyes. "No!" Dellin told him firmly, as
if he were a child reaching for a pot of boiling water. "No!
Let go!"

Ki saw him release the man. She saw it in Goat's face, in
the sudden slumping of his narrow shoulders. She didn't have
to turn to see the lynchman tumbled flat in the road like a

puppet with cut strings. But she did turn to watch Dellin
as he climbed down the box and slowly crossed to where
Willow lay.

He lifted the girl with an ease not entirely Human. He
spoke something over the limp form in his arms, and when
she began to stir, he set her carefully on her feet again.
Neither one of them paid attention to the man who lay in the
street, weeping silently. Dellin spoke softly to Willow as he
took her hand and led her toward the wagon. He brought her
alongside it, gestured her up toward the box. She lifted her
face and for a long moment her eyes locked with Goat's.

"No!" she cried out, in a voice low and harsh as a cat's
growl. Her eyes fixed on Ki and went wider. "I won't go
with you! I won't ride with traitors and freaks! I won't
become one such as he! I won't! I'd rather die!" She broke
free of Dellin's light touch, spun and was gone in a staggering run.

"She speaks the truth," Dellin said, and with a start Ki
knew his words were meant for Goat. The boy watched
Willow run away with heartbreak in his eyes. "She'd rather
die," Dellin went on mercilessly. "And she probably will, if
she keeps radiating it to the Humans around her. Thick as
their mindskins are, still a few will hear her, and enough will
feel her death-hunger to find a way to satisfy it. This," and
his sweeping hand included not just the fleeing girl, but the
smouldering city as well, "is what comes of Jore blood
misused, to a Human's end. This is what comes of Jore and
Human mingled without wisdom or conscience." His grave
accusation brooked no denial.

"You can't say all this is his fault!" Ki objected, and was
surprised at the depth of her feelings.

But Goat, his pale eyes wide, nodded with equally grave
acceptance. "Yes, Ki, it was."

"You are strong, and your Jore talent is great in you,"
Dellin observed.

Goat nodded again. With a strange humility, he added,
"Stronger than you, Uncle. And more talented."

Dellin stared at the boy, reevaluating him. When he spoke,
there was acceptance in his voice. "It is good for both of us
to recognize that before we begin. So, Gotheris. Now is a
deciding time. Will you go on with me, and learn? Or will

you flee, as that girl does, frightened by the wideness of the
plain she glimpses?''

Goat's silence seemed long to Ki. She listened to the
crackling of distant fire, the restless shifting of the horses in
their harness. ''I will not flee, Uncle,'' Goat replied at last,
and some small corner of Ki felt absurdly pleased, as if she
had made an unlikely bet with herself, and won.

''Remember that you have decided that.'' Dellin mounted
the box, took up the reins and shook them. Goat remained
where he was, leaning on the seat between them. He watched
the scorched buildings and toppled stalls as they passed them,
as if memorizing their outlines. Ki watched the hitch-lurch of
Sigurd's uneven stride.

She felt empty, she decided at last. She was cargo on her
own wagon, just a thing along for the ride to Villena. She had
felt too much in the last few days. Like a musical instrument
treated too roughly, the strings of her emotions were broken
and dangling inside her. No matter how they were plucked,
no further sound could be wrung from them. She swayed
slightly as the wagon rumbled down the street.

The town slowly changed to farm acreage. A field of
stubble had burned into a great black square. Goat spoke
suddenly. ''The thing I liked best about Vandien,'' he said
without preamble, ''was how he felt when he was angry
with me.''

Ki felt as if a bandage had been ripped from a wound
scarcely closed. But Dellin turned to the boy, and his surprise
was plain. ''What?''

''I didn't know, then, the difference between us . . .''
Goat fumbled for words. ''I couldn't separate what he felt
from what I felt,'' he said slowly. ''So his anger was mine.''

''So?'' Dellin prodded.

''He was angry at me because I was not . . . honorable. To
myself. He believed I had betrayed myself, by not being a
better . . . man.'' Goat spoke the word hesitantly, as if he
feared laughter. No one even smiled, and the boy took courage. ''A lot of folk have hated me. Or wished me dead. But
no one had been angry with me that way before. Even my
father: his anger was always full of sorrow, mostly for
my mother and himself, and how hard I made their lives.
But Vandien's anger believed I was cheating him and my-

self, by being . . . dishonorable. He made me feel that . . . that I was angry with myself, for being less than an honorable . . . man.''

Goat stopped speaking. The wagon creaked on, and Ki thought about the strangeness of the legacy Vandien had left the boy. ''At first, it was about . . . that girl.'' Points of color suddenly appeared on Goat's cheeks. His fingertip traced a knot in the plank seat. ''And I was angry back at him. Because he made me so uncomfortable about what I had done. But then . . . after Kellich . . . Vandien felt that way again. About himself as well as me.'' Wonder came into Goat's voice. ''It was as if he had claimed me, because he judged me as he judged himself.''

Goat touched Ki's hand shyly, to be sure she was listening. ''That was why I attacked that Brurjan. Because I thought he would have, and I wanted to do as he would have done.'' The boy's voice tightened. ''I'm sorry he's dead. I wanted to hear him say I had done the right thing.''

Ki clutched the boy's fingers briefly. ''You saved my life.'' She tried to give him what he needed. She couldn't say Vandien's name, refused to feel her grief. ''He would have said that you'd done the right thing.''

They passed a smouldering farmhouse. A flock of chickens, refugees from the fire, were taking dust-baths in the road. They squawked angrily as the passage of the horses disturbed them. Farther ahead a stray horse grazed by the road. They were almost abreast of it before Ki spotted the crumpled rider in the ditch.

''That's the smallest Brurjan . . .'' she began, but was interrupted by Goat's sudden cry. The boy sprang to the seat, and then leaped to the road from the moving wagon, to fall face down in the dust. He was on his feet and scrambling toward the body before Dellin could even halt the team.

''Gotheris!'' Dellin cried in rebuke and alarm as the boy put his hands on the body.

''Goat! Leave him alone, he's already dead!'' Ki added.

''He's not!'' Goat declared, and the hope in his voice stunned Ki until he lifted the oversized helm and bared the dark curls beneath it. Her heart slammed into her mouth. Emotions fountained in her, her anger, her fears, but she found herself in the road, and she knelt beside him, almost afraid to touch him. He was arrayed like a Brurjan, and his clothing was richer than anything she had ever seen, but it was Vandien.

"He's dead," Dellin said gently, but she paid no attention. His skin was cool, his arm a terrible grey, but she turned his face away from the dust and slipped her hand inside his shirt. Cold chain mail. She set her fingers to his throat, touched the light pulsing under the angle of his jaw. "He's alive!" she declared fiercely.

Dellin clambered slowly down from the wagon and came to stand over them. He did not stoop to touch the body, but Ki could almost feel the soft brush of his mind as he probed.

"Ki," he said at last, and there was infinite pity in his tone. She felt his touch on her thoughts, felt his attempt to soften the impact as he said softly, "It's only his body. He's not . . . in there."

"No!" Goat's voice was shrill in her ears, but more, it screamed within her as he pushed aside his uncle's comforting touch. She felt scraped raw as his mind-touch ripped away her half-formed acceptance of Vandien's death. "Don't let go!" he told her fiercely. "Hold on to his life for him!" His clutch at her feelings was as rough as his uncle's was skilled. It was like the embrace of a stranger, and she would have struggled against it if she had known how.

Her hearing had gone woolly. Someone whispered, "Stop. You'll only die with him, he's gone out of reach," but it was no one she knew and his words didn't matter. What mattered, she found, was sitting down in the dust and dragging Vandien's body half into her lap, cradling him against her as she put her cheek on his forehead. Holding onto him. Refusing to let him be dead. She brushed her lips against his hair. She held him closer, but despite her grip she sensed him slipping away.

"Too late," someone warned. "He's let go, no one can reach him now. Let him go."

"Which do you fear more?" Goat demanded of her. The boy's voice was strangled in her ears, but it rang out in her heart. "Decide. To love him. Or let him go."

She couldn't hold him and let him go. His body was warm against her; the rising scents of his hair and skin were sweet in her nostrils. She couldn't let him go. But she couldn't love him, not the way Goat made the word feel inside her, not without restraints and cautions. She loved the man, yes, she wanted him close to her, she'd die for him if she had to. But

that was not what Goat was asking of her. She could let her
love flow endlessly into Vandien without regret. But there
was another aspect. There was accepting wholeheartedly
Vandien's love, and depending on his love to be there. It was
not just admitting she loved him, but admitting he loved her,
and accepting what he offered. It was too dangerous to be that
vulnerable, it would hurt too much if . . . She felt him slip
another notch. Something inside her broke jaggedly. She
gasped, but the pain wasn't physical. She threw away her
caution, let the walls come down and her love go howling
after him. There was relief in releasing what she had withheld
from him and from herself. Needing him. Not just wanting
him. Depending on him in the same way he depended on her.
"Please," she begged of someone, not knowing who she
asked, nor what she asked for.

"You've reached him." There was amazement in Dellin's
voice. She suddenly felt his guidance enter the web of their
feelings. Deftly she felt him extracting Goat, and just for a
bare moment, as he left, she felt as a Jore would the network
she and Vandien had made and shared, felt it stretched tight
and hummingly alive between them.

Then there was only the man in her arms, his weight and
his warmth against her. She knew then only what she felt
toward him; what he felt toward her she would have to take
on trust, believing blindly that his feelings corresponded to her
own. It was suddenly a lonely and dangerous position to hold.
Caution bade her be wary, warned her not to care too much
that he cared for her.

"Don't let go now," Dellin warned her. He dragged Goat
to his feet, stumbled him toward the wagon. "Neither Goat
nor I could hold him for you now. Love him, or let him go."

She sat in the dust of the road, holding him. She lifted his
arms carefully onto his chest, clasped both his hands in one of
hers. The fingers of his sword arm were puffy and chill
against hers. The wound he had taken from Kellich? She
pushed his sleeve back. As her eyes traced the angry brand
down his tanned forearm, she winced. "What did they do to
you?" she asked him.

"Probably more than he'll ever be able to tell you about,
even if he can remember it all himself," Dellin replied for
him. The Jore healer crouched beside them. "It might be
wiser not even to ask." He rocked on his heels beside them.

"Is Gotheris going to be all right?" Ki remembered to ask.

Dellin nodded in his slow way. "He's tired. But he did well, for his first attempt. I see that my major task will be to teach the boy restraint and caution. He left himself no line of life to depend on. If Vandien had not come back, neither would Gotheris."

"But Vandien is back, and he's going to recover?"

Dellin looked at her pityingly. "You know he is, so why do you ask? Trust what you feel sometimes." After a long pause, he added, "You may find him somewhat changed."

Ki lifted a questioning gaze, but Dellin dropped his eyes to one side to keep her from reading them. "I could mute it for him," Dellin offered softly. "Hide the worst from him."

Ki heard what he was offering. It frightened her. What had they done to him, that Dellin would make such an offer? She pushed the idea away, and knew he felt her doing so. "I want him the way he is," she said firmly. Saying the words aloud helped her know they were true, "I don't always have to understand him. Sometimes we'll just have to trust each other."

Vandien took a slightly deeper breath. His mouth twitched. She held him closer. His eyes slowly opened. "I thought . . ." His voice was rusty. "I thought I was home."

"You are," Ki told him.

TWENTY

"Loveran is no longer a Human province. Does it feel strange, knowing you're responsible for a thing like that?"

A few heartbeats passed before Vandien answered. "No. Because I won't accept that as true. All of this would have happened without us, you know. Kellich would have killed the Duke, if we had never happened along."

"But we did." Ki watched the Brurjans trotting toward them, then glanced over at Vandien once more. Bad enough that he looked so damn good in the Duke's armor, on the Duke's horse. Did he also have to be aware of it? As the Brurjans closed with them, he lifted his hand in casual greeting. Both his sleeves were rolled back, but they scarcely glanced at the knife's scar. "Keklokito," one growled companionably in passing, and Vandien nodded. His white horse cut through their ranks, and the opening widened to allow Ki, riding Sigmund and leading Sigurd, to follow. She'd sold the wagon in Villena, as much out of disgust with it as for the coin. Sigurd's leg needed the rest from pulling anyway.

She waited until the sound of the Brurjan troops had faded behind her before she asked, "How's it feel to be a Brurjan legend?"

He made a noncommittal sound.

"What's it mean, anyway?"

"Lordly one," he said, quite seriously.

"I'll bet. How much farther to the border, do you suppose?"

"Doesn't matter, remember? No freight, no customers, no deadlines."

"No money," she pointed out.

"Has it been a problem so far?" he asked chidingly.

"No. But after we cross the border, Keklokito isn't going to have his Brurjan friends to depend on. Thank the Moon."

"They aren't that bad," he insisted again, and Ki snorted, but let it drop.

"I miss him," Vandien said suddenly into the silence.

Ki didn't need to ask who. "Dellin said there was something between you. A teacher bond. It's what made him keep looking for you after I'd given you up for dead. And he'll always be aware of you, through that bond . . . ."

"As close as I'll ever come to a son. And I'll never see him again."

"We don't have to go back north," Ki suggested.

"Yes we do." He cleared his throat. "I had to leave the boy. Dellin explained it to me that last night. As long as I was close by, Goat would never form a 'primary' bond with him. And he needed that bond to teach Goat, not just healing, but how to shield and protect himself."

"So, for his own good, you leave him."

"He understood."

"Is that what all those long talks were about in the back of the wagon while your body was shaking off the poison?"

"Dellin said it was more the effects of the Brurjan cure than the poison from Kellich's blade. She must have given me the full Brurjan dose."

"Could Keklokito have merited less?" Ki asked gravely.

He shot her a glance, but didn't smile. It was something she'd missed lately; it was harder to make him smile, and he seemed always to be thinking of something else. Was this the change Dellin had warned her about?

"Know what Goat said to me, the night before we left Villena?"

"What?" Ki asked tolerantly. Since they had left Villena, Vandien hadn't stopped talking about the boy, and repeating precocious things Goat had said. Oddly, she found she didn't mind hearing them. She'd even added a few of her own.

"He said, 'Your honor, Vandien, is what makes it possible for you to live with yourself.' "

"And can you live with yourself, now?"

"A little better than it was right afterwards. Goat assured me that my motives were always honorable, even when the results were appalling.'' Vandien paused, gave a small laugh. ''It's strange. The words of a child, and I take them so seriously.''

''He knows you very well.'' Ki couldn't keep a twinge of jealousy out of her voice.

''Well enough to know there's only one woman I'd burn a town down for.'' Vandien grinned suddenly. ''I think Goat would have helped me do it, too, if he'd had the chance.''

Old habit made Ki refuse to look at him. Then she caught herself and brought her eyes up to face him. ''Did you think I'd threatened Willow with less than that for your life?''

They rode side by side, as close as White could be persuaded to come to Sigmund. Something hummed between them, like a secret they both knew and neither wanted to speak. It was good.

CLASSIC SCIENCE FICTION
AND FANTASY

__DUNE Frank Herbert 0-441-17266-0/$4.95
The bestselling novel of an awesome world where gods and
adventurers clash, mile-long sandworms rule the desert, and
the ancient dream of immortality comes true.

__STRANGER IN A STRANGE LAND Robert A. Heinlein
0-441-79034-8/$4.95
From the *New York Times* bestselling author—the science
fiction masterpiece of a man from Mars who teaches
humankind the art of grokking, watersharing and love.

__THE ONCE AND FUTURE KING T.H. White
0-441-62740-4/$5.50
The world's greatest fantasy classic! A magical epic of King
Arthur in Camelot, romance, wizardry and war. By the author
of *The Book of Merlyn*.

__THE LEFT HAND OF DARKNESS Ursula K. LeGuin
0-441-47812-3/$3.95
Winner of the Hugo and Nebula awards for best science fiction
novel of the year. "SF masterpiece!"—*Newsweek* "A Jewel of
a story."—Frank Herbert

__MAN IN A HIGH CASTLE Philip K. Dick 0-441-51809-5/$3.95
"Philip K. Dick's best novel, a masterfully detailed alternate
world peopled by superbly realized characters."
—Harry Harrison